THE WRANGLING OF THE WREATH

SHILOH RIDGE RANCH IN THREE RIVERS, BOOK 10

LIZ ISAACSON

THE GLOVER FAMILY

Welcome to Shiloh Ridge Ranch! The Glover family is BIG, and sometimes it can be hard to keep track of everyone.

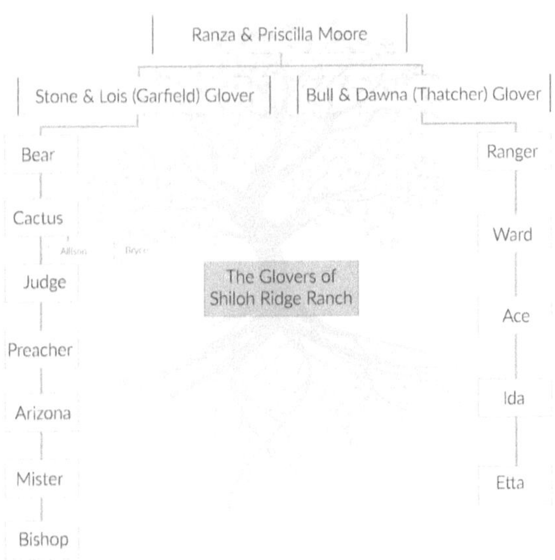

Here's how things are right now:

Lois & Stone (deceased) Glover, 7 children, in age-order: (Lois is now married to Donald Parker)

1. Bear (Sammy, wife / Lincoln (13), step-son, Stetson (3), son, Russell (18 mo), son, Heather (6 mo), daughter)

2. Cactus (Allison, ex-wife / Bryce, son (deceased) // Willa, wife / Mitch (14), step-son, Charlie (17 mo), son)

3. Judge (June, engaged)

4. Preacher (Charlie, wife)

5. Arizona (Duke Rhinehart, husband, living at the Rhinehart Ranch, just south of Shiloh Ridge / Shiloh (14 mo), daughter)

6. Mister

7. Bishop (Montana, wife / Aurora (19), step-daughter and married to Oliver Osburn, Robbie (15 mo), son)

Dawna & Bull (deceased) Glover, 5 children, in age-order:

1. Ranger (Oakley, wife / Wilder (2), son, Fawn (7 mo), daughter)

2. Ward (Dot, wife)

3. Ace (Holly Ann, wife / Gunnison (16 mo), son)

4. Etta

5. Ida (Brady Burton, husband / Johnny and Judy, (twins, 18 mo), son and daughter)

Bull and Stone Glover were brothers, so their children are cousins. Ranger and Bear, for example, are cousins, and each the oldest sibling in their families.

THE GLOVERS KNOW AND INTERACT WITH THE Walkers of Seven Sons Ranch. There's a lot of them too! Here's a little cheat sheet for you for the Walkers.

MOMMA & DADDY: PENNY AND GIDEON WALKER

1. RHETT & EVELYN WALKER
Son: Conrad
Triplets: Austin, Elaine, and Easton

2. JEREMIAH & WHITNEY WALKER
Son: Jonah Jeremiah (JJ)
Daughter: Clara Jean
Son: Jason

3. LIAM & CALLIE WALKER
Daughter: Denise
Daughter: Ginger

4. TRIPP & IVORY WALKER
Son: Oliver
Son: Isaac

5. WYATT & MARCY WALKER
Son: Warren

Son: Cole
Son: Harrison

6. SKYLER & MALLERY WALKER
Daughter: Camila

7. MICAH & SIMONE WALKER
Son: Travis (Trap)
Daughter: Due soon

THE GLOVERS KNOW AND INTERACT WITH THE several of the cowboys and their families at Three Rivers Ranch too... There's a lot going on in Three Rivers!

You'll see:

1. Squire and Kelly Ackerman

Mother / Father: Heidi (owns Ackermans bakery) / Frank

Son: Finn

Daughter: Libby

Son: Michael

Son: Samuel

2. PETE AND CHELSEA MARSHALL (CHELSEA IS Squire's sister)

4 sons: Paul, Henry, John, Rich

3. REESE AND CARLY SANDERS: THEY'RE THE admins for Courage Reins, Pete and Chelsea's equine therapy unit at Three Rivers Ranch.

CHAPTER 1

*M*ister Glover saw the outline of Three Rivers on the horizon, and something in his heart settled. Something he hadn't even realized had been kicking around inside his chest. He hadn't been terribly happy to leave Winterhaven, because he had friends there now. Brock put his dishes in the dishwasher every evening, and Josiah had given Mister some amazing advice about how to fall asleep faster.

He'd packed up and driven away, even when the boss wanted him to stay. Heck, he'd even been offered more money, and he'd have been paid the most out of anyone at Winterhaven had he accepted.

"I learned something, Dad," he whispered, the horizon blurring slightly in the heavy heat that had already arrived in the Texas Panhandle, though it wasn't even June yet. He'd learned that he could be a valuable resource—very valuable. He could put his head down and work without accolades. He could put up with a snoring roommate, and a messy cabin-mate, and a man who thought he was better than everyone else.

Not only could he put up with them, he could learn to love them for exactly who they were. In doing that, Mister felt like he'd learned to love himself better, flaws and all.

He smiled into the sunshine, and for the first time, a snippet in his letter from his deceased father made sense.

You'll need to go your own way, Mister. You've always done that, and it used to drive me and your mother insane. Then Grandmother would remind us of who you were, and we'd find a way to encourage you to seek and understand for yourself.

When he'd first read that paragraph, years ago, he hadn't known what his father meant. He'd never really thought he'd gone his own way. He'd had the opportunity to join the rodeo, because he was good with a rope and knew instinctively how to stay on a bull. So he'd joined.

He'd never really thought of it as "going his own way."

He'd returned to Shiloh Ridge, just like everyone else in his family. Cactus had gone to school for a long time, and he'd come back. Mister had too.

As his truck sped along the highway, Mister sure would like to ask Grandmother who she thought he was. How had she seen who he was when he was so young?

He wanted to honor his family name, do what was right, and be the type of person his grandmother had somehow seen, so long ago.

"I hope I'm at least better than I was," he murmured, though he already knew he was. He felt calmer inside, and while he had dreams and goals he wanted to accomplish, he didn't feel frantic to get them done.

He knew now that the joy came from the *doing*, not from the *finishing*.

His phone rang, saving himself from his inner thoughts, and he reached over to the infotainment screen and tapped to answer Preacher's call. "Tell me she's not having the baby," Mister said. Preacher and Charlie were due with their first child tomorrow, which was why Mister was moving back to Three Rivers and Shiloh Ridge Ranch today.

Despite the good life he enjoyed at Winterhaven with his cowboy friends and hard-working boss, Mister couldn't stand to be away from all the hustle and bustle on his family's ranch. He missed his brothers and sister and all of their spouses. He missed his cousins. He missed all the littles, and he'd missed eleven months of them growing up, changing, developing, and learning the wonders of mud, bugs, and baby calves.

In his opinion, cattle ranching—what they did at Shiloh Ridge—was better than dairy farming—what he'd done at Winterhaven. A quiet excitement brewed within him, and Mister couldn't wait to get back to the ranch and see all the changes. Bear had sent pictures of the house, but Mister knew from being gone this year that pictures and videos weren't anywhere near the same as seeing things in person.

A birthday party via video, where he could only see the chocolate cakes and the joy on his nephews' face? Or being there to taste, smell, hear, and bask in the familial spirit?

Yes, this year had been very difficult for Mister, and he thanked the Lord that he'd only felt it keenly in a few instances.

"She's not having the baby," Preacher said, chuckling. "Though she just glared at me *because* she's not having the baby."

"Oh, boy," Mister said, smiling. He pictured Charlie in the last selfie she'd sent him, and she had to be super uncomfortable. She'd told him to "hurry home" so he could "convince Preacher to let her start exercising or taking castor oil or something" to get the baby to come faster.

"We're just wondering where you are," Preacher said. "Charlie wants a few things from the grocery store, and I'm up to my eyeballs in the repasturization we're doing up here."

"Ward's got the whip cracking," Mister said, his grin only widening.

"That he does," Preacher said. "It's fine. It's good. But she can't drive to the store alone—"

"Yes, I can!" Charlie yelled, but Preacher just kept right on talking.

"—and I'm too busy to go. We thought you might be able to stop on your way through town."

"I can stop on my way through town," Mister echoed. "I can see it ahead of me. I'm maybe five miles out. Tell me what you need."

"Charlie will text you," Preacher said, and he sounded so happy too. So cheerful, and so…animated. For Preacher, that was saying something, as he preferred to live his life on the sidelines.

"Sounds good," Mister said. "I can't wait to see the new Kinder place too. It looks amazing in the pictures Bishop's been sending."

"It is pretty amazing what that man can do," Preacher said. "We're still a few months out from completion, but Montana told Char that they're actually *ahead* of schedule."

"They really are miracle workers," Mister said, his heart aching to see Bishop and Montana again. Their little boy Robbie had turned one over four months ago, and Mister had only been able to participate in watching the child blow out his single candle via video.

Judge, Preacher, and Ward had been the very best at keeping Mister involved in the family. He got to watch from afar all the birthday parties, the Sunday dinners, and the bridal shower for June, Judge's fiancée.

They'd set a date for August tenth to be married, and Mister knew that Judge had held off on setting a date until Mister had announced his plans to return to Texas. Guilt pulled through him, but Judge had told him August was the best time for June's family. It really had nothing to do with him.

"Okay, see you soon," Preacher said, and Mister let him end the call. A moment later the truck chirped a notification from the speakers, and a glance at the infotainment screen told him Charlie had texted.

"Read the text from Charlie," he said.

"Potato chips, the plain ones. Cool Ranch Doritos. Butter pecan ice cream. Thanks, Mister!"

Chips and ice cream. Mister grinned to himself, his need to get back to the ranch only doubling. He wouldn't have to dive right back into work, though summertime at Shiloh Ridge could make a man question his career choices. He'd take a few days to get moved home, go around and see everyone and everything that had changed, and then report to Ward and Preacher, the two foremen at the ranch, for work on Tuesday morning.

He continued his drive, pulling into Wilde & Organic only a few minutes later. The lot held plenty of cars for a Sunday afternoon, and Mister dang near fell over when he got out of the vehicle and had to breathe in the heat.

"My word," he said, gasping. "I'm going to die this summer." The weather hadn't really been better in Oklahoma, as it sat due east of Three Rivers, but he'd been driving in air-conditioned bliss for hours now.

He hurried inside the store and re-read Charlie's list. She only had a few things on it, and he quickly texted Judge to ask if he had anything he wanted. Mister wouldn't be moving back into the Ranch House, but he had planned for it to be his first stop.

Since Judge and June would be living there, and Bear and Sammy had moved into their new house a couple of months ago, there was room for Mister in the homestead. He'd be taking the suite Bear and Sammy had been living in, though Ranger had moved the ranch office and conference room across the landing to that area.

He'd needed the room for his own family, which had grown to four now. Bear and Sammy had four children and had needed a bigger place. Mister hadn't been able to come for the birth of their daughter, Heather, who they'd named after Sammy's sister. He couldn't wait to meet his niece, and he looked up from his phone, suddenly eager to get this shopping done.

Cactus had once told him that one of the best places to meet women was in the grocery store, but Mister had laughed him off. He wasn't looking to start dating anyway, and certainly not someone he met in the grocery store.

He hadn't met anyone in Oklahoma that had caught his eye, and Mister wondered if there would be anyone in Three Rivers that would. He'd grown up here and spent so many years of his life here. He felt like he knew so many people, though the town had grown a lot in the past several years.

An image of Liberty Bellamore filled his mind, and while Mister had thought she'd recede back to best friend status while he worked his days away at Winterhaven, he found that she hadn't.

He'd learned to control his frustration surrounding her, and he'd learned to enjoy their friendship again. He'd loved telling her about his life in Oklahoma, and he loved getting random pictures of the landscape around her. In fact, he smiled just thinking about her as he reached for a shopping cart.

"Welcome to Wilde and Organic," a woman said, handing him a quarter-sheet of paper. "We have half-pans of brownies on sale this afternoon."

"Sounds good," Mister said, taking the coupon. Charlie hadn't requested brownies, but Mister didn't know a Glover alive who would turn down a chocolatey treat.

He pushed a cart around, getting the things both Judge and Charlie wanted, then the brownies, and he finally just had the chips and Doritos left. He turned down the chip and snack aisle, the long row of bags of potato chips stretching in front of him.

"Plain," he muttered. Who liked plain potato chips?

"Mister?"

He turned toward the sound of the voice, already knowing who he'd find standing there. "Libby." She wore a pair of cutoff shorts with a red-and-blue-checkered tank top, with big work boots on her feet. Her hair wasn't braided or ponytailed, but fell around her face in beautiful brunette waves that made Mister's mouth turn dry.

She looked so much like the woman he'd known for decades. And yet…something about her was different too. Completely different, but he couldn't pinpoint what it was.

He also couldn't stop the smile as it bloomed on his face, and she dropped her basket with oranges and mint in it.

She laughed and grabbed onto him, pulling him into a

wonderful hug that had him closing his eyes in bliss and inhaling the scent of her hair, her skin, her clothes. She'd definitely been working outside today, because she smelled like straw, sunshine, and sweat. It was the best scent in the whole world to Mister, and he wished he'd been out on the ranch with her today.

He sighed and said, "It's so good to see you." He started to laugh, and he lifted her right up off the ground and spun her around. Maybe Cactus had been onto something when he'd said Mister could meet someone special in the grocery store.

He set her down, and she backed up. She bent to get her produce, and when her eyes met his again, a whole lightning storm started zapping in his chest.

"What are you doing here?" she asked, glancing at his shopping cart. "Are you back in Three Rivers for good?" The hope in her voice screamed in his ears, and Mister told himself it was because they were friends. Good friends.

Best friends.

She definitely fit in that box, but he could still feel her pushing and pulsing against the edges of it, wanting to become more. Maybe he just wanted her to be more, and that was him trying to break down the walls keeping her in the friendship position.

Not only that, he wasn't going to start anything with Libby he couldn't finish. Not again. He wasn't going to lose her because of his childish behavior and stubbornness. He wasn't going to pressure her to go out with him.

He wasn't going to ask her to set him up with anyone. He wasn't even going to make the first move.

He knew better now, so despite the thumping of his pulse and his own hope shooting toward the stars, he said, "Yeah, yep. Today's my first day back." He glanced at the chips in the rack beside him and grinned. "And wouldn't you know it? Everyone in my family is already putting me to work."

She chuckled and took in the groceries in his cart. "Getting brownies and ice cream is work? You've had it easy in Oklahoma, Mister."

He grinned at her, wondering if he'd heard something flirty in his name. He'd known her for so long, and he'd never heard anything off in her voice until Preacher had mentioned she'd asked about him.

He couldn't trust himself and his feelings right now, so he just said, "Nothing about being in Oklahoma was as easy as I've made it seem, Libs."

"No? What's been hard?"

Not seeing you in person, he thought, but he said, "Missing out on all the parties, the births, and the family stuff."

"You used to sometimes complain about the family stuff, and that was when it was a third of the size it is now."

Mister grinned at her, but he couldn't deny it. "I'm older now," he said simply. "I guess I didn't realize how wonderful it was to have so many people to enjoy life with." He wanted to ask her what she was doing later that weekend. Maybe they could go to lunch tomorrow. Lunch was an easy get-together, wasn't it?

You're not asking, he reminded himself, and besides, he couldn't commit to lunch—or any other date—because Libby had spoken true. His family was huge, and they'd all want to see him.

"Anyway," he said. "I just need to get these chips and get on up to the ranch. I'm not sure if you've ever been between a pregnant lady and her ice cream, but I know it's not a position I want to be in."

CHAPTER 2

*L*iberty Bellamore could only stare at Mister Glover's mouth as he spoke. He'd grown in a full beard, just the kind Libby liked. He'd likely shave it before Sunday, when she'd see him at church.

He was twice as handsome as she remembered, though he'd been sending her pictures as the beard had grown in. "I like the beard," she said, grinning at him. He'd grown one last year when he'd first left Three Rivers, but he'd shaved it after a while.

"Yeah?" He reached up and stroked his face, as if he didn't know he had hair there. "I'm thinking it's too hot for a beard."

"I'm sure you'll shave it soon enough," she teased. "You never did like that much facial hair."

"Yes, well, you dared me to see how long I could stand it this time. Goin' on five months now."

She giggled again and ducked her head, horrified at her

girlish, flirty behavior. Her mind screamed at her to *stop it!* and not only because she'd set very clear boundaries with Mister she wasn't going to cross again.

She cut off the sound and took a deep breath. Why had she come down this aisle? She was sure it wasn't because she'd seen this tall, dark, delectable cowboy studying the chips as if he couldn't read their English names.

"Are you going to make that tropical punch?" he asked, indicating her basket.

"Yes," she blurted out, seizing onto the topic. "I just… we're having a little picnic to celebrate Jack and Suzy's anniversary. I'm in charge of the punch, obviously." She lifted her basket, her face feeling so hot. Mister had to know more ingredients than oranges and mint were needed for the tropical punch he'd drunk many times.

"And chips," she finished lamely.

"Is your daddy makin' his famous spit-roasted pig?"

"Slaughtered it yesterday and everything." Libby smiled at Mister, enjoying this easy conversation. She needed it in her life. She craved it.

She also couldn't have it. Couldn't perpetuate it.

Get your chips and go, she commanded herself. *Quickly.*

Her family's news would reach Mister soon enough, if it hadn't already, but her legs literally shook at the idea of him finding out about Cory right here in the grocery store.

"Mildred's engaged," she said casually as she reached for the cheddar and sour cream chips she loved so much. She normally provided several different flavors of chips for her family to choose from, but she only carried a basket, and to get so many would require the cart Cory was filling with frozen lemonade, limeade, and orange juice.

"She is?" Mister asked, obviously surprised. "I thought you said she didn't like that guy that much."

"Oh, she's a big liar." Libby gave Mister a smile she hoped was friendly and not flirty and moved around his cart to get a bag of barbecue chips. "Once I figured that out, they were already talking about diamonds and dress-es." She gave an exaggerated sigh. "They're getting married in November."

"Right during the Country Christmas?" Mister's shock only made Libby's pulse bounce erratically.

"Right before," she said. "So yes, I'm pretty mad at her."

"Wow," Mister said as she picked up another bag of chips, this time the Maui sweet onion flavor her brother Cord adored. Was three bags of chips enough? Had this conversation lasted long enough? Could she walk away now?

Her mind raced, and Libby had never been good under pressure. She didn't like confrontation, and she had no idea how she could possibly fill Mister in on everything that had happened in the past month or two.

Their texts had been friendly; the type of thing she'd send to an acquaintance, not a deep, personal friend. As he asked another question about Mildred with a pinch of hurt in his voice, Libby realized that he didn't view her as an acquaintance. He'd expected her to share her big family news with him, even though he'd been living in another state.

After all, that was what Libby and Mister had been doing for decades.

"She's getting married at the Old Apple Mill," Libby said. "Our space at Golden Hour will already be set up for the Country Christmas." She glanced at him, not truly meeting his eyes. "So." She shrugged like that was no big deal, but Mister knew Libby would never get married anywhere but her family ranch.

She loved being a cowgirl, and she couldn't fathom a life without cattle, horses, and dogs in it.

"Where will she live?" Mister asked. "Are you going to lose that house you love?"

"No, Scott is a scientist at HealNow," Libby said, plucking a plain bag of chips from the shelf. "He has one of those nice, new homes on the north side of town. Kind of out by your sister-in-law's sister." She dared to look at him, and oh, how he made her heart pulse in her chest.

She stubbornly tamped against it, because she couldn't have feelings for this man anymore. It wasn't fair to him, and it wasn't fair to her.

And there's Cory, her mind shrieked.

"Bethany Rose and Doug Culver?" Libby said, providing the names for him. "There's a new subdivision out there. Scott lives out there, and since Mildred doesn't *really* work the ranch—not the way I do or Jack and Cord do—she's going to move in with him once they get married."

Mister edged closer to her, tugging on his cart from the front of it instead of using the handle. He hadn't picked up a single bag of chips yet, and Libby really wished he would. He came far too close to her, which only made her skin prickle and ripple with want.

"I'm glad," he said, his voice throaty and deeper now. He seemed...older. More mature. Wiser. She realized he didn't give in to every thought in his head, as she watched his emotions blaze through his eyes but his mouth stayed shut. Before he'd left for Winterhaven, whatever he'd been thinking would've just spilled from his mouth.

She also realized he hadn't told her a single thing about him. He'd been asking her questions about Mildred and her family and what she was doing at the grocery store. Before, everything was about Mister.

He'd conquered another bull. He'd won the National Championship. He'd gotten his shiny, bejeweled belt buckle in the mail and did she want to see it? He'd gotten an article accepted in a magazine.

Even when he'd first moved to Oklahoma, his texts had been about the farm, his roommates, and the work. Libby wasn't sure when they'd changed, but standing there in the snack aisle with him, she realized she hadn't heard about him or his life in quite some time now.

Months, probably.

"You love that house," he said. "Have you kept it red?"

"Yes," she managed to push out of her narrow throat. "I like the brick red."

"I know you do," he said. "You also like to switch

things up sometimes." He grinned at her and his gaze softened. "It really is so good to see you. I've missed you more than I realized."

Before she could answer, a man called, "Libby."

She looked past Mister's shoulder, wanting to lunge at him and tell him not to look. But he was already turning in the direction of the voice too.

Another man strode toward them, pushing the cart filled with the other items she needed to make the tropical punch, as well as provide all the sides for the family picnic. Cory had met her parents before, but Libby had not introduced him to the whole family.

That was happening today. In mere hours.

"Did you get the chips, darlin'?" Cory drawled, barely glancing at Mister. Funny how Libby couldn't get herself to look away from him.

His face transformed instantly, and she caught a momentary bout of shock before he covered it smoothly away.

"Howdy." Cory went right past Mister to her. "Four bags, honey? I don't think that's enough. You said Cord will eat those onion ones by himself." He took the bag of chips from her hand and twisted to put it in the cart.

"Hello," Mister said diplomatically, and that single word thawed Libby.

She did lunge forward then, stepping partially in front of Cory. "Mister," she said, clearing her throat. "Cory." She looked at him. "Cory, this is Mister Glover. Remember I've talked about him?"

Cory finally looked at Mister, and his eyes lit up. "Yes, of course. The friend in Oklahoma." He reached out to shake Mister's hand.

His eyebrows had furrowed, but Libby plowed forward. "Mister, this is Cory Blanchard."

"You *haven't* talked about him," Mister said, taking Cory's hand and pumping it a couple of times before releasing it.

Cory chuckled, as if nothing was amiss in this snack aisle. Nothing to see here. Only Libby's utter humiliation and embarrassment that she had feelings for someone she had no right to feel anything for.

"That Libs," he said. "She likes to keep things a little secret." Cory put his arm around her waist, and Libby wanted the floor in Wilde & Organic to swallow her right down. "She thinks a forbidden relationship is more exciting."

"Forbidden relationship?" Mister's eyes bored into the top of Libby's head, because she couldn't raise it to face him head-on.

"He's my boyfriend," Libby muttered, the words nowhere near loud enough to reach Mister's ears.

"I'm the boyfriend," Cory repeated, much louder. So loud it made Libby cringe.

Mister took a step back, but she still didn't dare look at his face. "So nice to meet you," he said, his voice diplomatic and guarded. "I should get these things found and on my way. My sister-in-law is due with a baby tomorrow, and I don't know if you've ever made a pregnant woman wait for her potato chips, but it isn't pretty."

He chuckled in a way that sounded natural to a casual observer. But Libby wasn't a casual observer. She knew the force behind the laughter and how much it took for Mister to do it.

When she finally got the courage to look up, Mister had retreated behind his cart and gripped the handle with both hands. "I just need to find the Cool Ranch Doritos...."

"Oh, they're down here farther," Cory said, so upbeat and so oblivious to Libby. He slid his hand away from her body and went down the aisle easily. He picked up the blue bag of chips and turned just as Mister started to go by her.

"Boyfriend?" he asked out of the corner of his mouth. "Seems like you've been holdin' out on me, my friend." He didn't slow down or stop as he walked by, and his words left a burning hole in her stomach.

She wasn't his friend, and he now knew it. Friends would've shared the news that they'd started seeing someone over two months ago. If they were friends, she wouldn't have blindsided him with a boyfriend in the grocery store.

Libby turned away from the two men exchanging chips and pleasantries. Her eyes filled with tears, and she loathed herself on a whole new level. *Why did he have to be here at the same time we were?* she thought.

Of all the times he could've stopped by to get chips for Charlie, why did You have to let it be now? Libby wouldn't get an answer from the Lord, she knew that. No matter how hard she tried to converse with Him or how many times she asked what she should do, she didn't get an answer.

This time would be no different.

"Let's see what we've got," Cory said. "You said at least eight bags, baby, and you have four."

She let him take her basket and move the chips into the cart. She let him pick out the rest of the chips while she studied cans of peanuts and cashews on the other side of the aisle. She couldn't let him see her crying, that was for certain.

Libby felt hollow inside, and she clutched her arms around herself, trying to keep all the pieces together. She'd lost her connection to God. She didn't feel worthy of His love anymore, and she didn't know what to do about it. She still went to church, but there was nothing there for her.

She was empty and floating through the wind, desperate for something or someone to hold onto, and no one came. Nothing appeared.

"Okay," Cory said, breaking into her thoughts. "Libby?" He put his hand on her hip, and she flinched away from him. "What's wrong? Are you okay?" He came around and stood beside her, facing her.

Looking up at him, she found concern and compassion in his dark brown eyes. He wore his hair a little too long, but she hadn't minded. He was a great kisser, and a lot of fun. He liked to go hiking and biking and while she wasn't terribly into outdoor sports, she did like being under the open sky and in the fresh air.

He wasn't a cowboy either, and Libby had thought she could make that concession, because he did possess good looks, and he worked hard, and he was kind to her. He cared about her.

She couldn't hide from him any longer. She couldn't hide from herself either. "I'm not feeling well," she said, her tears spilling over and tracking down her face. "I'm sorry, Cory."

"Hey, it's okay." He put his arms around her, and Libby let him.

"No," she said. "It's not okay."

"Why are you sorry?"

She drew in a deep breath and stepped out of his arms. It wasn't fair to take comfort from him. She needed to stand up and support herself. "That was Mister Glover, Cory."

He frowned as he peered at her. "Yeah, okay."

She shook her head, a fresh set of tears threatening to spill down her face. She pulled them back in and laced everything tight. She hated the crusty feeling of saltwater on her face, and she wiped it away. "He's my very best friend in the whole world. Or he was."

She knew she wasn't making sense. "I didn't tell him about us, because somewhere in the back of my mind, I was hoping that when he came back to town...."

Cory fell back a step, as if she'd pushed him. "You

were hoping when he came back, the two of you would become an *us*."

Libby nodded. "Yes," she admitted. "I've liked him for a long time." She looked up into Cory's eyes, which weren't nearly as warm now. "It's just a silly crush. I'm sure it'll pass."

She'd been telling herself that for five years now.

Cory sighed and looked across the aisle. A mother and her two kids came toward them, and neither Libby nor Cory moved, though their cart sat on one side of the aisle and they stood on the other.

She obviously knew something was wrong here, and she met Libby's eyes with her wide ones. Libby shook her head slightly, and the mother herded her children through the narrow space to get to the goldfish down at the other end.

"Well," he finally said. "What do you want to do? Do you want to break-up with me?"

Libby had no idea what she wanted to do. She thought of Cory, and how charming he'd been. He'd swept her off her feet when she'd least expected it, and she did have fun with him.

But seeing Mister….

No one was Mister Glover, and she knew that deep down in her core.

"Let's just go to the picnic," she said.

"I don't want to go meet your whole family if this isn't going to work out between us," Cory said, moving over to the shopping cart. He looked at her, his unspoken words loud enough for her to hear.

You have to choose, Libby.

Now.

Help me, she prayed, and Libby closed her eyes and thought about what she wanted her future to look like. Her therapist had her do these types of visualization techniques, and she'd gotten very good at them.

She did see the brick red house in her future. The ranch she loved, with the job she loved, wrangling cattle and setting up for the Country Christmas.

And when she went home, it was to a tall, dark, handsome cowboy who'd known her for so long, he knew her better than she knew herself.

"I don't think you should come to the picnic," Libby whispered.

Cory blinked, obviously surprised, and then he scoffed. "Fine." With that, he left the cart full of groceries right there in the snack aisle and walked out.

Libby stood there frozen for another moment, then she went over to the cart and steadied herself against it. Her breath stuttered out of her lungs, and her next thought was that perhaps Mister hadn't left Wilde & Organic yet.

Perhaps she could find him and tell him what had just happened and invite him to the family picnic instead.

She looked toward the end of the aisle, and then she hurried away from the cart of groceries, her goal singular: *Find Mister. Find Mister right now.*

CHAPTER 3

"Are you Mister Glover?"

Mister stopped in his flight from the grocer and turned to look at the teenager who'd just used his name. He immediately put a smile on his face, though the heat wouldn't allow him to stand out here on this blacktop and chat for long.

You have ice cream with you, he told himself even as he said, "I sure am," out loud.

The boy exchanged a glance with his friend. "I knew it." He grinned like he'd just discovered he could have cake for breakfast, and he added, "I just read your article in *Rodeo Today*. I'm a calf roper too."

"Are you now?"

"Do you have it?" the boy asked his friend, who gestured back toward one of the cars in the parking lot.

"In the truck," he said.

The first boy looked at him with pure hope pouring

from every pore in his body. "Do you have a minute? We have the issue with your article in it, and I'd love for you to sign it." He practically bounced on the balls of his feet.

Mister couldn't say no to that. He wouldn't, no matter the circumstance, and he said, "Sure thing. Where are you parked?"

"Right here," the second boy said, striding further into the lot.

Mister started to walk with the first boy. "So you rope? Are you doing junior PRCA? Something through the high school?"

"Junior PRCA," he said. "I'm the top qualifier for calf roping. Me and Jake do the team roping. We're third in the region."

"Wow," Mister said, truly impressed. "When are you guys doing rodeos this summer?" He liked to attend a handful of competitions, simply because a spirit and excitement hung in the air at a rodeo that Mister's soul craved.

"We have one tomorrow night," the boy said. "Right here in town."

"Fantastic," Mister said while the other boy bent into his vehicle. "I'm just getting back into town, so I probably can't make that work, but I'd love to come to some junior events." He'd been retired from the rodeo for about a decade now, but he still had an agent who booked him with some endorsement spots from time to time.

Nothing for a while, and Mister should probably contact Josiah and let him know he was back at Shiloh

Ridge, with more freedom in his life. Not only that, but Wyatt Walker had been bugging Mister to do a charity event with him. Wyatt had been a far bigger star than Mister had ever been, but he said God must've put them in the same small Texas town for a reason.

The teen emerged from his truck with a tattered copy of *Rodeo Today*. He held it up like a trophy and said, "I like your beard."

"Me too," the first boy said quickly.

"Thanks." Mister automatically reached to touch his facial hair. "Sure is hot, though. I'll probably shave before the Sabbath. My momma will probably fall down dead if I don't." He chuckled, though Mother didn't care if her sons wore "tasteful" beards. Her word, not his.

He took the magazine from the teen and then a pen. "What are your names?" He looked at the second boy. "He said your name was Jake."

"Yeah, Jake."

"I'm Karl."

"Jake and Karl...." Mister said slowly, scrawling out the names. He had a saying he used when he signed autographs like this. *Aim high. Shoot straight. Praise God.*

He wrote out the words and then added his signature with a flourish of an M and a G. He grinned at it, as he hadn't signed anything since leaving Texas almost a year ago. "There you go."

"Thanks so much," Karl gushed, taking the magazine and staring at it. He met Jake's eyes, and the two of them shared some insider secret Mister couldn't decipher.

"Mister," someone called behind him, and he turned back the way he'd come.

Libby picked up her step, jogging for a stride or two before settling back into a walk. His heart split in half, one part flinging itself right into the back of his throat and the other plummeting all the way to the soles of his boots.

"Excuse me, fellas," he said, flashing them another pro-rodeo smile. He felt the weight of the quart of ice cream in his plastic shopping bag as he took a few steps toward Libby. She wore pure anxiety on her face. It filled the air around her, and he could almost see a cloud above her head.

"Do you have a minute?" she asked, and it hit his ears the same way the request from the teenagers had. Unsure. Afraid. Stunningly hopeful.

"Of course," he said as diplomatically as possible. He lifted his arm as Libby approached and put it around her shoulders. "But not in the heat, Libs. Can we sit in my truck and blast the AC?"

She nodded, her swallow audibly punching him in the eardrum.

He took her across the aisle to his truck, opened her door for her, and steadied her as she climbed in. Behind the wheel, he nearly choked on the accumulation of hot air, and he got the engine started as quickly as possible.

He set the melting ice cream on the console between them and adjusted all of the vents to be blowing ice-cold air into the cab. Then he waited.

Libby's hands went round and round one another, and

Mister hated that with as much heat as the sun blasted into Texas that day. He reached over and took one of her hands in his. "Libby," he said. "It's just me."

"I broke up with him."

Mister sighed and looked out his side window. "You didn't have to do that." This Cory fellow had sure seemed interested in Libby. He'd been all smiles and darlin's and baby's.

"I did," she said. "He's not right for me."

"He sure seemed to like you. You're telling me you didn't like him?"

Libby didn't say that, and Mister honestly wondered what was going through her head. He gave her some seconds to respond, and she finally said, "I'm not ready to be with anyone else."

"Anyone else...besides who?" he asked, turning to look at her.

She met his eye too. "Besides you, Mister."

The sky could've fallen and he wouldn't have known it. He blinked and stared, his brain misfiring. Surely he'd heard her wrong. "I don't know what to say. I thought...." He swallowed, and he now had the loud gulp coming from his throat.

"I don't know what I'm saying either," she said. "I just know that seeing you, and then seeing him, and there's no contest. It's you. You win every time."

"But you don't want to be with me." Mister didn't like the shape or sound of the words as they came out of his mouth, because they were too true. He'd asked her out so many times. He'd begged. He'd apologized. He'd left town for a year, for crying out loud. All of it was in an attempt to figure out who he was and what he really wanted.

"I wish we could rewind," Libby said. "Just go back in time a few years, and I'd do things differently, and so would you, and everything would be better." She sighed and gently tugged her hand away from his. She cleared her throat. "I know you have ice cream and your whole family anticipating your return. I don't want to keep you from them."

Mister would stay as long as she wanted, but he kept that to himself.

"Maybe…maybe could we just pretend like we can rewind? Just me and you. We'll go back in our minds, and it will be like the last three years haven't happened."

Mister smiled, but she didn't look at him. "I don't know how to do that," he said.

"Yeah, I don't either." She sounded absolutely miserable. She reached for the door handle. "I just wanted you to know I broke up with him." She slid from the truck. "Can I call you later?"

"Of course."

With that, she closed the door and walked away. Mister sat in the air conditioning, completely confused and trying to figure out how to rewind time.

MISTER'S MIND FINALLY MOVED AWAY FROM Libby Bellamore when he reached the right turn off the highway that led up to Shiloh Ridge Ranch. He hadn't even completed the turn when all sorts of New hit him.

"Holy dairy cows," he said, easing his foot over to the brake. The truck came to a stop, and he simply stared at the development on both sides of the now-dirt road. To his left, barns and buildings had gone up, and the finest materials had been used. Another dirt road branched down through the buildings, and Mister let the truck drift toward that junction.

He looked down the road, where a big, beautiful homestead rose from ground that had previously been barren.

The windows glinted with light, and two men worked on the roof, bending down and doing something to make sure it was what it needed to be. Dirt and gravel mostly covered the ground, but he could see places where the lawn would go in.

The big garage-style doors on the equipment building stood open, and he could see a large, green swather parked inside. His gaze switched to the land beyond the new buildings, and he saw that it had been cultivated. Hay grew, and some fields were the pastures that Ward loved to use with his rotational ranching technique.

To his right, more storage buildings stood, including a large barn that had been painted a bright gray and had black trim along the doors and windows. "That's different," Mister said. He liked different, especially when it came to barns and ranches. The front of the barn bore enormous letters between the slanted rooftop, also painted black

SRR shone down at him, in their family's letter logo, something his grandfather had designed decades ago. A sense of generational pride filled Mister's chest, and his smile took up his whole face.

"Nice work, Bishop," he said to himself. "And Montana. You two are extraordinary." Mister thought all of his siblings possessed some sort of super power; Bishop's just happened to be in wielding a hammer and making wood bend to his will.

He continued up the lane and passed under the official sign, which welcomed everyone to the ranch. He wondered if they'd move the sign closer to the highway now, and he knew he wouldn't have to be in the dark for long. Nothing stayed too secret in the Glover family.

Preacher had tried his hardest to keep his girlfriend a secret, and out of all of them, he'd succeeded the most at keeping something under wraps. Of course, then he'd suffered through a horrendous car accident that still brought chills to the back of Mister's neck.

He pulled up to the homestead, though he knew Bear and Sammy didn't live there anymore. The huge house was still the epicenter of the ranch, and no less than four vehicles sat outside of it.

Including an ATV.

Mister eyed the machine as he snagged the grocery bag and headed for the front door. It opened before he even put a foot on the bottom step, and Ranger said, "The

Prodigal Son returns," with a smile the size of Texas on his face.

"Not true," Mister said as he started up the steps. "Trust me, there were no parties in Oklahoma."

Ranger laughed as he took Mister into a hug, and Mister could admit he missed embracing his brothers and cousins. He was much more touchy-feely than most of the Glovers, and he loved a good hug from anyone he could get one from.

"Come on in," he said. "Etta was alerted of your proximity, and she threw together some pizzas."

"Of course she did," Mister said, though he wouldn't say no to his cousin's pizza.

"We've got a new pizza oven," Ranger said. "Wood-fired. You're gonna love it." He led the way inside the homestead, and while the noise didn't knock Mister back on his heels, a buzz definitely streamed through the arched doorway that led into the kitchen and living area.

Etta appeared there, wearing an apron. She licked her finger and then opened her arms to Mister. He jogged the last couple of steps to her and lifted her right off her feet while the pair of them laughed. The past six months had found the two of them connecting in new ways, as they were now the last two people in the family without a significant other.

"Come make your pizza," she said. "Thirty seconds. Then I can fire it while you say hello to everyone else." She stepped back and beamed her brightest smile at him. Why she hadn't been able to find someone to fall madly in love with her, Mister would never know.

He followed her into the kitchen and handed the groceries to Preacher, who'd been hovering just out of sight. "You're a Godsend," Preacher said, clapping Mister on the shoulder before taking out the carton of half-melted ice cream and heading for the couch where his wife sat.

Mister detoured into the kitchen while Charlie called hello to him, and he let Etta sauce his dough with Alfredo. Then he piled on the chicken, bacon, olives, and ham and let her add a more-than-healthy amount of cheese.

"Ten minutes," she said, sliding the pizza onto a paddle and heading for the door. She went outside, and Mister's curiosity went with her. He poked his head out the door to find her sliding his pizza into a legit oven. She closed the lid and stepped over to a second pod and opened that door.

"Preach, yours is ready," she called.

"Comin'," he said from behind Mister. Etta pulled the pie out and started for the house. Mister got out of the way, and he marveled at the melty cheese and the scent of marinara and pepperoni as she passed.

Three pizza ovens took up the end of the deck immediately outside the door, and they looked like outdoor grills. They stood waist-high, so it was easy to get the pizzas in and out, and the doors were clear, so he could see inside. He peered through the glass on his oven, and he watched the flames lick up between the grill where his pizza sat on a silver tray.

His stomach grumbled, and he turned to go inside. He sealed the heat outside and bent down as Wilder spotted him and started running toward him. "Uncle Misser!" the boy cried out, his chubby toddler legs barely keeping him upright.

"Heya, bud." He scooped up the little boy, who'd turned two a few months ago. "Did you get a pizza from Auntie Etta?"

"Not yet," Oakley said, following her son. She embraced them both and took Wilder from him. "Your mother is bringing Fawn down, if you want to hold her." She smiled down at her son. "Come on, baby. Let's go make a pizza for you and me. Daddy already put his in."

"Cheese," Wilder said, and Mister chuckled at him.

Mother entered the kitchen, and she looked so happy carrying Ranger and Oakley's little girl in her arms. If possible, her expression doubled with joy when she saw Mister. "Oh, you're home," she said, and that summed it all up for Mister.

He moved toward her and she toward him, quickly passing Fawn to Ranger, and Mister had never felt more loved and like he belonged somewhere more than he did when his mother wrapped her arms around him and held him tight.

"Incoming," someone said behind him, and he released his mom to see Cactus entering through the deck door. "The whole gang is on the way." He grinned at Mister.

"Everyone?" Mister asked.

"Of course." Cactus drew him into a hug, and that too felt like coming home to Mister. "Didn't you know we look for every excuse to have a party around here?"

"The official welcome-home party is tomorrow," Etta said from the kitchen. "One o'clock sharp."

"She's not wrong," Cactus said. "But I can smell that pizza all the way out at the Edge, and I figured I might as well come in."

"Same," Ward said from behind him, and Cactus moved so Ward could welcome Mister home too. He should've known his homecoming would bring a crowd, and it did, as more and more of his siblings, cousins, and their spouses arrived at the homestead.

Mister didn't mind, because he thrived on the energy of a crowd.

When Bear finally opened the deck door and held it for his wife and child, then entered with his baby girl in his arms, Mister felt real tears prick his eyes. For some reason, Bear represented Shiloh Ridge to Mister, and he jumped to his feet from the table, where he'd already eaten half of his pizza.

"Bear," he said, and his eldest brother zeroed in on him. He handed Heather to Sammy and engulfed Mister in a rib-crushing hug. Neither of them said anything, but so much passed between them.

Bear held him and held him, just the way Mister imagined his father would have after he'd completed his year in the cowboy cabins. Once again, Mister thought, *I did it, Dad. I did it, and I'm so much better now.*

Bear finally stepped back and cupped Mister's face in his hands. "You'll come by tonight, and we'll get everything sorted. All right?"

Mister could only nod, and Bear patted his face and then turned toward the kitchen. "All right," he said. "I heard there was a chance I could make a dessert pizza...Etta?"

"The Oreos are already crushed up, Bear," she said without missing a beat. "Come make your cookie pizza."

CHAPTER 4

*L*ibby stirred the almond punch, the scent of lemons and oranges thick in the air around her.

Her mind had not thought of anything but measurements and Mister, and she wondered how she could possibly call him later today. What was there to say?

I'm not ready to be with anyone else.

She couldn't say that again.

"What a disaster," she muttered to herself as the front door opened.

"I'm here," Jack called, and with just three footfalls, he appeared in the back of the house. The living room took up the right half and the kitchen-dining-room combo took up the left. The two bedrooms sat down a short hall that ran off the living room, and a big storage room, a mud room from the side entrance, and a half-bath extended off the kitchen.

"Also, I just figured out where Frankie's been escaping

to all this time." He grinned at her and thumbed back toward the front door. "He's asleep out there on that fluffy rug on your front porch. Barely moved as I came up the steps."

"Really?" Libby asked. "I didn't know he did that." Franklin was technically Jack's golden retriever, but he had been spending more and more time with Libby on the ranch in recent months.

"Avoiding the heat," Jack said with a grin. "How's the punch coming?"

"I just finished," Libby said, reaching for the screw-top lid for the huge cooler she'd made the punch in. "Thanks for coming to get it." She couldn't lift the heavy container, and she'd called on Jack for help.

She'd been doing that for as long as she could remember, and her oldest brother had always been there when she'd needed him. Now, he smiled at her and took in the mess on the counter before returning his gaze to hers. "You look tired, Libs," he said.

"That's just what every woman wants to hear," she said, rolling her eyes. She picked up the teaspoons and measuring cups she'd used and started putting them in the sink.

"Are you okay?"

That was the question of the century, wasn't it? Libby felt the weight of the world resting on the back of her neck, her shoulders straining to hold it up. She'd never been able to hide much from her family, and the picnic was only thirty minutes away.

"I broke up with Cory," she said. Everyone would need the story once they got together, but Libby could practice her speech on Jack.

"You did?" He stepped closer. "Why? Y'all have been dating for months. I thought we were gonna meet him today."

"You were." She turned on the water in the sink. "And it's been two months. That's barely plural."

Jack didn't say that it was two months longer than anyone she'd been out with in the past five years, but the words somehow streamed through the kitchen anyway.

"What happened?" Jack stepped next to her, which only made Libby feel claustrophobic.

She looked up at her older brother. He'd been married for a decade now, and he had three kids, one of whom had just been born a few months ago. He had light brown hair while hers was a little darker, but the kindest hazel eyes in the world. Just like Papa.

She'd spent most of her explanations about Mister on Mildred, but it wasn't like Jack didn't know. "I ran into Mister Glover at the grocery store," she said.

"Oh, boy." Jack blew out his breath. "Today?"

She nodded as she rinsed the measuring equipment of the almond extract and sugar she'd put into the punch. "I just...when I think about my future, he's in it. No one else." She sounded absolutely miserable about that, because she was.

"Well, maybe that means something," Jack said, though his eyebrows had drawn down into a V.

"Yeah, I'm insane," Libby said. She turned off the water and left the rest of the dishes. "I just need to whip the cream for the key lime pie, and I'll be there with it and the chips. You go on ahead."

"You sure?" Jack asked. "I can stay, and you can tell me everything." He would too, and he'd listen and give her the best advice he had. Libby knew that, and she loved her brother fiercely for it.

She shook her head. "Mildred will demand the full story at lunch, and Mama will want to know too. I can't tell it twice."

"All right," Jack said with the pitch of doubt in his tone. "You come by the house if you need anything. A bowl of ice cream. A break from Mildred…."

Libby grinned at him, and they laughed together briefly. Then Jack lifted the heavy container of punch and Libby hastened to get the door for him. He lugged it down the front steps of the house Libby loved so much and put it in the back of his truck.

She turned toward Frankie, who really hadn't moved. "Come on, you lazy thing," she said to the dog. He lifted his head and looked at her like she had disturbed a great slumber. "Come get a drink, Frankie." He lumbered to his feet and trotted into the house, where Libby followed and closed the door, keeping out the heat and humidity.

She filled a bowl for Frankie, adding ice to the water, and set it in the mudroom where she wouldn't have to clean it up for a while. She got out the cream and started whipping it, adding a fistful of sugar and a capful of vanilla to make it sweet and delicious. With the tart filling in the key lime pie, it would be perfect.

She could just spread it over the solidified custard, but Libby filled a piping bag with the stiff cream instead, and she piped on beautiful ridged dollops that reminded her of clouds until the whole pie was covered.

Satisfied with the dessert, she slid it into the fridge and started taking the bags of chips out to her car. They'd eat at a covered, outdoor table Papa had built to hold them all, and Mama would have the misters going so it wouldn't be too terribly hot.

Libby had the hardest time getting herself to leave the house, though she'd started her truck and had the air conditioning blowing. Finally, when she risked being late and calling even more attention to herself, she said, "Come on, Frankie. Let's go."

With the pie in one hand and Frankie leading the way, Libby finally made it to her truck. The dog rode up front with her, and she trundled along the ranch roads and up to the main homestead, where Mama and Papa lived.

She parked beside Cord's truck, looped all the bags of potato chips around her wrist, and collected the pie. Mama had always wanted a long sidewalk edged with flowers, and the homestead definitely had one. Papa had put it in for her, and Mama spent hours in her yard, making it into a paradise in the Panhandle. She'd even won Yard of the Year once, a fact she wore with great pride.

Libby went up to the house and through it to the back

yard, where she found everyone had arrived ahead of her. Not surprising, given her reluctance to come. Cord carried his five-year-old on his shoulders while he put something on the serving table and Mildred sat at the long picnic table with her fiancé, Scott, their heads bent together as they likely talked about their upcoming wedding. They'd been engaged for eight days now, though it felt like eight years for how often Mildred spoke about their plans to get married.

Suzy, Jack's wife, had corralled their two older boys at the table, and she held their baby girl on her hip as she stood behind them, talking to Cord's wife, Anne-Marie. Libby couldn't see Papa, and the suckling pig hadn't made an appearance either, which meant he was probably down at the pit tending to it.

"Here she is," Jack said, noticing her first, probably because Frankie had trotted ahead of her and nosed his hand.

Mama flitted around the serving table, and she pointed at the end of it. "Chips down there, darlin'." She looked at Libby with fondness, which quickly switched to concern. "Where's Cory?" She took the key lime pie and placed it next to the pecan one she'd made. Of course. They couldn't have a picnic or barbecue in the state of Texas without pecan pie.

Libby cleared her throat, which seemed to bring all chatter to a stop. Even Jack's boys stopped arguing at the table. "Uh, he's not coming," she said, her voice sounding like she'd grated it to put on pizza later. "We broke up."

Mama's eyebrows shot up. "You broke up?"

"Why?" Mildred asked in near tandem, suddenly not at the picnic table anymore. Libby cut a glance at her, but she'd much rather look at Mama. Mildred would be able to see the truth whether Libby said it out loud or not, and that always unnerved her.

She'd lived with her sister for years now, and they knew each other so well. Libby did love Mildred, but she couldn't help feeling...abandoned. Mildred had said she didn't even like Scott that much until about two weeks ago. In fact, she'd told Libby three Sundays ago—nineteen days to be precise—that she was probably going to break up with him.

Now she was engaged to him, and Libby hadn't had a conversation with her sister without Scott present or the topic of all they talked about.

"He just wasn't right for me." Libby reached to start opening the bags of chips, something she'd seen her mother do at every picnic they'd ever had.

"I'm sorry, dear," Mama said, and Libby nodded.

She wouldn't be able to avoid Mildred forever, and sure enough, the moment she looked up, her older sister stood right there. She folded her arms, cocked that hip, and let her eyebrows do the talking.

Libby glanced at Mama, who pretended not to hear the silent conversation, but she wasn't doing anything now but moving dishes around.

"Fine," Libby said. "I ran into Mister Glover at Wilde and Organic this afternoon."

A gasp flew from Mildred's mouth, which might as well have been a stream of questions. *You did? What happened? What did you say? Did he ask you out? Do you still like him? Libby, when are you going to follow your heart?*

Libby would follow her heart when it came to Mister Glover when she could trust he wouldn't break it. No one knew Mister the way she did, and Mildred hadn't been there the night she'd seen him get three women's phone numbers, then kiss a fourth, and then brag about it to all of his rodeo cowboy buddies.

Libby had been there, and she'd been disgusted by his behavior.

It was ten years ago, she told herself, not for the first time. Not even for the hundredth time. Everything about that night was still so vivid in her head, and while she hadn't had feelings for the man at the time, she had just been played by a man exactly like Mister. She'd vowed then and there that she would *not* allow herself to be taken in by a charmer again. And Mister Glover was absolutely the worst kind of charmer in the world.

Nothing made sense in her head or her heart, and she didn't have words to explain it. Her past with Mister was fraught with potholes and experiences, some good and some bad. She didn't know how to sift through the bad ones to the good, and she didn't know how to make that man she'd seen in the dance hall and known to be a complete womanizer mesh with the one she'd run into at Wilde & Organic today.

No, they weren't the same person. Intellectually, she

knew that. Her heart didn't seem to know the difference, and it still screamed her vow at her every time she even thought about getting close to Mister.

She reached up and touched her lips, where Mister had kissed last year when he'd left Three Rivers. That had really messed her up, and she was still unraveling those emotions with her therapist.

"Did he ask you out?" Mildred asked.

"No, he did not," Libby clipped out, wishing Mildred knew when to drop things. She glanced at Mama. "What else do we need? Are we close to ready?"

"Just your daddy to bring up the pig," she said, turning to look down the hill from the back yard. "Oh, I see him." She busied herself with making more space for the pit-roasted pig, though there was already plenty.

"Did you ask him out?" Mildred asked, as if the conversation hadn't moved on at all.

"No," Libby said, shooting her a glare. "I'm not going to do that."

"I think you should." Mildred lifted her chin as if daring Libby to defy her. "The Good Lord knows it's time you got out of your own way when it comes to that man."

Libby wanted to spit something out about how the Good Lord had abandoned her, just like everyone else had, but somewhere in the back of her mind, she knew He hadn't. She also didn't want to come across as childish and petulant. "I should be paying you to be my therapist," she said instead.

"Girls," Mama said. "Not today, okay? Right here, Brit."

Papa arrived with the weight of the pig making his arms shake, and he slid the wooden board he carried onto the table with a grunt. A smile instantly filled his face and he looked at his wife and put his arm around her waist.

To Libby, they'd always been the perfect couple, a complement to each other in a way she wanted badly in her life. When she closed her eyes at night and pictured herself with a big, strong cowboy who could carry a whole pig up a hill for their picnic, it wasn't someone like Cory.

It was Mister Glover. Always.

"Let's say grace," Papa said, and they all moved over to the big picnic table. "Jack, would you?"

"Yes, sir," Jack said, reaching up to swipe off his cowboy hat. Libby positioned herself in the direct path of one of the misters, and she enjoyed the rush of cool air as her brother prayed. She bowed her head, but she didn't close her eyes, and while Jack spoke, she looked up and around at her family members.

They definitely possessed a faith she didn't have, and she mourned the loss of it. She needed to figure out where it had gone, and how she could get it back, because for the first time in her life, she felt like an outcast in her family. She hated that, and tears pricked her eyes.

Please, she prayed, maybe for the first time in months. *Please bless me to know what to do to come back to Thee.*

"Amen," Mildred said from beside her, her eyes immediately moving to Libby's. She searched and she *saw*, and that made Libby want to cry even harder.

Instead of abandoning her, Mildred looped her arm through Libby's and said, "Me and you, tonight. *Emma*. Popcorn and ice cream and truth."

Libby nodded, because she needed Mildred more than ever right now, and she'd felt like she'd lost her.

Mildred gave a final nod and watched as their nephews dashed by to get to the food first. "Really, Libby. What are you going to do about Mister?"

She shrugged, that nagging weight settling right around her neck again, almost like a yoke. "He said I could call him later."

"Okay," Mildred said brightly. "That's good. So you'll do that, and we'll go from there."

Because it was easier than arguing, especially after Mama had asked them not to, Libby nodded again. Deep down, however, she did not think she could dial Mister's number without being in some sort of drugged out condition.

She had been texting him while he'd been gone, and she stepped to the other side of the serving table and looked out over the farm. She lifted her phone and snapped a picture, capturing the perfect Texas afternoon from her perspective.

She sent that to Mister while Suzy argued with her boys about eating pie before pig, and she smiled when he responded almost instantly with, *I wish I was there. There's no better view of Texas than Golden Hour Ranch.*

Plus, my papa made that pig you love, she sent, teasing him.

Save me some if you can, he said. *I'll come get it tomorrow.*

She wasn't sure if he meant that or not, and Cord bumped her playfully and said, "Talkin' to your boyfriend? I heard you broke up with him."

She shoved her phone in her back pocket and smiled at her brother. "I did," she said, feeling stronger about the decision now than she had even ten minutes ago. "I hope I didn't hurt him too badly, but it just wasn't a good fit."

"We got a new junior rider today," Cord said. "He seemed like a nice guy."

Libby fixed her brother with a stare. "A junior rider? Really? What's he like, twenty-five?"

"He's twenty-six," Cord said coolly, his face one of stone.

Libby rolled her eyes, which made Cord laugh. "No thanks."

"Yeah, you're too good for him, Libs," Cord said as he loaded his plate with pork and potatoes. "Hang in there. You'll find someone." He lifted his head as Papa said he had an announcement, and so did Libby.

"Your mother and I are taking a cruise next month," Papa said, beaming out at the kids and grandkids. "We wanted you to know. We'll have been married for forty-seven years in August, and we're celebrating by going to the Caribbean."

Jack whistled through his teeth, and Libby added her whoops to those of her siblings. They quieted down quickly, and Cord said. "Anne-Marie and I have an announcement too. She's due in November."

"Oh, that's wonderful," Mama gushed, rushing at Anne-Marie. Libby grinned too, because she knew Anne-Marie had been trying to get pregnant for a long time now. Her only other child was already five, and Libby nudged Cord with her hip.

"Congratulations," she said.

"Yeah, thanks." Cord wore a smile that couldn't be erased, and Libby wondered what it would feel like to be that happy. She didn't know, but the idea that she should call Mister and find out if the kiss he'd given her last year, which had kept her warm and safe all these months, could help generate some of that happiness.

CHAPTER 5

"This is incredible," Mister said, gazing up at the two-story house. It seemed to be made of diamonds and steel, and it didn't seem like the kind of house Bear would like at all. It had taken him over a year to come to terms with knocking down the original homestead and building something that would take the family into the future.

It had, but the family had grown so much in the past several years that Bear had needed a place of his own.

"It's all done with reclaimed wood from here at the ranch." Bear spoke with a measure of pride, and he started down the sidewalk. "Sammy wanted a big yard for the kids, which I don't get. The ranch is hundreds of acres." He didn't sound happy about that. "So now I'm paying Brandon Rhinehart to come mow my lawn."

Mister chuckled as he walked with his brother. "You sound like a grumpy old man."

"I *am* a grumpy old man," Bear said, sliding him a smile and a look out of the corner of his eye. "I'm going to be fifty this year, Mister. *Fifty.*"

That did sound old to Mister, who was knocking on the door of thirty-six. "How many kids are you and Sammy going to have?"

"I think we might be done," Bear said. "This last pregnancy cost her a lot, and we've got three kids under the age of four. Plus Link, though he's a huge help most of the time. If I can get him away from Mitch." He went up the front steps to the beautifully carved door.

"Micah did this, didn't he?" Mister asked, reaching out to trace the elegant swirls. His eyes caught on some letters in the wood, and he easily picked out GLOVER among all the lines and circles.

"He did," Bear said. "Bishop and Montana did a lot of coordinating with the sub-contractors, and Bish came over lots of times to help out."

"Preacher's place must've kept them busy."

"Beyond busy," Bear said. "That's how we got all the wood from the shop." He chuckled and reached to open the door. "If Bishop hadn't been so distracted with five billion things down the hill, I know he wouldn't have agreed."

"Sneaky." Mister stepped into the air-conditioned house first, getting a blast of pure sugar in his nose. "Wow. What is that?" The smell was familiar, but he couldn't place it.

They'd stepped into a wide foyer, but it wasn't like at

the homestead, where the rest of the house couldn't be seen from the front door. This house opened up instantly, with carpeting running from several feet in front of Mister to the far right wall. Couches and bean bags filled the living room, and a huge television hung on the wall above the fireplace.

The dining room took up the back corner of the house and blended into the kitchen, where Sammy stood twirling her arm in a huge, tin bin. Wafts of what looked like cotton lifted out the bin, and Mister grinned. "She's making cotton candy."

"We get no sleep around here," Bear said dryly. He closed the door behind him and called, "Hey, baby. We're here."

Sammy looked up, her expression open and wide before she let it dissolve into happiness. "Daddy's home." She looked down at her side and handed a smaller person the stick of cotton candy.

Smiles came running around the island, his little legs pumping hard. "Daddy!" He held up the blue cotton candy like a spear. "Momma made cotton candy! It's bwue!"

Bear chuckled as he swooped his son into his arms. "It sure is, bud. Are we eatin' sweets before dinner?"

"Momma said I ate my pizza."

Sammy approached with another stick with a big, puffy cloud of cotton candy on it. "Hey, Mister." She handed him the treat and hugged him again. When she stepped over to her husband, she said, "I put fish in the oven for dinner, and I didn't feel like fighting with him." She stretched up and kissed him, and Mister sure did like watching Bear's love for his wife and kids.

"He ate his whole pizza," Bear said, smiling at her with so much adoration that Mister almost sighed. He couldn't help thinking of Libby, and he looked into the kitchen to find a clock. She'd asked if she could call him later, and he'd said yes.

He had serious doubts that she'd call. Libby had never been good at taking the first step or making the first move. He'd teased her for years about her shyness as they'd grown up together, and at that moment, it was just one more thing he regretted when it came to Liberty Bellamore.

He started toward the kitchen, where he found Russ playing with a set of measuring cups on the floor. Mister crouched down as the little boy looked up, and Russ's face brightened with recognition. He didn't speak much, but he was only eighteen months old and he had an older brother who never seemed to stop talking.

"Hey, baby boy," Mister said, picking him up. "Come sit with me in the living room." He didn't particularly want fish for dinner either, and he told himself he didn't have to stay. After the pizza party that afternoon, he'd moved his few boxes into the upstairs bedroom of the homestead, and Mister suspected he'd get behind the wheel of his truck and go pick up a bag of hamburgers for dinner.

"How long until dinner?" Bear asked.

"Fifteen minutes," Sammy said.

"Mister." Bear nodded to the left, where a double-wide doorway sat. "Let's get this done, and then you can go get your pizza."

"I'm not going to get pizza," Mister said, detouring toward the office. A hallway stretched off the kitchen, and he assumed the master suite sat down there. A set of steps went up between the office entrance and the hallway, and surely the other bedrooms waited up there.

"Burgers and fries then," Bear said with a grin.

"Maybe," Mister said, not wanting to concede the point. It annoyed him that Bear knew him so well when he felt like he'd changed so much.

Bear settled at his desk with Smiles on his lap, happily munching on his cotton candy. Benny, their black and white family dog, made a groaning noise and came out from underneath the desk as Bear said, "Sorry, bud. I didn't know you were there."

The dog flopped on the ground in front of the desk and rested his head on his front paws as if Bear had wounded him terribly. Mister grinned at the dog and sat in one of the chairs before the desk, settling his nephew on his lap.

"I'm going to put you on Ward's crew," Bear said, and he plucked a folder from a stack on his desk. "Preacher is doing a lot more down the hill, and he's working with Judge and Ace, and he's in the process of hiring several more cowboys. Ward's doing all the herds and pastures, and he needs a lot of help with the new land down the hill." Bear smiled and tapped his computer. "When we met, they fought over you, you should know."

"I'm just another body," Mister said.

Bear met his eyes, so much seriousness in his. "That's simply not true, Mister. You care about this place, and that means something. You're a Glover." He slid the folder to the edge of the desk. "These are all the forms you need to take to the bank to get my name off your account. You'll be back on the payroll this Friday, and if you're unhappy about the living situation at any time, you can come to us and say so. I don't expect you'll want to live in a single bedroom and bathroom for long."

He raised his eyebrows, but Mister didn't know what to say. "It's fine," he said. "I'm not sharing with someone who snores, so." He shrugged and grinned.

"There's other places for you," he said. "The Top Cottage is open. There are plots of land for another house. When you get married, you'll especially want somewhere of your own."

"That's a long while off," Mister said. "I'm not even dating anyone."

Bear's eyebrows went up, but he only said, "Okay. The four of us meet every week, and we have special appointments for anyone who needs them."

"I'm aware," Mister said, as he'd made one of those special appointments to meet with Bear, Ranger, Ward, and Preacher when he'd made the decision to leave Shiloh Ridge last year.

"Come by anytime," Bear said, rising to his feet. He came around the desk and the two brothers embraced again, the two little boys between them. "C'mere, Russ.

Uncle Mister has to go." He took the littler boy into his other arm, and Mister wanted to take a snapshot of him holding his two sons, that warm smile on his face.

"Thanks, Bear," Mister said, and he slipped out the front door. He checked his phone at the top of the porch steps, and it was with a long sigh that he continued back to his truck. Libby hadn't texted. She hadn't called.

"She's not going to," Mister said. "If you want to talk to her, you'll have to initiate it." He started the truck at the same time his phone chimed.

A smile sprang to his face at the picture from Libby, and his emotions went round and round as he realized he'd jumped to conclusions. "Later" could mean so many things. It didn't mean by the end of the day or anything.

He sat in his truck and texted with her for a couple of minutes, telling her he'd come get some of her daddy's famous suckling pig tomorrow. She didn't respond, but he didn't let his melancholy get him down.

The double bacon cheeseburgers helped with that, even if Mister did eat them alone, in the cab of his truck, while the people of Three Rivers bustled by on the other side of the windshield.

It's at 1, HE TYPED OUT AS THE CLOCK TICKED TO twelve-fifty. *Don't worry about it. I just thought if you weren't busy, you could come. There's going to be a million people there, and no one will care if there's one more.*

I'm sure that's true, Libby said. *I have that pig you wanted, but I'm not sure I can make it today.*

It's late notice, Mister said. *We'll get together another time.*

Libby took several seconds to respond, during which Mister started to feel antsy about going inside the homestead. This was his homecoming party, and he really shouldn't be late to it. Someone knocked on the window, startling him, and he turned to face Ace.

He rolled down the window and grinned at his cousin. "You're not going in?" Ace glanced over to his wife, who came up beside him with their son on her hip. "At least we're not the last ones to get here."

Gunnison, their son, sniffled and hiccuped, and he's obviously been bawling in the very recent past.

Mister reached to open the door just as his phone chimed at him. He couldn't help looking at it, and he saw Libby's name on the screen. When he met Ace's eyes, he saw that Ace had seen her name too.

"I'm coming," he said. "Just talking to Libby."

"That's good, right?" Ace asked, backing up as Mister slid from the truck.

"I'll take him," Mister said, reaching for Gunnison. "And yes, I guess it's good." He didn't get into all the particulars of how Libby had broken up with her boyfriend because of him and how confusing that was. Mister had wrestled with several problems in the past year, and he'd been able to make them line up and see them for what they were. Only then had he been able to move on, recognizing that yes, he'd once been a spoiled, self-serving rodeo star, but that now, he was someone different.

He didn't think only of himself the way he once had. He didn't scope out a room for the prettiest woman the moment he walked into a bar or restaurant. In fact, he didn't go to bars anymore. He'd never been much of a drinker, but he did love dancing with pretty women, getting their phone numbers that he never used, and kissing them down dark hallways.

Embarrassment tunneled through him every time he thought about that person he'd once been. It usually only lasted a few seconds or minutes, because the Lord had made it known to him that he had repented, changed, and didn't need to worry about those instances anymore.

Libby does, he thought, and he immediately prayed that her heart would be softened toward him, if at all possible. *I just want us to be friends*, he added. *I like having her in my life, and I need to know if there's anything I need to do to make her feel comfortable around me.*

"He might scream at you," Holly Ann said, passing over Gun. "He's not very happy right now, because he has a little cold."

"Are you sick, buddy?" Mister asked, taking the boy. The dark-haired child had such a mild demeanor, and he snuggled into Mister's shoulder, no scream in sight. He grinned at the child and then Ace and Holly Ann.

"Let's make a run for it," Ace said, grinning. "Maybe we can enjoy the party for once." He took his wife's hand and they started toward the homestead.

"Thanks, Mister," Holly Ann called over her shoulder, and Mister had his answer to his prayer.

He needed to thank Libby. "For what?" he asked, looking up into the sky as if the answer would form in the clouds. She'd been his best friend for years and years, and once again, Mister knew what he needed to thank her for.

He looked down at his phone to see what she'd said, and her answer was far better than a message in the sky.

Church tomorrow? Maybe you'd like a quieter row to sit on. I'll be by myself.

Sure, he tapped out. *Church tomorrow.*

He wasn't sure he'd count sitting through a sermon as a date, but with some semblance of one on the horizon, he found it easier to breathe, easier to take the first step toward the homestead, and easier to think he might find happiness someday.

CHAPTER 6

*L*ibby loved driving the big lawn mower around the ranch, and she'd just finished clipping the sprawling lawn surrounding the main homestead. She did all the lawns here at Golden Hour, including her two brothers', hers and Mildred's, and all the common areas down by the big commercial outdoor area where they ran their Country Christmas.

It took her a whole day to get all the grass cut, and it was one of her favorite days of the week. She could put in her headphones, bask in the warmth and light from the sun, and get tangible work done.

Sometimes, when she really needed to work through a difficult problem, her mowing days allowed her mind freedom and space to roam. She always found the answers she needed, and today, her mind had been moving back and forth between two subjects: Mister and her relationship with the Lord.

She'd agreed to meet the man at church tomorrow, and so she'd go. But she had no real hope of feeling anything there. It felt like the heavens had been closed to her for so long, and she also felt like she was ready to open the door again.

To both God and Mister.

A tremble ran through her stomach, but Libby tamped against it. She wasn't going to go into things nervous. Not this time. She wanted to wipe the slate clean with Mister —and herself—and to do that, she couldn't bring baggage from the past that made her anxious.

I want to do the right thing, she thought as she maneuvered the mower off the dirt road and onto the grass at Cord's house. He and Jack lived right next door to one another, and Libby had often felt left out of the friendship between their wives. She'd gotten over it, as she and Mildred were only seventeen months apart and the best of friends too.

All four women got along fine when they were together, and Libby couldn't expect to be everybody's best friend. She loved her sisters-in-law, and they took care of her and her parents with kindness and great care. She couldn't ask for more. It made sense that they shared a bond as newcomers to the Bellamore family and the ranch, and Libby's thoughts moved to the ranch wives up at Shiloh Ridge.

They had a community up there too, and while Libby had been invited to join them, she'd felt out of place and uncomfortable doing so.

Something clanked, and Libby immediately lifted her foot from the gas pedal and pressed on the brake. She muttered something about how Cord never cleaned up his lawn for Libby to mow, despite the reminder texts she sent, and let the mower come to a halt.

Sure enough, behind her on the lawn sat a now-partially-chewed-up baseball bat. "Great," she muttered, climbing down from the big seat that made her feel like a queen on a throne. Silly, she knew, because who would want to be queen of lawn mowers? Libby, that was who.

She went back and picked up the bat, tossing it into a nearby wheelbarrow. She pushed that around, collecting other items from the lawn that would wreak havoc with her mower, including a soccer ball, a length of garden hose, her nephew's bicycle, and a rake that had been left too close to the edge of the garden.

She stowed it all in the wheelbarrow for Cord and Anne-Marie to find later, and she started back toward where her mower sat waiting for her. The grass shone like emeralds in the sun, and sweat slipped down Libby's face. She reached up to wipe it, her eyes going closed for a moment.

The next thing she knew, pain flared through her ankle and knee, which both buckled. She threw her arms out to catch herself as she fell, but there was nothing to grab onto. She hit the ground with her knees, her hands, and then her chin before she was able to stop her forward momentum.

Instant humiliation ran through her, and her first

thought was to jump right back to her feet and pretend like everything was A-okay.

It only took two seconds for her to realize that wouldn't be happening. Echoes of pain throbbed through her knee, but it was really her ankle that screamed a warning at her. *Don't get up!* it said. *Stay here. I can't bend.*

She rolled over so she wasn't face-planted in Cord's too-long grass, and she told herself the feeling of getting her behind wet was just because the grass was hot. It sure felt wet, and Libby ran her palm along the tips of the grass, as if sitting on the wet ground was her biggest problem right now.

It did seem a little wet, and Libby huffed in frustration. Cord was supposed to modify his watering schedule so it wouldn't be wet when she mowed. Wet grass took up more room in the bag, and she had to empty it more often. Annoyance sang through her with the speed of her pulse —about the same way the waves of discomfort flowed up her leg and down into her toes.

She looked at her right leg, as if there would be a diagram outlined on her skin, telling her what she'd strained and done and how long it would take to heal. She ran her hands down her thigh to her knee, and it seemed okay. Twisted a little, sure. Both knees bore a bright green grass stain, but Libby had been touched by much dirtier things around the ranch.

She reached up and wiped her chin too, getting a little green there. "Great," she muttered. She had a lawn stain on her face. "That better come off before church tomorrow," she told the sky and the white, puffy clouds moving through it.

The air had gone dead, and that meant a suffocating breath for Libby. She took it and looked down at her ankle. It had already started to swell and bruise. Alarm pulled through her, and she didn't think she'd be able to stand without something to support her. In the middle of Cord's lawn, with everything now picked up, she had nothing.

She remembered her phone as the hard outline of it against her behind made itself known, and she pulled it from her pocket. Her first instinct was to dial Mildred, because the sisters had taken care of each other for so long. Mildred had even attended a year of nursing school before returning to the ranch after a devastating break-up. She never had returned to school, and she'd come up with the Country Christmas idea that year.

"What's up?" Mildred asked after only one ring. Her voice sounded chipper and upbeat, probably because she was going through their inventory for their Sunday Farmer's Market in a cool, dry, dark storage shed.

"I fell at Cord's," Libby said, feeling cold inside. She didn't handle getting hurt very well, and a measure of shock started to roll through her. "I hurt my ankle, and I don't know if I can get up."

"I'm down at the Country Barn," she said. "I'll be there in a few minutes. Are you bleeding?"

Libby looked at her free hand, and yes, she saw a scrape there. How did someone scrape their hand on blasted blades of grass? Sometimes Libby felt made of glass. One wrong touch and she shattered.

"No," she said anyway. "But my ankle is already swollen to twice its size, and it's turning blue."

"Blue?"

"Purple. Whatever color a bruise is."

"It sounds broken," Mildred said, all of her chirpiness now gone. "The skin isn't broken?"

"No."

"Don't try to get up," Mildred said in her Mom-tone. "I'll be right there."

Anne-Marie came out of the house a few seconds later, and she carried a water bottle in one hand and her phone in the other. "Yes, she's right out front," she said before hanging up. She rushed toward Libby. "Mildred called. Are you okay?"

"I don't know," Libby said, bracing her palms against the grass as her sister-in-law arrived.

"It's so hot," Anne-Marie said. "Drink something."

"I'm okay," Libby said. She carried water on the mower, and she drank all day long. She looked to where it waited for her, the thought of not getting her day of freedom under the sun overwhelming her with frustration.

Anne-Marie tucked her golden hair behind her ear, and Libby had the thought that she should dye her hair. She'd never done much experimenting with hair color, but Anne-Marie was a stylist, and she had a new color every few weeks.

"Do you think my hair would take blonde?" Libby asked.

Anne-Marie looked at her with surprise. "What?" Her eyes slid back down to Libby's ankle. "Honey, I think this is broken. Look at that bump." She pointed, and Libby winced though she hadn't touched it.

The thought of her touching it had Libby in a near-panic, pain pouring through her already. "Don't touch it," she practically shouted.

"I didn't," Anne-Marie said, but every cell in Libby's body trembled anyway. Her sister-in-law wore a look of sympathy, and she added, "Yes, I think you could do blonde. We could streak it and it would be amazing." A kind smile accompanied the words.

"You really think so?" Libby asked.

"I really do." Anne-Marie sat back on her haunches. "I could do it for you this week. I had one of my little granny clients pass away, and she doesn't come anymore."

"Oh, right," Libby said. "Esther. So sad."

"She was the cutest lady," Anne-Marie agreed. She took a big breath. "Anyway, there's a spot on Wednesday morning open if you want it."

Libby almost said no. She wasn't going to change her hair. But something inside her really wanted to. If she really wanted to move forward into the future without anything from her past holding her back, why shouldn't she change her hair?

"Okay," she said. "What time?"

"Ten-thirty," Anne-Marie said. "Then Suzy and I have lunch. You should join us. Tell Mildred too."

"Okay," Libby said, though she wasn't sure if she or Mildred would stay for the lunch. But maybe she would. Libby was tired of getting the same old things she'd always gotten. She wanted to try new things and see what happened. "Thanks, Anne-Marie."

They both looked up at gravel crunched under tires, and relief filled Libby as her sister jumped from the truck. She came toward Libby, worry on her face. She knelt in the grass as she said, "Hey." She took one look at Libby's ankle and said, "We have to go to the hospital."

"No," Libby said, her heartbeat bouncing up into her throat. "It's not that bad." She reached for her sister. "Help me up. I just need to work it out."

"I don't think so," Mildred said, and she held out both of her palms in the universal gesture of *stop! Stay there.* "It's broken, Libby."

"I just tripped on a divot," she said. "People don't break their ankles doing that."

"Some do," Mildred said. "I'm calling Cord and Jack."

"No," Libby said again, more forcefully this time. "They don't need to come in off the ranch for this." She reached for Anne-Marie and then Mildred. "You guys can help me to the truck. I'll go to the blasted hospital."

"Wait for Suzy," Anne-Marie said. "She's coming."

Sure enough, Suzy arrived less than a minute later, out of breath as she said, "My goodness. Libby, are you okay?"

"Her ankle is broken," Mildred said firmly. "We need to

get her to the truck, and I'm taking her to the hospital. I'll call Mama from there."

No one dared to argue with Mildred when she spoke in that tone, and the three of them managed to help Libby to her feet while she could only help them with one leg and two arms. She tried to test her weight on her right leg, but there was no way she could even press her toes into the ground.

She cried out, and she had to accept that yes, she'd broken her ankle. So she hobbled to the truck and let the others help her into it. Mildred got behind the wheel, and while her sister was usually a crazy driver and Libby only rode with her if absolutely necessary, the drive to the hospital passed in a blur.

In fact, Libby thought she might have zoned out, because she opened her eyes when Mildred said, "Wake up, Libs. We're here."

THREE HOURS LATER, LIBBY SAT UP IN HER hospital bed, her half-eaten lunch on a tray in front of her, and almost her entire family filling the room with her. Her ankle hadn't been broken, but fractured. Thankfully, it had not been bad enough to require surgery. She'd been relieved when the doctor had delivered that news, and tears pricked her eyes again as Mama finally returned to the room.

She'd gone back to the ranch to get Libby her favorite

pillow, because the doctor did want her to stay until evening, just to make sure the walking cast they'd done would be enough to hold the ankle. If not, he might need to put in a pin—a surgery—and then do a full plaster cast.

"Here you go, darling," Mama said, tucking the pillow behind Libby's head. She pressed her lips to Libby's forehead, and Libby enjoyed the motherly comfort her mom gave so freely. "You're so blessed," she whispered. "The doctor just stopped me in the hall and said it could've been so much worse."

Tears shone in her eyes as she smiled down at Libby. "The Lord is so good to have watched out for you in that one moment."

Libby's first thought was to smile and nod and close her eyes. Maybe then her family would leave her alone to rest. After all, she never got out of a day's work on the ranch, and pure exhaustion ran through her from the x-rays, the waiting, the pain, and now the delicious drugs they'd given her to make the pain abate.

But instead, she truly looked at her mother, and she thought about what she'd said. Her mother's faith filled the room, and Libby got a little taste of it. She grasped onto it with both hands and tried to bring it closer to her. She couldn't live on borrowed faith for long, but somehow seeing and hearing her mother's testimony that God watched out for her, Libby's dormant faith stirred.

It grew, almost like it was raising its head after a long time asleep.

"Let's go," Jack said, meeting Libby's eyes. "She should rest while she can."

"I'll stay with her," Mildred said. "I was very nearly done with the sorting, and we're ready for market tomorrow."

"I can help out tomorrow," Suzy said. "I know Libby usually goes to the Farmer's Market."

"Thank you," Libby murmured while Cord said he'd finish the mowing when he could, what with the lawn mower in his yard and everything. Her family took turns hugging her and saying good-bye, all while making plans to cover what she did around the ranch for the next few days.

"After that, we'll figure out what you can and can't do, okay, Peanut?" Papa asked, kindness in his voice, but concern in his eyes.

Libby nodded, her tears too close to the surface for talking. Everyone filed out, except for Mildred, who held up her phone. "You know who you should call to come keep you company?" She put the device on the tray with Libby's food, not naming any names before she too hugged Libby, promised she'd be back that night, and left the room.

Libby looked at the phone, one single person in her mind's eye. The same man who'd been featured there for many, many months now.

Mister Glover.

reacher Glover bent down and smiled into the phone his brother, Bishop, had set up for Aurora and Ollie. They'd wanted to welcome Mister back to the ranch, even though they weren't even here. Preacher understood their feelings of wanting to be close to their family, especially since they'd moved across the country only days after getting married—and only seven months after graduating from high school.

"Hey, Preacher," Aurora said, her smile as beautiful and as wide as he'd ever seen it. "Charlie hasn't had the baby yet, has she?"

"Not yet," Preacher said.

"She's due today, right?" Ollie asked, pressing in close to his wife. He wore joy on his face, and Preacher knew exactly what it was like to be newly married and in love. Ollie and Aurora were also young, and both of them doing amazing things at the school they'd chosen to attend in South Carolina.

"Today, yes," Preacher said. "Any petitioning you can do to get that baby to come today would be much appreciated. She's pretty miserable."

"We'll pray for you," Aurora said, and Preacher gave her a thumbs up before moving to go sit by his very pregnant wife. He'd helped her onto the couch several minutes ago, and then he'd gone to help Bishop bring in the cookies he'd made for Mister's official homecoming party.

One of Mister's favorite treats in the world was oatmeal chocolate chip cookies, and about three hundred of them currently sat on the kitchen counter. Zona and Ida worked behind the counter, layering meat and cheese onto two, six-foot long pieces of bread Ida had ordered and picked up at the grocery store on her way to the ranch.

She mixed Italian salad dressing into pasta, vegetables, and the little cubes of cheese Preacher liked so much, and she set the bowl of salad on the counter. "What else?" she asked, but Preacher lifted his arm around his wife and let those in the kitchen handle the food.

He felt like he handled so much otherwise, and it sure was nice to come to the homestead and get fed sometimes. Even an hour or two with someone else in charge recharged him.

Not everyone had arrived yet, but there was still plenty of chatter among the few who had. Ace entered with a "Hey, howdy ho," and his wife, Holly Ann. They were followed by Mister, who lifted Gun over the back of the couch and gave him to Oakley.

"Hey, Gunny," she cooed at the boy. He giggled and buried his face in Oakley's chest, which was just so cute. Preacher grinned at them, and Oakley looked over to him and Charlie. His wife had her eyes closed, and Preacher watched her chest rise and fall, marveling at how she could sleep right now.

She was incredible to him, because Charlie wasn't a big woman in the least. She barely stood a couple of inches over five feet, and she hadn't carried much extra weight before her pregnancy. Now, she rested her hands on her bulging belly, and Preacher couldn't wait to meet their daughter.

"Etta," Oakley said, raising her hand with a phone clutched in it. "Your phone is ringing."

All of the women in the kitchen went silent, and Preacher's eyebrows went up.

"Is it LaMar Anderton?" Charlie asked without opening her eyes.

"Oakley," Etta said, plenty of warning in her voice.

"It's LaMar Anderton," Oakley confirmed.

A squeal rose up from the kitchen, and Etta hurried around the island to take the phone from Oakley. "All right, enough," she said, and she swiped on the call as she headed for the foyer. "LaMar," she said, her voice much more refined than it was a moment ago. "How good to hear from you."

"Oh, boy," Preacher said, chuckling. "What is that

about?" He knew Etta had been dating a lot. Everyone knew that. He didn't know about this guy named LaMar, though all of the women obviously did.

"She met him a couple of weeks ago," Charlie said, her eyes coming open. "He's very handsome and very available, and he seems to be interested in Etta."

"She seems interested in him," Preacher said, his defenses going up. He couldn't stand to see his cousin hurt again, but he did want her to be happy. She'd risked so much already, and he quickly prayed for her. *Bless her with a clear mind and help her to find happiness.*

Beside him, Charlie groaned, drawing his attention. "Okay?"

"Mm." She shifted on the couch, definitely trying to find a more comfortable position. The house continued to fill, and Etta came back after a few minutes and began whispering furiously with Ida and Zona in the kitchen.

Bear's family arrived, and then Ward and Dot came in and sat beside Preacher. Charlie kept pressing on her stomach and moving this way and then that. Preacher's concern grew, but every time he looked at her, she let him know she was fine.

They didn't have to say much to communicate, and when Zona said, "All right, everyone. It's time to start," the Glover clan quieted down. It always took several long seconds for conversations to wrap, and just when it went all the way silent, Charlie gave a sharp cry of pain.

Everyone looked at her, including Preacher. "Babe?"

"I'm fine," she said, lifting one hand to wave others off.

"Really, I was just sitting up, and I pinched that stupid nerve in my back." She pushed herself to the edge of the couch but didn't stand up.

"Stay here," Preacher said. "I'll get you something to eat."

"I need to sit on something hard," she whispered back as Zona welcomed everyone and said Bear was going to say the family prayer and then they could eat. "Cookies first, if you want," Zona said with a smile. "There's plenty of milk to go with them."

"All right." Mister clapped his hands together and rubbed them as if he'd eat the entire platter of cookies by himself. Several people twittered, but Preacher couldn't look away from his wife for longer than a few seconds.

She'd turned a little bit paler than usual, and a fine sheen of sweat had broken out along her forehead. He met her eye again, his eyebrows going all the way up, asking, *Are you okay?*

She nodded and Bear started praying. "Lord, we're so grateful to have Mister home with us again. We thank Thee for his safe travel, for all the lessons he learned, and for all of this delicious food Thou has blessed us with. Please bless the hands that made it with the things they need to be happy. Help us to look for ways to serve one another here at the ranch and to do the same with our friends and neighbors in the community. Bless Charlie and Preacher to have the baby real soon, and that all will go well. Amen."

"Amen," Preacher said along with several others. He

immediately got to his feet and said, "Stay here," in a more forceful tone. "I'll get whatever you want."

Charlie nodded in short little bursts of her head, and that set off an alarm in Preacher's head. He wasn't sure what it screamed, so he turned and went around the couches to get her a plate of food.

"Any announcements?" Bear asked just as Preacher stepped into the kitchen again, and Cactus stepped forward.

He held up one hand. "I know the wolves are circling." He grinned at the two teen boys only inches away from the oatmeal chocolate chip cookies. "Willa and I just have a quick announcement. We want more kids, but we've decided to go the route of fostering."

A murmur ran through the family, but Cactus wore such a grand smile. He did love kids, and it seemed like his heart had endless room for them. "There's a few classes we have to take and then we'll be able to give a home to children who need it."

"That's great," Ace said, and he patted Cactus on the back.

Preacher agreed, and he grinned and went to congratulate his brother on his way to get his wife some food.

Mister loved chicken nuggets and macaroni and cheese, and Preacher couldn't really argue with the diet of a twelve-year-old boy. He put several nuggets, a scoop of hot pasta, and then one of the cold salad onto a plate, picked up two cookies, and returned to Charlie.

She accepted the plate with a smile and said, "I'm fine.

Help me up and over to the table. I can't eat on the couch."

Preacher took the plate from her again and put it on top of the piano. He quickly returned to Charlie and helped her to her feet with strong hands on her arms and lower back. "There you go, baby. Nice and slow."

"Oh, it's easier to stand," she said. "Maybe I can just eat at the piano."

"No, come sit at the table." He led her over to the table and she slid into the end seat. He gave her the food, and she beamed a grateful smile up at him.

"Thanks, Preach. I'm okay."

"Okay," he said, and he went to get his own food.

He stepped into a conversation with Ward and Judge, who said, "I don't know. I won last year. It feels like I should just go out with that."

"But what about all of those decorations?"

"They're fine in the basement." Judge put a healthy amount of chicken nuggets on his plate while June scooped pasta salad onto hers in front of him. "No one lives there but me. June and I won't need the room for a lot of years, if we ever need it."

"He's going to do it," June said. "He just needs a few more months to gear up."

"I bet you're right," Ward said. "Once an idea strikes, Judge, you won't be able to stop yourself."

Judge chuckled, and Preacher nodded. "He's right," he said. "You love the Christmas lights."

"I just don't want to lose again," Judge said. "It'll feel

like I'm going backward, and I'd rather not feel like that."
He looked at Preacher and smiled. "Have you and Charlie
decided on a name?"

"No," Preacher said, glancing over his shoulder to his
wife. Mother had sat near her, leaving a spot for Preacher
between them. Love for both of them filled him, and he
turned back to the conversation. "She doesn't want
anything too masculine, because she doesn't like her
name. I don't like her old-fashioned ideas."

"I thought Ruth was really cute," Ward said. "And you
know, Etta and Ida are old-fashioned, and they wear their
names really well."

"Ruth is adorable," Dot said from the other side of the
island. "Just think, Ruthy Glover. She'll be so blonde like
you and Charlie, and she'll be the cutest little girl." She
grinned down the line to Preacher.

He smiled back and shook his head. "I guess Ruth is a
good name," he said.

"I had a great-grandma Ruth," June said. "She had real
fire inside her."

"Not sure you've met Preacher and Charlie appropri-
ately," Judge said, grinning. "He's the coolest of us all."

"Not true," Bishop said, reaching between Judge and
Preacher to get another cookie. "You should see him when
you tell him it's going to be another month before he can
move into his house."

"Hey, I was nice," Preacher said. "I'm allowed to be
frustrated to be living out of boxes for yet another thirty
days—while I'm bringing home a new baby and trying to

figure out how to be a dad and a husband *and* keep up with Ward's insane schedule for getting the pastures done by fall."

Judge, Ward, and Bishop all blinked at him, and Preacher rolled his eyes. "If anyone says anything about how many words I just said, I swear you'll see fire."

Down the line, Dot started to laugh, as did June. That didn't exactly please Preacher, but when Ward's wife turned and looked at him, she said, "You tell 'em, Preacher. And look at that, they all listened to you."

They shuffled down the line, and Preacher picked up the big serving spoon for the mac and cheese.

"I'll get you in the house before the Fourth," Bishop promised before he went to sit down.

"I'll hire some temporary help for the pastures," Ward said.

"Thank—"

"Preacher," someone called, enough alarm in their voice to make him mute and spin. A few people stood around where Charlie had been sitting, and Preacher tossed his plate and headed back toward her.

"She's in labor," Sammy said.

Zona knelt at Charlie's side. "Her contractions aren't very close together, but it's a long way to the hospital."

"Let's go," Preacher said, thinking of the baby bag Charlie had tucked behind the front seat of the truck before they'd come to the party. She was prepared; he was ready. It didn't matter where they took their daughter home to, and he dropped into the chair beside Charlie.

She had only cried once or twice in all the time he'd known her, but she had tears in her eyes.

"Babe?"

"Help me up, Preach," she said. "I think we should go to the hospital."

Preacher didn't waste a single second. He stood and said, "Mister," who happened to be the closest man to him. The two of them got Charlie to her feet and helped her out to the truck.

"I'm sorry, Mister," Preacher said after slamming the passenger door. He grabbed onto him and added, "Try to get them to wait a couple of hours, at least. Finish the party. We already said we didn't want everyone down there, but I know how they all are."

"I'll do my best to delay them as long as possible." Mister grinned at him and stepped back. "Now go have your baby."

Preacher grinned, his nerves vibrating through his whole body. He ran around the front of the truck and got behind the wheel. "Ready, baby?"

"Mm hm." Charlie said, her legs straight out in front of her. "This doesn't feel great, but at least I know now that it's a contraction."

"I'll get us there as fast as possible." Preacher put the truck in gear and got it moving toward the town of Three Rivers. "You keep talking to me. Now's not the time to go silent, okay?" He kneaded the steering wheel and glanced at her over and over.

"Okay," Charlie said. "I'm okay. I'm okay." She seemed

to be trying to convince herself, and her breathing increased. She kept track of the time between contractions and by the time they got to the hospital, they were just under three minutes apart.

Preacher hurried inside to get help, and he ran up to the first woman he saw at the information desk. "My wife is in labor," he said.

"Let's get her a wheelchair." She indicated a row of them to his right, and he grabbed one.

Preacher forced himself to walk back to the truck, and he helped Charlie into the wheelchair. "I'm okay," she said. "You go park the truck, and I'll wait here."

"I'll call up to maternity," the woman from the information desk said. "She can sit with me, and if they come get her before you're back, I'll tell you where they've taken her."

Preacher hesitated, because he didn't want to leave Charlie's side. He also couldn't leave his huge truck in the drive-through entrance of the hospital, idling. He nodded once and leapt back into the truck while the woman wheeled Charlie inside.

He found the first parking spot he could and dashed back inside. The woman sat alone at the information desk, and she looked up as he ran toward her. She rose to her feet. "They came and got her two minutes ago. She's on her way up to delivery. Third floor."

"Thank you," he said as he dashed by. He punched the elevator buttons and paced in the car as it rose. He ran toward maternity and said, "Charlie Glover?"

"She just came in," a nurse said. "She's in two, I think."

"I'll take you," another woman said, turning to go back the way she'd come. Preacher followed her, gulping great lungfuls of air and trying to calm down. He had to be calm for this. Charlie had told him she'd be freaking out, and she needed one of them to be rational in the delivery room.

The nurse opened the door and gestured for him to go inside. He took a deep breath and ducked through the doorway to find his wife in a bed. "Preacher," she said, reaching for him, and Preacher hurried to her side.

"I'm here," he said, taking her face in his hands. "I'm here, and we're going to have a baby today." He grinned at her and kissed her, and she trembled in his arms.

"Okay," a man said, and Preacher turned to see their doctor walk in. "It's a good day to stop being pregnant." He grinned at the pair of them, and when Preacher looked back at his wife, she wore her game face.

"That's right," she said. "I'm ready to be done with that. Let's have this baby."

CHAPTER 8

Mister pulled up to the hospital and found a parking spot far out in the lot. He'd rather just walk than drive up and down the aisles, then try to swing his king cab deluxe Texas edition truck into a narrow stall. This way, he could just pull through and everyone was happy.

With the vehicle out of gear, he reached for his phone, which had chimed a couple of times on his drive down from the ranch. He'd managed to keep everyone up at Shiloh Ridge for another couple of hours, and then Sammy had said she couldn't stand not being at the hospital, and she'd started loading up her family.

Mister expected his texts to be from her or Bear, who'd left about a half-hour before him. They did have to take their kids to her parents' house, because no one knew how long it would take Charlie to have the baby, as it was her first.

But the texts were from Libby. A smile popped onto his face, and he swiped to get to the messages. The first one was a picture, a game they'd been playing for a year. This one made him frown, because it looked like…. "A hospital room," Mister murmured.

He looked up and out of the windshield, then quickly back to her texts. *You'll never guess what happened today.*

What in the world? he asked, and then he tapped on the picture. It expanded, and he could see her foot now—her cast foot—when he couldn't before. He tapped to call her, and she picked up before the first ring even finished.

"I fractured my ankle," she said by way of hello.

"You're kidding," he said, surprise filling his chest over and over again.

"I wish." She sounded miserable. "The doctor is supposed to be by in a couple of hours, and then I should be able to go home."

"I'm at the hospital too," he said. "Preacher and Charlie are having their baby."

"Oh, that's great," Libby said.

"Yeah, so what room are you in? I'll come see you."

"You know what would be really amazing?" she asked, lowering her voice.

Mister grinned, liking her mischievous tone. "What?"

"If you could sneak me in a cheeseburger. And a Diet Dr. Pepper."

He chuckled and shook his head. "Your wish is my command."

"Check on Charlie first," she said. "I mean, it's four

o'clock. I can wait for a bit."

"I'll keep in touch," he said, and the call ended. He got out of the truck, torn in two directions. He wanted to rush off to Burnt Ends and get Libby her favorite cheeseburger and soda pop. He wanted to be there when Preacher brought out his new niece. He'd missed so much in the past year, and he wanted to be at the hospital with his family as a new Glover came into the world.

He strode toward the hospital entrance, telling himself that Libby wasn't going anywhere. Not only that, but somewhere in the back of his mind, he knew she'd need some help, and he could be the one to provide it.

"Thank you," he whispered as he entered the hospital. He'd been around for some of the births, and he knew how to get up to the waiting area for the maternity wing, and he wasn't surprised to find a flock of Glovers perched on the couches when he made it there.

"Nothing yet?" he asked Ace as he sat down next to him. Bishop sat on his other side, playing a game on his phone.

"Not yet," Ace said, yawning.

"Uncle Mister," Smiles said, racing up to Mister. "Look at this." He held up a bouncy ball the color of green slime. "Momma bought us toys from the machines."

Mister grinned at his nephew. "You lucky boy." He knew better than to pick up the boy and try to hold him right now. With a ball in his hand, Smiles needed freedom to throw and run. "Better not bounce it too high."

Smiles did exactly that, completely bobbled trying to

catch the ball, and went scampering after it as it bounced away from him. Sammy watched him while she held Heather, and Bear kept one eye on Smiles too while he talked with Ward and Cactus.

Ward held Russ, and Mister gazed around at the family, marveling at how many parents didn't have their own kids. From what he could see, only Sammy held her daughter, and Oakley held hers. Aunt Dawna had Gun on her lap, and Holly Ann held Robbie, Bishop and Montana's son.

Judge cradled Chaz, Willa and Cactus's boy, in his arms, and Dot held Arizona's daughter over her shoulder as she slept.

Pure contentment flowed through him, and he lifted his phone to take a couple of pictures. He sent the best one to Libby while Ace's breathing besides him evened and deepened. How he could sleep with so much energy in the air, Mister didn't know.

Ace startled when Cactus said, "There he is," in a loud voice. Like many others, Mister got to his feet and looked toward the mouth of the hallway. Preacher walked really slow, his eyes trained down on the baby in his arms.

She'd been wrapped in a pink blanket, and she wore a soft green cap on her head. Mister's whole heart turned to marshmallow, and for the first time in his life, he wanted a child. Truly wanted one of his own. He'd loved getting to know his new in-laws, and he loved his nieces and nephews. But until that very moment, he had not considered himself as father material.

He did now, and he moved forward to see the little girl. Preacher could talk loud if he had to, but he normally didn't have to. People listened to him when he spoke, because he didn't make a big deal about being in the spotlight.

"Look, Betty," he said, placing her against his chest, facing out at everyone. "Your family came to meet you."

A sigh moved through Mister's soul, because the little girl was so precious and so darling. She kept her eyes stubbornly closed, but Mister could see the long, slender Glover nose right in the middle of her face.

"Her name is Betty Susanne Glover," Preacher said, pure joy radiating from him. "I lost the battle on the old-fashioned name. Charlie says Betty means 'God is my oath,' and I didn't know how to argue with that."

"She's perfect," someone whispered, and Preacher passed his daughter to Mother. He beamed at the two of them, and then Bear said, "Stand there with them, Preach. I'll take your picture."

"How did Charlie do?" Dot asked. "She was a little nervous."

Preacher smiled for his picture before saying, "She did great. She's doing great. They said I could bring Betty out real quick, and then she's going to try to feed her. Then you can start to come back."

Mother bent down and kissed Betty's forehead and passed the baby back to Preacher. "Just a few more minutes," he promised, retreating back the way he'd come.

Mister stepped over to Mother and linked his arm through hers. She patted his forearm as she sighed wistfully. "I love being a grandmother," she said.

"She was pretty perfect." Mister grinned as Preacher went through the door and disappeared. "Would it be okay if I snuck away, do you think?"

Mother looked at him. "Where are you going?"

"Libby fractured her ankle, and she's here in the hospital."

Mother's face turned to alarm. "I'll make her something for lunch tomorrow, and you can take it to her."

Mister grinned from ear to ear. That would surely win him some points with the beautiful brunette. *You're not trying to earn any points,* he told himself, but he agreed with Mother. "That would be great, Momma. Thanks."

"There will be plenty of time to congratulate Preacher and Charlie," she said. "You're not even leaving the building."

"I might drive her home," Mister said, and his mind caught on the fact that she wanted a cheeseburger.

"You go take care of her," Mother said, releasing his arm. "She needs you more than Preacher does right now. I mean, look at us." She turned to face the Glovers, and when Mister did too, he could see the enormity of them.

The family really had grown so much in the past five years. He could hardly recognize some of his siblings and cousins for how much they'd changed, especially Judge. Mister held no ill will toward his brother anymore, and he walked over to him and gave him a hearty hug.

"Where you goin'?" Judge asked, as if he knew Mister was about to leave.

Mister stepped back and looked at his brother and then June, who had come to the homecoming party and then down to the hospital with her fiancé. "Libby called me."

Judge's eyes widened. "She did?"

"What did she say?" June asked, pressing in closer to both Judge and Mister.

Mister knew Judge hated it when he talked about Libby, but he told himself it was different. Mister wasn't complaining about Libby this time. He wasn't frustrated she wouldn't go out with him. He was…hopeful.

"She hurt her ankle today," Mister said, feeling like the Lord had answered one of his prayers in a pretty terrible way. But an answer nonetheless. "She's here in the hospital, and I'm going to go see how she is."

"Wow." Judge glanced at June, and they clearly had something to say. Mister waited, and Judge finally said, "You tell him."

"I did some work at Golden Hour a couple of days ago," June said. "Something for their Country Christmas coming up."

"Mm hm." Mister had no idea where this was going, so he didn't interrupt by saying actual words.

"I heard her talking to Mildred, and it was pretty clear they were talking about you."

Mister shook his head. "I don't want to know."

"It's not bad," June said, glancing at Judge. They both seemed nervous.

"It's okay," Mister said. "I'd rather not know. She—" He cleared his throat. "She broke up with her boyfriend yesterday, and she said some stuff to me...I'm just going to play her game. Whatever she wants, until I figure out where I went wrong and can fix it."

"So we still like this woman." Judge smiled at him, no judgment in sight.

Mister saw no reason to deny it. "I still like this woman. Lord help me, I tried not to like her. I prayed that she'd leave my head every day for the past year. She hasn't. She's still there, and every time I even think about her...." He shivered in an over-exaggerated way, and June giggled.

He grinned back at her and Judge. "So I'm going to go get some cheeseburgers, because she requested one, and then I'm going to go sit with her. Simple."

"Sure," Judge said. "Sounds simple." He chuckled as Mister waved good-bye and walked away.

Twenty-five minutes later, Mister knocked on a closed door—the number of the one Libby had given him. She called, "Come in," and he inched open the door.

When she saw him, her face, which was pale and drawn, lit up. "Praise the heavens," she said. "I'm starving."

He chuckled as he entered the room and closed the door behind him. Hospital rooms didn't lock, and he wasn't sure if she was on a restricted diet or not. He put the brown paper bag containing her cheeseburger on the tray in front of her and set the Diet Dr. Pepper beside it.

Then, without thinking, he brushed his fingers along her forehead, moving her bangs out of the way, and bent to place a kiss in the space he'd cleared. "How are you feeling? Are you in much pain?"

She blinked those gorgeous eyes up at him, and Mister lost himself in the deep, dark depths of them. Fantasies swam through his mind, all of them featuring a kiss from Libby. He'd kissed her before—twice, actually—and one of them had been somewhat passionate if a little rushed. The last time he'd kissed her, it had been sweet and chaste—a good-bye kiss before he'd left for Oklahoma.

Libby's eyes blazed at him, and Mister couldn't read what she was trying to say. Her mouth moved into the words, "Thank you, Mister," and that broke the spell between them.

He cleared his throat and backed out of her personal space, mourning the distance between them now. "Sure," he said, his voice stuck behind the lump in his throat. He opened the bag and took out a burger before retreating to the only other place to sit in the room—a recliner that had been pushed against the wall.

Only five feet separated them now, but it was a safe distance. A non-kissing distance. A best friend distance.

"The doctor said I could go home as soon as I could get a ride," she said. "Would you take me?"

"Of course," Mister said.

"Thank you." She unwrapped her burger, the air between them turning from charged to comfortable. "Now, tell me all about Preacher's baby."

CHAPTER 9

*L*ibby looked up from her tablet when the doorbell rang. "That has to be Mister," she said to Mildred, who groaned as she pushed herself to the edge of the love seat. Libby had slept on the couch, because she was afraid she'd get in bed and not be able to get out.

Mister had brought her home last night, where she'd found Mildred and Scott cuddled together on the couch, watching a movie. She'd busted their romantic evening right in half, taken their spot on the couch, and barely moved since.

"It could be Scott," Mildred said. "He said he'd come by after church." The two of them had stayed home from church that Sabbath morning, because Libby took some strong painkillers that made her vision spin and her stomach sick.

Mildred went down the hall to the front door, and by the sound of her shriek and laughter, the man on the front porch belonged to her. "I'll be back in a little bit, Libs," she said, hustling back into the living room. "You're okay here alone for like a half-hour?"

"Yes," Libby said, though the word felt coated in poison. Scott came down the hall too, wearing a big smile that matched Mildred's, and Libby swallowed against the bitterness rising through her chest. It so wasn't fair to be so jealous of Mildred. She deserved to be happy too, and she hadn't dated anyone in so long.

Scott treated her like a queen, and Libby could see the love in his eyes every time he looked at her sister. So she put a smile on her face too, and she said, "Hello, Scott."

"Hi, Libby." He lifted a white pastry box. "I brought fruit pizzas."

"Thank you," Libby said, her taste buds doing a little dance inside her mouth. "I love fruit pizza."

"Mildred said you did."

Mildred finished putting on her shoes, and she linked her fingers through Scott's. "We're just going to take a quick walk. It's too hot to go far."

"Mister is bringing lunch," Libby said, lifting the remote. "I've got an action-packed movie playing. I'm fine." She smiled her sister and Scott out of the house, and then she sighed, her lips falling right back into a straight line.

She stared at the TV, but the movie didn't interest her. It was just noise in the background. She jabbed at the button to turn it off at the same time Mister called, "Libby? I'm coming in."

"Come in," she called, and his footsteps came closer, the front door slammed shut, and then he walked down the hall, clearly wearing cowboy boots.

He entered the living room carrying a huge pot with both hands, still dressed in his church clothes. Her heartbeat kicked into second gear at the sight of those black slacks and that white shirt. His tie had been loosened but not removed completely, and it too was black, white, and silver.

Mister sure knew how to make himself look good, and Libby's stupid hormones fired desire through her at the speed of light. It so wasn't fair that she couldn't get over this man. It wasn't fair to him or to her, and she wondered if she should just do what Mildred had suggested and get out of her own way.

"It smells good," she said.

"It's just hamburger stew," he said. "Mother made it, so don't be impressed by me. I'm just the delivery boy." He put the soup pot on the stove and exhaled as he turned back toward her. "I told her it's not really stew weather, but Momma thinks soup is a year-round food."

Libby grinned at him. "I'm sure it'll be delicious."

Mister came back into the living room. "I couldn't tell her no, you know? She sends her best wishes." He smiled as he sank into the recliner next to the couch. He put his elbows on his knees and looked at her. "I told her I'd bring it, and I brought it. I can't be lyin' to my momma."

"Definitely not," Libby agreed, completely charmed by this man. He was and always had been a momma's boy, which had made his tour with the rodeo all the more surprising to Libby.

Before either of them could say another word, his phone rang. Mister pulled it from his back pocket and looked at it. "It's Wyatt Walker." He met Libby's eyes. "He's been trying to get in touch with me for a couple of weeks. Do you mind?"

"Not at all."

"Two minutes," he said, standing. He swiped on the call and said, "Wyatt Walker," followed by an immediate laugh. The sound filled the whole house with happiness, the booming quality of it making Libby's own smile appear and be the most genuine it had been in months.

"Yeah, I'm back in Three Rivers," Mister said as he opened the back door and stepped out onto the deck. He closed the door, and while Libby could still hear his voice, she couldn't make out the words.

Wyatt Walker, she thought. *The Rodeo King.*

He'd made quite the name for himself since retiring from the rodeo. He'd ridden for much longer than Mister had, and he had brand sponsors in clothing, nutrition, and even jewelry. He had his own line of western wear, and he was still one of the nicest, most giving men in Three Rivers.

Libby simply had a bad taste in her mouth that she couldn't get rid of when it came to rodeo cowboys. She'd hated Mister when he'd ridden the circuit, and she'd hated entertaining his friends when they came through town.

The back door opened again, and Libby glanced at the

clock. It really had been two minutes. "Sure thing," Mister said. "I'll see you Wednesday." He hung up, pocketed his phone, and looked at Libby.

The same lightning-hot charge that had filled her hospital room last night roared to life again. With their eyes locked, they seemed unable to stay away from one another, and Libby told herself to close her eyes. That would break the connection, the same way her voice had last night.

Instead, her fingers drifted up to her forehead, where she pushed her bangs aside. Mister had kissed her there last night, and she wanted his mouth six inches lower, right above hers. Her lips tingled, and every cell in her body trembled with anticipation.

"Do you want to eat?" he asked, breaking eye-contact and heading into the kitchen. "I'll dish us up something to eat."

She let him do that, and when he handed her a bowl of his mother's fabulous hamburger stew, Libby didn't dare look at him again. So many thoughts raced through her mind. So many emotions stormed through her chest.

"There's a container of the pork in the fridge," she said. "Don't forget to take that when you go."

"Okay." Mister took a bite of his soup. "How long can I stay?"

Libby looked at him again, blinking. "As long as you want." She gestured to herself with her spoon. "This is what I'm doing today."

He smiled at her, the gesture so kind. It didn't hold the

playfulness his smiles sometimes did. It wasn't one that would be followed by loud laughter. He was...calmer. Gentler. More mature.

It was the second time she'd thought that about him, and she wanted to believe it so badly.

"You don't need to get up and move today?" he asked. "I have to say, I distinctly remember the nurses telling you to get up and walk as often as you can."

"I can't walk," she said, perhaps a bit too harshly. "I hate the crutches." She glanced at the walking boot Mildred had put next to the TV cabinet. "The boot hurts. It squeezes too tight. The doctor said I could wait until the swelling goes down to put it on."

"I could be your crutch," he said. "We'll go to the barn and back."

She knew exactly which barn he was referencing, and it was the one she'd tried to hide behind last year when he'd come to say he was moving to Oklahoma for twelve months. He hadn't been gone quite that long, but every day had felt eternal to her.

"Fine," she said, clearly not happy about having to do what the nurses had told her to.

"Fine," Mister echoed, grinning at her with that edge of mischievousness in his eyes. "Do you want to hear what the pastor had to say today?"

"If I must." Libby put a bite of soup in her mouth, wishing she had this recipe. It was just big chunks of carrots, potatoes, and hamburger in a tomato-based broth, but it was delicious. Salty and tangy and sweet at the same time.

"He said the Lord accepts us right where we are," Mister said. "I liked that." He kept his head down as he stirred his soup and took another bite. "Sometimes I think I'm not what I need to be, you know? And there's this struggle between where I am, and where I want to be, and I can't reconcile it."

"What do you do about that?" Libby asked, her voice on the outer edge of a whisper. She felt like that all the time, and she had no idea how to even begin building the bridge from where she was to where she could feel comfortable with the Lord.

"I usually read my daddy's letter," he said. "Go to the cemetery and talk to him. Go see Bear. Spend time doing what I know is right and good."

She looked at him, but he still had his focus on his bowl.

"Stuff like that." He looked up. "What do you do?"

"Nothing," she said honestly, looking away from him. He was too powerful and too good for her to hold his gaze. "I don't know what to do, so I end up doing nothing, and then I find myself even further from where I want to be." She swallowed, only half of her soup gone but she didn't want to eat any more.

"Libs," he said, but Libby just shook her head, her eyes burning.

She lifted her bowl toward him, a clear indication that she wanted him to take it. He stood and did so, taking both of their bowls into the kitchen. The house strained with tension now, but Mister plowed right on through it. "Come on, girl. Let's get you up and outside."

"You make me sound like a cow," she said, looking up at him.

He grinned down at her. "Only if you're the most beautiful cow in the state of Texas." He reached for her, and Libby let him help her stand. She steadied herself against the strength of his arms, and then his right hand slid along her waist, and he inched closer to her.

"Where do you want to be?" he whispered. "I'll help you get there."

Libby clung to him, mostly because she only had one good foot to balance with. She hadn't told anyone, even Mildred, about how spiritually stunted she'd become. She'd always been able to tell Mister anything, though she'd been holding back with him since that fateful day almost a decade ago.

Get out of your own way, she thought, and she looked up at him. He gazed down at her, and with only a few inches of movement on both sides, she could be kissing him.

"I feel completely removed from God," she admitted. "He doesn't hear me, or I don't hear Him. There's something...off. I don't know how it happened, and I don't know how to fix it." She pulled back on her emotions, sniffling and reaching to wipe her eyes.

Mister pressed his lips to her forehead and held her close. "I know how that feels, Libs."

"You do?"

"Keenly."

"What did you do?"

"Well, once I ran away to Winterhaven for a year." He chuckled. "Another time, I kept pushing myself and pushing myself and I ended up with a broken femur."

Libby suddenly saw the parallels between her fractured ankle and his devastating rodeo injury. "I wasn't pushing myself," she said. "I was just mowing the lawns."

"I didn't mean to imply you were doing anything wrong," he said. "I think…I think the Lord sometimes hits us with things to remind us that He's there. That He's aware of us. I didn't know it at the time, but by the time my leg had healed, I knew I'd been injured as a way for the Lord to reach through all the noise, all the haze, all of my stubbornness and say, 'Enough, Mister. Time to go home.'"

He grinned down at her, and Libby once again felt something she hadn't in a while—the stirring of her spirit, telling her that he'd spoken something true. She stretched up and brushed her lips along his cheek, feeling him press into her touch with more pressure.

"To the barn and back today," she said nearly in his ear. "And will you come tomorrow and help me with a few chores?"

"Absolutely," he whispered back, pulling back a little. He met her eye and added, "I see you, Libby. I hear you."

She pressed her eyes closed and nodded, some parts of her that had been dark, dreary, and dead coming back to life with those simple words. "Thank you, Mister."

CHAPTER 10

$\mathcal{M}$ister pulled up to the brown and white barn at the same time Libby scootered inside it. She could get around fast on that thing, and he grinned to himself as he put his truck in park. He got down and held the door open for George, Dot's hound dog who he'd brought with him this afternoon.

A couple of days had passed since he'd taken her a steaming hot pot of soup in the middle of the summer, and today was Libby's first day back out on the ranch. Mister took a deep breath of the hot air, getting the scent of straw, dust, and horses that only came when in Texas. Even in Oklahoma, the ranches smelled different.

Libby came out of the barn, and when she saw him, her face lit up. "I thought I heard a truck. Took me a second to turn around." She gave a light laugh, and it was all Mister could do not to jog toward her and sweep her into his arms.

Number one, best friends didn't do that. Number two, she was mostly immobile, and there would be no sweeping for a while. Number three, he wasn't going to be more forward than he'd already been.

Libby had been pretty forward too, but he didn't know what to do with the things she said. As he continued to cover the ground between them, he realized she probably thought she'd tossed the ball into his court. And he was holding it.

"Hey." He reached her and took her into a light hug. "The scooter is awesome, right?"

"Whatever prompted you to think of it was a stroke of genius," she said, patting him on the shoulder blade. "Thank you for bringing it. It alleviated a lot of my fear about being able to get around the ranch."

Mister stepped back and tucked his hands in his back pockets. "And bonus, you didn't die on the ramp."

"Almost," Libby said, bending down slightly to pat George. "Mildred wanted to film it, and that would've been a disaster." She laughed again, and it did Mister's heart good to see her in such great spirits. Their walk on Sunday had been a forlorn affair, and it had taken far too long to get to the barn and back. He'd known she wouldn't be able to get anything done around the ranch on crutches, and that night, when he'd gone to take a vat of hamburger stew to Aunt Dawna in her long-term care facility, he'd seen an older gentleman using a walker with a seat.

He'd sat down while waiting for the elevator, and he'd

wheeled himself onto the car with Mister without standing. He'd done some research when he'd gotten back to the homestead, and sure enough, he'd found a walker of sorts for people who didn't want to use crutches. Libby propelled herself around with her good leg, her knee resting on the scooter's pad.

"How's the ankle?" he asked.

"Good," Libby said. "Hardly hurts if I keep up with the pills."

"But not the codeine," he said.

"No," she said. "That puts me right out." A gorgeous smile had his heart pulsing around in his chest like it wasn't connected via arteries or veins, and his breath caught somewhere in the bottom of his lungs. "I'll admit, I take it at night." She reached up and tucked the wispy hair that had fallen out of her ponytail behind her ear.

She looked back and down to it. "I've been wearing the boot at night too. It's too clunky and makes me too slow out here on the ranch." She sighed and looked at him again. "But it's nice to be able to walk."

"What about this Friday night?" he asked. "How do you think you'll be feeling then?" He reached up and lifted his cowboy hat, letting the heat of the sun reach his skin. He put the hat back on, because the last thing he needed was a sunburn.

"I don't know," she said, looking up at him. Her thick eyelashes fluttered, and while she didn't wear makeup she'd just have to sweat off while working, Mister thought she possessed a natural beauty that he'd like to wake up next to every single day.

"Uh, if you're feeling well," he said, about to blow his vow to himself right out of the water. He'd told himself a thousand times that he wasn't going to ask her out. And yet, here he was, about to ask her to dinner.

He sighed and looked away, gazing across the dirt lot where the guests would park during the Country Christmas Festival. It soaked in the heat and pumped it back into the air, creating waves he could visibly see.

"I told myself I wasn't going to do this," he said. "But I can't stop thinking about what you said in my truck in the grocery store parking lot."

Libby cleared her throat. "I was a little stressed."

He brought his eyes back to hers. *I'm not ready to be with anyone else.* "Are you saying you said something you didn't mean?"

"No," she said slowly.

Anyone but you, Mister.

He drew in a deep breath and organized the words in his brain and mouth before he even thought about talking. "If you're feeling well enough, I'd love to take you to dinner on Friday night."

There. The statement was out. Dinner. Friday night. That said date from here to the Southern border.

"As a date?" Libby still asked.

"Yes." Mister brought his eyes back to her and tried to stay as steady as possible.

Libby's smile told him she had been waiting for him to

do something with the ball she'd bounced his way. "All right," she drawled in that sexy, Texas accent, and relief poured through Mister.

"Yeah?" he asked, a ridiculous amount of hope filling him. "I'll come pick you up. Six-ish?"

"Okay," she said. "That should work."

"If you don't feel well, no big deal," he said. "I'm sure Momma will make you something I can drop by."

Libby shook her head, her smile fading slightly. "Do you cook, Mister?"

"I can," he said. "I just don't like it."

"I don't either," she said. "When Mildred moves out, I'm going to have to stock the freezer with my favorite heat-and-eat meals."

"At Winterhaven, I got really good at going to the grocery store and getting stuff from the frozen section. I love the veggie fried rice, and I could add some corn to it —remember how we ate corn for every meal?" He chuckled and kept talking. "And grill up a couple of chicken breasts, and bam. Dinner."

"We have a grill on the back deck," Libby said.

"So I'll stock up on the frozen fried rice for Friday night, just in case you don't feel like going out." He grinned at her, feeling himself slipping into flirtatious-rodeo-cowboy mode. He pulled back on that personality, because he didn't like himself when he allowed that part of himself to come out.

It might have gotten him a lot of women's numbers and dates in the past, but Mister wasn't looking to do that anymore. He already had Libby's number, and she'd already said yes to a date on Friday night.

"All right," he said. "So where do you want me this afternoon?" He looked toward the entrance to the barn. "Are we riding?"

"Nice try," Libby said, moving forward and taking a big arc to turn herself around. "We're cleaning out the six-stall this afternoon. I was just coming in here to get my gloves."

"Great," Mister said brightly. "I'll take a pair of gloves too."

"HEY, HEY, THERE HE IS." WYATT WALKER ROSE to his feet as Mister came to a stop inside the pancake house. He'd suggested breakfast for lunch, and Mister wouldn't say no to bacon, eggs, or pancakes at any hour.

He laughed as the hostess got out of the way, because obviously Mister was here with Wyatt. The two men embraced, each clapping the other on the back, and Mister sure felt like he was someone special to Wyatt.

Of course, Wyatt made everyone feel like that, and Mister knew he wasn't special.

"Come sit down," he said, stepping back. "I just barely ordered coffee."

"It's far too hot for coffee," Mister said, following Wyatt back to the booth along the front windows. The waitress appeared, and he said, "I'd love some iced sweet tea."

She handed him a menu, and said, "You got it, sir." She batted a pair of thick eyelashes, like Libby's, and walked away. Mister tore his gaze from her swaying hips. He'd seen this tactic before, and ten years ago, he'd have gotten her number before ordering his food.

He wasn't twenty-three anymore, and in fact, a sliver of embarrassment dug at him for his behavior in the past. He had treated women badly, without any intent to get to know them before he kissed them, and zero intention of any sort of real commitment.

All he could do was pray that his changes had been profound enough and deep enough to warrant forgiveness. And be extremely grateful his mother had never seen him pick up women in a bar or restaurant. She'd have been mortified, and Mister's stomach felt like ice at the prospect of her finding out.

He cleared his mind and looked at the menu, though he'd eaten here loads of times. "How's life?" he asked Wyatt, who also held a menu in front of his face.

"Good," Wyatt said with a grin. "Real good. Marcy's gonna have a little girl in a couple of months."

Mister beamed at his friend. "That's great, Wyatt."

"It's really great," he said dryly. "If the baby was a boy, she said she'd—well, it wasn't pretty." His face turned a bit pink, and he cleared his throat. "But it's a girl. She wanted a girl, and well, I try to give her what she wants."

"Sounds like a solid plan," Mister said, grinning at Wyatt. "So a rodeo demo?"

"Yeah." Wyatt shifted in his seat and looked up. "I've done demos in the past, usually for trainers or brand reps, but I was thinking since you guys do your community outreach programs, and you have tons of contacts with the schools, we should do something for the teens actually interested in rodeo."

Mister nodded along for a few seconds. "Etta does all of our school programs. She doesn't do much in the summer."

"We can do them at Shiloh Ridge or Seven Sons. I can call the teacher," Wyatt said. "I just don't want to do it myself. Number one, you're the genius with a rope. I can barely throw one, especially after my last surgery."

"You fellas know what you want?" the waitress asked.

"Yeah, I'll take the country fireman's breakfast," Wyatt said without looking at the menu. He handed it to her. "Pancakes and bacon."

"Yes, sir," she said. "And for you?"

"I'll take the short stack," Mister said. "Double bacon. Scrambled eggs."

"All three syrups?"

"Blueberry for me," Wyatt said.

"Yeah, I'll take 'em all." Mister handed her his menu too, and she walked away. This time, there wasn't much sway to her hips, and Mister was glad he hadn't fed anything he shouldn't have. He focused on Wyatt again and said, "I'd love to do demos for teens actually interested in the rodeo."

"They could be classes," he said. "But I don't know about that. What do you think?"

"Classes implies someone has to pay," Mister said. "Like a lesson. And what are we gonna do with that money?"

"Donate it to the high school rodeo program?" Wyatt suggested. "I mean, I benefitted from that program. You did too."

Mister thought about Jake and Karl, the two teens who'd asked for his autograph in the parking lot last week. "Yeah, there's a great program at the high school. We should talk to Etta. She'll have things we need to think about."

"I'd love to talk to Etta more," Wyatt said. "You guys do horseback riding lessons up there, don't you?"

"Yeah," Mister said. "My niece used to do that, but I'm pretty sure Bear hired someone to keep them going after she moved away to college. I'd have to look into it all."

Wyatt nodded and reached up with both hands and wiped them down his face. "Do you want to, Mister? It suddenly feels like a lot. I was thinking a few summer demos at the rodeos that come to town."

"Maybe we should just do that, then," Mister said. "We know the guys who put on the rodeos, right?"

Wyatt grinned, and he looked less tired when he did that. "Yeah, I get free tickets to every one. I'm takin' Daddy to the next one, because it turns out that Marcy doesn't like the rodeo as much as I do." He chuckled and shook his head. "I can't fathom why."

"Maybe because you don't even sit down long enough to watch an event?" Mister guessed, grinning too. "I saw you at the last one. How long did you stand there and sign autographs?"

"Not that long," Wyatt said, which only caused Mister to burst out laughing. The whole time, if Mister remembered right. No wonder his wife didn't want to go to the rodeo with him. She sat alone the whole time.

"Is there a rodeo this weekend?" Mister asked, thinking he'd heard there was.

"Yep," Wyatt said. "If you need tickets, let me know."

"I got an email from Baby Ray." Mister looked up as the waitress set his plate of pancakes in front of him. "I'll contact him if I want to go." He wondered if he'd be swamped the same way Wyatt was at a rodeo. He wondered if he could get Libby to go with him on a date two nights in a row....

As he tucked into his bacon and pancakes, he wondered if exposing her to the rodeo world—and the man he so easily slipped into being when he went to that world—was a good idea in the first place.

CHAPTER 11

*L*ibby scanned herself from head to toe, her gaze lingering on her ankle cast. She couldn't wear a shoe on her right foot, but Mildred had bought her a brand-new pair of socks for her date tonight with Mister.

"A date with Mister," Libby murmured, running her hands down her torso, trying to get her stomach to iron flatter. Of course it didn't, and she cocked her head and admired her dress. It was a cool black number that fell all the way to her ankles, with enough fabric to cover her leg and keep her decent, even with her knee on the padded platform of the scooter.

Mister had promised they wouldn't have to walk very far, and she sent up a prayer that he'd remember who he was going out with. Liberty Bellamore, a woman who didn't like having very bright lights on her.

She didn't want to park in the handicapped space, for

example. She'd been zooming all over Golden Hour this week, and she could make it from any space to any entrance. She didn't want to use crutches, because she wasn't very good at it, and ninety percent of the time, she felt like she might pitch forward and fall flat on her face.

She wouldn't mind hanging on Mister's arm, and she'd cinched the walking boot over her foot and ankle. She'd been wearing it more and more, and she did like the mobility it afforded her. Mister had been a pure blessing the past five days, showing up in the afternoons to help her finish up any chores she hadn't been able to get done from the morning.

He'd gone up on the barn roof to fetch Frankie yesterday, and today, he'd hauled all the trash bins to the end of the lane for tomorrow morning's pick-up.

Things that Libby used to be able to do without thinking, she now had to consider. Could she get up in the silo and spread things out a bit more? Could she dig through boxes, twisting and turning and lifting, to find the one she needed with last year's flyers for the Country Christmas in it?

Could she even stand to make coffee in the morning? Not without the boot.

She turned away from the mirror and went toward her bedroom exit. Down the hall she hobbled, hoping she really could make it to a table and enjoy a delicious steak dinner, her injury tucked out of sight.

Her pulse pounced through her body at the thought of getting in Mister's big ole truck. Then at getting out. She sighed and pushed her hair off her forehead, pausing as she started to go through her purse for the third time that evening.

"Lord," she said, and then she simply stalled. Her mind quieted, and the words Libby wanted to say disappeared. She hadn't spoken to the Lord—truly spoken to Him—in a long time. She'd tried so many times, only to feel unworthy.

Today, she didn't feel like that. Today, she closed her eyes and listened to the hum of the refrigerator a few feet from her. Today, she knew He hadn't abandoned her. He'd simply been talking very quietly, and her life had gotten too loud to hear Him.

"Surely you don't care about a dinner date between two people somewhere in Texas," she whispered. "But if at all possible, I would love for this date to go really well for both me and Mister."

She swallowed, her eyes flying open as the doorbell chimed, filling the house with a song from *The Sound of Music.*

Libby's heartbeat rolled through her body like thunder, and she turned toward the hallway as Mister said, "Just me, Libs."

"Coming," she called, and she held onto the counter as she turned to go that way. He beat her into the back of the house before she could leave it, and when he saw her, he came to a dead standstill.

Something glinted in those dark eyes, and he quickly

reached up and swiped that midnight black cowboy hat from his head. "My," he said, and that was all.

She kept hobble-clopping toward him, her boot making terrible plastic-on-wood sounds as she did. Her smile took over her face, because he wore a pair of clean jeans that made his legs look ten times as long as they were. He'd tucked a brown, black, and white plaid shirt into that, and fixed everything up nice around his waist with a belt, the buckle of which didn't have any sequins or gems on it.

The silver shone like a beacon, however, an image of something like mountains on it. She tore her eyes from his waist and slid them up to his. "You look good enough to eat." She tacked a laugh onto the end of the statement as a smile lit up his face too.

"Thank you, darlin'." He swept one arm around her as she arrived in his personal space. Her left leg felt tired from the extra work it had to do, but she ignored the relief flowing through her at being able to use some of his strength and steadiness. "You look like a million bucks." He bent down and took a deep breath, his nose only inches from her neck. His lips brushed there, and he sighed. "You ready?"

"Yes," she said. "I'm not bringing the scooter or the crutches. I've got the boot on." She stepped back and balanced on her left foot, then lifted her skirt so he could see. "Mildred bought me these new socks."

He grinned down at them and looked into her eyes again. "They have horses on them."

"So very Texan, right?" She reached for his hand, and

his fingers slid through hers effortlessly. She wished everything about their relationship and past had been so easy, but she banished the thought. No, Libby didn't want easy. She wanted real, and sometimes life wasn't easy. Sometimes relationships got really complicated. Sometimes a woman needed to get out of her own way so she could see what she really wanted.

"And bonus," she said as he turned to take her down the hall to the front door. "I get two wears out of them before they need to be washed."

Mister laughed, the sound floating up and into the ceiling, where Libby hoped she could access it later. "You always look for the silver lining."

Libby did like looking on the positive side of life. She'd sort of forgotten that the past couple of years, as it sure had seemed like doom, gloom, and disaster had been waiting for her around every corner.

Mister stepped slowly with her down the stairs, talking about something one of his nephews had done that day. "He doesn't talk, right? He's got all these louder, older boys around him all the time. Well, today, he looked right at Smiles, and he said, 'Mine.' Everyone sort of froze, and then we all burst out laughing."

"I guess he didn't want his brother to take his doughnut."

"Well, anyone who gets between a Glover and their sweets is asking for trouble." Mister reached to open the passenger door.

Libby looked at the foot runner, and she thought she'd

better use her left leg to push her up and into the truck. She made a few stutter-steps to get the correct leg in position, and then she stepped up. Mister's hand stayed right on her hip, even sliding a little lower as he pressed to help her.

Heat exploded through her body, and the moment she started to sink into the seat, he pulled his hands back. "Sorry," he said under his breath, slamming the door closed in the next moment. She watched him round the truck, his face flaming red.

Libby stared at him as he got in, as he buckled, and as he started the truck. "You're...different."

"I should hope so." He cut a look at her but didn't let his gaze linger.

Libby smiled, her adoration of him expanding. "I've seen you touch women like that before," she said.

"Not for a long time," he said quickly, putting the truck in reverse and backing out of the driveway.

"Not that long," she said. "You went out with Allison, what?" Her mind blanked.

"Allison?" he asked, looking at her now as the truck rumbled down the dirt road toward the highway. "Libby, I went out with Allison four years ago."

"Then it was..."

"Then it was no one," he said. "Maybe some flirting here and there. Then I started asking you out. Then I went to Oklahoma, and there was no room for dating there." He cleared his throat and shifted in his seat. "I'm actually a little nervous about this."

"Me too," Libby said. "I prayed that it would go well."

"Did you now?" He eased the truck to a stop. "And?"

"And what?"

"And how did you feel?"

"I...." She shrugged. "I have no idea. I guess we'll see."

"I guess so." He made the turn west and started accelerating. "I thought we'd go to Porterhouse. Is that all right?"

"Just fine," Libby said, knowing Mister would take her to a steakhouse on their first date. Three Rivers had several, and Porterhouse was one of the best. Perhaps the very best one. She loved their chicken cordon bleu bites, and she could practically taste the bite-sized nuggets stuffed with cheese and ham, fried until crisp, and served with a creamy, cheesy sauce.

"How did you feel when you prayed?" he asked. "You said you were kind of coming back to that." He glanced at her again, this time reaching over with his right hand to take her left. "Is this okay?"

"Okay," she said. "And I felt okay too. I felt...like I maybe just need to listen better, and I'll be able to hear God again."

"Listening can be really tough," he said. "At least for me. My mind gets goin', and I have all these ideas of what I could or should do. Sometimes it's really loud in there, and no one can get through."

Libby nodded along. "I know how that feels."

He drew in a deep breath and pushed it all out. "Preacher and Charlie are home with baby Betty."

"That's great," she said.

"When's the last time you went up to Shiloh Ridge?" he asked, glancing at her again.

She adjusted her hand in his, trying to think. "A while," she said. "Maybe over Christmas? When you guys had that party."

A grin popped onto his face. "Ah, the party. We danced at that party."

"I remember." Libby looked out the window, her memories with Mister so strong. It had actually been a going-away party for him, and yes, she'd gone. Yes, she'd danced with him. Yes, she'd laughed, and they'd texted over the past five months.

"No dancing tonight," he said.

"No," she agreed. "You were a little rusty anyway." She swung her attention back to him. "I remember you being much lighter on your feet…before."

"Are you kidding me right now?" He looked at her, then back to the road. Her, the road. He laughed and shook his head. "Wow, the lady insults my dancing skills, and she can't even let me prove her wrong."

"I'm just saying," she said with a giggle. "I've seen you do better."

"I'm old, Libby."

She laughed harder. "You are not. You're thirty-five."

"My body hurt from all the corn farming." He grinned at her, but Libby just shook her head. She loved being with Mister when it was this fun, this carefree, this real. They settled into silence, and that was okay too.

The twenty-five minutes from Golden Hour to the outskirts of Three Rivers passed quickly, and Porterhouse sat on the southern side of town, one of the last restaurants before the suburbs took over. An older building housed it, with an ancient water tower off the back of it.

"Looks like they're having a wedding," he said, looking left as he went by.

"I think this would be a great place to have your wedding dinner," Libby said.

"Yeah? Why's that?" He swung into a parking space and put the truck in park.

"Because they have an amazing buffet," she said, her nose getting a hint of browned meat and something full of flavor. "Salads, meats, sides. I had a friend host her luncheon here, and it really was spectacular."

Mister nodded. "I'll come help you out." He slid from the truck easily, and Libby took the few seconds between then and when he opened her door to arrange her purse and clutch it tightly.

So far, so good, she thought, and she added, *Thank you,* just as Mister opened the door. He reached up for her hand, and she slid her right one into his. She turned her legs and let her left one dangle down farther than her right. She went past the runner, aiming for the ground in a single leap.

She took it, but the ground was a bit farther than she'd anticipated. She stumbled forward, and Mister caught her. She put both hands on his chest, and nothing else mattered after that. She wanted him to hold her while the earth swayed around them. Or maybe they were swaying.

She closed her eyes and let her fantasies play out, the way they had been for *years*. Five long years. She knew what his hands felt like. They were rough and gentle at the same time. Large and strong. She knew what he smelled like, but she took a deep breath of his spice, woods, and fresh water scent.

She knew how his voice sounded, but the deep, throaty quality of it still lodged in her ears when he said, "You okay, sweetheart?"

Oh, he really couldn't call her that and be playing fair. She shook her head and said, "No."

"What do you need?" He stayed close, keeping her almost right against the open door and the runner of the truck.

She opened her eyes and looked up at him. She'd put on makeup tonight, for the first time in a long time. She wore gold hoops in her ears, something she normally only did to attend church. She felt soft in body but strong in mind, and her eyes dropped from his to his mouth.

"I need you to kiss me," she whispered.

Surprise colored Mister's expression, only staying for a single, split-second heartbeat. He leaned down, his mouth first landing against her forehead. If that was what he called a kiss, Libby would seriously riot.

He'd just started to slide his lips lower when someone said, "Mister Glover? Is that Mister Glover?"

He pulled away, and Libby blinked into the bright light

of the evening sun. It would linger for hours yet, and fool-ishness filled her that she'd created this little pocket of the world where only she and Mister existed.

A trio of men approached, all of them made of smiles for miles and meters. "It *is* Mister Glover." One of them laughed, and in the next breath, he stepped into Mister and shook his hand in quite a vigorous fashion. "I've been a fan of yours for a long time. I heard you lived 'round here."

Mister laughed, the sound a little jarring from all the jiggly hand-shaking. Libby wanted to fade right back into the truck, but when he glanced over his shoulder to her, his eyes begged her to come join him.

She stepped forward awkwardly, because that was how Libby moved now. She linked her arm through Mister's the moment the man released it.

"Nice to meet y'all," he said. "I'm just here with my—girl." He hitched a smile onto his face, and if any of them heard the pause and then the near-explosion on the G-sound of *girl*, they didn't indicate it. In fact, only two of them looked at her.

"Excuse us," Mister said, easily closing the door behind him and gliding away.

"We can stay," Libby said out of the corner of her mouth.

Mister lifted his key and pressed the button to lock the doors. "Nope."

"Do you know them?"

"Nope."

"They're fans." Libby tried to look up at him and hobble along with him, but she nearly fell again.

"I've met two of them before," he said. "They're fine, and I'm not in the mood to sign autographs." He glanced at her. "Thanks for rescuing me."

Libby nodded, though she wanted to scoff. She hadn't rescued him. He'd walked away with a semi-strange explanation. "I'm your—girl?"

"Buckets," he said, reaching for the door handle to enter the steakhouse. "No, of course not." He paused and looked at her. "I'm sorry I said that. I didn't know what to put there."

Libby looked up at him, that intimate pocket of space getting created between them again. Every time they looked at one another, it sure did feel like the rest of the world disappeared. She wasn't going to go insane and ask him to kiss her in broad daylight again.

This time, a smile found its way to her face, and a giggle trickled out of her mouth. "Buckets? What does that mean?"

"It's how we used to swear on the corn farm," he said with a grin. "There are buckets and buckets and *buckets* of corn everywhere. Trust me, it's a swear word." Those eyes danced with flames and fun, and Libby basked in Mister's energy, something she'd always enjoyed doing.

"Good to know."

He chuckled and led the way inside, his hand in hers firm and welcome. People milled about, obviously waiting for a table, but Mister stepped through the crowd to the hostess podium, and not thirty seconds later, he and Libby had been seated at a booth with a single red rose in a vase between them.

"Wow," she said. "I feel like I'm with a real celebrity."

Mister grinned and unwrapped his silverware to lay his napkin in his lap. "I made a couple of phone calls is all."

"Impressive," she said, and Libby *was* impressed. She'd not gone on any dates with Mister and his numerous women, and she wondered how much of this he'd done for someone else already.

Does it matter? she asked herself, pushing against the bitter feelings that had started in her stomach. Something told her that it did, because she didn't want to end up like one of those women—cast aside, thrown away, once Mister found them uninteresting.

At the same time, a voice inside her head told her not to dwell on the past and to enjoy her time with Mister right now, in the present.

"Cordon bleu bites," the waiter said, sliding a tray of golden, fried morsels onto the table. He left without another word, and Libby blinked at Mister.

"Did you put in our whole order?"

"No, ma'am," he said. "Just these, because you said they were your favorite."

Libby gaped at him while he picked up one of the small plates on the table and placed it closer to her. "Like, ten years ago."

He laughed lightly. "Come on. Not that long ago."

"Eight then."

He looked up from the plate which held the food making her mouth water. "Are you saying you don't like them anymore?"

"No," she said.

"Great, then let's eat." He put three bites on her plate and nudged the sauce closer. "And I believe you had a story about a calf I needed to hear."

CHAPTER 12

*E*tta Glover ran her fingertips down the silky blouse the color of violet in the rainbow. It was a bit too bright for her, but Etta had been trying to say yes when her first instinct told her to say no.

"That one's great," Dot said, and Etta turned toward her. "What do you think of this one?" She held up a forest green blouse to her chest. It had swirling pink and white flowers throughout it, making the green brighter.

A grin covered Etta's face. "It's gorgeous. It's totally you." Dot owned a landscaping company, and the floral blouse fit her perfectly.

"It's good enough for a bridal shower, right?" Dot looked down at the blouse. "It might be the last thing I can wear before—" She cut off, her head jerking up. Pure panic poured out of her eyes, and Etta wondered if she should ask Dot to continue or let her off the hook.

She loved her sister-in-law, and since Etta had been

living up at the ranch, right next door to Ward and Dot, she'd gotten close to her.

"Are you pregnant?" Etta asked, deciding to go with the direct route. All Dot would have to do is nod or shake her head. Before she could do either, Oakley arrived, saying, "Etta, Ida's about to burst into tears," and shoving a crying Judy into her arms.

Dot eased away, lowering the blouse and ducking her head so she didn't have to look at Etta.

"Etty, Etty," Judy said, hiccuping. "Etty, snack."

"I'm sure your mama brought snacks." Etta smiled softly at her niece and pushed her hair back off her head. "Did she do these piggies for you?"

Judy reached up and touched the pigtail on top of her head. When Etta had stopped by to ride with Ida and the twins, she'd already exclaimed over Judy's hair. The little girl had been happy and giggly then, only about an hour ago.

"Piggy," she said.

"That's right," Etta said, swinging her purse up to the top of the clothing rack where she stood. Oakley had turned right around to go back to Ida, who stood several yards away with her double-stroller, bent over it, doing something. As Etta watched, Oakley handed her another wet wipe.

Dot had migrated a safe distance away, where Etta couldn't talk to her unless she used a loud voice, which she wouldn't do in the department store.

"I'm sure I have a snack in my purse," she said to Judy,

who sniffled among all of the hope now filling her wide, blue eyes. Etta dug around, her fingers catching on a plastic baggy of Cheerios.

She tugged it out from under her wallet and opened it. "Here you go, baby." She tugged the bag away from the little girl's chubby fingers. "Judy, you have to stop crying."

"No crying," she said.

"No crying," Etta repeated. "Your mama just needs you to eat your snack and be good, okay?" She touched her forehead to the little girl's. "If you can do it, Auntie Etta will bring you home with her, and we can have a cupcake tea party."

Joy filled her at the smile on Judy's face. "I good," she said, her voice so solemn and so cute. Etta loved her so very much, and she gave the eighteen-month-old a hug.

"Okay," she said. "Let's go see what your mama needs."

At the stroller, Oakley held Johnny on her hip while Ida rose. "Okay," she said, blowing out her breath. "I think I got it all."

"What happened?"

"Oh, Johnny spilled his milk all over everything, including Judy and her snack." Ida looked beyond stressed, and she reached up and pushed her hair off her forehead. "This is why I don't leave the house."

"You're doing fine," Etta said. "We need something new for June's bridal shower. I'll take them for a bit while you look."

Ida met her eyes, so much gratitude streaming from

her. At the same time, Etta saw the wobble in her twin's chin. "Don't cry," Etta said.

"Have you even found anything?" Ida asked.

"Yes," Etta said, though that wasn't quite true. "There's a blouse over there I'm going to try on." She bent to strap Judy into the left side of the double stroller. "Judy has her snack, and she promised she'd be good." She clicked the buckle and twisted to reach for Johnny. Oakley relinquished him to her, and Etta strapped him into the stroller too.

"I'll take them and go try it on while you look." She nudged her twin out of the way, ignoring the dubious looks. "And if Judy's good, I told her we could have a cupcake tea party at my house tonight, so I hope you have no plans."

"When do I ever have plans?" Ida asked, and it took a well-trained ear to hear the bitterness in her question. Etta had spent her whole life with Ida, and she heard it. She glanced at Oakley, who'd turned her back and currently leafed through a rack of tops.

"Does it have to be a blouse?" she asked, turning as she pulled out a black tank top. "Look at this." She held up the shirt to her body, and Etta did like the old-fashioned rose that looked like it had been weathered.

"That's cute," Ida said. "I could never pull it off, but you do just holding it up to yourself." She put a smile on her face, and joined Oakley at the rack.

Etta pushed the stroller out from between these racks and over to where she'd been looking. She tugged two or three blouses off the bar and hooked them over the handlebars of the stroller, barely allowing them to stop as she did.

"Okay, babies," she said, pushing them toward the dressing room. "I'm going to model for you." She went into the largest fitting room and locked the door. Johnny blinked his dark blue eyes at her, and Etta took a few of Judy's Cheerios and put them on his tray.

"What do you say, buddy?"

"Fank you," he babbled, already reaching for the cereal.

Etta grinned at him and quickly tried on the first blouse. Five minutes later, she'd chosen one, and while it wasn't her favorite article of clothing she'd ever put on, it didn't matter. If she didn't want to wear the light blue blouse with tiny white stars on it to the bridal shower, she could go find something else on her own. Or buy something online and never leave her room under the stairs at the homestead.

She kept the twins entertained—and well-fed—until everyone had found something they liked enough to buy.

"All right," Oakley said, grinning as Dot turned from the register with her bagged blouse. "Lunch?" She tapped and swiped. "Back of the House is getting rave reviews on Two Cents, and I think we should try it."

Etta said nothing, because she'd been to Back of the House a couple of nights ago. Another disastrous first date that wouldn't yield a second.

"I'm in," Ida said, and she reached for the stroller. 'Thanks, Etta. I can take them." She took a couple of steps with Oakley, and then added, "Oh, did you get my text about Mike? You never said if you'd go out with him."

"I got it," Etta said, giving her a glare-glance out of the corner of her eye. "I don't want to go out with him."

"He's a great guy," Ida said. "Just moved in down the street. Works for that new pharmacy on the bottom floor of the hospital."

"I'm sure he's fabulous," Etta said, sighing. They exited the department store to bright sunshine, and Etta reached into her purse to find her sunglasses.

"I think Etta is done with blind dates," Dot said from her left, and Etta gave her a grateful look as she slid her sunglasses into place. They'd had lunch last week where Etta had told Dot she didn't want to be set up anymore. Ida loved finding men for Etta so much that she hadn't been able to tell her sister yet.

"I don't know how you do it," Oakley said. "Dating is so exhausting."

That was the perfect word for how Etta felt. "Yes," she said. "It is."

"So what are you going to do?" Ida asked, clicking her keys so her minivan would unlock. "You're not using the app again, are you?"

Etta started to help her get the twins unbuckled and into their car seats. "No," she said. "I'm not using the app." She handed her bag to Oakley, who moved toward the back of the vehicle to put their purchases back there.

"So—"

"I'm not going to date," Etta said, cutting off her sister.

"I need a break. I'm done. I've been going full blast for a long time." Over a year. Maybe two years. Etta wasn't sure. She knew she felt like she'd been swimming in circles in the middle of the ocean, waiting for a rescue boat or plane to spot her and come get her.

No help came, despite the best efforts of her sister, herself, and even her Aunt Lois, who'd set up a date for Etta with one of her new husband's nephews.

Tyrell had been one of the least disastrous dates Etta had been on, but there was no spark between them. Not even a fizzle.

Her latest crush, LaMar Anderton, had called a lot, but when it came to going out…he hadn't seemed too keen on that. Etta suspected he'd only started talking to her on a dare, and she was far too old for such games.

"Done?" Ida asked, as if she didn't know what that word meant.

Etta lifted Johnny out and set him on his feet. "Get in, bud." She pushed the stroller toward Dot, who started to fold it up. "Yes," she said. "I'm just going to focus on the community outreach programs and my family. I have plenty of nieces and nephews and opportunities to mother."

She met Dot's eyes. "Right, Dot?"

"Yes," Dot said, ducking around the back of the van with the stroller. Etta sighed, because she'd at least tried. Dot obviously wasn't ready to take the bait, and she turned as she heard Oakley talking.

"Yes, we're on the way," she said, and she came around

the back of the van. "See you soon, Holly Ann." She lowered the phone and added, "Holly Ann and Bethany Rose have a table at Back of the House," Oakley said. "I told them we were on the way."

"Did they find anything at Hector's?" Ida asked, heading for the driver's seat.

"She said they did," Oakley said, and they all started piling into the minivan. Etta let the others chatter around her, because she simply needed the silence for her own vocal cords.

"AH, HERE HE IS," MISTER SAID AS THE DOORBELL rang at the homestead. He jumped to his feet like his chair had caught fire, and Etta concealed her smile as best as she could by stirring the pulled pork.

Mister sure seemed to have a man-crush on Wyatt Walker, who'd just arrived at Shiloh Ridge for their planned meeting. He and Mister wanted to do some roping and riding demos, and he'd asked Etta for her help in knowing the best way to go about doing them.

Since she ran all the school programs and community outreach classes, she knew the right people to talk to in order to get things listed in the community bulletin, on the website, and with the teachers at the high school.

Laughter echoed into the kitchen from the foyer, and Etta stepped over to the fridge and pulled out the bowl of potato salad she'd made that morning. She'd just set it on the counter next to the buns she'd cut five minutes ago when Wyatt and Mister entered the kitchen.

"Etta, you know Wyatt Walker," Mister said. "Wyatt, my cousin, Etta."

"Pleasure, ma'am," Wyatt said, and Etta smiled at him and shook his hand.

"It's good to see you again, Wyatt." The Walkers had come up to the barn for family weddings in the past, and while she wasn't besties with Wyatt, they'd certainly met before. "Do you want to get food, and then we'll talk?"

"Food is always good," he said, taking in the spread on the counter. "This is a feast."

"I have some packed up for your family," Etta said. "Mister said Marcy is pregnant again? She'd probably like a meal she didn't have to make." She kept the smile on her face, because if there was anything that brought Etta joy, it was feeding other people.

"She'll probably start crying," Wyatt said with a smile. "I'll text her right now." He did that and then the three of them made themselves pulled pork sandwiches, put potato salad on their plates, and Etta added a healthy handful of corn chips to go with her salsa too.

"So," Wyatt said after they'd chitted and chatted and eaten. "Mister said he ran the idea by you. Tell us all the holes we need to fill."

Etta reached for the folder she'd prepared for the meeting. "If you just want to do simple demos, all you need is a way for people to sign up. I'm assuming you'll have an attendance cap?" She looked between Wyatt and Mister.

They looked at each other, both of them with raised eyebrows. They clearly hadn't even thought of an attendance cap. Etta suppressed her sigh, realizing this consultation was going to be much more work than she'd first anticipated.

So what? she asked herself. *What else have you got to do?*

The answer to that was nothing, and helping Wyatt and Mister give value to the community and showcasing rodeo as a career was a good thing. Etta tried to surround herself with good things, because it gave her something to focus on besides the things she wanted but didn't have.

"I'd suggest starting with demos," she said. "Then there's no money to collect. You could do age-appropriate sessions, with kids maybe twelve to sixteen, who are just starting out in the rodeo. And one with kids who are in the junior program looking to level up. And then any interested adult." She looked up from her paper to take in Wyatt's and Mister's reactions.

"I like that idea," Wyatt said.

"We definitely need an attendance cap," Mister said. "Can we make a form that closes when the maximum number is reached?"

"You can, yes," Etta said. "Or you can simply let everyone sign up and then perhaps make additional sessions based on interest level."

"I like that idea too," Wyatt said with a grin. "We should've talked to Etta ages ago."

Mister beamed at her too, and Etta did like hearing their praise. "I told you she was the one who'd know."

Cactus Glover lay with his wife, Willa, in his arms, his eyes closed but sleep a ways off. She hadn't fallen asleep either, if the way she kept rubbing a slow circle on his forearm meant anything.

He loved her with his whole heart, and he loved the life they'd started together a few years ago. He wished he didn't have more room in his heart to love, but he did. Willa simply couldn't physically go through another pregnancy, and a man could only have so many dogs.

They'd just finished making love, and he murmured, "I love you," before pressing his lips to her forehead.

"Love you too, Charles." She shifted in his arms and pressed a kiss to his mouth. "Rosita is coming tomorrow morning."

"I remember," he whispered. "I got out all the vaccinations for the dogs."

"Thank you." She settled back into his embrace, and

the two of them breathed in and out together. "After the home study, it's really just about the classes," she said.

"I liked the one last night," he said. It had been on loss and grief, and every class was taught by a DCFS staff member, as well as a current foster or adoptive parent. Cactus wanted to foster-to-adopt, because he wasn't sure he could handle getting attached to a child and then having to let them go again.

They'd been cautioned against that exact thing, but Cactus didn't know how to interact with a child without wanting the very best for them.

"I did too," Willa said. "Let's see what Rosita says tomorrow. They know we want kids that have the potential of being adopted."

"Yes," Cactus said. "We'll see what she says." He wasn't the most patient man on the planet, and he reminded himself of something he'd learned in therapy a few years ago.

Only worry about what you can control.

He couldn't control the news Rosita would bring with her tomorrow. He and Willa had started in the foster parent program only a few weeks ago, and they'd already gone a long way. Their application had been accepted instantly, and they'd passed all the criminal and background checks in only a day or two.

They'd been attending classes a few times a week, because the state of Texas had a real need for foster parents right now, and the DCFS department in the

Panhandle was trying to get the training done as quickly as possible.

Willa had been taking a first aid class through the Three Rivers community center, and she was nearly finished with the certification. That would help them with their quest to get children into their home.

Cactus closed his eyes once again. *Bless us to be willing to do whatever Thy will is,* he prayed. He used *us* when really he meant himself. *We have so much, and if we can help a child, that's all I want.*

Chaz, their son, had just turned a year old in the spring, and Mitch was almost fourteen. Cactus already felt like he had to know everything when it came to raising kids, and he'd sure like to have more feet running around here, calling him Dad and Willa Mom.

He thought about the baby he'd buried, and while he contributed monetarily to the Heart Association, specifically for research and care for congenital heart defects in infants, he wanted a more tangible way to honor his son. He wanted as many children in his life as he could get.

His nieces and nephews weren't in short supply, and their parents let Cactus take them whenever he wanted to. Willa simply went along with him, because she knew how important it was to him to let the love he felt come out. She loved kids too, and Cactus thanked the Lord above every day that he'd found his soulmate.

After all, he'd thought that would never happen again.

T HE FOLLOWING MORNING, THE HOUSE SMELLED like cinnamon and bacon, and while Cactus would've liked another ten minutes to get the dirty dishes currently sitting in the sink cleaned up, the doorbell rang.

"She's here," Willa said needlessly. She looked at Mitch and Chaz, who'd both just finished breakfast. "She's early."

"They never come when they say they're going to," Cactus said, frowning. He didn't like that, because he loved a schedule and sticking to it. But the DCFS wanted to see what a home was really like. Today, Rosita was going to see a one-year-old with a syrup beard and more pancake stuck to the floor than he'd gotten in his belly.

Tank barked, and Cactus shushed him instantly. "Stay," he told the dogs. "Right there, Galaxy. Stay."

He wiped his hands on his jeans and went to answer the door while Willa stepped over to the sink to get the washcloth. He pulled open the door to find Rosita standing on the porch, along with another man he hadn't met yet.

"Cactus," she said pleasantly.

"Good morning, Rosita," he said, stepping back. "C'mon in. We're just finishing breakfast."

"It smells amazing," the man said, entering the house.

"This is my boss, Thomas Millhouse," Rosita said, entering second and closing the door behind her. "He wanted to come along this morning, because I've been telling him about you and Willa."

"Nice to meet you, sir," Cactus said, surprise coloring

him on the inside. He thought he did a pretty decent job of masking it in his voice. He turned toward the kitchen, where Willa stood at the highchair, trying to get Chaz to cooperate with getting his face de-stickified.

The baby whined and cried, of course, and Cactus saw the two dogs waiting. "Are you dog-averse?" he asked. "I can put Tank and Galaxy outside. Frost stays with Mitch. He's his hearing dog."

"Not at all," Thomas said. "I've got a couple of dogs myself." He grinned at the canines and moved further into the house.

"Willa," Cactus said following him. "This is Thomas Millhouse."

"Lovely to meet you," she said.

"Pastor," he said with a smile as Gal came over to sniff him. He bent down and scrubbed behind her ears. Her eyes closed in bliss, and Cactus smiled at the animal. He'd let them sleep in the bed with him if it didn't bother Willa so much.

"You've got just the two kids?" Thomas asked, glancing up at them.

"Yes," Cactus said. "Mitch will be fourteen soon. Chaz is only one."

"Eighteen months," Willa said. "Just the right age to think he can do things he can't really do." She laughed lightly and tried to sneak-attack him with the washcloth. It worked too, and she got more syrup off his chin before he could protest or turn away. "Go wash up, baby," she told Mitch, signing as she said it.

"Mitch is deaf," she said, also signing that. "This is Mister Millhouse. You remember Rosita." She indicated the staff member they'd been working with. She'd been out to the house before.

Hi, Mitch signed. *Can I take the dogs out to the golden field after I wash up?*

Willa looked at Cactus, who wanted to say no.

"I think you should take Chaz over to Uncle Ace's," Cactus told the boy. "You said you would, and then you can grab Link and see what chores Uncle Bear has for you two to do today."

Mitch's face fell, and he looked away from Cactus. He tapped him on the shoulder to get him to look at him again. "*Then* you can take the dogs to the golden field. After the chores are done."

His face lit up again, though it wasn't quite as bright as before. *Okay*, he signed. *Can we take the scooter?*

"If you wear the helmets," Willa said. "Let me get Chazzy all cleaned up." She turned to the little boy and kept signing as she spoke. "You have to get cleaned up, or Brother can't take you to play with Gun. Do you want to play with Gun?"

"Yeah, yeah," Chaz said, straining against his restraint in the highchair.

Cactus took the washcloth from her and went to get it warmer and wetter while she bent to pick up the pancake pieces off the floor. With that done, he handed her the washcloth and said, "I'll get his clothes."

He went into the boy's bedroom and opened the top

drawer of the dresser Bishop had built for his son. He pulled out a pair of shorts and dug around for a T-shirt. Back in the main area of the house, he found Chaz out of his seat, wearing only his diaper, and Willa saying, "Sorry. We should've gone with a non-syrup breakfast the day you guys were coming."

Thomas had taken a seat on the couch, and Tank, the devil, had jumped up next to him. He sat in the man's lap, for heaven's sake.

"Tank," Cactus barked at the dog. "Come on, bud. Down."

The dog reluctantly got down, but the important thing was that he got down. He flopped on the floor in front of the couch, as if Cactus had ruined his life by making him give up Thomas's lap.

"Sorry," he said to Thomas. "He has personal space issues."

Thomas simply chuckled and waved away the apology. "I've got one that gets up on the counter. He once ate a whole meatloaf. Boy, was my wife mad."

"I bet she was," Willa said, scooping Chaz into her arms. He immediately squirmed to get down, squawking like a baby bird.

Willa muscled him into Cactus's arms, who said, "Come on, buddy. You're going with Mitch, and that means you have to get dressed." He quieted then, and Cactus sat in the recliner and pulled on his shorts and helped him get his head through his shirt. "There you go. Run and find your shoes for Daddy."

The little boy ran off toward the back door, and Cactus sighed before looking at Rosita and Thomas. "We're not quite ready for the day."

"It's why we came when we did," she said with a smile.

"Do you feed them a hot breakfast every morning?" Thomas asked.

"Heavens, no," Willa said, signing though Mitch wasn't in the room. It was such a habit for the two of them, and she seemed to realize she didn't need to do it. She glanced at Cactus and slipped her hands into her pockets. "I sent Mitch out to get the scooter ready."

"How many of you live up here at the ranch?" Rosita asked. "I was trying to count the houses."

Cactus needed his fingers to count too. "Uh, let's see," he said, looking at Willa. "We all live up here except for Ida and Brady, and Aunt Dawna."

"And your mother," Willa said, reaching for his hand as she sat on the end of the couch closest to the recliner. "There are twelve Glover siblings and cousins. Bear's the oldest, and he and his wife build that new house on the way out here to the Edge."

"Judge and June will live in the Ranch House," Cactus said. "They're getting married in another month or so."

"Ward and Dot live in Bull House," Willa said. "Oakley and Ranger, Mister, and Etta live in the homestead."

"Ace and Holly Ann have a house overlooking the bluff," Cactus said. "Just down the road from the blue barn. Bishop and Montana live behind the barn."

"And Preacher and Charlie are moving into the new house near the highway next weekend," Willa finished.

"Oh, Zona lives just over the hill with her husband, Duke Rhinehart. So she doesn't live here."

"She's very close though," Thomas said.

"Very close, yes," Cactus agreed.

"I'm assuming y'all get together often." Thomas crossed his legs oh-so-formally.

"Seems like every day," Cactus said dryly.

"Cactus," Willa chastised.

"What?" he asked. "I just like living out here, that's all." He looked at Rosita and Thomas. "My family is big and loud. Everyone needs a break sometimes."

"You want a bigger family," Willa said. "That's why we're doing this."

Embarrassment filled Cactus's face. "Of course, yes." He cleared his throat. "I love my big, loud family. I just like living at the Edge too."

"It's very peaceful out here," Rosita said, exchanging a glance with Thomas. "Well, we're here to finish up your home study," she said. "And because you've already started PRIDE, and we have an immediate need."

Cactus swallowed, and he glanced at Willa. She wore her concern right in her eyes, and her hand in his squeezed.

"Three kids," Thomas said. "Their mother passed away last year, and their father just got indicted for a federal crime. He'll be tied up in jail and court and who knows what will happen with that."

Cactus swallowed. "They have no other family?"

"The mother's mother. She's eighty-eight, and she can't care for them."

Willa cleared her throat and shifted on the end of the couch. "They don't—"

A honking noise came from the back door, and Chaz squealed.

I'm ready, Momma, Mitch said from the back door. *Is Chazzy ready?*

"Let me get his shoes on," Cactus said, swooping the little boy into his arms as he tried to run by. "Shoes first, bud. Then you sit real still while Mitch drives you to Gun's." He slipped his son's feet into his shoes and followed him out the back door. Mitch fitted the baby helmet onto Chaz's head and helped him climb into the car seat Cactus had fashioned onto the front of a motorized scooter.

All Mitch had to do was stand up on it and drive it, the way any teenager would do. He did that, started the scooter up, and the whining buzz of the gas-powered engine filled the air around the house.

"Be safe," Cactus called to them, making his signs big. "Don't leave Frost in the dust."

Okay! Mitch signed back, and then they took off, the little cocker spaniel running alongside the scooter.

He turned back to the house and nearly ran into Thomas. "He just motors off?"

"Yeah," Cactus said. "I'm sure Willa's texted Holly

Ann. He should be there in ten or fifteen minutes, and she'll text us."

"My son has a scooter like that." He turned and went back inside.

Cactus looked up into the wide, Texas sky and said, "Thy will. I will follow it," under his breath before he rejoined everyone in the house.

Willa hadn't moved, and neither had Rosita. "The kids could be adopted," she said, twisting to look at him as he approached. "But they can't guarantee that, obviously. The father might be acquitted, for example."

Cactus didn't like the sound of that. He wanted kids they could work toward adopting, so he didn't have to give them up at some future date.

This isn't about you.

The words entered his mind, and he knew they came outside himself. He met his wife's eyes and bent down to kiss her forehead. "Whatever the Lord will give us, right?"

She nodded, and when their eyes met again, Cactus could see and feel her love for him. He felt like the luckiest man in the world in that single breath of time, and as he settled into the recliner again, he said, "How soon would we need to take them?"

"They're ready," Rosita said, her smile growing and growing. She looked at Thomas. "What do you think?"

"I think *I'd* like to come live up here," he said, chuckling in a robust way. He sobered and leaned forward, his elbows resting on his knees. "In all seriousness, I think if you two are willing, those three kids would be very lucky to come live here for a while." He exchanged a glance with Rosita. "It won't be easy. They have been up, down, and around. They've had very little stability since their mother's death."

"How old are they?" Willa asked.

"Nine, seven, and four," Thomas said. "Two boys—the older ones—and a girl."

Willa looked at Cactus, and it was obvious from the clear-eyed gaze she wore that she wanted these children. Cactus wanted them too, crazy as it sounded. If there was anything life at Shiloh Ridge was, it was stable. The work that had to be done day-in and day-out could bore a man to death, and there were plenty of good examples of men and women here.

He looked back at Thomas as Willa said, "We'll take them, if you think we're ready for them."

Rosita grinned and bent to pluck a folder from her briefcase. She extended it toward Willa. "If you can get these things, we'll have the children ready on Friday."

"Friday," Cactus echoed. Two days.

Willa flipped open the folder, and Cactus peered over her forearm. *Separate beds for each child* sat at the top of the list, and he looked back at Rosita. "Can the little girl sleep in the same room as the boys?"

"They prefer to be in the same room," Rosita said. "For now."

Relief filled Cactus. Right now, Mitch had his own room, and so did Chaz. That only left one more bedroom, and Cactus had honestly thought they'd start fostering with a single child. But three siblings.... He suddenly wasn't sure he and Willa could handle them.

"This will allow us to keep the siblings together," Thomas said. "We feel that's very important for them, as they've been through so much already."

"Yes," Willa said, clearing her throat and closing the folder. "We can get all of this by Friday."

There was no way she'd even had time to read the whole list—he'd seen words all the way down the page—but Cactus felt the exact same way. He'd do whatever it took to get every item on that list by Friday so he could keep the three siblings together.

CHAPTER 14

Mister strained to get the corner of his end of the bunk bed aligned. "It's not far enough," he said, releasing his grip. He looked down the length of the bed to his brother, who had both sides in on his end. "It's got to go left more."

"Maybe I can rotate it." Cactus lifted out the right pin that had gone down into the frame, which allowed Mister to pull his corner to the left.

"Yeah, there." His pin slid right in. "Can you get it?"

"Not quite," Cactus said, straightening and stretching his back.

"Let's try it at the same time." Mister hefted his end out, and Cactus inched the frame back his way.

"Yeah?"

"Let's drop it." Mister said, and he pushed on the bottom bed frame, and pulled on the top one, and he got the pins aligned. "I'm in."

"Me too."

Mister pressed the pin in, and it was definitely a tight, scraping fit. But it went in. Cactus used the rubber mallet to get his seated properly and stepped to hand it to Mister, who did the same. They both sighed simultaneously, and when their eyes met, Cactus grinned at Mister.

"Thanks for coming to help."

"Of course," Mister said. "Preacher's been lettin' me go down to Golden Hour in the afternoons, so I was already done around here."

"Yeah, how's that going?" Cactus asked, turning back to the two twin mattresses that leaned against the wall. "Is Libby's ankle healing up?"

"She's doin' real good, yeah." Mister hadn't talked a lot about Libby, to anyone. If there was someone he'd confide in, it would be Ward or Preacher, but Cactus sure knew how to keep a secret.

He didn't ask pressing questions about the relationship, which Mister appreciated, and together, they got the mattresses on the frames and the beds made up with the bright blue bedding. It matched, top and bottom, and after Mister emerged from the bottom bunk, having tucked the sheets and blankets against the far corner, he groaned.

"I'm too old to be bending like that."

Cactus scoff-laughed. "You don't get to talk about being old."

"Here's the pillows," Willa said, arriving with an armful of them. She let them fall to the floor as her eyes rounding. "Oh, Charles, it's beautiful." She stepped into his side, and he put his arm around her. "It's…real. There are going to be little humans sleeping in those beds."

Mister smiled at the tender looks on both of their faces. He wasn't sure he knew how to open his heart the way Cactus and Willa were, but then he remembered how easily he'd taken to Mitch and Lincoln. He sent up a prayer that the transition would go smoothly, and if anything, that the new children coming to the ranch weren't overwhelmed by the sheer number of Glovers.

"Yeah," Cactus said, reaching for the first pillow. "So where do you think all of these are going to go?" He grinned at his wife. "Each bedding set only came with two pillowcases."

There were easily more than four pillows on the floor, and Mister reached for one too. He took off the plastic sheath that protected it and reached for one of those said pillowcases.

"You can never have too many pillows," Willa said, turning. "Let me get the rest, and I'll bring in the extra cases too."

"The rest?" Cactus called after her, but she'd already walked away. Mister noticed the limp in her stride, and he remembered why she and Cactus were becoming foster parents. His brother loved three things in this world: Kids, dogs, and super dark chocolate.

He grinned as Cactus muttered about too many pillows, thinking he could probably add Willa, family, and God to the list of things Cactus adored.

The thing was, kids and dogs loved Cactus too.

Instantly and fiercely, if the way Tank and Gal kept poking their heads into the room said anything. Cactus cared about them, and he took care of them, and children and animals could feel it.

They finished up the pillows, putting four on each of the three beds in the room, and Mister retreated to the corner where the door sat. He stood beside Cactus and admired the room. "They're going to love it," he said. The single bed opposite the new bunk had a pink Strawberry Shortcake bedding set, as the notes Cactus and Willa had received had said the little girl coming to their home that evening loved that particular doll.

A brand new Strawberry Shortcake doll even leaned up against the pillows, and Mister's heart expanded at the care and precision with which Cactus and Willa were going to welcome the children to their family.

"What else do you need?"

"Cactus?" someone called from down the hall, and Cactus turned that way.

"Nothing, Mister. Go take care of Libby." He stepped out of the room. "Down here, Bear." He turned back and nearly rammed into Mister, who'd started to follow him. "Thank you, Mister." Cactus grabbed onto him and held him tight for one, two breaths, and then he released him as Bear filled the end of the hallway.

"We've got all the food," he said. "Sammy's filling the fridge."

"Right," Cactus said. "Mother brought a few things

too, so we'll probably have to put some in the unit out in the barn."

"There's no way this is fitting," Sammy called from the kitchen, and Mister basked in the energy of life on this ranch. He hadn't felt like this at Winterhaven, and truth be told, he didn't feel like this at Golden Hour.

He went with the other brothers into the main part of the house, where Sammy stood in the kitchen, peering into the fridge. "Charles," she said, and that was all.

"I'm going to tell Mother not to bring food?" he grumbled. "It's fine. I have a fridge in the barn. Load me up." He held out his arms, and Sammy slid a sheet pan of potatoes into it, then topped that with one of cookies.

"The rest is still in the truck," Bear said.

"You guys act like we haven't eaten in ten years," Cactus said, nodding to the back door. Bear went out first, leaving Mister to shake his head at their back-and-forth about how everyone in the family wanted to help, and he and Willa better not hoard those kids out here.

Sammy sighed and wiped her hand across her forehead before she zeroed in on Mister. "Heya, Mister." She stepped over to him and hugged him. "I have a tray for you too."

"You do?" He stepped back and smiled at his brother's wife. "What is it?"

"Come see." She grinned and headed for the back door. "Are you still okay to watch the kids on Monday night?"

"Yep," he said, following her. "Would you care if Libby came with me?"

Sammy spun back to him, her eyebrows sky-high. "Libby Bellamore?"

"Is there another Libby I've been pining over for two years?" He chuckled. "You know I'm seeing her." Everyone knew. He hadn't tried to keep it a secret, and he and Libby had been out four times now. He went down to Golden Hour to help her every afternoon. She'd asked him to kiss her a couple of weeks ago, but they'd been interrupted, and Mister hadn't found the right time or place to try again.

He knew he didn't want it to be in a parking lot. Or on her front porch. He wasn't sure why he wanted this ultra-romantic moment with her, and he certainly didn't know how to create it. His relationships in the past hadn't necessarily been focused on creating memories and romance, but with Libby, he found he wanted both.

"I'm just...." Sammy shook her head. "I thought she'd put you in the friend zone."

"I'm creeping out," Mister said with a smile. "It's slow. Libby seems unsure about something." He led the way down the steps to the back driveway where Bear and Sammy had parked. Lincoln sat in the ancient swing, his baby sister on his lap.

"Okay, Link?" Sammy called.

"Yeah," he said back. "Cactus said Mitch can't come over tonight."

"He's getting three new brothers and sisters," Sammy said, detouring that way. "Of course he can't come over tonight."

Mister reached the tailgate, his phone buzzing in his pocket. He pulled it out to see Libby's name on the screen. His heart pulsed, and he swiped on the call. "Hey, beautiful."

"Are you on your way yet?" she asked, ignoring his endearment.

"Not yet," he said. "I'm still out on the Edge helping Cactus and Willa." He gazed down at the pans of food that still needed to go somewhere. He got out of the way as Bear, Cactus, and Willa returned.

"Okay, good," she said. "I hate to ask, but could you stop and get something for me?"

"Sure. What do you need?"

"Well, it's more like a want."

Mister grinned into the summer sky. "All right."

"It's one of those frozen mango lemonades from the Bilge." She hung onto the last syllable, and Mister burst out laughing.

"You made it sound like you needed some major painkillers in a major way," he said between chuckles. "You just want a treat."

"It'll ease my pain," she said with a touch of haughtiness in her voice. "It's so hot today."

He stood in the shade, and the Edge had some level of wind always attacking it. "It is," he agreed. "I'll be down in a bit."

"Thanks, Mister."

"Sure thing, sweetheart."

"Oh," she said. "Real quick. You're sure I don't need to wear anything special for the rodeo tomorrow night?"

"It's a rodeo, Libs."

"You're a rodeo celebrity."

"I am not," he said, though he supposed he had been. Four National Championships would say he was. His right leg sent a phantom pain through him, reminding him that the life he'd once lived was over. Ended. Gone. Done.

Not worth having.

"How big is the belt buckle you're going to wear?"

He smiled and shook his head. "Not that big."

"Is it going to have diamonds on it?"

"No," he said. "They don't have real diamonds, Libs."

"Anything sparkly, then?"

"No." He didn't wear his championship belt buckles. He wasn't even sure where they were right now. Probably in a box somewhere. "It's going to be a perfectly normal night, with a perfectly normal couple. We'll go to dinner, we'll go watch some rodeo, and then we'll drive home."

Easy. Mister thought about kissing her, and nothing seemed easy then.

"Okay," she said.

"Okay. See you soon." He pocketed his phone, and Sammy approached the truck, now carrying Heather on her hip.

"That one's yours," she said, indicating a brownie pan full of exactly that. Brownies. "Double chocolate."

"You're a saint," he said, lifting the pan and leaning to press a kiss to Sammy's forehead. "Once again, I'm disappointed you're already married to my brother." He grinned at her and kissed his niece too. "I'm going to take these to Libby's. Maybe some chocolate will earn me a few points."

"Let me know if that works," Sammy called after him. "I can make more."

Mister waved over his shoulder, his smile wide. He wasn't going to ask his sister-in-law to make more brownies for him. He didn't need to earn points with Libby. He needed to figure out what her hang-up was and address that in a calm, mature, adult way.

MISTER GOT OUT OF THE TRUCK AND TOOK A long, deep breath of the Amarillo night. "I love the rodeo," he murmured. He'd been to many since his injury had forced him into retirement, and there was nothing like a dark night with bright lights over the stadium. Nothing like the scent of hamburgers frying and red licorice hanging in the air. Nothing like the announcer's voice, and the way the dust lingered in the air after a ride, and the energy pouring off every living thing who'd gathered for the event.

He went around the front of the truck and opened Libby's door for her. She'd waited for him, and he reached up to help her down. She wore the walking boot all the time now, and in another three weeks, she might be able to get rid of it completely.

Her rosy perfume added to the scent of the rodeo, and

he grinned at her as she found her footing. He took her hand in his, closed her door behind her, and started toward the stands. Most people never saw the behind-the-scenes at a rodeo. The part where the cowboys and cowgirls hung out, where they kept their horses, where they watched the events in a tent so they'd know how everyone's runs went.

Mister knew, and he automatically looked right when the majority of the crowd moved left. At other events, he'd longed to go down the path less trod, but tonight, that pull didn't come.

He didn't want to be part of the rodeo anymore. It had been cleansed from his system, and a small, private smile touched his soul and then his mouth.

"Can we get some candy?" Libby asked, drawing him back to his new reality. It was one he wanted badly—this woman on his arm all the time. The ability to see her every single day. Tell her that he didn't want to go back, that his focus was now forward on becoming the best man, husband, and father he could be, doing the best he could at his job and in his community, and making sure he stayed close to the Lord.

He took another deep breath of the rodeo, and exhaled it all out. "I'm not your daddy," he said. "If you want candy, we can get candy."

She grinned at him. "I want one of those three-foot licorice ropes."

He laughed and steered them over to the concessions

stand. Plenty of people milled about, because the pre-events were still running. He wanted to see the barrel racing—he loved barrel racing—and the roping, of course. As a former roping champion, he loved watching the cowboys throw their ropes. He could still remember the adrenaline that propelled a man out of a saddle on a moving horse.

He'd loved working with his horse too, because most people didn't realize that the horse did a ton of work in the calf roping event. It had to explode from the gate at exactly the right time, and it had to come to a complete stop and then back up to help the cowboy get that calf down and tied.

Mister had loved his rodeo horses, and he did experience a moment of missing them.

They got their candy, and while Mister held out his hand for his change, he heard his name behind him. He didn't want to turn and see who it was. He could pretend he hadn't heard, right? Surely the Lord wouldn't smite him for that.

Libby had turned already, and he took a moment to tuck the dollar bills back into his wallet, slide it into his back pocket, and then pick up their goods. Only then did he turn, and he went left instead of right.

He'd taken two steps, not even clearing the condiment table, when he spotted Lucky Gillroy and Yarn Thompson.

No, he thought instantly. *Please, Dear Lord, no.*

"Mister Glover," Lucky said, his swagger exactly the

same. He dang near knocked over the table with all the relish on it as he barreled toward Mister. He wrapped him up in a hug, causing Mister to drop his tub of cotton candy.

"Lucky," he said, laughing. "What are you doing here?"

"It's a rodeo, man," he said, stepping back. His smile rivaled the glory of the sunrise, and Mister had seen him use it on plenty of unsuspecting women.

Yarn bent to pick up the cotton candy, taking an extra moment to examine it. "This is what you're eating?"

"It's the rodeo," Mister said, taking it back from him. "Are you guys competing?" They couldn't be, unless they'd gone to roping only. Only the younger men could do the bronc and bull riding. The body took a real beating, and the riders only lasted a few years.

That, or a man ended up like Wyatt Walker, with severe back problems and years of surgeries. Mister had only had three on his leg to try to get it right, and he thanked God every day that he hadn't had to endure more.

"Nah," Lucky said. "But we've got guys here tonight."

"Guys?" Mister felt Libby come up beside him, and he glanced at her.

"Yeah, we run a coaching facility," Lucky said, plenty of pride in his voice. His whole face lit up. "You should join us." He turned to Yarn. "Shouldn't he? We don't have anyone with the roping skills of Mister."

"You should," Yarn said. "It's great money."

"I have a job," Mister said, putting a smile on his face that stretched strangely. "Libby, this is—"

"There's plenty of women," Lucky said.

Libby pulled in a breath so loud Mister could hear it above the crowd. He looked at her, the heavens opening before him.

Mister looked back at Lucky and Yarn, their idiotic grins irritating him to the very core. He wanted to slug those stupid smiles right off their faces and tell them to grow up. Maybe he'd been a player in the past.

My word, he thought. *There's no maybe about that, Mister.*

But he didn't want that life now. He couldn't believe men his age did. He stared at Lucky and Yarn, both of them with hope in their eyes, and he felt completely removed from them. A thick, clear partition went up between him and them, and all the noise around him faded into silence.

He existed alone, and Mister had felt like this often at Winterhaven. This clarity had come to him when he'd prayed and asked to know what his life should be. What *God* wanted his life to be.

Everything rushed back at him, and he said, "I'm not into that anymore, sorry." He watched their faces fall, but he did not feel bad. He didn't feel weak. If anything, having the Lord on his side made him more powerful and sure. "I'm working my family ranch, which I love. I'm looking for a good woman to spend my life with. In fact." He looked to his side, but Libby was gone.

"She was right here." He scanned the crowd, catching her hobble-step as she disappeared around one of the grandstands.

"Excuse me."

"Mister, wait a second," Lucky said, but Mister didn't wait a second. He needed to get to Libby, and fast.

CHAPTER 15

*L*ibby's chest felt like someone had poured liquid nitrogen into it. Every breath cracked something, and the summer evening air went down ice-cold.

"Libby," she heard behind her, and she slowed to a stop. She couldn't outrun Mister, and unless she wanted to act like she was twelve years old and hide in the bathroom all night, she'd have to face him sooner or later. Not only that, but they had a ninety-minute drive back to her house, and she had no other way home.

She clenched and unclenched her fingers, trying to knead her way toward a solution. "Help me," she prayed, more words piling behind those. "Help me be honest with him."

Things with Mister had been going extraordinarily well in Libby's opinion. He was prompt for their dates. He cleaned up spectacularly. He showed up at the ranch every afternoon to help her, though Libby was getting through her chores almost by herself now. He was a perfect gentleman when they were together, and Libby had fallen more and more in love with him with every passing day.

When he wasn't Rodeo-Mister, he was dang near perfect.

"Hey," he said, arriving at her side out of breath. He circled around to stand in front of her. "You ran off."

"Mm."

He studied her face, but Libby looked at something on the horizon past him. She couldn't quite meet his gaze, because of that perfection that existed inside him. She hated feeling inferior to him. She didn't clean up as nice. She had to wear this walking boot everywhere. She was still struggling with her faith, though it too had grown over the past few weeks. The process had been slow, and she'd told herself over and over to be patient. A garden took all summer to grow. Faith was no different.

"I don't want to be here," she said.

"Then let's go."

She met his gaze then. "Really?"

"Really."

"Can I keep my licorice?"

"Once again, I'm not your father." He passed her the licorice, and Libby gripped the crinkly plastic like it alone could save her. "Let's go." He didn't take her hand this time, and he didn't go back the way they'd come. She didn't think they could get out on this end of the stands, but Mister's long stride didn't break.

He got further and further ahead of her, as she couldn't

walk very fast in the boot, and he spoke to a cowboy at the fence line. He opened the gate for Mister, and he waited for Libby to walk through in front of him. Cattle and horses surrounded them, and Mister said, "This way, Libs," before taking off again.

He walked angry, and Libby supposed he had every right to be. Amarillo was a long way to come for nothing, and her own guilt needled at her.

No, she thought. *It's not your job to please him.*

She wanted to be his partner, not his pleasure.

At the truck, he opened her door and helped her up. He got behind the wheel and started the vehicle so the air conditioning would begin. "Are you going to say anything?" he asked.

"Yes." She cleared her throat, trying to find where to begin. It sure seemed like everything had started a decade ago. "Remember when you were the featured guest at the grand re-opening of Rivers?"

"Vaguely," he said with wariness in his voice.

"I remember it."

"You weren't there. It was a private, ticketed event."

Oh, but she was. "Yes, I was," she said. "I went with Mildred and Suzy. She and Jack were dating at the time, and he wanted to impress her. I called the publicity director and said you and I were friends, and he gave us tickets."

Mister swiveled his head and looked at her, shock coloring his expression. "You never told me that."

"I think...." She took a breath and told herself to be

brave. "I know. I *know* that was when things changed for me. I just keep going back to that night in my head. Over and over and over."

"What did I do to upset you?"

Tears pricked Libby's eyes. "This is so stupid."

Mister reached across the console and took her hand in his. "It's not. It's bothered you for ten years. Let me fix it."

"What if you can't fix it?"

"I certainly can't if you don't tell me." He pushed his breath out. "Though I bet I can guess." He looked away, and he pulled his hand back too. "Libby, I was...I was not a good man back then. I would not be surprised by anything you said, to be honest."

"You worked the room, but I think you were supposed to do that."

"I was."

"I sat in this corner booth, sipping champagne, while you got three women's numbers, then followed this other woman down the hall and kissed her." She could still taste the bubbly alcohol as it burned her throat. She could still remember the way her mind had conjured up other scenarios where Mister acted like women were objects for him to admire and use.

"Then, you went back to your table and told all your rodeo buddies about it. Laughed about it, like she was just some conquest."

"I'm so sorry."

"I'd just broken up with Marsden. Remember him?"

"The guy who told you that women should be seen and not heard? Oh, I remember that dude." He spoke with disdain and a level of fury Libby hadn't expected.

"Watching you," she said, staring out the windshield into the darkness. "I vowed right then and there that I would never be that woman. I would not exist just for some man's pleasure, and I would not ever, *ever* allow a man to take advantage of me the way you did those women."

"Libby."

"I didn't like you at the time," she said. "I mean, we were friends and all, but it was like there was this new type of spotlight on you, and it made everything so harsh. It showed me things about you I hadn't seen before."

She shook her head, and she wished her memories would fall out as easily. "Then you got hurt, and you came home, and you started all the surgeries and healing." She lifted her hands and let them fall back to her lap as if they were too heavy to hold up.

"And you changed, and I know you've changed. I started developing this crush on you, and it won't go away, and I don't know. I just...I can't help thinking of that night and wondering if you're really different, or if I'm going to get that man at Rivers at some point. I don't want that man."

"I hate that man," Mister said, plenty of power behind his voice.

"You reminded me of him just now," she said. "Talking to those guys."

"I'm not going to take some job training rodeo hopefuls," he said.

"There's plenty of women," she said.

"Libby." He sighed. "I wish I could go back in time and slap myself upside the head." His head hung down now. "I did so many stupid things back then. For one, my daddy would be real ashamed of how I used the Glover name. For two, you saw me at my worst, and I hate that."

Libby's chest stormed, breaking up the ice from the liquid nitrogen and flinging it all away.

"I'm not that man anymore," Mister said. "I promise you with everything I have, I'm not him. Can't you see I'm not?"

Libby looked at him, and with her eyes adjusted to the darkness, and some sliver of orange light coming in from the street lamps in the parking lot, she could see him.

Clearly.

"Surely you've done things in the past you wish you could change," he whispered. "Surely you've grown up and changed and become someone you're more proud of."

She nodded, released his hand, and moved hers to cradle his face. "My head knows you've changed. My heart is struggling to believe it."

He closed his eyes and leaned into her touch. "Tell me what to do to fix it."

"I don't know." Hearts didn't work like that. They didn't whisper things Libby could hear and understand.

He took a moment to breathe. "Before you left, I tried to introduce you. I told them I loved working my family ranch, because I love my family. I told them I was looking for a good woman to spend my life with, and then I went to introduce *you*."

Libby smiled at him, but his eyes were still closed. "I'm sorry I left. I panicked."

He opened his eyes and looked at her. "We don't have to come to the rodeo."

"You love the rodeo. It's part of who you are."

"No," he said. "It was part of who I *once was*. I'm not that man anymore." He shook his head and she dropped her hand. "I'm not, Libs. Maybe even a year ago, I still was. I was so angry at you for refusing to go out with me, as if you *had* to simply because *I* wanted you to." He focused out the windshield too. "But I've learned so much this year. So much about myself, and so much about relationships, and so much about what I really want my life to be."

"And what's that?"

"I just want a simple life." He reached up and took off his cowboy hat. "Before, I wanted to be the best. I needed to be in the spotlight. I was the National Champion. Now?" He shrugged and lifted the hat over the seat and dropped it in the back. "I just want a house with a porch that has a view of the ranch. I want a dog. I want a good woman at my side, and I want to laugh with my kids when they show me painted rocks. I want to yell at them to be safe when they ride their bikes to the pond, and I want to show up at my huge, loud family events and have everyone be glad I'm there."

Libby's eyes burned, because it sounded like a very good life. The kind she wanted too.

"When you say, 'the ranch,' does it really matter which one?" she asked.

He looked at her then. "I suppose not," he said. "Yours, mine, ours. Whatever. I want space. I want trees. I want…there's so much I want. I'm a selfish man, and I'm working on that. I swear I am."

"I don't think wanting trees makes you selfish," Libby said with a smile.

Mister did not smile. In fact, he sniffled, and Libby had no idea what to do with that. He reached to put the truck in gear, and he backed out of the stall he'd parked in earlier. "Let's go home."

Libby wanted to apologize for dredging up the past. At the same time, it had needed to be done, and she didn't know if she'd have ever been brave enough to do it had they not run into those two men.

The drive happened with low country music for company, and when Mister finally pulled up to the red house Libby loved with her whole soul, she sighed. He got out and helped her down, then steadied her up the steps to the porch.

She couldn't end the night with so much silence, so she grabbed onto him and hugged him as tightly as she could. "I am working with my heart," she whispered, her lips so close to him they caught on his ear. "I swear I am. I'm trying to coax it along so it knows you won't hurt us, and you won't shatter us, and you aren't that man anymore."

"I'm really not," he whispered back. "I've worked so hard to overcome him, and I'm glad part of you can see it."

"I can see it," she said. "I can hear it. I'm working on *feeling* it."

He nodded against her shoulder and pulled back. "Thank you for telling me. I've known there was this wedge between us, but I didn't know what it was." He kept his head down, and Libby wanted to tell him, *Chin up, Mister. The sun will come out tomorrow, and everything will be okay.*

Instead, she said, "Babysitting on Monday night? And then Bear's birthday party next weekend? I can still do both of those with you?" She heard the insane hope in her voice, and surely Mister did too.

He looked at her and nodded. "Absolutely. I'm glad you even want to."

"Did you not hear the part about how I've had this insane crush on you for years?" She offered him a smile, which he took and returned.

He leaned down and pressed his lips to her forehead. "See you Monday." He started for the steps, and Libby watched him go.

"What about church tomorrow?" she asked.

He paused and half-turned his head toward her. "I think I need to sit alone tomorrow, if that's okay."

"Okay," she said, but she didn't want him to be alone.

His boots clunked down the steps, and Libby stood on the porch while the engine roared to life and he drove away. In that moment, she realized that Mister learned and grew while he was alone, when he didn't have anyone else to rely on but himself and the Lord.

"Bless him," she prayed into the night, feeling her words get all the way to heaven and right into God's ears. "Bless us both now that the truth is out." She opened the door and went inside, knowing it was too early for Mildred to be home.

"Help my heart heal," she continued to pray out loud. She knew once it did, she'd be willing to offer it to Mister, and that sent a shiver of fear through her. Still, she continued to pray that the Lord would be mindful of and watch over her and Mister, though she didn't dare ask Him to help them end up together.

In that regard, she knew they'd have to work things out for themselves.

ard Glover turned as his wife, Dot, groaned as she eased herself into the dining room chair. "That bad?" he asked, concern spiking through him.

"I shouldn't have gotten down and done those roses yesterday," she said. "That's all." She gave him a smile carrying mostly weariness, and Ward turned back to the stove. He kept his head down for a couple of extra seconds, feigning the need to check the eggs.

Truth be told, he'd already turned off the flame beneath the pan. "Eggs and coffee?" he asked.

"Yes, please, baby," she said, and Ward sure did like the presence of this woman in his life, in his house, on his ranch.

He served her breakfast, noting that she put salt on the eggs before tasting them, and she poured cream in her coffee—no sugar. He grinned at her and sat at the table with his own plate of eggs and his own mug of coffee.

Their eyes met, and the conversation they'd been having for a couple of weeks now came right back to life. "I'll slow down," she promised.

Ward didn't say he'd heard it before, though he'd heard it before. "I'd like to tell everyone."

"I know."

"Tell me again why we can't?"

Dot put a forkful of eggs in her mouth, took her time chewing, and swallowed. "I don't know. I just—I hate the Glover spotlight."

"I could just text it out."

"You do and you're dead to me." She spoke with a level of strength Ward hadn't heard in a while.

He grinned at her. "Then you'll have ranch wives popping over one at a time."

"And I'll have to explain it fifteen bajillion times." She stabbed her fork toward him. "And they'll bring food we don't want."

"Hey, speak for yourself, love." He chuckled as she cocked her head with an exasperated look in her dark eyes, saying, *Really Ward?* "I love those oatmeal bars Oakley makes."

His phone chimed, and he glanced at it, suspecting it to be one of two people. Preacher, who'd beat him out to the ranch this morning, or Jed, the cowboy Ward had put in charge of the repasturization. They had a whole crew of cowboys and cowgirls working on their fields this summer while the cattle were out in the wild hills. Ward couldn't help it if the ranch needed to be cleaned up a little, or that it was painstaking work to fix fences, clean out weeds, and keep rotating their chickens, turkeys, sheep, and horses through the fields.

Sammy's name sat on the screen, which caused a blip of surprise to move through him. She rarely texted the whole family string unless she was responding to something someone else had said.

He swiped to read the text. "Oh, right," he said. "Bear's fiftieth birthday party is on Saturday." He looked up hopefully. "Maybe we could tell everyone then. We do family announcements at parties."

To his surprise, Dot nodded. Joy burst through Ward. He got up and leaned down to kiss his wife, enjoying the heat in her lips from her coffee. "I love you, Dorothy. I will tell them you don't want the spotlight on you for very long." He would take all of it if he could.

But she was the one who was starting to show the evidence of their growing family. She was the one who'd make him a father in only five short months. She was the one who'd become his first thought in the morning and his last at night before he fell asleep.

"Are you going to shower while I'm gone?" he asked. "I have to run out and talk to Jed for a minute."

"Yeah," she said. "But don't be long. I hate walking into the chapel after they start."

"I won't make us late again," he promised, and he knew he better keep it. He reached for his cowboy hat and wished he could bottle the air conditioning to take with him. The July heat in Texas could make a man wither in a day without proper hydration, and Ward grabbed an enormous bottle of water from the fridge before he left.

He walked out onto the ranch from his front porch, going past the stables on his right and the barns and sheds on the left. He loved the new firepit he and Dot had put in, and he came out and built a fire there often. He loved watching the dancing flames and cooking a hot dog until it had some black char on the skin.

He thought about how his life would change in only a few short months, and a smile bloomed over his face. He wanted all of the changes that had come his way and that were coming. He and Dot had been married for a year now, and by the time their baby was born, it would be almost eighteen months.

She hadn't wanted to start a family right away, claiming she wanted time for just the two of them. She worked quite a lot at her landscaping company, and as one of the foremen on the ranch, Ward certainly had plenty to occupy his time. He and Dot had consciously made time for one another, something he adored about being married to her.

When she'd told him she was pregnant, it was like the Lord had added an extra layer of light to Ward's life. He'd been so happy, and the high of that still hadn't worn off. He hoped it never would. He wasn't the most kid-friendly of cowboys around the ranch—that honor went to Judge or Cactus or Mister. A lot of the kids liked Bishop and Ace too, and of course, Etta was the absolute favorite of all the children and babies at the ranch.

It was no wonder, as she invited them to sleep over with her. She sat in rocking chairs and read their favorite books to them over and over—and over. She saved treats for them and brought them gifts from the time they were born.

Ward couldn't wait to share his baby with Etta, and it had been very hard for him to keep Dot's pregnancy a secret from her and Ida. Ward was quite close to his twin sisters, and he'd wanted to tell his family about the baby for a couple of months now.

"Ward," a man said, and Ward pulled himself out of his thoughts. He wanted to tell his mother too, because she'd been aging steadily in the past year, and he thought she might not be with them much longer. Sadness darkened his joy for a few moments, but he pushed it back.

Mother had lived a good life. He'd miss her terribly, but he understood the circle of life, and he didn't want her to continue to live with sickness and pain.

"Jed," he said, finally spotting the man when he waved from inside one of their smaller equipment sheds just off the path where Ward walked. "What are you getting?"

"Some wire patches," he said. "We lost six chickens overnight. Foxes."

Ward sighed and reached up to wipe the sweat from under his hatband. "You know it's foxes?"

"Found the fur in the broken fence, yes," he said. "We need stronger protection around the coops. This patch might hold for a couple of days, but we need that heavy-duty stuff."

"Yeah, I know." Ward looked southwest, toward where the chicken coops sat, though he couldn't see them past a bank of trees and another long barn that housed their hay. "I'll get down to the farm supply store tomorrow. We'll pull over Damien, Royce, and Max and get it done."

"Maybe Preach can spare a man or two for a day."

In the middle of July? "I'll talk to him." Ward would, but he didn't think he'd be able to pull any men from Preacher's agriculture crew. Not with all the additional acreage down on the new part of Shiloh Ridge.

"All right," Ward said, sighing. "Load me up. Wait, let me text my wife. Maybe she can get down to church with my brother this morning. This sounds like we're going to be a while."

"There's a significant hole in the fence," Jed said, giving Ward a sympathetic look. He reached for a pair of wire cutters while Ward pulled out his phone and called Dot.

"Hey, hon," he said.

"You're not going to make it."

"We lost six chickens to foxes." Ward sighed. "I have to help Jed get that patched up. Could you call Ranger?"

"Yeah," Dot said with a sigh. "Sorry, baby."

"It's okay," Ward said. "Take good notes, and you can give me the sermon this afternoon." He grinned into the sunshine, his heart lifting at the thought of spending a Sabbath Day afternoon alone with his wife, in the air conditioning, while she talked to him about spiritual things.

"Love you, Ward. Don't let another task keep you out there. Fix the fence and come home."

"Yes, ma'am." He grinned and added, "See you after church." He ended the call, realizing he'd given himself four or five hours before his wife would be home from church. He faced Jed again. "All right. I'm yours for a few hours. Let's talk about that north section that's giving us trouble."

CHAPTER 17

*A*ce Glover carried his son as he and his wife, Holly Ann, hurried up the steps and into the church. With the summer sunshine blazing through the stained glass windows, little pockets of red, blue, and green touched the lobby.

He kept moving, even though he'd like to take a moment and enjoy the simple things in life. Sometimes Ace felt like his life was too busy, and he needed a way to find the reins and pull on them. Hard.

Thankfully, this year, Holly Ann had already talked to Bethany Rose about being Santa Claus during the holidays. She still worked a lot with her catering company, something Ace wanted her to keep doing if she wanted to.

"Right there," she whispered. "On the left. Sit by Duke."

Ace spotted his cousin-in-law and met his eyes. Duke instantly turned to Arizona, his wife, and they inched down to make room for Ace and Holly Ann. The choir had already finished, and Pastor Corning had just arrived in front of the mic.

Ace breathed heavily from all the rushing, which he hated. Holly Ann had been sick that morning, just like the past week or so, and he'd done his best with Gun. As he settled the little boy on his lap, Ace swept his fingers through his son's hair to get it to swoop correctly.

Holly Ann set the diaper bag on the floor and pulled out a bottle, handing it to Ace. They'd skipped breakfast— he hadn't felt well and Holly Ann had lost hers—and Gun hadn't eaten more than a couple of bites of crackers on the way down to town.

Ace held the bottle for Gun, who was distracted by Duke and Zona's daughter, Shiloh. The little girl had just learned to walk last month, and she stutter-stepped around her daddy's legs to Ace's, her big, dark green eyes soaking up everything.

She was a sober child with a quick smile, and Ace bent down and scooped her into his arms too. "Heya, girlie," he whispered to her as he settled her on his left leg. "Look, Gun, It's Shiloh. Be nice."

Gun could have a heavy fist, as he didn't know his own strength, and he reached for Shiloh and touched her face softly.

"Good boy," Ace whispered. "Say, 'hi Shiloh.'"

"Hi, Shy," Gun said, as he was still learning how to talk. He was almost eighteen months old, and Holly Ann insisted that he said more than Ace thought he did. She could understand words where he only heard vowels and consonants, and Gun was a happy, bubbling baby.

Shiloh reached for Gun's bottle, but the boy wasn't sharing. He pulled it back and leaned back into the crook of Ace's arm, sticking the bottle in his mouth.

Duke reached over and handed Shiloh a sippy cup, and she did the same thing—relaxed into Ace and leaned her head back to drink her juice. Ace could've died and gone to heaven right then. He wasn't the brother everyone called in an emergency, but they seemed happy when he showed up, ready to help.

He wasn't the Glover that all the children loved, though Aurora had come to sit on their back deck plenty last summer. Ace loved his cousin Bishop, and he and Holly Ann did a lot with Bishop and Montana. Holly Ann babysat for the other ranch wives if they needed it, and Mitch had been scootering in Chaz to play with Gun all summer long.

Something buzzed inside Ace that he couldn't name. Holly Ann was pregnant again, but she probably wasn't due until February or March. They wouldn't tell the family for months. Their life marched forward, with long days on the ranch and delicious food coming out of their kitchen for other people's events around Three Rivers.

A pain sliced through Ace's stomach, and he coughed. He'd been sick to his stomach for the past month or so, and he'd thought it was just sympathy sickness to go along with his wife's morning sickness.

He looked up to Pastor Corning, needing the comfort

he usually found in the man's sermons. "…listen to those still, small promptings. Sometimes they come from the Lord, but sometimes the Lord works through others. He allows them to say things that you need to hear. That doesn't mean they're not important or that you should ignore them. We usually know when we hear something about its truthfulness." He smiled around at the congregation, and Ace let his eyes wander along the backs of heads too.

Most of the other Glovers sat in three rows near the front of the chapel. Right in the middle section, which had the longest rows and could therefore fit the most people. He saw Bear and Sammy sitting side-by-side, Bear's arm around her shoulders. Next to them sat Cactus, then the three dark-haired children that had come to the ranch only two days ago.

Ace hadn't met them yet, because Cactus and Willa wanted to introduce their foster children to the family in stages. He understood that, because even meeting a couple of families could be overwhelming.

Cactus, Willa, and their five children were coming for dinner tomorrow night, and Ace suddenly couldn't wait. He watched Willa turn toward the little girl they'd just gotten and hand her something.

"If there's something you doubt," Pastor Corning said, "Take it to the Lord in prayer. He'll always answer you."

Ace believed that with his whole soul, and he took a moment to think about what he needed to take to the Lord. Admittedly, his prayers had grown somewhat stale, as he prayed for the health and safety of his wife and son, his brothers, sisters, and cousins, and himself.

Yourself, he thought, a bolt of lightning zinging through his mind. He didn't feel well, and he hadn't for at least a month now. *There's more to this than sympathy pain.*

The thought entered his mind, rooted right in, and wouldn't let go. He tried to push it away, force it out, and it would not go. Fear bloomed in his chest, and he pulled in a breath loud enough to make Holly Ann on his right and Duke on his left look at him.

His wife raised her eyebrows and took Gun from him. She leaned into him. "Are you okay?"

No, screamed through his mind. He wasn't okay, and as the prickles moved over his scalp and down his neck, he knew it.

He simply *knew* it.

He didn't want to frighten his wife, because plenty of panic still paraded through him. Their house sat in a little clearing and on a bluff overlooking the rest of the ranch below. Trees surrounded the property they'd been gifted, and just on the other side of the north wall of foliage sat the family cemetery.

His father had died young. So had his uncle Stone. Bear, who was turning fifty this week, was older than his father had been when he'd died. They'd both suffered from and ultimately passed from prostate cancer. Bear had been diligent in getting tested—and in encouraging every male in the family to do the same.

Ace had never done it.

He swallowed, everything in his life collapsing. He wasn't old enough to have cancer…was he? He'd be forty next year, and even as he tried to reason his way through his fears and doubts, he knew his father had been diagnosed at about the same age Ace was now.

Absolute fear gripped his every organ, and he slid Shiloh back to her father. "I have to get out," he said, his voice barely low enough to be considered a whisper. He stood and stepped past his wife as she asked him again if he was okay.

No, he was not okay.

He only had to move past a few rows to get out of the chapel, and he did so quickly. Out in the lobby, he found a couple of mothers with their fussy babies, and he gave them cursory smiles. The little jewels of light danced on the floor, and Ace focused on a particularly golden one.

He drew in a deep breath, feeling calmer and more centered now. He walked over to the doors that he'd walked through only a few minutes ago, and stepped outside. "What do I do?" he prayed, looking up into the hot sky. "Go to the hospital right now? Make an appointment? How do I tell my wife?"

His questions grew increasingly quiet, until he was whispering his pleas to heaven above. He closed his eyes, imagining that glinting light to still be dancing through his vision.

Make an appointment entered his mind. *Be honest.*

Being honest was ultra-important to Ace, and he couldn't hide anything from the family. No, he wanted them to know, because then they could pray for him. He figured it would be better to have two dozen people begging God for his good health than just himself.

He opened his eyes and turned to go back inside just as the door opened. Holly Ann emerged from the church, her concern written clearly on her face. She'd given Gun to someone else, as she'd arrived alone. "Ace, honey," she said, stepping right into his arms. "What's going on?"

"I don't feel good," he said, holding her tightly. He needed to keep her close so he wouldn't have to be alone. "I need to go to the doctor and make sure I'm…okay."

She pulled back, alarms loudly screaming on her face. "What is it?"

"I don't know," he said. "But my daddy died young from prostate cancer. My uncle too." She knew this; they all knew it. Was he the only one who hadn't gone in for screenings, thinking he was too young?

"Do you think it's that?" she asked, that unadulterated fear he'd experienced inside marching through her expression now.

"I don't know," he said again. "The pastor said to go to the Lord with questions, and I thought about what I needed to know about and ask the Lord. I haven't been feeling well, and my prayers have become these sort of rote, *keep us safe, bless us with good health* types of things, and I thought—I'm not well." He cleared his throat and ran his hand through his hair. "I sort of spiraled from there, but just now, out here where I can think clearer, I feel like I just need to make an appointment and go get the tests done."

Holly Ann studied his face, her eyes searching his. "Are you sure?"

"Yes."

"I'm going to have another baby soon," she whispered, her lovely, navy eyes filling with tears. "I can't lose you."

Ace cradled her face in his hands, wanting to reassure her that she wouldn't. That he loved her from now until the end of time, and they'd always be together. He touched his forehead to hers, both of them closing their eyes.

"Maybe we should just go to the hospital today," she whispered.

Ace didn't respond right away. He thought about what the pastor had said—others could act as the voice of the Lord—and then he thought about how he should handle this scary situation. Once again, the thought of, *Just make an appointment* entered his mind.

"I don't think that's necessary," he said. "I'll call the doctor first thing tomorrow morning, and we'll go together."

She gripped his shoulders tightly. "If you're sure."

"I'm sure." His stomach ached, but it had been doing that a lot lately.

"Okay," Holly Ann said. "Do you want to go back in? I'm sure we could move Gun's seat to Zona's truck, and they could bring him home."

Ace pulled away from his wife and looked at the church. "No, let's go back in."

They went in together, and Ace thanked God that he had a partner to go through this life with. He couldn't imagine having to go to the doctor alone, and he kept his arm around Holly Ann as they filled the doorway that led back into the chapel.

Their spots a couple of rows down waited for them, but as he stood in the back, he could see Mister a few rows in front of where he'd been sitting.

He was alone.

A frown tugged at his soul, because Mister had been sitting by Libby Bellamore for the past couple of weeks. They almost always sat near the rest of the Glovers too— or her family.

Today, he found Libby sitting with her sister and Mildred's fiancé, clear across the chapel. His eyes traveled right back to Mister, who'd bowed his head.

Go sit by him, flowed through Ace's mind. He gave his wife a squeeze and whispered, "Mister's all alone. I'm going to go sit by him for a minute." He took the first step, and he went right past Duke and Zona to Mister's pew.

He slid into it and sat a couple of feet away from his cousin. Their eyes met, and Mister wore such gratitude in his. He held out his fist, and Ace bumped his knuckles. Nothing was said aloud, but lots got exchanged between them.

The pastor kept talking, but Ace couldn't focus. After a

few minutes, he heard his boy start to fuss, and he turned to look over his shoulder.

"You can go," Mister whispered. "I'm good now."

Ace looked at him. "You weren't good before?"

Mister gave him a tight, carefully controlled smile that didn't reach his eyes. "I was as soon as you sat down. Thanks for coming, but I'm really good now."

Gun wasn't having whatever Holly Ann was trying to do to help him, and Ace nodded. "Love you, brother," he said, though he and Mister were cousins, not brothers.

"Love you too," Mister said, and Ace stood up. He slid onto the end of the row where his wife held Gun on her lap while she rifled through the diaper bag.

"Hey, bud, hush up," Ace said, taking the boy. "Look, Momma's got your pacifier." She handed it to him, and Ace plopped it in his son's mouth. Not fifteen seconds later, the boy fell asleep in Ace's arms, and he leaned into the strength of his wife's arm as she put it around his shoulders.

He'd call the doctor tomorrow, and he'd be brave. He'd figure out why he didn't feel well, and he'd do whatever it took to get better. He didn't want to miss a single moment of his children's lives, and he wanted to be with Holly Ann for a good long time to come.

He wanted to pray that God would heal him, but the words wouldn't come. Instead, he thought, *Help me to be brave and accept Thy will.*

CHAPTER 18

Sammy Glover avoided a shallow pothole in the path, her destination just up ahead. If Jed wasn't in his cabin, she wasn't sure what she was going do with the frosted cupcakes in the basket under her stroller.

She loved getting out on the ranch and interacting with the men and women Shiloh Ridge employed. She'd felt so alone in the world before becoming Bear Glover's wife, and she didn't want anyone who came to this ranch to feel that way.

Thus, she'd spent the morning making a batch of cupcakes, four of which now rode in a box for Jed, whose birthday was tomorrow. She tried to get out to the people on their actual birthday, but she was watching both Robbie and Gun tomorrow morning for Montana and Holly Ann. That would give her five children under the age of four, and she might be called Superwoman by her husband, but it wasn't actually true.

The remaining twenty cupcakes the recipe had produced sat on her kitchen counter for her husband, Mister, and Libby. She had arranged an evening out with just her and Bear, something they hadn't done in months. At least since Heather had been born.

"Momma, look," Smiles said, pointing with one finger. "That bird just took off out of that tree!" Everything seemed to delight the child, and as the oldest—and with Bear as a father who demanded his children speak so he could understand them—Smiles did talk extraordinarily well.

Russ barely made a sound, because Smiles talked for him. Heather was only four months old, and she'd just started babbling her da-da-da's and her ma-ma-ma's.

"Yeah," she said, giving her oldest biological son a smile. "What kind of bird is it?"

"I don't know," Smiles said. "We can look it up in that book Gramma brought."

"Good idea," she said, starting to sweat in the noon-day sun. She'd go inside the cabin and leave the card and cupcakes if Jed wasn't there for lunch. The cowboy cabins came into view, and the sight of Sammy's destination brought relief to her aching legs.

She only went down to the mechanic shop once a week now, but that day had been a few ago now. She couldn't blame her aching body on getting up and down from under a vehicle. No, that belonged to the stubborn tractor she'd worked on yesterday.

She loved engines and cars, trucks, and tractors, but

her family life had replaced a lot of the things the mechanic shop had fulfilled for her. In truth, she should sell it to Jason Essex. He'd worked for her for over a decade now, and he was a brilliant mechanic. He knew all of the systems, all of the customers, and more about machinery than anyone else.

In the front of the stroller, Russ, her eighteen-month-old, squawked about something. Sammy peered over her three-year-old, who perched on the runners of the stroller right in front of her, and found the little boy shoving his sister's hand away from his tray.

"Russ," she said. "Soft."

"No," he said, about the only thing she could decipher.

Sammy slowed the stroller, praising the Lord that they'd entered the shade of a big tree. "Bud, grab a couple of those crackers and give them to your brother."

Smiles reached into the cup holder and tossed the crackers up to his siblings just as Sammy stopped. She sighed, especially when getting hit in the head by a flying goldfish wasn't Russ's idea of brotherly kindness.

"I meant to take them around to him," she said.

"Oh." Smiles grabbed another handful and jumped down from his standing spot. He put the crackers on the tray in front of Russ and said, "There you go, baby." He grinned at him and looked at Sammy. "What about Heather?"

"She can have some too." Sammy handed him the crackers, and Smiles fixed his sister up right too. He saved back one of the crackers and ate it himself before starting down the path without getting back on the stroller.

Sammy went after him, catching him easily, what with his little, short legs. "You can walk yourself if you don't start to stray," she said. "The moment you do, you're back on the runners."

"Okay, Momma," he said cheerfully. He'd stray off the path before they reached the cabin, she was quite sure. Smiles didn't have a care in the world, and Sammy both admired him and envied him for that.

Her phone rang just as she reached the cabin, and she quickly swiped on the call from Oakley, her very best friend here at the ranch. "Oak," she said. "What's up?" She bent to get the cupcakes out from underneath the stroller, keeping one eye on Smiles, who'd seen a butterfly and had gone after it.

"I think I'm going to do it," she said. "I'm going to list Mack's for sale."

Sammy paused with the box in her hand, her mind completely blank. It was quiet here on the ranch, though she could hear the evidence of work happening some-where in the distance. "You are?"

"I have two little kids," she said. "Ranger is beyond busy with Two Cents and all the financial things around here." She sighed. "I feel good about it. It feels like it's time."

"I'm glad," Sammy said, her own soul restless to know if she should do the same with her mechanic shop. "Lis-ten, I'm just dropping off some cupcakes for one of the cowboys, and then I can come by. Do you have any lemon-ade? It's so dang hot today." She found Smiles crouched down at the next cabin, and she decided that was fine.

"Sure," Oakley said. "I just put Fawn down, and we can chat more about Mack's. I just wanted you to know. You've helped me so much with it."

"I have not," Sammy said with a scoff. She started up the steps. "In fact, I don't think I've helped at all."

"You've sat with me and listened to every side," Oakley said. "It helped get things straight in my head."

"Okay," Sammy said. "I have all three kids with me. We won't stay long, especially if Fawn is asleep." She still had to clean up the kitchen from that morning's baking and shower and get ready for her hot date with her husband that night.

"See you soon," Oakley said.

Sammy pocketed her phone and knocked on Jed's door. Boots sounded behind it, and the almost-birthday man himself opened the door. He stared at her and then switched his eyes to the cupcakes.

"Happy birthday tomorrow," she said, feeling some-what stupid as he hadn't smiled. She extended the box of cupcakes toward him. "Those are all for you. You don't have to share on your birthday." He did live with two other cowboys, and he'd likely share with them. But she wanted him to know he didn't have to.

He took the box, finally looking up from the white-frosted cupcakes. "How'd you know it was my birthday?"

"My husband owns the ranch," she said with a smile.

"He lets me sneak a peek at the applications of the men and women he hires. I put the birthdays in my phone. That's all I see, I swear."

A smile started across Jed's face. "Well, thank you, Miss Sammy. This is real nice." His voice broke on the last word, and Sammy's heart flew out to him. Jed had only been at the ranch for about eight months, which meant he hadn't been here for his birthday last year.

"You'll come to Bear's birthday party on Saturday, right?" she asked as he turned away without inviting her inside the cabin. She wouldn't go anyway.

"We'll see," he said.

"We'll be there, Miss Sammy," a man called from inside. Rufus came forward, a huge smile on his face. "Me and Jim. Wouldn't miss it."

"Great," Sammy said with a smile. She leaned closer. "Is he okay?"

Rufus checked over his shoulder. "I'll see if I can get him to come on Saturday," he muttered. "He's having a hard time, because I guess it was just about a year ago that his wife walked out. He hasn't heard from her since."

Sammy's pulse vibrated through her body. "Oh, no. How terrible."

"I guess they're still married, and it's just hard."

Sammy couldn't even imagine, though she'd been through some hard things in her life too. The death of her sister and her husband in one fatal accident, for example. Suddenly becoming a mother to her nephew.

"I'll bring some brownies by later this week," she

promised, and Rufus simply shook his head as Jed returned.

"You don't need to do that," Rufus said. "Heaven knows you're busy enough."

As if to prove it, Smiles yelled, "Momma! *Momma?!*"

He'd wandered off, of course, and Sammy hadn't been watching. "Excuse me," she said.

"Thank you, Miss Sammy," Jed said, stepping out onto the porch as Sammy turned to leave it. "I'll help you find him." They went in opposite directions when they reached the bottom of the steps, and Sammy heard Smiles laughing a few seconds later.

Jed came around a cabin a couple away with the little boy in his arms, both of them grinning like they'd just done something naughty and hoped to get away with it.

"You strayed," she said to Smiles as Jed passed him to her.

"Sorry, Momma," he said, squishing her cheeks.

She couldn't stay mad at him for longer than four seconds, and she set him down. "On the runners. Go on, now." As he went, she sighed and looked at Jed. Without thinking too hard about it, she took him into her arms and hugged him. "I hope it's a really amazing birthday."

"Thank you, ma'am," he said, holding her tightly the way only a man in pain could. He stepped back quickly and cleared his throat. "I sure do like it here."

"Shiloh Ridge is a fantastic place," she said with a smile. "Do come on Saturday. Bear will want you there." She gave him one last smile and headed back to her kids.

She would make brownies later this week, because she hadn't made enough last time to take around to everyone.

Mister had gotten a pan, as had Cactus and Willa. She'd split a pan between Zona and Duke and Ollie and Aurora. She'd frozen theirs and mailed them overnight so they could have a weekend treat. They'd both texted her their thanks, and she loved sending them surprises, because she remembered what it was like to be young and in school, without time to make desserts like brownies.

She'd taken a pan to Montana and one to Holly Ann, the two busiest women around the ranch. Neither of them had started working less after having their sons, and Sammy admired them so much for all they did for the ranch, their businesses, and their families.

Her birthday treats were a nice way to let the non-Glover cowboys and cowgirls know she saw them and appreciated them, but she figured everyone could use a brownie just for no reason. She knew she could, and as she headed to Oakley's, she sure hoped she could find a brownie mix in the pantry she could make that very afternoon.

"THEY'RE HERE," BEAR CALLED DOWN THE HALL as the doorbell kept ringing.

"I hear it," Sammy said under her breath. She bent her head to put on her second earring, and then she started down the hall from the master suite to the living room.

Mister was hugging Bear, a wide smile on his face. When he stepped back, he moved to Libby Bellamore's side, easily taking her hand in his.

Their eyes met, and oh, wow, Sammy almost got knocked down by the awkwardness in the exchange. They both seemed so...nervous, and she hated that. Mister had liked Libby for so long, and the road between them had been quite rocky from what she understood.

"Hey," she said breathlessly, still rushing though she was ready now. This day had gone by so quickly, the hours slipping away like steam rising from a pot. "The kids haven't eaten yet," she said. "Sorry, I meant to have that done for you, but I lost track of time at the homestead."

"There's brownies," Bear said, and Sammy smiled at him. The children couldn't eat brownies for dinner.

"They can have them after they eat," she said, stepping past him and into the kitchen, where she pulled open the fridge. "They can have hot dogs or mac and cheese. Smiles will tell you what he wants. Russ just goes along with it." She tossed a package of hot dogs on the counter. "Heather has a bottle, and she does have one made up. You just have to heat it up. Microwave for ten seconds. Shake. Repeat a couple of times. Make sure it's not too hot and not just pockets of hot. She'll go to sleep shortly after that."

"I've babysat before," Mister said.

Sammy wanted to challenge him with questions like, *Three children, Mister? A baby of only four months? Two children who can't speak and tell you what they want?*

She raised her eyebrows at him, all those questions and more streaming into the air, unspoken.

"Smiles and Russ then take a bath together," she said, picking up a piece of paper she'd prepared. "They can choose their unders and pajamas. They go to bed at eight-thirty."

Libby took the paper from her. "Heather is in bed about eight, and her pj's are in the top drawer. I can handle her." She grinned at Sammy, all the anxiety and awkwardness gone. "Don't worry, Sammy. I won't let him kill them."

"Hey," Mister said, looking at Libby like she'd betrayed him. She grinned at him, and his face dissolved into happiness too. Oh, he liked her, and he liked her a lot. It sure seemed as if Libby liked him too, and Sammy hoped they could work things out between them.

"Uncle Mister!" Smiles came racing in through the back door, his brother toddling along behind him.

Mister turned toward him and laughed as he lifted the boy into the air. "Hey, here's my favorite nephew. What are we having for dinner tonight?" He scooped Russ into his other arm. "And my other favorite nephew. Hot dogs or mac and cheese?"

"Hot dogs *and* mac and cheese!" Smiles yelled, and Russ added his voice to the fray in babbled agreement.

Bear laughed, and that only fueled his sons to be louder than him. Sammy shook her head and turned to get Heather out of the bouncy chair where her father had put her. "Hey, my darling." She smiled softly at the little girl, seeing so much of her sister in her, though that wasn't really possible.

Still, Sammy and Bear had named their daughter in honor of her sister, and Sammy loved them both with a fierceness she hadn't known before the girl was born. "You be good for Auntie Libby tonight," she said, turning to pass the baby to Libby. Their eyes met, and Sammy froze. "We just call everyone auntie or uncle."

"It's okay." Libby took Heather, her face lit up like the sun. "She's so beautiful, Sammy. Thanks for letting me come."

They both looked into the kitchen where Mister was saying they could absolutely fry up some hot dogs and mix them into the macaroni and cheese. Sammy shook her head, reminding herself that it was good for her boys to have babysitters. It was good for them to have someone else give them exactly what they wanted, because she hardly ever did.

"Good luck," she said to Libby, who giggled. Then Sammy swept into the kitchen and kissed her little boys. "You be good for Uncle Mister. You do *exactly* what he says."

"Yes, Momma," Smiles said, grinning of course.

"No fighting him on bedtime," Bear said, plenty of warning in his voice. "If you're awake when Momma and I get back, it won't be fun for you."

"Da-da-dad," Russ babbled.

"Thank you, Mister," Sammy said, linking her arm through Bear's. "Let's go, baby. They're fine here."

They went out into the garage, where Sammy let Bear open her door and help her up into the truck. He leaned into the doorway and touched his lips to hers. "I love you, Samantha," he said. "Thanks for arranging this night out for us." He grinned, and she saw so much of their little boys in his expression. In some ways, though Bear was turning fifty years old this week, he was still a little boy at heart.

And she loved that heart. It loved wide, and it loved big, and it loved deep.

"I love you too, Bartholomew."

He ran his hand down the side of her face, then her thigh. "This dress is fantastic. You look amazing."

"Good," she said. "Because today has been crazy-busy, and I don't feel amazing." She smiled at him. "And thank you."

He backed up and closed her door, then went around to the driver's side. "Locke's?"

"Yes," she said. It wasn't her favorite restaurant, but Bear adored the buffalo sliders and the bacon-and-sour-cream-loaded mashed potatoes. And it was his birthday. "You look great tonight too, my love. Did you get a new hat?" She looked up to the ultra-wide-brimmed cowboy hat perched just-so on his head.

"It's one of Wyatt Walker's," he said. "Mister brought it just now."

"I like it."

"Me too." He reached for her hand and kissed the back of it.

She squeezed his fingers. "All right. You're fifty now. Wow. What are you going to do in this decade?"

"Survive my children?" He looked at her, and the two of them started laughing together. They had such a good life together, and Sammy was so, so grateful for it.

After they'd quieted, she said, "The kids are coming tomorrow at eight-fifteen. Ace has to be at the doctor at nine. Bishop and Montana are going with him and Holly Ann."

Bear swallowed and nodded. "I'll come home after our morning meeting so I can be there when they come pick up Gun and Robbie."

Sammy nodded. "And we'll pray for them."

"That's all we can do right now," Bear agreed. "We'll know more tomorrow."

CHAPTER 19

Bear Glover knew his wife didn't love the food at Locke's. The service was somewhat slow too. But she acted like she'd rather be nowhere else than with him at this restaurant, because he loved it. So much of what Sammy did on a day-to-day basis was for someone else. He worked a lot around the ranch, and he had dozens of people to oversee and worry about, but he knew what his wife did.

He knew about the brownies she mailed to Ollie and Aurora.

He knew she drove down to town and took Montana's aunt and uncle dinner when she'd heard Uncle Bob was sick.

He knew she visited his mother—and hers—on a weekly basis, whether it was easy or not. She simply loaded up all of the children and went.

"Let's go," he said the moment she put the last bite of cheesecake in her mouth.

She looked at him in surprise. "Already? I just finished." She reached for her glass of water and took a sip. "You usually like to sit for a minute."

Bear's body vibrated with his need to get home and relax. He loved going out with just him and Sammy, because they didn't have to fight with the kids or clean up a huge mess after they'd eaten.

"I'm worried about Ace," he admitted. His cousin had come over yesterday afternoon after church, and he and Holly Ann had asked Sammy if she could watch Gun while he went to the doctor. He'd admitted he'd been nauseous and sick for a little over a month, and he hadn't done any of the standard screenings yet.

He was only thirty-nine years old, and honestly, Bear hadn't done them at that age either.

"There's nothing to worry about yet," Sammy said. "Rushing home when we're finally out isn't going to help."

"I know." Bear reached for his cola and finished it off. "Maybe I just want to get you home so we can be alone there." He grinned at her, and Sammy smiled right on back.

"Do you really think the boys will be asleep?"

"They better be," he said. "I think Mister knows how to get them to do what he wants."

"Yeah," Sammy said dryly. "Twinkies."

"Whatever works, I say," Bear said. Maybe he hadn't always thought that way, but the more children they had, the more Bear was willing to offer treats and rewards to get his children to fall into line. How his mother and father had done it with seven kids, he'd never know.

Of course, Dad had died young, and all of his kids had been nearly grown up by then. Bishop, as the youngest, had just graduated from high school. Bear was still having children in his fifties.

"I don't know if I want more kids," he said, and that made Sammy's eyebrows shoot up. Previously, they'd talked about having as many as they could, as fast as they could. His wife was much younger than him at only thirty-seven, and she could probably give him at least two more children. She'd never said she didn't want to, but her pregnancy with Heather had been harder than the others.

"No?" she asked, lifting that water glass again. "What's changed?"

"*I've* changed," Bear said, maybe a little too forcefully. He always had to remind himself that Sammy was his wife, not one of his employees. Just because she worked in the maintenance shed whenever one of their tractors or vehicles had a problem, didn't mean she was on the payroll.

"I'm old," he said softer. "Fifty, Sammy. I'm *fifty* years old."

"Not until Thursday," she said with a smile.

"I don't want to be seventy when my kids graduate

from high school." He leaned forward and took both of her hands in his. "We have boys and girls. They're wonderful children. Do *you* want more?"

Sammy blinked, obviously thinking about it. "I don't know," she finally said, pulling her hands back when the waiter arrived to clear the dessert plates. He left the bill, and Bear reached for it.

"I thought you wanted a lot, so I haven't given it much thought. We just built a new house."

"We needed the house regardless," Bear said, pulling out his credit card. "I don't know, Sammy. Think about it. I feel complete. I feel like our family is amazing. Four kids. Us. A dog. A lizard. Probably more pets, knowing Link and Smiles." He smiled then and tucked his card into the billfold. "If you don't feel like we're complete, that's fine. We can keep having more kids. I just...I don't know. The last few weeks, when I come home, I feel like it's to the family I'm meant to have."

"I'll think about it."

The waiter came and whisked off his card, returning only a minute later. "Thanks for coming in," he said, and Bear tucked his card back into his wallet.

He started to get out of the booth, glad when his wife slid out too. He took her into his arms and held her, glad she had been at his side for most of the past five years. "Remember when you made me all of those birthday cards?"

"We were dating," she said, taking his hand and

starting for the door. "I love birthdays. I hope this one is the best yet."

"I loved that. I think I knew then that I was in love with you." He touched his lips to her cheek as they left the restaurant.

Back at the house, he stepped into the kitchen after Sammy, everything dark except for the light above the stove. The TV didn't flicker. There wasn't a single dirty dish in the sink, on the counter, or the stovetop. Silence poured through the house.

"My goodness," Sammy whispered. "Where do you think they are?"

"They've all been kidnapped by a...an alien mom, who then cleaned up before beaming the lot of them into her spaceship," Bear said, looking around the whole room. The kitchen, the dining room, the huge living room. Mister and Libby weren't there. His brother's truck still sat out front, so they had to be here somewhere.

Sammy giggled quietly and stepped into his arms again. She kissed him, and Bear sure did like that. Their lives didn't come with a lot of silence or a lot of privacy, and he loved it when he got both at the same time. "Let's find them, and then tiptoe to bed."

She slipped away from him and toward the back door. He heard voices, and he figured Mister and Libby had been sitting on the back porch, so he loosened his tie and went up the steps to check on the kids.

Sammy likely would too, as she liked seeing their chests rising and falling while they slept before she came to bed, but maybe Bear could convince her that he'd done as good of a job as she could. Such a thing was literally impossible, but both Smiles and Russ were asleep in the room they shared. Baby Heather was snoozing comfortably in her crib, and while Link's room came with a stench only a teenage boy could produce, he too was asleep.

Bear snapped off his lamp, which he left on nine nights out of ten, and went back downstairs. Mister and Libby stood at the door, and Bear moved toward them. "Thank you," he said quietly, engulfing them both in a tight hug at the same time. "I don't know how you did it, but thank you."

"They're adorable children," Libby said, and Bear thought perhaps he needed to see his kids that way more often. Sometimes the evenings felt more like a chore than a happy family life, and he regretted that.

"Bye, Bear," Mister said. "Love you, brother."

"Love you too." He held the door as they left, then he closed it and turned toward Sammy.

"I think I might have interrupted something important with them." She gave him a smile and stepped into his arms.

"Mister'll figure it out," Bear said. "He's always been really good with women." Bear didn't mean it as a negative thing, only that Mister had never lacked for someone to hang on his arm, and he had plenty of experience with women. Whatever he and Libby had been doing on the back deck, Bear was sure Mister could pick up wherever they'd left off.

In his own love life, Sammy reached for his tie. Bear had already unknotted it, so it sat loosely around his neck. She pulled it free as she stepped away, a look in her eye that told Bear she wanted him to kiss her.

"The kids are all asleep," he said. "I checked." He followed her and reached for her, taking her effortlessly into his arms again. "Do you want to go check?"

"No, sir," she whispered, kissing him. "I want you to take me to bed."

"I can do that," he whispered back, leaning down to kiss his beautiful wife.

BEAR ENTERED TRUE BLUE FROM THE BACK, having just come in from off the ranch. The air conditioning kissed his skin, making him sigh in relief. He normally didn't mind working outside in the summer— he'd done it plenty—but the heat this July had been something he'd never experienced before.

A round of laughter sounded from the huge hall where the family had parties, meals, weddings, and movie nights. When Bishop, his youngest brother, had come up with the idea to renovate this barn into family space, he'd been truly inspired.

Bear peeled his gloves from his hands and dropped them on the side table, which happened to hold several other pairs. They made him smile, and he removed his hat only to find all the hooks above the table taken. He turned to the other side and managed to find a spot for his hat. The men's restroom sat on this side of the doorway that went into the hall, and Bear ducked in there to wash his hands and face before he had to make an appearance at his fiftieth birthday party.

Knowing his wife, she'd have invited every cowboy in town, and a tremor of unease hit Bear's heart as he turned on the cold water. He reminded himself that he liked parties, and he loved his friends from other ranches. They took care of one another around Three Rivers, and while they hadn't had quite the need to do that lately, if one arose, he knew he could call on the Rhinehart's, the Walker's, the Ackerman's, or the Bellamore's. Plus a whole lot of other people.

He scrubbed his hands with soap in the icy water, rinsed, and then splashed water on his face too. He ran his wet hands through his hair, glad he'd asked Sammy to cut it last night. He liked it shorter on the sides and top, even though his gray had started to shine through.

He actually liked it, and he gave himself a bright, blue-eyed smile before shutting off the water. His phone chimed, echoing in the bathroom. Before he could even look at it, the device started to ring.

His wife's name sat there, and he swiped the call away as he exited the restroom. He took a few more steps and the hall expanded before him. Sammy faced the doorway, frowning at her phone. She tapped and lifted it to her ear again, looking up. Her eyes caught his, and Bear ignored his phone as it started to ring.

She ended the call and started toward him. "There you are," she said.

He leaned down and pressed a kiss to her cheek. "The chutes took forever."

"Everyone else beat you here." She grinned up at him, and he could look into her eyes forever and see something new every other second.

"I'm slow now that I'm fifty," he teased.

She giggled and turned back to the crowd, linking her arm through his. "Announcements first?"

Bear surveyed the group, noting that people stood in pods around the hall. The tables and chairs had been set up, but only a few people had taken them at the moment. Mother sat with her husband, Don, and Aunt Dawna. Penny and Gideon Walker had claimed a table, and they spoke with Ollie and Aurora.

Bear's heart beat quicker seeing the young college students here. It was a big deal for them to come all this way, and he felt honored that they'd come to celebrate with him. He'd have to make sure he got over there to hug them both and ask how things were going in South Carolina.

June and Judge stood with her daughter, Lucy Mae, and they talked with Bishop, Montana, and Montana's aunt and uncle, Jackie and Bob.

"Yes," he said. "Announcements first. Ace wants to go first and get it over with."

"Ward grabbed me a minute ago and said he had something," Sammy said.

"Mister does too," Bear said, and that caused Sammy to look at him.

"He does? Is he going to propose?"

Bear shook his head even as he found Mister. He had his head tipped back, laughing about something with Wyatt Walker, his wife Marcy, Libby, and Rhett Walker. "I don't think so. It's something else."

"Anyone else?" Sammy asked.

"I think Cactus wanted to introduce his kids," Bear said, searching for them. He couldn't see them. "Are they here yet?"

"I saw them somewhere...." Sammy searched the hall too. "Oh, there's Willa. In the kitchen." Even as she spoke, Willa exited the kitchen, her hand holding the four-year-old girl's they'd had for a week now. She smiled down at her, and the little girl grinned back at Willa, then took a bite of the cookie she'd been given.

"You're here," Cactus said, appearing at Bear's side.

"Where were you?" He hugged his brother and offered his arm back to his wife.

"I was helpin' the boys get ready." He grinned at the two boys who stepped to his side. "They got new pants that were too long. Aurora worked her magic on the hems, and we were just changing in the back room."

Bear surveyed the two boys. "You guys look great." He grinned at Cameron, the oldest, and Kyle, the younger boy. "Are you ready for this?"

"We've met almost everyone," Cameron said.

"Not the Walkers," Cactus said. "They own Seven Sons, and they have a lot of kids and brothers too."

"Squire's here too," Sammy said. "He brought Pete, Reese, Garth, and Cal."

"I see Preacher talkin' to Beau from Three Rivers too," Bear said.

"Duke's family is here," Cactus said. "Remember, he married my sister, and they own the ranch just south of us?"

Libby moved toward the door, and her sister entered, along with her two brothers and her parents. "The Bellamores just arrived," Bear said, lifting his hand to acknowledge Brit, his smile expanding. "They own Golden Hour."

"And Mister is dating Libby," Kyle said. "We met them last night."

"That's right," Cactus said, grinning at the boys. "So, are we starting, or what?"

"Waiting for you, Charles," Sammy said with a touch of dryness in her tone. She glanced around, obviously looking for someone. "I need to talk to Holly Ann and make sure she's ready." She bustled away to do that, and Bear extended his hand to shake Brit's and then his wife's, Gabi's.

"Thanks for coming," he said.

"Fifty is such a big year," Brit said with a grin. "Plus, you Glovers know how to throw a party. When Libby told us about it, I cleared my whole schedule." He laughed, and Cactus and Bear joined in.

"These are my new boys," Cactus said when Brit

looked at him. "Cameron and Kyle. Boys, this is Mister Bellamore. He owns Golden Hour Ranch."

"Nice to meet you," both boys said in chorus, and Bear grinned. He knew Cactus hadn't coached them to say that; he'd probably just told them what they could say when they met someone new, and since children wanted Cactus to like them, they obeyed.

"I'd heard you'd had more kids. A little girl too, I think Libby said." Brit shook the boys' hands and grinned at Cactus.

"Yeah, she's over there with Willa. Her name's Lynn."

"All right," Sammy said into the microphone, and Bear cleared his throat. He was going to have to step into the spotlight any moment now. "I need my husband up here."

"Excuse me," he said, tugging on the collar of his shirt. He should've taken a leaf from Cactus's book and brought fresh clothes for this party. He joined his wife at the front of the hall while the last of the chatter died.

"Thank you so much for coming to celebrate Bear's *fiftieth* birthday!" Sammy beamed at him and started to clap. That only caused all the cowboys in the barn to try to raise the roof with their voices, and when the cheering and applause stopped, a baby cried somewhere in the building.

Probably his, though Bear couldn't find Heather at the moment.

"There's plenty of food, as Holly Ann, Montana, Oakley, Dot, Zona, Ida, and Etta have been cooking for days. I thank them so much for that." She touched her hand to her lips and blew the kiss out into the crowd. "I'm grateful for everyone who had to drive out here to celebrate with us. It means a lot to me, and I know to Bear too."

He raised his hand, his smile stuck in place.

"We're going to start with some family announcements, and if there are last-minute additions, from anyone here, that's fine. Then we'll sing and then we'll eat. Cakes are at the back, and you can have dessert first if you'd like."

Bear watched as Bishop waved both hands and pointed at the five birthday cakes in the back of the hall like he was bringing in airplanes.

Sammy left the mic, and Bear shuffled out of the way with her. They stayed near the front as Ace walked up to the mic, his son in his arms. He cleared his throat, and he looked white as a ghost. Bear thought, *Help him.*

The news wasn't bad, and Bear already knew it. He did know how hard it was to make big announcements, however, so he sent all the good vibes he had toward his cousin.

"I've been pretty sick for the past five or six weeks," he said, clearing his throat again. The mood in the barn went down a couple of notches. "Holly Ann and I went to the doctor, and thankfully, it's not too terrible. It's Celiac disease, which basically means anything with gluten gives me trouble." He put a smile on his face that strained around the edges. "It's a good thing my wife is a professional chef, and she's already been working on things I can eat. In just the few days since I've known, I've been eliminating gluten, and I feel a lot better."

Gun reached for the mic, and Ace pulled him back so he couldn't get it. "Anyway, that's all." He took a step back and then lunged forward again. "But my daddy and my uncle died from prostate cancer, and I hadn't done any of the screenings. I thought that might be it, and I think everyone should get those tests done." He raised his free hand. "Okay, now I'm done."

He left the mic, and his brother, Ward, took his place. "We'll pray for you, Ace," he said, and Ward took his wife's hand as she joined him. Bear took one look at Dot and knew exactly what their announcement was.

"She's pregnant," Sammy said, gasping. "How did I not know this?"

Bear grabbed onto his wife's hand and kept her at his side even as she tried to go toward Dot. "Let them announce it," he whispered.

"Dot and I are…." He looked at her. "Having a baby!" they said together, their mouths both right at the microphone so the words shouted through the barn.

"Yeah!" Bear yelled, clapping his hands and sending another round of rowdy cheering up to the rafters.

Ward hustled Dot away from the mic, and Cactus took his place. "Willa and I are foster parents to three amazing kids," he said. "They came last week, and while we don't know if we can adopt them—"

"And we won't know for a while," Willa interrupted, grabbing onto the mic and twisting it slightly toward her.

"We're hoping to in the future," Cactus said. "God willing." He waved to them, and all of their kids came off the sidelines of the crowd. "So we have Mitch, of course." Willa signed everything her husband said. "And Chaz. And now we have Lynn, who's four, Kyle, who's seven, and Cameron, who's nine. They're all working with me up here at the ranch this summer, and they'll be at school in the fall. They've met a lot of you, and we just wanted to say thanks for all the food and all the help we've gotten as we've been getting them settled into our home."

He too cleared his throat and hurried everyone away from the mic.

"I guess I'm next," Mister said, and he waved someone out of the crowd too. Wyatt Walker could part seas, and apparently people, because they all made way for him. He joined Mister, and the two of them grinned at one another.

"Wyatt and I are going to do a series of rodeo demonstrations starting next week and running through the fall. They'll be for kids, teens, and adults, and we're going to do half of them here at Shiloh Ridge, and half down at Seven Sons. Etta is helping us with the website right now, and we're going to launch it on Monday. So if you've got kids or you're interested yourself, watch for that."

"It'll be out on Two Cents too," Ranger yelled, his voice not nearly as amplified.

"Right," Wyatt said. "Ranger's pushing it out on Two Cents too, so you can get more details there." He lifted his hand in a wave, and he and Mister blended back into the crowd. Well, as much as two former rodeo champions could blend into a crowd.

"Anyone else?" Sammy asked, raising both hands. No one came forward, and she nodded to someone. The lights in the barn went out, though plenty of sunshine still poured in through the windows.

She pointed to someone else, and the whole crowd turned around as if they'd gotten a memo Bear hadn't. Bishop now stood on a chair, and he lifted both hands into the air.

"Come on, baby," Sammy said, taking Bear around the edge of the crowd so he stood at the front once again. Someone had lit candles on all five cakes—ten on each one —and Bear grinned at them.

"Happy birthday to you," Bishop began to sing as he waved his arms. He was no chorister, but the whole crowd joined in, filling the barn with their joyous, beautiful voices.

Tears touched Bear's eyes and pure gratitude and joy infused into his heart. He didn't sing, obviously, and when the song finished, he felt every eye on him. He didn't know what to say. There were no words for the outpouring of love he felt in the barn right here, right now.

He stepped out from the crowd and turned back to them when he reached Bishop on the chair. In what had become unspoken Glover fashion, he lifted his fist and touched it to his heart, bowing his head for a moment.

When he looked up again, everyone in the crowd

repeated the gesture back to him, men, women, and children alike, all honoring him for simply surviving another year on the earth. He didn't deserve it, but he acknowledged it.

"All right," Bishop yelled. "Let's eat!"

CHAPTER 20

Mister took a piece of the gluten-free chocolate cake as a show of solidarity for Ace. He and Libby had spots at the table with him, and when he turned from the cake tables, he found Libby with a piece of the strawberry shortcake, chatting with her sister-in-law, Anne-Marie.

She looked over shoulder and met Mister's eyes, smiling as she did. He walked toward her, forking off a bite of cake before he'd gone too far.

"The first demo is next Friday afternoon," she said. "I think it would be perfect for Quincy."

"How old is he?" Mister asked, arriving where the women stood.

"It's Jack's son," Libby said. "He's eight. He'll be nine in December."

"Oh, sure," Mister said, swiping up another bite of

cake. "We're inviting eight-year-olds. We want it to be for kids who might actually want to then go on to participate in the rodeos."

"You can be five and do mutton busting," Anne-Marie said.

"Yeah, but this is more than that," Mister said. "We might be starting some classes for kids and teens too, either here or at Seven Sons. We're still working with Etta on it. She and Ida already do some outreach classes with the high school rodeo kids. Wyatt and I want to add to that, not take from it." He put the cake in his mouth while Anne-Marie said she was going to tell Suzy about the demo next week.

She put her hand on Mister's forearm and said, "Thanks, Mister. You're the best," before walking away.

He met Libby's gaze, his eyebrows going up. "The *best*, she said."

Libby smiled as she shook her head. "I'll have a word with her about making your head bigger than it already is."

"Oh, come on," he said with a chuckle. "I've been nothing but humble with you."

"All right, all right," someone said into the microphone, and Mister looked toward the huge windows at the front of the hall. Ranger stood there, up on the small stage Bishop had made for a past wedding. "The dancing part of tonight's party is about to start. Get your cards out, get your smiles on, get your dancing shoes ready!"

"Oh, boy," Libby said. "I think that means it's time for me to sit down."

"Nonsense," Mister said, piercing an ultra-large piece of cake. The gluten-free wasn't bad, but had he known he'd stand up to eat it all, he'd have gone for the triple chocolate fudge flavor. "You're practically out of that boot, and I've seen you do way more than dancing in it."

He stuck the cake in his mouth, took her plate with her half-eaten cake on it, and piled it on top of his. A few quick steps to the trashcan and back, and Mister bowed at the waist. "May I have this dance?"

"The music hasn't even started yet," Libby said, her eyes glowing like live coals.

"Bear and his mother are going to lead us in the first dance," Ranger said, and Libby's eyebrows shot straight up.

"Fine," Mister said, edging to the side along with everyone else. He grabbed onto the table he'd been sitting at, and along with Ace, they moved it to the edge of the hall. That done, he took Libby's hand and squeezed while he waited for Bear and Mother to start the dance.

After only a few beats, Bear dipped Mother, which caused a huge squeal to come from all the women in the barn, and then he twirled her to her husband. Mister had never heard Mother laugh like that, and she looked so blissfully happy in Don's arms.

Sammy stepped into Bear's embrace, and he called, "Come on, everyone. This isn't a show."

Mister stepped out of those waiting on the sidelines, glad he wasn't the only one. Ranger and Oakley, Rhett Walker and his wife Evelyn, Ward and Dot, and Gideon and Penny Walker all did about the same time he did.

By the time he and Libby had claimed a patch of floor and had started swaying, several more couples had joined them, including Montana and Bishop, Aurora and Ollie, and Ace and Holly Ann.

He smiled at Libby and brought her closer while still keeping his arm out to the side. He didn't need to put on a show either, not here with all of their ranch neighbors, dozens of children, and all of his siblings and cousins watching.

He felt himself free-falling with this gorgeous woman in his arms, and he tried to get himself to slow down. They hadn't talked much more about the rodeo and the man he'd been while running that circuit, though they had had a pretty serious conversation on Monday night, after they'd put Bear's kids to bed.

"Parenting," even for a couple of hours, with someone else's kids, with Libby had been extremely fun for Mister. He'd enjoyed watching her read to Smiles and Russ, and then admiring her as she'd held Heather and rocked her back and forth while the baby drank her bottle. She'd put the baby to bed; Mister had tucked in the boys.

They'd gone out onto the back deck to talk, and Mister could admit he'd thought a lot about kissing her there. He might've been able to get the job done too, if Bear and Sammy hadn't gotten home before eleven.

He hadn't been able to work up the gumption to do it on Libby's front porch, because he'd kissed far too many women on their front porches. It meant nothing to him, and he wanted his next first kiss with Libby to be special. Important. Life-changing.

Maybe he could kiss her tonight, after the party. His mind stuck on that, when he really wished it wouldn't. He didn't want to be constantly thinking about kissing her. Libby possessed more to her than a pair of extremely kissable lips.

"Has Mildred said anything else about moving up her wedding?" he asked, trying to get the idea of kissing Libby out of his head.

"Not since last weekend," she said with a sigh. She looked left and right, and Mister spotted her dancing with her fiancé over by the main entrance to the barn.

"I can come help with the Country Christmas if she does," he said. "I already come down there every day as it is."

"I know," Libby said. Her dark eyes fired cannonballs at him. "But the Country Christmas is something Mildred and I have done for years. Ten years, Mister. She can't just abandon it in July."

Mister wanted to argue with her that of course she could. And Mildred probably would. Scott Hamblin had obviously flipped something for Mildred, and he was now more important than the Christmas Festival she'd worked on with her sister.

He'd seen it happen to plenty of people over the past

five years. Sammy barely worked at the mechanic shop anymore. Oakley only went down to Mack's Motor Sports once a week. Montana did all of her construction right here on the ranch; her business hadn't done anything outside the borders of Shiloh Ridge since she'd finished the library remodel, years ago.

Charlie didn't make her liquid nitrogen ice cream at fairs or weddings anymore. Willa had stopped preaching when Chaz had been born.

"People's priorities change," he said quietly.

Libby sighed and tucked herself more fully into his arms. "I know, and I hate it."

"What if your priorities changed?" he asked. "What if you met someone you fell madly in love with, and you started having kids, and well…. What if the Country Christmas just wasn't important anymore?"

Libby pulled away. "You think the Country Christmas isn't important to her anymore?"

Mister looked over to where Mildred clung to Scott. "No, Libby," he said still in his quiet indoor-voice. "I don't. I think her priorities have changed, and I think she's hoping you'll give her permission to be in love with Scott and marry him and spend her life with *him* now."

Libby looked toward Mildred too, and Mister swayed and danced her that direction so she could see her easier. It took until the end of the song for her to sigh and say, "I think you're right."

She looked back at him, and Mister found the worry

and the sadness in her expression. "Let's grab a piece of cake and get out of here," he said.

"Really?"

"Yeah, really." He stepped away from her and led her over to the birthday cakes. The large crowd had really done a number on them, but he got a piece of the triple chocolate fudge he wanted, and Libby said she wanted more of that strawberry shortcake, and Mister added a slice of the vanilla bean with raspberry whipped cream.

He looked out at the dance floor, but no one cared what he did. It wasn't his fiftieth birthday party, and he'd already hugged both Bear and Sammy. "Come on," he said, heading for Oakley, who stood over on the side, trying to soothe her fussy baby.

"Hey," he said when he reached her. "Libby and I are headed out. We can take Fawn if you want to stay and enjoy yourself?"

Oakley looked up at him, pure hope in her eyes. Ranger, who stood behind her, started nodding with vigor. Mister grinned at him and looked at Oakley, his eyebrows raised. "Would you? She'll probably go right to sleep. She wouldn't nap this afternoon, the diva."

"I'll take her," Libby said, reaching for the baby. "I had Heather out like a light on Monday." She smiled at Oakley, who readily relinquished the baby into Libby's arms.

"Thank you," Oakley said with such a force of gratitude that Mister could only smile back at her. He and Libby left the barn, him carrying the cake and her carrying the baby.

"I don't have a car seat," he said.

"We can walk. It's just down the lane."

"Mister," someone called behind him, and he and Libby turned simultaneously to see Preacher striding toward them.

"Where are you going?" he asked, out of breath.

"I just need some quiet," Mister said. "The party was awesome, really." He glanced at Libby. "We're just taking Fawn back to put her to bed. Oakley said she didn't nap today."

Charlie came outside too, her baby girl strapped to her body with a sling. Betty was only six weeks old, and considerably less chubby than Fawn, who still sniffled in Libby's arms.

"Will you take Betty?" she asked. "Did they say they would already?" She looked at Mister. "It's fine if you can't."

"I can," he said at the same time someone else did. He looked past Preacher and Charlie to Etta, who'd just come outside too. Beau Peterson walked a step or two behind her, and she glanced at him. "We could, right? She just needs to be driven around and she'll fall right asleep." She didn't wait for Beau to answer, and Preacher's eyebrows had flown right off his face anyway.

Mister's surprise shot into the sky too. Beau and Etta? He had to be a decade older than her—just like Noah Johnson had been—but Beau had never been married. He had no kids.

But...Beau and Etta?

Mister looked at Preacher while Etta started helping Charlie with the straps on the sling. "Are you two going out?" he asked.

"No," Beau said at the same time Etta said, "Not tonight."

"Then what are you doing?"

Etta glanced at Preacher, plenty of withering power in her eyes despite the briefness of the look. "He said he knew a place we could see the stars, and I said I wanted to see them. We're just going for a drive."

Preacher cocked his hip and folded his arms. "Going for a drive," he repeated, plenty of sarcasm in his voice. Mister grinned, because he was about to go wild on Beau. They played video games together and had been friends for years. And years. He likely knew Beau's dating tactics, and the panicked look on Beau's face confirmed it.

"Etta, this man is trying to get you alone," Preacher said.

"I'm thirty-six years old, Preach," she said. "I know when a man is hitting on me." She finally released the baby and scooped Betty into her arms. She gazed at the infant girl with love and adoration, her expression quickly morphing when she looked at Preacher. "I'm a grown woman, and if I want to go for a drive with a handsome cowboy, I can."

"Not with my daughter."

"Fine," she said, pushing the baby into his arms. "Mister said he'd take her."

"Sorry," Mister said as Fawn started sniffling and

crying again. "I think one baby girl is our limit." He looked at Libby, who grinned at him like they'd become co-conspirators.

"Preacher," Charlie said, her voice set on desperate.

"Fine," Preacher said, frowning. "Take her. Charlie will get you the car seat." He stepped between Etta and Beau. "I want to talk to this *handsome cowboy* for a second."

"Come on, Preach," Beau said with a chuckle.

"Yeah, you come on with me," Preacher said, stepping in the opposite direction of Charlie and Etta, who moved down the row of parked trucks to get the car seat.

"We best get out of here while we only have one baby," Mister murmured, and he and Libby turned to head down to the homestead.

Once there, Mister opened the fridge and got out a bottle for Fawn. Oakley had texted to say she had a couple made up, and Libby settled into the rocking recliner in the living room to hold her and feed her.

The silence in the homestead fed Mister's soul, and the chocolate cake made him drowsy with happiness. Libby took the sleeping baby upstairs and returned, snuggling right into his side with her strawberry shortcake. "This is nice," she said.

"It is," he agreed. They'd talked about kids on Monday, and they both wanted children. Mister decided to move right ahead as if they could really plan for and have a future together.

"If you get married," he said, speaking slowly. "Where

would you want to live? Golden Hour? That little red house you love? Or somewhere else?"

"It depends," Libby said.

"On what?"

"On what the options are." She took another bite of cake and swallowed it. "If my husband has a big house like Scott does, then maybe I'd move in with him."

"Let's say your husband-to-be has the potential to have any kind of house he wants. You could help design it. Right now, he doesn't have a house, but the potential is there. Then what?"

Libby straightened and looked at him, her eyes searching his as she took another bite of cake and put it in her mouth. Mister's eyes dropped to her lips, watching with pure desire coursing through him as she licked the creamy frosting away.

Her mouth moved, but he had no idea what she'd just said. She twisted away from him to set her plate on the table beside the couch. "Is that what you're saying?" she asked, those words getting through.

"What?"

She faced him again, something deep and sparkly in those brown eyes. She leaned toward him and ran her fingers up the side of his face. She'd invited him to kiss her on a previous occasion, but tonight, Mister didn't wait for the words. He could see her feelings on her face, and he cupped her face in both hands and lowered his mouth to taste hers.

He'd kissed her sweetly once, and a little roughly

another time. This time, he started slow and picked up speed when she responded to his touch. She smelled like fresh cotton and dryer sheets, and she tasted like sugar and strawberries. He wanted more and more and more, and thankfully, Libby kept kissing him and kissing him and kissing him.

CHAPTER 21

*L*ibby felt like she'd been waiting for her whole life to be kissed the way Mister Glover currently kissed her.

His touch sparked her heart into going *whizz-bam-boom!* over and over again.

His mouth stroking hers testified of how careful he'd be with that fizzing, whizzing heart. This was no conquest kiss. This was the touch of a man who knew how very fragile, how very important, and how very special she was.

He pulled away far too soon, though Libby felt like she'd lost an hour to kissing him. "Libby," he said, his voice throaty and husky and making her name sound like it had come straight from heaven. He ducked his head, and Libby lifted his chin with her hand.

Then she could kiss him again, which she did. She found herself wanting to be closer and closer to him, but she couldn't get any nearer physically. The kiss slowed, and the emotional closeness she craved finally kicked in.

His fingers ran through her hair and down her back, and Libby liked that. He kept his hands in appropriate places, and she adored that he respected her. She broke the kiss this time, sucking at the air to try to get enough.

Mister's breath labored as well, and she giggled as they both quieted.

"I've been wanting to kiss you for ages," he whispered, kneading her back to his side.

"Same," she admitted. She'd been kissed by other men before, but none of them had opened the doors to Libby's soul the way he just had.

"I'm falling in love with you," he said next, and that made her heart do a backflip. "It's strange and wonderful, and I've never been in love before. Mother says I'll know how it feels, and I think it feels like…this."

Libby didn't know what to say, because she'd been steadily falling in love with Mister for years. Now that she'd gotten the truth out about what she'd seen and who he'd been, she felt like she'd started to heal. The festering sore in her heart had been cleansed.

"What did you think about at church?" she asked. He'd sat alone, and he'd not told her anything about last Sunday yet.

He exhaled and ran his fingertips up and down her bare arm. "How much I've changed," he said. "How much you have. How much my family has. How much Three Rivers has."

She gave him space and silence to keep talking.

"Some stuff is easy to see, you know? Like the HealNow building. It wasn't there a couple of years ago, and now it is. Three Rivers has grown a ton. I can look at Bear and see the changes. He's married now, with four kids. He doesn't even live here anymore. In fact, I live in a room where he used to live with his family." He chuckled. "I can *see* the family and how big they are, how we keep expanding with every wedding and every birth."

"Some things are easy to see," she agreed.

"I can see changes in you. You've always been smart and kind, but you're...more mature now. You want to do what's right, and I'm not sure I noticed that before, though you might've always been that way. You love your family. You want someone to love you for who you are. You're more creative than I knew, and you're a better cook than I thought." He grinned and tilted his head down to look at her. She kept her gaze forward, though a small smile did touch her lips.

"You're dedicated to your ranch, and for some reason I can't fathom, you like mowing the lawn." He laughed now, and Libby joined in. "You love fruit in all its forms, and you love flowers, and you want a man who will treasure you, take care of you, and support you." He cleared his throat. "There's so many things about you I know now that I didn't realize before. I'm sorry about that."

"You don't need to be sorry," she murmured.

"I'm different too," he said. "I don't get nearly as upset about things, and it takes longer if I do. I feel like I'm more patient. I'm more willing to let my brothers be who they are than I was before. I'm more inclined to listen instead of speak, though I've always liked being in the spotlight, and I still do."

Libby smiled then, a hint of heat pricking in the back of her eyes.

"I want to help my family if I can," he said. "Even a couple of years ago, I didn't feel like that. I love Texas, and I appreciate the land we have here. Before I went to Winterhaven, I didn't even realize how amazing Shiloh Ridge is. I didn't know what I'd been blessed with. I feel like I have some indication of it now, at least."

"Do you want to know what I see that's different in you?'

"Absolutely."

"You're wiser," she said. "More mature." She sat up and slipped her fingers into his. "You're still loud, because you're a Glover, but you have this softer side too. One I got to see as your friend, but that you kept hidden from others. Others get to see it now, like you offering to take Fawn for Oakley, who was struggling with her."

He simply looked at her and swallowed. "Do you think I'm still a player?"

"No," she whispered.

"Do you think I'm going to use you and toss you away?"

"Of course not." Libby took a deep breath. "I know you're not the same man you were in that restaurant. I know it. I can see it. I *feel* it."

Relief painted over his handsome features, and Mister allowed a smile to touch his lips. "That's great news, Libs." He leaned toward her again, and she met him halfway for a sweet, chaste kiss. "You can trust me," he whispered. He leaned his forehead against hers and then pulled away.

"My dad wrote me a letter before he died," he said. "In it, he said I was one of the most trustworthy cowboys he knew, and that I should make sure everyone around me knew they could trust me." He sighed and shook his head. "I don't know how he could've possibly thought that at the time he wrote the letter. I was the rodeo cowboy then, and surely he saw all of the things I was doing wrong."

"I think parents can see into the heart of someone."

"My grandmother could," he said. "She gave me the name Mister. She'd say, 'Get over here, Mister. Don't make me ask twice.' And I'll have you know that I did. No one disobeyed Grandmother." He shivered. "She was scary."

"But you loved her."

"We all did," he said. "Completely. Because while she made us use vinegar to clean her fridge, she also made the most amazing birthday cakes. She'd invite us to her house on our birthdays and cook all our favorite foods. Just us. No one else in the family, and when you have a lot of brothers and sisters, doing anything alone is magical. She made us feel seen and heard, and I loved that. I might not have known that's what she was doing, but I do now." He looked at her. "I want you to know I see and hear you."

Libby's heart melted for this man. He was completely

different than he'd been before, and he did have a very good heart. "I know that, Michael," she said.

He smiled at her. "Only Sammy and Mother call me Michael."

"If Sammy gets to, I should," Libby said, grinning back at him. She inched closer to him, pleased when his eyes drifted closed as if anticipating kissing her. "I see you too, Mister."

"Oh, now, you can't say it like that," he murmured, reaching up to thread his fingers through her hair. He laughed, and Libby did too.

He kissed her again, silencing her giggles, and completely erasing any of her lingering doubts. He pulled away when a woman said, "Oh, we're interrupting."

Libby wanted to bury her face in Mister's chest while it burned, but he casually looked over the back of the couch. "Hey, Etta," he said.

"Sorry, Mister."

"It's fine." He offered her a smile and Libby dared to turn and look at her. She carried Betty in her arms, and Beau stood a pace or two behind her. "We're just talking."

"Looked like kissing," Beau said with a grin.

"Yeah, well, there's some of that too." Mister chuckled and indicated the couch. "I can go upstairs if I want to kiss her again."

Etta gave Mister and then Libby a look that said, *Don't you dare leave. I'm so sorry I had to interrupt, but don't you dare leave.*

"Come put something on TV," Libby said. "I'm sure we can find a nice romantic comedy or something."

"Perfect," Etta said with relief in her voice while both Beau and Mister groaned in tandem.

LIBBY PUT THE ENTIRE CROCK POT ON THE TABLE and sat down. "Mildred, after we pray, I want to talk to you about the Country Christmas."

Mildred looked up from her phone, her eyes big and round. "Okay."

"Do you want me to say it?" Libby folded her hands in her lap, calmer than she'd felt in a long, long time. When she texted with Mister, she felt calm like this too. When he kissed her, she could drift away on puffy, cotton-candy-clouds and never come down. When she thought about having a future with him, a certain giddiness spread through her, but she also stayed perfectly collected.

"Sure," Mildred said, turning over her phone and setting it up by her glass.

Libby nodded and took a deep breath. "Dear Lord, we thank Thee for this food. We're so grateful for air conditioning, and we ask Thee to bless those who are suffering without power right now. Help us to serve them if possible, and help those working to restore the power that they'll be safe and work quickly." She took a deep breath, beyond grateful for the power they had at Golden Hour.

Texas had been hit hard with a heat wave this summer, and the power usage had been through the roof.

Timed outages had occurred all over the state, and some customers never got their power back this morning.

"Bless me to speak with a clear mind, and bless Mildred to speak from her heart. Amen."

"Amen," her sister said. Neither of them reached for any utensils, serving or otherwise. "What's on your mind?"

Libby did reach for the tongs she'd put in the crock pot then. She grabbed a couple of chunks of potato and put them on her plate. She wanted the pot roast, and she inched up and peered into the pot to get it.

"Tell me truly," she said, her focus on the meat. "When would you like to marry Scott?"

"Tomorrow," Mildred said with a laugh.

Libby put the meat on her plate and turned the tongs so the handles faced Mildred. She met her sister's eyes and smiled too. "Sooner rather than later, right?"

"Yes," Mildred admitted. "Mama says we can be ready by September, and I'm thinking I'd like to move it up."

They started their major set-up for the Country Christmas in September. Libby's first instinct was to panic and tell Mildred there was no way she could leave on a honeymoon, divide her attention between moving and planning, and deal with a new husband while they put on their annual festival.

She took a deep breath and reached for the help of the

Lord. To her great surprise, He whispered in her ear exactly what to say. "I think you should do it then."

Mildred froze with the tongs in mid-air. "Really?"

"Really," she said. "I can get Mister to come help me with the Country Christmas. The cowboy is down here every afternoon anyway." She giggled and picked up her fork.

"Yeah, the cowboy is down here every afternoon to *see you,*" Mildred said, continuing to put roasted potatoes and carrots on her plate. "Maybe you should marry him in September."

Libby's chest went cold. "Bite your tongue."

"Why?" Mildred asked. "You've loved him forever."

"No," Libby said instantly. "I've had a crush on him. Thought he was handsome. I'm just barely starting to even, maybe—and I'm not saying I am—fall for him." She frowned, sure she'd felt herself falling last night when he kissed her beside the far fence, away from prying eyes, after they'd gone horseback riding.

That had to be a fluke, she told herself. The meat didn't have enough salt, and she reached for the shaker. He'd said she was a better cook than he'd thought at his brother's birthday party a couple of weeks ago.

Yes, she saw him every day. He spent most evenings with her after they finished their work around the ranch too. He kissed her every single time before he left. It never got old.

"Mildred," Libby said, immediately sticking a bite of roast in her mouth so she'd have time to think.

"Hmm?" Mildred stood and got a spoon from the drawer so she could get some au jus from the pot.

"How did you know you were in love with Scott?"

Mildred beamed at Libby, and she hated the older-sister-all-knowing look in her eye. "Forget it," she said.

"No," Mildred said, her smile softening. "I don't know how I knew. I haven't dated nearly as many men as you have." She sighed and pushed her food around on the plate. "I liked being with him. He made me feel…amazing about myself. He looked at me with stars in his eyes, and when I stopped and thought about what my future held, he was in it."

"Did you pray about him?"

"Yes," Mildred said simply. "It feels right to be with him." She took a bite of her roast and potatoes, as she loved mixing foods and never ate anything by itself if she could avoid it. "How do you feel about Mister?"

"I don't know," Libby said, forking up a chunk of potato. "I'm trying to reconcile a few things, and I'm trying to figure out how I feel."

"He's a good man," Mildred said. "When I see the two of you together, I see the stars in his eyes."

"Do you?" Libby searched her sister's face. "I haven't seen that."

"That's because you don't know how amazing you are," Mildred said, her eyes aglow again.

"I don't feel all that amazing," Libby said. "Maybe when the boot comes off."

"This week, right?" Mildred asked, reaching for the bowl of green salad.

"Yes," Libby said, her foot suddenly weighing twice as much. "Mister's taking me."

"Of course he is," Mildred teased. "Because he's in *love with you.*" She sang the last three words, and Libby just laughed and shook her head. But she couldn't help wondering if Mildred was right. She didn't know, but she was going to look straight into Mister's eyes and see if she could spot stars the very next time they were together.

CHAPTER 22

Judge Glover blew out his breath and reached for the cufflinks Bear held toward him. "This is good, right?"

"Judge," Bear said.

"You've been waiting to marry this woman for five years," Cactus said from Judge's other side. "Of course this is good."

"Why wouldn't it be good?" Bear asked.

"I'm just nervous," Judge said, turning to look at himself in the mirror. "It's going to be fine."

"More than fine," Cactus said, grinning at him. "The best day of your life."

"I just feel like I'm choking," he said, pinning the cufflink in place and reaching for his collar. "Did y'all feel like this?" He looked at Bear in the mirror and then Cactus. The three of them were the only men in the dressing room right now. Judge hadn't wanted the whole big show. Not only that, but the dressing room at the Cider Vineyard, where June had booked their wedding, could only hold about ten people.

Seeing as how Judge had way more people than he could bring into the room, he'd decided he'd been getting dressed by himself for forty-four years, and he could do so on his wedding day too.

That didn't fly with the Glover men, and once Ward had found out, he and Preacher had created a schedule. They'd started in the room with him, and they had the tuxedo he now wore.

Bishop and Ace had already been in the room, and they'd brought him his polished shoes—a brand new pair.

Mister had delivered a not-available-for-sale cowboy hat he'd gotten from Wyatt Walker's formal western wear line that hadn't launched yet.

Duke and Brady, the brothers-and-cousins-in-law, had brought him a handkerchief his mother had embroidered with a double-J logo. One for June and one for Judge. He had it tucked into his pants pocket right now, and he'd actually thought about framing it and putting it up in the Ranch House.

Behind him, Ranger opened the door and slipped inside. "Got it." He held up the boutonniere, his smile as brilliant as the bright red rose with lots of little white flowers surrounding it.

He joined Cactus, Bear, and Judge in front of the mirror, and Judge turned to let Ranger pin the flowers to his lapel. Cactus worked on one cufflink and Bear the other, and Judge turned his back on the mirror and faced the men in his family.

"I'm ready."

"You've been ready for a while," Bear said with a grin. He glanced at his watch, a great big silver thing that made Judge wonder how he lifted his arm. "It's time."

Judge took a deep breath. "Okay." He started for the door when no one else did, and he opened the door. Mother stood there, her husband not far from her. Judge stepped right into her arms, tears pricking his eyes. "I don't want to cry at my own wedding," he whispered.

"Your tears make you strong," she whispered back, and Judge pressed his eyes closed to keep the water inside. He could allow the emotions to storm through him without letting them out, and he determined—once again—to do that. He did want to feel the things he authentically felt, and he was done feeling ashamed of himself.

He stepped back from his mother and let her cup his face in her weathered, aged hands. "You are my favorite," she said, beaming at him.

Judge grinned at her, knowing all of her children were her favorites. "Thanks, Mom."

"Don," she said, and he came over. "We're ready."

"We'll get in line," Bear said, and he led Cactus and Ranger out of the building. Judge watched them go, and then he linked one arm through Mother's and one through Don's. They exited the building too, and the vineyard and gardens expanded in front of him.

Rows of chairs mirrored the lines of grapes further out,

with vines woven through the backs of them. Ribbons and pink flowers adorned the vines, and the whole thing seemed sophisticated and simple at the same time.

The audience rose, and Judge smiled at his guests. He, Mother, and Don walked down the aisle as pretty music filtered through the speakers. The altar in front of him bore a Texas longhorn skull that had leaves, flowers, and feathers making it beautiful, and it had been attached to the front of a chest-high table that looked like a brown leather saddlebag. It had been stitched with colorful thread in a floral pattern, and Judge reached out and traced his fingertip along the petals of a sunflower.

He bent and kissed his mother's cheek, gave Don a hug, and reached to shake Pastor Corning's hand. Then he turned to face back down the aisle, his pulse rioting against the cool air kissing his neck.

He looked up, not realizing the wooden trellises had essentially created an outdoor room. More vines, more flowers, and air conditioning units that blew air down onto the guests. June had gotten this venue for free, as she'd done all of their Internet capabilities and upgraded their networks for the past five years. She knew the owner well, and the moment he'd found out about their engagement, he'd offered the vineyard.

Judge wanted whatever June did, and it was actually pretty nice to get off the ranch and have a wedding outside True Blue, the barn up at Shiloh Ridge where so many Glovers had gotten married.

June's mother and her daughter walked toward each

other, one coming from the left and one from the right. They met in the middle, paused, and started down the aisle. Men started streaming in from the left, walking behind the last row of chairs. Women came in on the right, and Judge and June had asked them to stop at the end of the aisle for a couple of seconds.

That way, their photographer could capture each couple, and Bear and Sammy did exactly what they'd been asked to do. They then walked down the aisle, where they greeted Judge and found seats. Their children had been given to a couple of Sammy's mechanics, and they passed Heather to Bear and Russ to Sammy while Judge looked at Cactus and Willa down at the end of the aisle.

They both wore brilliant smiles, and Cactus's dogs walked in his wake as he made his way down the aisle. June had specifically requested that he bring his dogs, and Tank wore a tuxedo shirtfront on his chest while Galaxy wore a sparkling white dress with puffy sleeves over her shoulders.

Ranger and Oakley met in the middle, joined hands, and came toward Judge. He grinned back at them, so grateful for their friendship and example in his life. Oakley took Fawn from Mother, kissed Judge's cheek, and went down the front row to take a seat next to Aunt Dawna, who held Wilder on her lap. Ranger took his son from his mother before he sat down.

Ward and Dot came next, and she looked happy beyond belief. Judge and June had attended dinner with them last night, and Dot had admitted she'd been scared to have a baby, and that fear had stolen some of the joy from her for the first few months of her pregnancy. She wore her silver dress well with her baby bump, and she seemed to shine like the stars Judge had used in his Christmas light show last year.

This year, he and June had been working on the wedding for the past couple of months, and he hadn't even given a thought to his light show. He wasn't sure he'd do it this year, because he wanted his focus to be where it should be: on his new wife and step-daughter. He'd be lying if he said he didn't want a baby right away, and he and June had talked about starting their family extensively.

Preacher and Charlie walked toward him before Judge realized they were, and he blinked his focus back into the moment. Preacher was his very best friend, and Judge's smile wobbled on his face. Preacher saw it, because Preach saw so much. He stepped right into Judge and gripped him tightly. "I love you, brother," he whispered, and Judge could only nod.

They took their seats as Ace and Holly Ann walked down the aisle, baby Gun's hand in his mother's. Judge didn't care if the kids participated in the wedding, but most couples had chosen to pass them to friends or other family. Both Ace and Holly Ann hugged Judge, and Arizona and Duke Rhinehart met and strutted toward Judge.

His parents held their daughter, and Judge accepted his cheek-kisses from his solitary sister.

Mister met Libby Bellamore in the middle, and Judge could see the love he had for her, plain as day on his face. Whether anyone else could or not, Judge didn't know. He'd spent a lot of time analyzing Mister over the past several years, and he looked and acted like a completely different man. Judge hadn't argued with him in a long, long time, and he was so grateful for that.

He could still remember Mister's apology before he'd left for his new job in Oklahoma last year, and it had made a real impact on Judge, changing him for what he hoped was the better.

I'm sorry I wasted so much time not *saying I'm sorry.*

Judge didn't ever want to withhold an apology and lose time with a loved one because of it. He'd been much quicker to admit he was wrong and rectify a situation since Mister had said that.

Mister grinned the whole way down the aisle, Libby's hand tucked into his elbow. Her walking boot had come off a couple of weeks ago, and she walked without a limp or a hitch in her step at all. Judge grinned at both of them, unsurprised when Mister laughed loudly and pulled Judge into a hug. He clapped him on the back in a most informal way and grabbed onto his shoulders.

"I'm so happy for you," he said, not bothering to keep his voice down. Mister never did, and he reached for Libby and indicated she should go in front of him down the row where they sat next to Ward and Dot.

Bishop came next, Montana right at his side. They spent their days side-by-side too, and Judge loved his youngest brother with a fierceness he hadn't realized until the past couple of years. He faced situations fearlessly, and he'd spent a lot of time over the past six months teaching Judge how to be a step-dad. He'd prayed, and he hoped he could be half the man Bishop was.

They met Ollie and Aurora at the end of the aisle, Aurora carrying her half-brother Robbie. As a family, they took a seat in the second row, and Judge smiled at the lot of them. He appreciated Oliver and Aurora making a second trip to Shiloh Ridge after they'd come for Bear's birthday party.

Finally, the twins arrived, Ida coming first with her husband, Brady. Etta walked right behind her, meeting her date in the middle. They carried Ida's twins, and Etta looked radiant and beautiful in her sparkly dress and holding a toddler.

Judge had met her date for the wedding, and he liked Chris Gabriel despite the man having two first names. He and Etta had been out a few times now, and the most important thing was that *Etta* liked Chris enough to bring him to this huge family function so early in the relationship.

She passed Johnny to Ida before she took Judge into her arms. He gripped her tight and neither of them said anything. Nothing needed to be said between them, because he understood Etta's desires and fears on a deep, personal level.

The music changed, and Judge released his cousin. She went to sit by her date, and Judge reached up to straighten his bow tie. He blew out his breath slowly, and the door he'd come through opened to reveal his bride-to-be.

She stepped outside carefully, her feet in heeled shoes she'd confessed to him she hoped she could walk in. Her father exited behind her, and June's sister took a moment to flare out the skirt of the wedding dress while June smoothed down the fabric in the front and took her father's arm.

She was the most beautiful woman in the world, and Judge felt like he was seeing her for the first time all over again. His heartbeat kicked at him exactly the same, and his mind told him he better figure out how to get and keep this woman in his life.

It sure had taken longer than Judge had thought it would, but he still thanked the Lord for the woman and the way he reacted to her. She was made to fill all the holes in his life, and she did so effortlessly.

When she was ready, she looked down the aisle. Her eyes met Judge's, and her entire countenance lit up. Her smile could've blinded a man twice over, and Judge felt like the luckiest man in the world as she and her father made their way toward him.

She kissed her daddy's cheek, and he passed her to Judge. He kissed her cheek too, tucked her against his side, and whispered, "I love you, June-Bug."

"I love you too, Judge."

They turned toward Pastor Corning, and he grinned at them from the other side of the altar. "That was fantastic," he said. "I have loved being part of the Glover family, and

I'm sure everyone could feel the love they have for one another as they entered."

He looked only at Judge and June, and Judge felt dozens of eyes from all the people they'd invited. June knew a lot of people around town, and Judge had asked Bear for his Christmas card list, and he'd invited everyone on it. All the cowboys from Seven Sons, Three Rivers, and Golden Hour. Duke's family had come. Holly Ann's sister and husband.

"I understand June's daughter is going to read her vows." Pastor Corning raised his eyebrows at June and then Judge. They both twisted to find Lucy Mae, and she came forward.

She stood next to June and pulled a paper from her pocket. Judge gave her his best *you-can-do-this* smile, because he knew she was nervous about this.

"My mom has been my best friend since I knew what that concept was." She smiled at her mother, the gesture somewhat shaky on her lips. Judge tightened his hand in June's, her own nerves radiating off of her. "She gave up a lot for me, including a lot of dates with a lot of men. I never noticed her caring all that much—until Judge Glover.

"He was the first man she said yes to in a dozen years, and even though she put him off and put him off, I could tell there was something about him that really called to her."

She took a deep breath and gave Judge a tearful smile. He prayed she would have the strength to continue, though he hadn't heard these vows. "From the moment I met Judge, I could see how much he liked my mother. He has more patience than any man I know, and I'm thrilled she finally opened the door to her heart all the way so he could walk into our lives."

Lucy Mae refolded her paper and tucked it away. "Judge, you complete my mom in a way she didn't even know she needed. She loves you more than servers and modems and networks, and that is saying a whole lot."

Judge chuckled and shook his head, but June nodded. He'd felt her love for him, and it was real and deep, and he didn't doubt it for a moment.

"Judge has asked his cousin Etta to read his vows for June."

Etta appeared at his side, no notes in her hand. He reached for her, hoping this wouldn't be too hard for her. She'd insisted it wouldn't be, but Judge had his doubts all the way up to this moment. She took a deep breath as he hugged her, and then she said in a loud, clear voice, "Judge loves June with everything he has. I knew it pretty early on, when he wouldn't ask anyone else to dinner, despite his many opportunities to do so. Once he met June, he seemed to know she was the one he wanted to get to know better.

"I saw Judge in some of his worst moments when it came to June, and it became obvious to me how deeply she'd embedded herself into his heart when he threw away his phone and got a new one after she'd broken up with him." Etta smiled at him and then June, and Judge wondered where she was going with this.

"We made all these plans to meet someone new at the Christmas activities, and even as we did, I knew Judge wouldn't do them with me. I knew he'd find his way back to June, because they really are made for each other."

Etta paused for a moment that became two and then three. Judge looked at her and found her emotions storming across her face and making her chin tremble.

"He loves her the way a woman wants to be loved, and I hope she knows how very lucky she is to have found a man who feels the way Judge feels, and who loves as completely as Judge loves. It's something beautiful to see, and I can only hope to find a man like him one day." Etta nodded, and Judge put his arm around her and squeezed her.

"Thank you, Etta," he whispered.

She wiped her eyes and stepped back to her seat.

"Let's get these two married," Pastor Corning said. "Juniper Hailey Nichols, do you give yourself to John Eric Glover, to be his legally wedded wife, for now and for all eternity?"

"Yes," June said in a strong, perfect voice.

"John, do you give yourself to Juniper Hailey Nichols, to be her legally wedded husband, for now and for all eternity?"

"Yes," he said, some measure of relief moving through him.

"I now pronounce you husband and wife," Pastor Corning said. "You may kiss your bride."

Judge turned toward June, the audience behind them already applauding. The whooping and whistles, cat calls and clapping, made him smile and laugh, but nothing was going to keep him from kissing his wife.

He drew her into him and pressed his lips to hers, curved as they were. She laughed against his kiss, finally kissing him properly. He wanted more, but he recognized now wasn't the time. So he broke the kiss and faced the crowd, then started down the aisle while everyone kept celebrating.

Once he and June and her puffy dress had made it through the door and into the quiet hall, he looked at her. She looked at him.

He breathed in and reached for her as she moved toward him. "I love you," he said.

"I love you more." She touched her lips to his, and Judge thought kissing her before had been tremendous. But being married and kissing his wife...that was the best thing in the world.

Mister waved to Judge in the front yard as he drove by. His brother lifted his arm in a wave then used his hand to wipe his face. The heat hadn't abated while he'd been on his honeymoon with June, and since they'd gone to Hawaii, they hadn't caught a break from the soaring temperatures.

He had reindeer, Christmas trees, and shiny, silver stars all around him, and Mister chuckled to himself and reached to turn up the air conditioning in his truck. He'd finished his Shiloh Ridge chores for the day, eaten lunch with Cactus's family, and now he needed to get down to Golden Hour to help Libby with the same thing Judge was currently dealing with: A theme for her Country Christmas Festival.

She and Mildred usually came up with the theme together, but her sister had decided to move her wedding up. Since that decision had been made, Libby said Mildred barely worked around the ranch anymore at all. She had appointments with florists, to get her dress altered, to taste cakes, and to sample menus.

She and Libby's mom left the ranch almost every day while Libby was out cleaning horse stalls—her morning chore—and she didn't see her again until evening. Sometimes not even then, as Mildred went to see her husband-to-be after he finished working.

Mister didn't mind Mildred being gone more. She'd acted like a warden for Libby for a lot of months before he'd left to work at Winterhaven, as she was fiercely protective of her sister. Mister hadn't wanted to cause grief for either of them; he'd just wanted to talk to Libby.

He did plenty of talking to her now. Plenty of kissing too, and a smile touched his face as he went around the east side of the ranch, where Bull House and the homestead stood, and then started down toward Preacher's new place.

One more week, and Preacher and Charlie would be in the farmhouse. Bishop was just finishing the final walk-through and inspection this week, and then come Saturday, Mister would be at the Top Cottage, helping to load their belongings into the back of his truck. With everyone helping, it shouldn't take long.

Mister looked down the newly paved lane that ran past the sheds and toward the house. It sat proudly in the sun, and the first word his mind came up with to describe it was *expensive*. Nice. Beautiful.

He could only hope to have a house that nice all to

himself one day. "Maybe you won't even live at Shiloh Ridge," he murmured to himself as he eased to a stop at the highway. Hardly anyone came this way in the middle of the day, and Mister turned onto the road, drove about a mile, and then turned right to head further east.

Golden Hour sat another five minutes down the road, and he arrived at Libby's at the same time he saw Frankie going inside. The front door closed behind the dog, and he suspected she'd just gotten home for lunch.

He'd already eaten, but he didn't mind sitting with her while she did. They didn't even have to talk. He parked and got out, climbed the steps and knocked.

"Come in!" she yelled from inside, and Mister did just that.

"It's me," he said, kicking off his cowboy boots next to the ones she'd discarded by the front door too.

Frankie barked and came skidding around the corner from the kitchen. Mister grinned at him and clapped a couple of times while Libby said, "It's just Mister, you dumb dog."

He crouched down and gave the golden retriever a good scrub around the ears and along his ridged head. "Hey, boy. Get on any roofs today?"

"He tried," Libby called from the kitchen. "I had to put the ladder up."

Mister chuckled, straightened, and went into the kitchen. Libby glanced at him while she poured sweet tea into a glass, and his mouth watered. He wasn't sure if it was at the sight of her or the cold drink. Probably both.

Her cheeks bore red patches from the heat, and she wiped her hair back with a sigh. "Do I have to go back out this afternoon?"

"I thought we were going to go through your festival," he said. "Can I have some of that tea?" He stepped toward her, his hand easily sliding along her waist and bringing her flush against his chest.

She took a long drink of tea, and Mister waited his turn to touch those lips. The moment she set her glass down and looked at him, he kissed her. Mm, yes, her mouth was cool and sweet and wonderful, and he could kiss this woman for hours and never get bored.

She broke the kiss after several long seconds and said, "There's plenty of tea."

"Thanks."

Libby fiddled with his collar, her focus there. "I was thinking about something."

"Sounds dangerous," he said, not making a move to get a drink. Not with her touching him the way she was.

She flashed him a smile. "This might be kind of crazy, but I was thinking about doing a rodeo theme for the Country Christmas this year."

Mister's eyebrows did react with surprise, shooting right up toward his hatband. "Rodeo?" She didn't like the rodeo. In fact, Libby *loathed* the rodeo.

"You and Wyatt are drawing quite the crowds for your demos," she said. "People like the rodeo." She stroked her hands across his collar to make it lie flat, and then continued with her hands down over his shoulders and biceps.

"*You* don't like the rodeo."

"I bet you know a lot of people who could come do things," she continued as if he hadn't spoken. "We could have those mechanical bulls that kids could ride. Adults too. There could be pony rides—those are always popular. Maybe a couple of live demos by real rodeo cowboys...." She trailed off, sucked in a breath, and started up again.

"It wouldn't have to be you and Wyatt, though I'd love it if you'd both come do something. The Country Christmas runs for twenty-three days, from December first to December twenty-third, and maybe we could get different men and women to come on different nights. It would be a draw for people to come back more than once, or come on the night their favorite star is going to be there."

Mister's mouth fished, opening and closing, while he tried to think of how to respond.

"I've already got The Yellow Rose of Texas coming the first weekend, and the Lone Star Dads coming the second. They'll be huge too, so we wouldn't even need rodeo cowboys those nights. The musical entertainment will pull people in."

"The Nationals are in December," he said. "In Vegas."

"I don't want current rodeo people," she said, finally stepping out of his arms. "I was thinking men and women like you and Wyatt. Brynn Greene up at Bowman's Breeds. Her and her husband could come. They both ran in the rodeo and won things. She could even do something for her business."

"You've thought a lot about this," he said, watching her as she opened the fridge and bent to pull something out.

"Are you hungry?" she asked.

"I ate with Cactus, Willa, and the kids." He looked at the container. "But that looks like cake, so yes, I'm starving."

She grinned at him, and he grinned at her, and Mister knew then that he'd do whatever Libby asked him to do. If she wanted a rodeo-themed Country Christmas, he'd call everyone he'd ever known in the rodeo to come to Three Rivers and make it happen for her.

The woman had roped his heart completely.

He may have kissed a lot of women in the past, but he hadn't loved any of them.

He loved Libby Bellamore. If he couldn't be with her, he didn't want to be with anyone.

He swallowed, his heart suddenly beating and booming and banging against his ribcage like a wild animal trying to escape. Was all of that true? Was he in love with her? Would he really be alone forever if he couldn't have her at his side?

"Mister," she said, and he blinked to find her standing on the other side of the island. How she'd gotten over there, he had no idea.

"Yeah." His voice came out strangled, and he cleared his throat. "Yeah, what?"

"Grab a couple of forks." She gave him a sexy grin, as if she knew what currently ran through his head, his heart, and his whole soul.

"Forks, yeah." His fingers fumbled over the drawers in her island, but he managed to yank one open. The silverware inside sloshed around, making a terrible metal noise. He cringed, didn't look at Libby, and picked out two forks.

He rounded the island to sit next to her, a single piece of cake for them to share between them. He met her eyes, his heart doing that bass-drum-booming again, and he leaned down, glad when she tilted her head up.

"I missed you," he murmured just before he touched his lips to hers in a sweet kiss.

"We saw each other yesterday," she whispered, kissing him a little stronger after speaking.

True, but he'd still missed her that morning. He didn't like waking up alone, in a house with a lot of people in it, but not her. He smiled, because he didn't want to say any of that, and that broke their kiss.

"All right," he said as she took the tip of the cake onto her fork. He gathered a bite too and looked at it. Yellow cake, with a layer of cream, then covered in chocolate frosting. He'd bet good money that her mother had made this, and even more that it would be delicious. "I bet I can get a couple of guys to come for your rodeo-themed Christmas thing."

"Yeah? Only a couple?" She took another bite of cake and watched him eat his. "I bet you still talk to quite a few of them."

Mister shrugged. "Not as often as you think."

She looked at him with hope streaming through her expression, lighting up her eyes and making her angelic. "Could you maybe find out how many we could get?"

"Sure."

"Then I'll know if this theme is worth pursuing or not. I mean, if there's not going to be anything rodeo about it, I can't really advertise it as a Rodeo Christmas Extravaganza."

Mister burst out laughing, his joy so full. Libby giggled with him, but as soon as the cake was gone, she got up, gathered a notebook and a pen, and said, "Okay, now, let's start with a list of ideas. We can assign a facility to them as we go, or wait and see what we come up with."

She looked at him expectantly, and Mister simply blinked back at her.

"Mechanical bull riding," she said, starting to scrawl the idea onto the paper. "Your turn."

"Uh…churros?" he guessed.

"Ooh, yes," Libby said. "The food should match that at a rodeo too." Her pen scratched a line down the middle, and she started writing food items on the right-hand side of the paper. Mister had the very real feeling he'd just gotten way in over his head, but at the same time, there was nowhere else he'd rather be.

"Then let it fly," he called from the fence. LeRoy, the man he'd picked from the crowd to come try to throw the rope after his demo, did what he said. The rope did fly through the air, but it missed the mark.

Still, the man turned toward Mister, a beaming smile on his face.

"Nice one," Mister said as the rest of the demo participants clapped. "You had nice form." He turned back to the rest of the group. "Did y'all see how high his arm was? It's a feel thing. Now." He started toward the dummy calf, which was really just a big ottoman with a cow's head on the front of it.

"Wyatt, who is not a roper, but who's done quite a few demos with me now, tell 'em why it didn't make it far enough."

"The release was too late," Wyatt said dutifully. "That's a feel thing too, I'm learning. I release when Mister yells, but it's always that half-second too late."

Mister bent to pick up the rope and take it back to LeRoy, who still stood where Mister had told him he should. He gave him the rope while Wyatt demonstrated the whirling of it, the high arm, and then he said, "You almost want to release it before you think you should."

"He's right," Mister said in a quieter voice, one only LeRoy could hear. "I'm not going to yell this time. It comes out of the hand on the upward round." He lifted his arm and moved his wrist. "Then see? It flies up and out and it'll make it this time."

"All right," LeRoy drawled, plenty of doubt in his

voice. He was an older gentleman who'd come to a few demos now. Mister had recognized several faces in today's crowd and that brought a smile to his face. He'd really enjoyed the past couple of months of demos and lectures with Wyatt, and it seemed like the community did too.

School started next week, and he and Wyatt would be going to the junior PRCA class the very first Thursday to talk about careers in rodeo. They'd do a couple of demos, and Wyatt still had the idea to hold classes in the future.

Today's demo was about half-lecture and half-demo. At the end, they'd let everyone try their hand at throwing the rope and hitting the mark.

Mister retook his spot against the fence; Wyatt finished talking; LeRoy started to whirl and twirl the rope again. Mister's muscles tensed, because he'd have thrown it by now. On the back of a horse, with the calf sprinting away from him, his horse in hot pursuit, he didn't have time for that extra loop around.

Just when he thought LeRoy wouldn't throw it without some indication from Mister, he did. It came out a little sloppy, but it had the distance. It hit the calf dummy, and people started cheering even though the rope slipped off the left side and only hung on the right horn.

Mister grinned and clapped too. He'd gotten the height and the distance. He could work on the aim from there.

"All right," he said, turning back to the crowd. "We have about half a dozen ropes. Who wants to try?"

Nearly every hand shot into the air, and Mister liked

that there were men and women at the demo, and everyone seemed to want to give throwing a rope a try.

He met Wyatt's eyes, the two of them having an entire conversation in the space of a breath, and then Wyatt started handing out ropes.

Mister opened the gate in the fence to let people inside, and surprise darted through him when he caught sight of Libby near the back of the crowd. She met his eye too, and he edged through the people to get to her.

"What are you doin' here?" he asked, taking her into a hug.

"I wanted to come see what you do during these," she said. "I've never been to one." She stepped back and admired him, then looked past him to the arena Wyatt had set up at Seven Sons Ranch. "That was incredible."

"You wanna come try?" he asked.

"I think Wyatt handed out all the ropes."

"You can use mine," he said, pulling it from his back pocket.

Her eyes widened. "You just said a cowboy doesn't let anyone use his rope."

"Yeah, well, I guess that makes you special." He handed her the rope and led her through the crowd. Libby couldn't even get it above her head, which made him laugh. She kept trying, finally getting it high enough to throw. She did, but it only went a few feet.

They laughed together, and she returned his rope to him. "How about you demonstrate again? I liked watching that."

He tucked his rope away, no more demonstrating for him. At least not right now. "I have to go help a couple of others. Are you going to stay? Or should I just come by after like we'd planned?"

Libby started to climb the fence to take up a seat on the top. "I'll stay. With the wedding so close, I need some of that mashed potato casserole from Southern Lovin'. Will you take me there for dinner?"

"Absolutely," he said, catching the stress on her face and in the set of her shoulders before she cleared it away. Mister went to help someone with their throw, his mind churning around Mildred's wedding.

It's almost over, he told himself. Then Libby wouldn't be so distressed, and her life could get back to normal. At least he hoped so.

CHAPTER 24

*L*ibby let her mama finish buttoning her dress before she smoothed her hands down the front of her body. She hated wearing long dresses, because they made her look shorter than she already was.

"You're gorgeous," Mama said, gripping her shoulders with both hands as she smiled at Libby in the mirror.

"Thank you, Mama." Libby leaned her head against her mother's, more than ready for this wedding to be over. She loved her sister, and Libby wasn't sure how to live in the little red farmhouse without Mildred. The past few months had been so...silent in the evenings, despite Mister coming over most nights.

Her smile only grew with thoughts of Mister, and a sigh slipped through her lips.

"Maybe you and Mister will get married soon," Mama said, grinning widely too.

"I don't know, Mama," Libby said, though her mother

had always been extraordinarily gifted at reading Libby's mind.

"It's serious, right?" Mama stepped away from Libby and reached into the bucket to get the wrist corsage. She already wore hers, and she handed this one to Libby.

She adjusted it on her wrist, admiring the deep blue rose, which had obviously been dyed. Mildred adored navy blue and sparkles, and it felt like the whole wedding was made of those two things.

And apples, as Mildred had chosen the Old Apple Mill as her venue. The crisp, sweet-tart scent of apples infused everything here, including this dressing room. Mildred sat in front of another mirror, still in her slip. Libby's cousin worked around her, weaving some of those sparkling blue flowers into Mildred's hair, and Anne-Marie and Suzy were helping one another finish getting ready.

Then they'd all help Mildred into her dress, and the show would begin.

"I suppose it's serious," Libby said, pushing her corsage a bit to the left so one of the longer leaves didn't rub against the back of her hand. She looked up, nerves prancing through her the way ponies did in parades. "How do you know if it's serious? How did you know you were going to marry Papa?"

"Oh, well, Papa swept me off my feet," Mama said with a laugh. "We only dated for two months before he proposed. We were married within six months of knowing each other." She smiled fondly and shook her head. When her eyes came back to Libby's, she sobered.

"You've known Mister for a long time," she said. "You know who he is. He knows who you are."

Libby couldn't hold her mother's gaze. "Yeah, I know." And she did. She knew Mister had morphed and changed. She knew he kissed her with the soft lips of a man falling in love. She herself had been drifting and floating and falling for what felt like months, and then years.

"Are you saying you don't love him?"

Libby's gaze flew back to her mother's. She hadn't admitted how she felt about Mister to anyone, not even herself. "I don't know," she said. "That's what I'm asking you. How do you know true love, and not just some... infatuation? A crush?"

"Libby." Mama smiled at her. "You just know." She smoothed Libby's hair back the way she'd done countless times when she'd been a child. "Have you two talked about the future?"

"A little bit," she admitted. "He asked if I wanted to stay in the red house. We've talked about kids and if we want them. He knows I'd never want to get married anywhere but at Golden Hour. That kind of stuff."

"Sounds like serious stuff," Mama said.

"He invited me to his big family party next month," she said quietly. "Only the ranch wives go to that." And really serious girlfriends. Fiancées of the Glovers. She wasn't engaged to Mister, and she had to admit she was important to him. Important enough for him to invite her to a party six weeks in advance.

He claimed no one missed it, ever. It was the one thing

that held great significance for all of them, and he'd said in his throaty, *I'm-about-to-kiss-you* voice that he wanted her there. She'd agreed to attend; she'd kissed him.

Dear Lord, she thought. *Am I in love with him? Like, all the way, legit in love with him?*

Yes.

The word just entered her mind, making her eyes fill with tears and her heart start crashing around inside her chest.

"Ready," Lucinda said, stepping away from Mildred. Libby looked past her mother to her sister, glad for something else to focus on.

"I'll get the dress," Mama said, turning toward Mildred too.

"I'll get the shoes," Libby said, ducking around the corner to the entrance closet, where she'd stowed the shoebox. From there, the activity in the bridal room really picked up, and not twenty minutes later, Mama led the way out into the hallway.

Papa stepped away from the wall where he'd been waiting, and he slid one arm around Mama with a smile. "Ready?"

"She's ready," Mama confirmed. She tipped up to kiss her husband's cheek, and Libby did the same.

"Hey, Papa," she murmured. "You'll walk me down the aisle when it's time, right?"

"Of course, sweet pea. I've been waiting my whole life to do this." He grinned at her, the gesture quickly switching to Mildred as she came out of the bride's room.

Stars could not shine brighter than her sister today, and Libby felt her excitement and love for Scott permeate everything.

She wanted to be that bright with love for someone. She wanted to bask in that glow, experience that high, and wield that excitement.

As Mildred's maid of honor, Libby had to march down the aisle in the very front. She'd asked Mister to escort her, because she didn't have any unmarried brothers, and Mama wasn't in the wedding party.

The moment she saw Mister's face, everything cleared in her soul. He grinned at her, but the power of it only touched his mouth. His eyes saw things she tried to keep hidden from others. He offered her his arm, and she gratefully slipped hers through it.

"Hey," he whispered, bending his head to speak right at her ear. "Are you okay?"

"Yes," she whispered back. "Just hold me tight, okay?"

"I'm right here," he said, this solid piece of man at her side. He'd always been steady and strong—that much about him hadn't changed. He'd always been confident and dashing and quick on his feet. Those things hadn't changed either.

In the past, he might've noticed Libby's emotions, and he might not have. She'd witnessed him gloss over her several times, usually with that bright smile and his eyes roaming as he looked for someone he wanted to ask out. Then he'd ask Libby for that woman's number, and he'd leave an event like this with a new girlfriend.

Today, he hadn't looked anywhere but at her.

"We're first," she said as the others lined up behind them. "We just have to wait for the signal from Judge." Yes, Mildred had asked Mister's brother to marry her and Scott. She'd been to a couple of the Glover weddings where he'd officiated, and she liked the things he said.

Libby could admit that she did too. She also knew Mister and Judge hadn't gotten along all that well in the past, as Mister often came to her to blow off steam. They'd been best friends for so long, and Libby felt the box she'd always put him expand and reform.

How it had taken that long, she wasn't sure.

Judge nodded at her, and Mister cleared his throat. "Here we go. Ready, Libs?"

"Ready," she confirmed. They walked down the aisle together, and Libby plastered a younger-sister smile on her face for all of Mildred's friends, their family, and Scott's side of everything. With Mister at her side, the journey was easy, and she even laughed as he grabbed onto Judge in an informal show and banged him on the back.

They then took their seats, as Mildred wanted her and Scott to be the only people at the altar.

Libby's emotions stayed safely dormant—until Mildred and Papa stood at the end of the aisle alone. The music changed to something upbeat. Mildred's favorite song, which happened to be *Fun, Fun, Fun* by The Beach Boys.

The electric guitar picked through the tune that everyone seemed to know. Mildred started down the aisle in short, almost dancing steps, and Papa held her hand above her head while she twirled in a circle on the chorus.

At the altar, Scott laughed, and beside her, Mister started singing, "Fun, fun, fun, till her daddy takes the T-bird away."

Mildred made it to the end of the aisle, and she and Scott bee-bopped together, and when the lead singer went into his high vocalizations, Libby relented and sang along too. She giggled and danced at her seat, glad the sentimental and overpowering emotions that had surged had gone back into her stomach.

"Well, that was amazing," Judge said, his grin as wide as Mildred's. Everyone took a few seconds to settle into their seats again, and Libby leaned right into Mister's chest, his arm draped halfway across the back of her chair and halfway across her shoulders.

She loved the feel of him supporting her, and not just physically. She turned her head as if she wanted to say something to him, and he automatically leaned down to listen. A smile filled her soul, and Libby shook her head. She didn't have anything to say to him.

Not anything she could say right now, at least, because she wasn't going to profess her love for him in whispers at her sister's wedding.

"In my family," Judge said, drawing Libby's attention back to him. He did have a soothing voice, and she noticed several of the other Glovers in the audience sit up a little straighter. Her father had known Bear his whole life, and as he ran the ranch, Papa and Bear helped one another a lot.

When the tornadoes had hit Three Rivers a handful of years ago, Bear had brought every Glover to help get Golden Hour cleaned up. They'd gone up to Shiloh Ridge to help. Libby and her family had been there when the Glover's had suffered a landslide a year or two ago.

"Our daddy wrote us letters," Judge said. "Before he died. It was a really sweet blessing to receive years later, and I've been thinking a lot about my own marriage and this letter from my father lately." He looked at Mildred and Scott.

"And I see the two of you here, and Mildred with her father, and I think that relationship is so tender." He touched his hand to his heart as if about to pledge something. "I often give a bit of advice before the ceremony, and when I asked Mildred and Scott what they wanted me to say, they told me I could say whatever I wanted."

"Oh, brother," Mister muttered beside her, and Libby's smile only grew. "Here we go."

"They'll probably regret it," Judge said. "But here goes. I was an adult when my daddy passed away. I remember keenly how much he loved my mother. I remember how devastated she was. I've seen her fall in love again, get remarried, and incorporate this new love into all of our lives. I've seen them look at each other."

He gazed around at the people gathered at the wedding, and Libby took a deep breath when his eyes skimmed over her and Mister. They stopped on his brother for a moment, Judge's smile widening slightly.

The scent of apples hung in the air, and the breeze made the leaves above them rustle in the September evening. Libby did like this venue, and it felt...peaceful and serene. Quiet enough for someone to contemplate deep things.

"I was only married last month myself," he said. "I had the opportunity to watch nine of my family members get married before me. Make that ten, as one of my niece-in-laws got married over Christmas. Ten other weddings. Ten other couples. I've seen the way my brothers and cousins look at their wives. I've seen the way their wives look at them. I see it on a lot of faces here today too."

Judge's eyes came right back to Mister and Libby, and she wondered what she showed on her face.

"It's love in its purest form, and I can feel it coming from the two of you. I see it on your faces as well. My best advice to you is to remember it. Remember how this feels, right here, right now. Remember this love, and how deep it is, and how much you want to be with your spouse. Sometimes, when life gets busy and things get hard, it's easy to forget. Don't forget."

Libby thought that was perfect advice, especially for Mildred, who did forget things sometimes just in her everyday life. She smiled at her sister as Mildred turned toward Scott and leaned into him.

"All right," Judge said, taking another deep breath. "Let's

get the ceremony done. That's why we're all here in our best clothes, right?" He smiled at Mildred and Scott, performed the ceremony, and pronounced them husband and wife.

As Scott laughed and kissed Mildred, Libby's tears made another appearance. This time there were no beach boys, no snazzy songs, and nothing to distract her from crying. She told herself it was okay to cry at her sister's wedding, and she stood next to Mister and clapped.

When she could, she hurried forward and embraced her sister, saying, "I'm so happy for you. I love you so much."

"Love you too, Libs," Mildred whispered, her voice choked and her hold on Libby tight, tight, tight. She pulled back, her beauty radiant and her smile still beaming with brightness. "You'll be okay in that house without me."

Libby nodded, because she was worried about going to sleep there alone, and waking up alone, and just being alone all the time.

Then a warm set of fingers slid between hers, and Libby knew she wasn't alone.

Mister was at her side. He hugged Mildred and then Scott, and the couple made their way into the crowd to keep accepting congratulations. Libby stayed out of the way, which was where she preferred to be.

Mister moved over to Judge and gave him another hearty hug. They talked for several seconds, and when Mister turned back to Libby, he looked a little perturbed. The emotion fled quickly as he returned to her side, and

Libby simply held onto him so he'd know she was there for him if he wanted to talk to her about anything.

He'd done that for her over the course of the past year, and she was so grateful for it. Her soul felt renewed, and her spirit felt full, and Libby's heart pulsed with life and energy. She turned into Mister and said, "Come help me check on the food, okay?"

"Sure," he said easily, and she led him away from the crowd. Once they were out of sight, she spun back to him and kissed him, causing him to stumble a little.

He chuckled as he righted himself. "You don't need to check on the food, do you?" he murmured, his lips tracing along her neck.

"No, sir," she whispered.

"Mm." Mister kissed her then, and Libby knew without a doubt that she loved him and wanted to be with him. Now she just had to figure out how to admit it out loud.

CHAPTER 25

"Hey, hey, you made it." Mister got to his feet the moment he saw Porter enter the diner.

Porter Hangford's face transformed into a smile too, and he stepped toward Mister. He shook his hand the same way he always had—with plenty of pump—and turned back toward the door. "We went to the wrong place a minute ago," he said. "Let me get Dave and Austin."

"Yeah, sure," Mister said, his chest feeling a bit hollow.

"Is that all of you now?" the hostess asked, and Mister turned toward her.

"Uh, no. There's still a woman coming. Libby Bellamore? She'll be here soon."

The woman nodded and handed him four menus. "You can order whenever."

"Thanks." Mister waited by the door for the cowboys to come back, and then he led them to the table where he'd been sitting for ten minutes. He reminded himself that he knew these men. They weren't active in the rodeo anymore, and he didn't have anything to prove to them.

He sat and handed out the menus. "We can order whatever. I'm paying."

"You don't have to pay," Dave said, peering at the laminated sheet in his hand.

"Yeah, well, I am," Mister said. "It's easier that way, and it's a business expense besides." He smiled around at them, suddenly so glad they were here. "Look at you guys. You had to pay to get here."

"I drove," Porter said. "From Austin. It wasn't hard."

"I appreciate it," Mister said. "And I'm going to pay for lunch."

"It's three o'clock in the afternoon," Austin drawled. "It's not lunch."

"It's not dinner," Mister shot back, grinning at the cowboy. He was a couple of years older than Mister, and he'd been present when Mister had broken his leg on his career-ending ride. They'd stayed in touch over the years, and Mister hadn't been surprised when Austin had immediately said yes to coming to Three Rivers for a Christmas festival.

Porter hadn't taken much to convince either, but Dave had required some real cajoling. Mister had done it too, because he wanted to give Libby the sun, the moon, and the stars. Or at least five rodeo stars for her Country Rodeo Christmas Extravaganza.

"Howdy, boys," a waitress said. "Drinks?"

They went around and put in their drink requests, and

Mister said, "We have one more coming. She'll want a Diet Coke." He tapped the empty seat between him and Dave.

"Sure thing." The woman walked away, and Mister looked at his friends again. His smile withered when he saw their faces. Dave's dark eyes yelled questions at him, and Porter reached up and ran his hand through his hair. That wasn't good. That was his tell for *I'm about to ask a hard thing and I need to have something for my hand to do.*

Mister had seen it before.

Austin had already asked Mister about Libby, and Mister had his answer ready.

"So you and this woman," Porter said when the others remained quiet. They'd obviously staged this little intervention. Mister simply leaned back in his chair and folded his arms. He'd had plenty of conversations about women in the past. "You like her?"

"Yes," Mister said simply.

"How long you been dating?" Dave asked, actually reaching for a phantom glass of water.

Mister smirked at him as he pulled his hand back. "I don't know. A few months."

"You don't know?" Austin scoffed and chuckled. "He told me since June."

"Four months is a long time for you," Porter said, and Mister wanted to leap across the table and get in his face.

"I'm not the same person I was before," he said. "Look at you. You got married. Are you the same?"

"No," Porter said thoughtfully, a slight frown appearing between his eyes. "You're right. Sorry, Mister."

"Even after you left the rodeo, you didn't settle down," Austin said, pointing out a fact Mister didn't need pointed out. "Four months is a long time for you, Mikey. It's okay to admit it."

"I have admitted it," he said, glaring at Austin. "I would appreciate you guys not bringing up my dating history with Libby."

"She doesn't know?" Porter asked, glancing at Dave.

"She knows," Mister said. "It's...it *was* a sore spot for her, and I don't need to go rubbin' it again."

"Fair enough," Dave said, looking up when the waitress arrived with that glass of water. He took a drink of it, waited until she left, and added, "Are *you* going to get married?"

"You say it like it's an impossibility," Mister said, annoyed at Dave.

"I'm so sorry," Libby said as she rushed into the diner. He rose to his feet to greet her, stepping around the other cowboys to do so. "You would *not* believe what happened."

He put one hand on her hip and smiled at her. "It's fine. They were late too. No problem."

She swallowed and pushed her hair back. It did look a little disheveled, and when she felt it, she tugged the ponytail holder out of it and shook her head to get the hair loose.

"You're fine," he whispered, turning in the next

moment. "Here she is, fellas. The genius behind the Country Rodeo Christmas, Liberty Bellamore."

She blinked at him once before turning back to the table. "I'm so sorry I'm late. I have this Houdini dog, right? He likes to climb ladders onto roofs and balance on the top rung of fences. That kind of thing. Well, today, he did his fence crawl, and he unlatched a gate. We had sheep from here to Oklahoma." She shook her head and took the empty seat.

She looked at the soft drink there and then up to Mister as he sat down too. "Did you order this for me?"

"Yep."

"Thanks, baby." She grinned at him and lifted the soda glass to her lips. "Have you ordered?"

"Not food," he said, warmth flowing through him like hot lava. Libby didn't have a lot of endearments for him. She liked him, he knew that. If Libby didn't like someone, they knew it too—and he'd been on the receiving end of that.

He was the one who brought food and gifts for her, not the other way around. She hadn't come up to Shiloh Ridge much since he'd gotten home at all. He didn't mind, because she'd broken her ankle and needed help. He could help her, and she was coming to the angel tree celebration in another month or so.

The waitress returned, and they put in their food orders. Libby bent and took a folder from her purse. "All right," she said. "You told them it was a business lunch, right?"

"It's not lunch," Austin said, and that caused Libby to blink-blink, blink-blink.

"I told them," Mister said, chuckling between the words. "Ignore him. He's never eaten a meal at the right time."

"It's hard to do in the rodeo," Austin said. "You sleep through breakfast, and train through lunch."

"Compete through dinner," Porter said with a smile.

Libby looked like she'd been hit with a load of bricks, and Mister put his arm around her shoulders. "Okay, I should introduce you. Right next to you is David Warburton. He's a two-time National Champion in the PRCA Rodeo, and the man can ride bulls no one else even thinks about riding."

"Once," Dave said with a grin. He tipped his hat at Libby. "Not for a while now."

"Austin is next to me," Mister said, smiling at Dave for a moment before switching his gaze to Libby. "You recognize him, yeah?"

"Austin Goodnight," she murmured. "He won the year before you."

"The *four* years before me," Mister said. "He was one of my best friends on the circuit. He was there when I went down on Lonely Rider."

Libby nodded. "I've seen that video. He's a lot...." Her voice trailed off, but Mister really wanted to hear how she'd finish that sentence.

"Younger," Austin said, lifting his cowboy hat a couple

of inches off his head. "And I had more hair back then too." He grinned at Libby, and she relaxed.

"And Porter Hangford," Mister said, indicating the blond man across from him. "He can ride a bronc like no one I've ever seen. He's the true horse whisperer."

"I am not," Porter said.

"Runs an equine training facility in Austin," Mister said without missing a beat. "So he really is."

"What kind of training facility?" Libby asked. "And can you really come here for three weeks in December?" She folded her hands over her folder. "You all can?"

"Yep," Austin said. "I'm bringing my daughter, and we're going to stay up at Shiloh Ridge." He cut a look at Mister. "Mister says he's got a cottage I can stay in."

"All ready for you," Mister said with a smile.

"I'm bringing my family," Porter said. "I'm married with two kids now. We're looking for a rental. My wife's sister is in Amarillo, so she's thrilled."

Libby nodded and switched her gaze to Dave. He wasn't married, and as far as Mister knew, he never had been. "I'm going to stay with Mister," he said. "In the homestead."

"Just you?" Libby asked.

"Just me," Dave said with a smile. "We can't all find beautiful women like you to go out with us."

"Okay," Mister said quickly, hating Dave in that moment. "She's *my* girlfriend already, you idiot." He grinned at Dave, though his eyes felt like they could throw fire at the man.

He looked at Libby, and thankfully, she was smiling too. He could see the thin veil over her nerves, and he didn't like it. "Why don't you tell 'em what you were thinking, sweetheart? You're so much better at it than I am."

She nodded, cleared her throat, and opened the folder. "Okay, so the Country Christmas is an evening event. We serve a big chuckwagon dinner, and then there are activities, booths, and entertainment. I have a band coming in on each of the three weekends, and I was thinking you rodeo stars could be the entertainment during the week."

"So you'd have weekends off," Mister said.

"Right," Libby said, tag-teaming with him. "Weekends off. And we'd only do the demos or shows for no more than an hour. So it's an hour each evening, Monday through Thursday."

"Four hours a week," Mister said. "And the most amazing Christmas season in the best town in Texas."

Porter scoffed, but Mister simply kept on smiling. He'd already gotten them to come to Three Rivers for this meeting. They'd come do the Country Christmas—and that would surely earn him a for-certain place in Libby's heart.

Now, if he could just keep Dave from saying something stupid, he'd have it made.

MISTER SIGHED AS HE SANK ONTO LIBBY'S couch. "Thanks for feeding me," he said. Since Mildred's wedding, he'd been staying later and later at Libby's house. She let him run his hands through her hair and tell her she'd be okay there alone that night.

She texted him once he got home, and he usually had a text from her no matter how early he'd gotten up too.

"Anytime," she said. "I'm pretty good with a slow cooker."

"I've never had scalloped potatoes out of one." He grinned at her and lay down, resting his head in her lap.

She threaded her fingers through his hair and sent sparkles and shivers through his body. He sighed out the day and closed his eyes. He didn't have anything to say, so he said nothing, and Libby seemed out of words tonight too.

His rodeo friends had only come into town for a few days, and Libby had shown them the facilities here at Golden Hour. They'd gone over their contracts. They'd even done a few demos for what they could do for the shows at the festival.

Mister actually missed them, and he missed the rodeo. It had a special piece of his heart, and when he saw the cowboys and smelled the dust, he couldn't help feeling like he'd gone home.

He was home at Shiloh Ridge too, and definitely home in Libby's arms.

"Oh," he said, opening his eyes. "I brought my letter." He sat up and dug in his back pocket. He'd stowed his in an envelope, and it flapped as he extended it toward Libby. He'd told her about it, of course, but she'd asked about it after Judge had mentioned the letters at Mildred's wedding.

He'd also told Mister that he could see the same love and adoration on his face that he saw on Bear's, Cactus's, Ace's, and everyone else. Mister hadn't wanted to deal with his brother at the wedding, and he hadn't seen Judge much since.

With October here, both he and Libby were in the thick of setting up their Christmas shows. Judge had won last year, and the pressure to do so again seemed to have addled his brother's brain.

"I don't have to read it," she said, turning and putting the letter on the side table. "Just tell me what's in it."

Mister had read his letter so much, he had it memorized. Snippets of it, at least. The stuff that had helped him through the past few years.

"My dad told me to go my own way," he said, laying down in her lap again. "He said it's something I've always done, and that he and Mother had to learn how to encourage me to seek my own understanding."

Her fingertips traced his jaw, and he smiled up at her. "You're growing your beard again," she murmured.

"Just a little," he said. "Because I got up too late to shave this morning."

She smiled at him, the moment sweet and tender and everything Mister wanted in his life. "You do go your own way. You always have."

"I wasn't sure what it meant," he said. "But I guess he's right. I do like to know things for myself, and I do like to do things my own way."

"Even though Bear is right sometimes."

Mister chuckled, because Bear was right a lot of the time. "Even though Bear is right sometimes," he agreed. He breathed in, and he could still smell the milk and cheese and meat she'd made for dinner. "Dad said that I was saved to come into the family near the end so I could help the others."

You're almost last in our family, the letter actually read. *There's only Bishop after you, and he looks to Bear for everything. A couple of the other brothers look to Judge, but you have Glovers who need your support. It's okay to operate in the background, Mister, but I know that's hard for you.*

I encourage you to work on it, if you can. Remember that Preacher wants to feel important too, as does Arizona. You have the power to make sure they can be heard in the family. Judge bears a lot of burdens for the family. Lift him up if you can.

"It was really humbling," he said quietly. "My dad telling me all this stuff that I could do, and me realizing I hadn't done any of it."

"I'm sure that's not true," Libby said.

"It's true," he said. "I started to change even more after the letter. I couldn't get along with Judge, and I'm still hot-headed sometimes." A small smile touched his lips. "But I'm working on that, Libs. I swear. Going to Winterhaven helped a ton, actually."

"I'm glad you went then."

"Me too."

He sensed her leaning over, and he kept his eyes closed as she kissed him. Mister could lose hours in this house with her, in quiet, soft moments like this. She didn't let the kiss last long, and Mister mourned the loss of her touch when she pulled away.

"What else?" she asked.

"He told me Grandmother gave me the nickname Mister because I was always getting in trouble." He smiled and looked up at her. "I guess I was pretty disobedient every time she watched me, and she once found me in her kitchen after I'd dumped out two bags of flour." He smiled, remembering doing that.

"Why would you do that?"

"Flour was fun," he said. "You could draw pictures in it and stuff. It's like dirt, and little boys love dirt."

"My word, Mister." She giggled and threaded those magical fingers through his hair again.

He sighed, his smile stuck in place. In that moment, Mister was the happiest he'd ever been in his entire life. "She used slightly more colorful language," he said. "But after that, it was, 'listen here, Mister,' or 'don't you dare, Mister.'"

"You got your nickname because you were always in trouble," she said, still laughing.

"That's right."

She curled her fingers around his ear, the gesture loving and gentle. "Anything else?"

"Let's see." Mister took a breath and enjoyed her

touch. "Just good advice. He told me to remember who I was and what name I carry. I didn't do that very well in the rodeo, but I've been trying harder, especially since I got the letter."

"Mm."

"He told me to not be afraid to love my family and my wife."

Libby took a moment, and then she asked, "Why would you be afraid to do that?"

Mister knew why, but he still struggled to come up with the right words, in the right order. "Let's see. Hand me the letter, would you?"

She did, and Mister removed it from the envelope and scanned the paragraphs. He'd seen Bear's letter and Bishop's, but no one else's. Compared to theirs, Mister's was about the same length.

"Here it is," he said, his eyes catching on it. "Don't be afraid to love your brothers. They need it, and they'll need it specifically from you. Arizona tries so hard to keep up with all of you, and she needs to know that she's loved just how she is. You can give her that, because you have a big heart."

Mister paused for a moment now, just as he had when he'd first read his letter. He'd never considered his heart all that big, but he did love his family as they grew, and grew, and grew.

"Someday, you'll find a good woman to marry. She'll need you to tell her how wonderful she is. Don't be afraid to do that. I didn't for a long time, and Mother finally told me I better start speaking my feelings and telling her I loved her. I learned then to tell her and you kids how much I loved you, how very important you were to me. I wish I'd started doing it sooner."

He cleared his throat. "He never really did say he loved us until I was maybe seven or eight."

"Good for your mother for telling him."

"Mother is an extraordinary woman," he agreed. "The letter says, Don't be afraid to love, Mister. It's not a weakness, and it's not something that makes you less of a man. If anything, it makes you stronger and better."

He refolded the letter and slipped it back inside the envelope. She took it from him and returned it to the table. "You loved your dad."

"A whole lot," he said, letting his eyes drift closed. "Libby, I...we've been friends forever. Do you think we could ever make a marriage work?"

She didn't answer, and after several long moments, Mister opened his eyes. She gazed down at him and said, "Yes, Michael, I think we could make a marriage work."

He reached for her, and she leaned down, and this kiss felt explosive and subtle at the same time. He'd been steadily falling for her, and with his true name said in her voice, and the careful stroke of her mouth against his, he landed all the way in love with her.

Now he just had to figure out how to keep her in his life for good.

*L*ibby watched David Warburton whistle through his teeth, sending the blue heeler across the stadium she and Mister had created for the rodeo events. Though the Country Christmas wouldn't open for another six or seven weeks, Libby had already decorated the fences by looping pine boughs through them.

She'd make sure the bright red bows stored in the barn were hung before opening day. The Country Christmas was an evening event, with the first round of dinner being served at five, and the second at seven. That allowed them to host over two hundred people per evening. Mildred, though she'd been very busy on her honeymoon and then setting up her new life in Scott's house on the other side of Three Rivers, had not abandoned Libby completely.

She was still making the maps and brochures for their guests, as she always did. She'd also been working on their website, as their ticket sales usually started the day after Halloween.

In fact, after Dave's show today, Libby needed to meet her sister in the office they'd always used in the storage barn.

"Then Porter would come out and do a horse demonstration," Dave called from the arena. He dropped from the gate he'd just swung closed and dusted his hands together. He grinned at Libby as he came toward her.

"Okay," she said.

"It's only about thirty minutes," Dave said. "We can split up and do individual chats, like Mister mentioned, if you'd like."

"I'm not sure yet," Libby said, climbing down from the fence. She gave him a smile. "Thanks, Dave. This gives me a better idea of what will be happening. We can make sure we advertise it correctly."

He nodded as his phone rang. He plucked it from his front shirt pocket and said, "Oh, it's Mister now." He swiped on the call, and though Libby would've normally excused herself, she stayed. "Hey, Mister." Dave grinned into the sky, and thankfully, now that autumn had truly arrived, the temperatures had started to relax a little bit.

Not much, as it wasn't Halloween yet, but slightly, which Libby was grateful for.

Dave laughed loudly and turned away from Libby. "Yeah, let's go tonight. That sounds fun."

Libby searched her memory for what Mister was doing that night. They usually spent their evenings together, almost always here on the ranch. If they weren't at her house, it was because Mister had taken her to dinner somewhere. They didn't have plans set in stone, because they seemed to just happen after they finished their work for the day.

"Yeah, Austin will be here by then," Dave said. "Porter's flying in on the red eye. He's renting a car to drive here."

Libby had asked them all to come again—and she'd offered to pay their way up to the Panhandle—to get promotional pictures. She'd booked Whitney Walker, because the woman could photograph anything, and she'd been using Whit for her images for the Country Christmas for years now.

Three former rodeo champions would go right at the top of their website, that was for sure.

Libby ducked through the rungs in the fence just as Dave said, "Yeah, I'll come up to Shiloh Ridge. See you then." He ended the call and added, "Are we done, Libby?"

"Yes." She turned back to him. "Thank you so much, really. I have a great idea of what you guys mean now." She gave him a smile, and he returned it. She went toward the barn, something storming in her chest.

She didn't need help around Golden Hour anymore, but Mister still came down every afternoon. She expected him to be waiting for her when she finished talking to Mildred, and her stomach twisted at the thought that he wouldn't be.

"What does that mean?" she asked herself, wishing she

could take her individual feelings out of herself and examine them subjectively.

She entered the shed, and Mildred's classical music filled her ears. Libby wouldn't choose songs without lyrics, but she could admit the strings had been known to soothe her when she felt seething.

Right now, she took a deep breath, held it, and blew it out as she went down the aisle in the shed to the office in the back of it. The sisters had installed a small, room-sized air conditioner in the window, and that kept the office at a comfortable temperature for meeting and talking.

"Libs," Mildred said, her expression brightening when she saw Libby in the doorway. She reached to turn down the music and then gestured her forward. "Come look at this."

Libby caught some of her sister's enthusiasm, and she hurried to her side, pulling the second chair around to the right side of the table. She'd seen this surface covered with hundreds of maps in the past. Before that, it had housed boxes and boxes of new decorations, or stacks of notebooks—Libby and Mildred's notes from previous events.

So many good memories had been made right here at this table, and Libby's pulse did a hop, skip, and jump as she sat down and looked at Mildred's desktop computer screen. She turned it further toward Libby and said, "Look at the animated banner Scott helped me make."

Country Christmas Extravaganza came up on the banner, not so flashy and fast as to give a person a stroke, but a nice smooth motion. The font was festive and fun, just what they'd always aimed for. The Country Christmas appealed to families, as they hosted children's events and crafts, fed everyone the same food, and promised holiday magic, ranch-style.

The background was black, with twinkling stars that changed to colored Christmas lights right before Libby's eyes. A smile started way down in her twisted stomach, evening it out and making her doubts and worries go dormant.

"Wait for it," Mildred said, drawing out the words.

Libby didn't have to wait long, and she had no time to ask what she was waiting for. The word *Rodeo* appeared, pushing Christmas and Extravaganza further apart as it slanted between them. This font held all the bumps and bobbles of a rope, with stars for the usually-circular holes in the letters that had them.

Joy burst through Libby. "Wow," she said.

"Right?" Mildred giggled and looked away from Libby's reaction. "I love it. Like, love it. And we can put the picture of our stars right here." She pointed to the empty spot on the screen. "And I'm going to put a BUY TICKETS button right at the top."

"Right at the top?" Libby asked, still watching that animated banner. The dates of their festival had come up below the title, and then the word *Rodeo* disappeared first, as did all the other words.

The lights turned back into stars, and then the whole thing started again.

"I've been doing some research," she said. "Two Cents has their most important item right at the top. Most apps do."

"This isn't an app."

"But people don't want to try to figure out how to buy tickets. It should be easy and obvious." She shuffled some papers in front of her. "I've been working on the promotional language. Tell me what you think."

Libby took the pages and started to read. *Bring the whole family for a fun, festive holiday evening…rodeo-style! Celebrate our ten-year anniversary by joining local rodeo celebrities Wyatt Walker and Mister Glover as they team up with three more retired National Champions for a Christmas celebration to remember.*

"This is amazing," Libby said, because Mildred had always been very good at hitting the right emotional notes in her promotional copy.

Get tickets during the week to mingle with the stars, enjoy a delicious chuckwagon feast, and experience the holidays in a way only Texas can offer. Then, come back on the weekends to dine and dance with our top-tier bands! Featuring The Yellow Rose of Texas, The Lone Star Dads, and Card Dalley—recently voted Texas's Rising Guitar Star—you'll need to book early to make sure you get a seat in our outdoor stadium!

Impress a date, provide a memorable Christmas for the kids, or just get out of the house and enjoy yourself…it's the perfect year to saddle up and join the cowboys and cowgirls at Golden Hour Ranch for a Country Christmas Rodeo Extravaganza!

Libby looked up. "This is perfect."

"Really?" Mildred looked away from the screen and at Libby with hope in her eyes.

"I don't think the 'the' is capitalized in 'the Lone Star Dads,' so we should check that. Other than that, it's perfect."

Mildred started tapping on the keyboard, and sure enough, the band name was simply Lone Star Dads. "Should I take it out completely?"

"I think people always say 'the' in front of it," Libby said. "It's just not capitalized."

"Okay." Mildred clicked and double-clicked over to her promotional document, changed the single letter, and saved the doc. She moved the cursor further up and took a moment to read. "Okay. What about naming Wyatt before Mister?"

"That's fine," Libby said. "Wyatt is a much bigger star than Mister."

Mildred searched Libby's face, genuinely concerned. "Is he?"

"I think so?" Libby didn't know how things were ranked. "Wyatt's been retired for less time. He won and won and won, and he has his own clothing line now. He's got products on TV. He has to live in a gated community."

To her, Mister seemed…normal, while Wyatt was definitely a celebrity. Of course, she'd seen Mister signing autographs in the parking lot at Wilde & Organic not that long ago. He'd won plenty of belt buckles and trophies— and money. He'd also been her best friend for years before he'd left town for the rodeo, and he was so *familiar* to her.

"I'll ask him." She fired off a text to him, knowing he'd just been on the phone. Her stomach growled, which meant it was almost lunchtime, and she knew he went around to his siblings' or cousins' houses for lunch to see them and eat with them.

Put Wyatt first, Mister said. *He's much more famous than I am.*

"He said to put Wyatt first."

"Okay," Mildred said, "Let's take a look at the map." She stood and moved over to the huge whiteboard they'd had Jack nail to the wall a decade ago, when they'd first started the Country Christmas festival.

But Mister had texted again, and Libby's chest had iced over. *I'm going out with Dave and Austin tonight. That okay?*

"Libby?"

She looked up at her sister, realizing she still had her knowledge and expertise to draw on. "Look at this text." She handed her phone to Mildred, who frowned before she'd even read it.

"Okay," she said.

"Why is he asking me if it's okay if he goes out with his friends?" Libby took her device back, almost hoping the words would've changed simply by Mildred reading them. They hadn't. "And what's he going to do if I say no?"

She would never say no. Mister was a grown man, and she wasn't his mother.

"He's just making sure you'll be okay alone," Mildred said. "He's been over there every night, hasn't he?"

"Yes," Libby murmured, still gazing at his text. Thoughts swirled through her head, and she didn't like any of them. She wanted to ask him where he, Dave, and Austin were going. She wanted to ask if Mister would be looking for a new girlfriend. She wanted to ask him if he really wanted to marry her and settle down.

They'd been talking more and more about it, and while neither of them had uttered the words *I love you,* Libby had felt them teeming inside her—and inside him.

She drew in a deep breath and employed her trust. She trusted Mister. He wasn't the same man he'd been when he'd been besties with Dave and Austin in the past.

Sure, she typed out, her fingers moving fast and striking at the send button like a snake.

If you don't want me to, it's fine, Mister said almost instantly, like he was waiting to see what she'd say before he sent the pre-typed message. *I know you don't like being home alone at night.*

It's okay, she sent back. *I don't expect you to come babysit me every night.*

Her phone rang, and Mister's name sat on the screen. She got to her feet and met her sister's eye. "It's fine," Mildred said, a hint of worry riding in her expression. "Go talk to him."

Libby swiped on the call as she walked toward the door. "Hey."

"It's not babysitting," he said, his voice on the outer edges of frustration. "I come down there, because I want to be with you."

Libby exhaled when she reached the non-air-conditioned hallway. "I know. Bad choice of words."

Mister let a couple of seconds go by. "We're going to Chips and Fish."

"Sports bar."

"They're showing the quarter-final event out of Montana tonight," he said, his voice guarded. "I won't drink, as usual. I'm not going to pick up any women."

"I didn't say you were." Just because she'd had a moment of doubt meant nothing. She hadn't said anything to him. "You don't need to ask me for permission to go out with your friends."

"I do, if I want you to know I'd rather be with you than them."

"Then why ask?"

"I like my friends too. But Libby, if you're not okay with it, then I won't go. *You're* more important. *My relationship* with you is more important to me." Mister could say all the right things; Libby had seen him do it before.

He's not the same, she told herself. *He's not the Mister Glover from that night.*

He was Michael Glover with her, and she had fallen in love with him. She had to trust him. "I think you should go," she said, the words scraping her throat though they came out in her normal voice. "I need to learn how to stay in that house alone."

"Do you?" he asked.

"Yes," she said quickly. "Because we're not married, and it's unreasonable for you to come down here every night and stay with me until we're both so tired we fall asleep."

"I like it," he said quietly, the bluster in him all blown out. That had happened far faster than Libby had ever experienced, and she seized onto that fact as further proof that Mister wasn't going to do anything tonight she wouldn't like.

"I want to marry you," he said next, his voice even softer, like he'd pulled the phone away from his mouth before speaking. "I'm in love with you, Liberty."

Her heartbeat filled her throat and ears, and she opened her mouth to say something. Anything. He chuckled, and she could just imagine him shaking his head. "Wow, I hate myself for saying it over the phone." He sighed, the laughter drying right up. "I'm on my way to you now. Will you be done with Mildred in ten or fifteen minutes? We can continue this conversation then."

Libby turned back to the office, the door of which she hadn't closed. "I don't know." Her voice sounded numb to her. "We're in the shed office. Just come in."

"Will do." The call ended, and Libby let her arm fall to her side.

"Libby?" Mildred said a few seconds—or a few minutes, Libby wasn't sure—later. She put her hand on Libby's arm. "Are you okay? Is everything good with Mister?"

Libby turned toward her sister, her eyes wide. "He said he loved me," she whispered.

Mildred lit up like one of the fourteen Christmas trees

Libby would start setting up at the beginning of next month. "That's wonderful, Libs. I'm so happy for you." She drew Libby into a hug, and Libby clung to her sister.

"Do you think he meant it?"

Mildred pulled away like lightning, crackling and popping with displeasure. "Liberty Mae Bellamore," she said, her voice snapping too. "Of course he meant it. That man has been in love with you for a long time, and you better start believing it before you lose him."

She shook her head and turned back to the office. "Now come on. He's going to be here soon, and you'll be useless for the rest of the day. I need your help with this map for ten minutes." She marched into the office as if Libby had been holding up her production time for days and weeks.

Libby followed her, starting to come out of the stupor she'd fallen into when Mister had said, *I'm in love with you, Liberty*, and *I want to marry you.*

She helped Mildred with the map, glancing toward the door every time her sister turned her back to write on the white board. Finally, when she turned, she found Mister standing there. He wore his usual clothes—jeans, cowboy boots, plaid shirt—this one yellow, black, and blue—and that giant cowboy hat that shaded his face and neck while he worked outside.

The air got sucked right out of the room, because Mister had a tendency to do that with his larger-than-life personality and stunning good looks. His eyes crinkled along the edges as he smiled, and Libby ran toward him as he chuckled.

He caught her around the waist, and she cradled his face in her hands as she pressed into him. "Did you really say that over the phone?"

"I'm so stupid," he murmured. "Forgive me." He touched his lips to her neck and then her cheek. "But I did say it, and I'll say it again. I love you."

Libby searched those blue, blue eyes, trying to find any hint of untruth. She found none, and she begged the Lord to help her believe everything Mister had said. To believe *in* Mister. "I love you too." She kissed him, sending fireworks through her whole body.

And while the Lord didn't confirm anything for her in that moment, Libby had come far enough in her relationship with Him to know that He hadn't left her alone to navigate this world. If being with Mister wasn't right, Libby would know eventually.

At the moment, it felt absolutely right, and Libby kissed him and kissed him and kissed him so he would know how she felt. After that, all she could do was hope and pray that her feelings hadn't been tricked and that her heart wouldn't get shattered.

CHAPTER 27

*E*tta kept adding the caramel popcorn balls into the bin she'd take out to the barn and pass out later. A third-grade class was coming to the farm that morning, and Etta would lead them through the equipment shed to show them the harvesters and tractors. She'd talk about what the ranch did in mid-October to finish getting the corn and hay in, though they'd keep harvesting for several more weeks.

They'd done well at Market Day last month, and Etta had spent plenty of time in the kitchen here at the homestead then too. There were a lot of cowboys and cowgirls to feed after Market Day, which took a few hours in the morning before all the semis left and their cattle got taken and sold.

If they had excess hay, they sold it starting in November and through the winter, when most ranches in this area weren't able to produce their own. With all the extra fields that had been planted down the slope from the main ranch, Shiloh Ridge had plenty of excess alfalfa this year.

Etta paused and started counting the remaining popcorn balls on the counter. She'd made enough to give to everyone who came to help Preacher move into his new house this weekend too. A sigh leaked from her lips, and she took three balls out of the bin and put them back on the counter.

"One more day," she told herself. "One more group." Then she had the weekend off, and she didn't have any school groups coming up to the ranch next week. She did have one appointment at the junior high, and she'd go there and do a demonstration for the home economics class. It would take twenty minutes, and then the students would try to recreate her recipe for sweet and sour meatballs.

She always brought her easier recipes in the fall, and the eighth graders wouldn't have any problem making the meatballs. In truth, mashed potatoes were much harder, as students were always impatient and didn't let them cook enough to become fluffy and creamy when whipped.

She thought about what she'd told Ida weeks ago. She was done dating. She needed to be. The attempt with Beau Peterson had been disastrous.

She'd been out with Chris Gabriel a handful of times, even taking the man to Judge's wedding. The moment she'd mentioned anything serious, he'd shut down, and

Etta didn't have time for men who didn't want a wife and family.

Etta grunted as she lifted the bin, but she got the job done. She hurried outside to her truck, slid the bin into the back of it, and got behind the wheel. The children would be here soon. Third grade was one of her favorites, because the students were inquisitive and kind, without much attitude. They mostly stayed with their teacher and the other chaperones, and Etta and Shiloh Ridge had hosted Mrs. Lambert several times.

At the big blue barn Bishop had renovated, she found Ida's car parked there. Her sister had taken a big step back from the ranch's community outreach programs when her twins had been born, but they were coming up on their second birthday soon, and this year, she'd come back with a vengeance.

Ida came outside as Etta killed the engine in her truck, and the two sisters smiled at one another. "Morning, Etta," Ida sang, her smile so pretty in the morning light.

"Good morning."

"I'll get the clipboard," Ida said, moving to the passenger side of the truck. Etta collected the popcorn balls and got them inside, where Ida had already set up a table. The kids started and ended in True Blue, which made it easy for teachers, parents, and bus drivers to all end up in the right place.

They never wandered far on the ranch anyway, but it was nice to tell everyone, "Look for the big blue barn, just down from the giant house." She hadn't had any lost adults or children since True Blue had been finished.

"All right," Ida said. "Three third-grade classes."

"Yes," Etta said. "Do you want to lead the tour?"

"Sure," Ida said, her eyes hooking onto Etta's. "Are you all right?"

"I'm tired," Etta said, reaching up to rub her hand along her forehead. "I was just up late making the banana pudding. If you could do the tour, I'd really appreciate it."

Concern sparked in Ida's light blue eyes. "Of course I can. You should go lie down."

"I don't need to do that. I'll just trail along at the end and make sure the stragglers keep up." She smiled at Ida. They'd both been doing the school field trip tours for long enough to know there were always kids lagging behind.

"You've been working yourself too hard," Ida said, looking at the clipboard again. Etta had prepared it with arrival times, teacher names, the number of students, and departure times. "Heaven forbid we don't feed five thousand people after we get Preacher and Charlie moved tomorrow."

"I like cooking," Etta said in a feeble attempt to defend herself. "Besides, Holly Ann did the main dish. I only made the dessert."

"Mm hm," Ida said, still set on protective-sister-mode. "And I'll bring pecan pie, and Bishop will have chocolate mousse." She looked at Etta. "If you're tired, you didn't have to make the banana pudding."

Smiles and Wilder had been in the kitchen with her,

along with Cactus's new boys, Cameron and Kyle. Etta had enjoyed showing them how to separate eggs and make custard, and she loved giving the small boys a taste of the creamy, sugary pudding. "I wanted to make it," she said without explaining how much joy the children had brought her. Ida already knew how much Etta loved kids; she came down from the ranch and babysat for her sister every single week.

"Is Johnny saying anything yet?" Etta asked.

"Just da-da," Ida said, her frown deepening.

"He'll get to mama soon enough."

The air brakes on a bus hissed into the barn, and both sisters turned toward the entrance. "Show time," Ida said, striding that way first. Etta followed her with slightly less bounce in her step.

Outside, Mrs. Lambert stood on the bottom step of the bus, her back to the barn. She yelled instructions for the kids, and when she turned and looked over her shoulder, her smile widened. She came down to the ground and over to Ida and Etta, but no children followed her.

"Hello, ladies." She laughed and hugged them both. "Rows in the barn?"

"Yes, please," Etta said, returning her smile and feeling her energy perk up a little bit. Mrs. Lambert waved toward the bus, and the first children started to disembark from it. Etta smiled at each individual one, and kept saying, "Welcome to Shiloh Ridge Ranch," as they streamed by her.

About halfway through the unloading, another bus

arrived, and more students spilled from it. Etta noticed a man who'd crouched down beside a blonde girl with curly hair, and she glanced at Ida. Sometimes the kids got hurt, and Etta had a plastic bag in her pocket with alcohol wipes and Band-aids.

"It's A-okay," the man said, his voice deep and comforting. He straightened, and Etta's heart stuttered in her chest. She hadn't met this man before, and she wondered if he worked at the school or if he was a parent.

Has to be a parent, she thought, because she knew everyone who worked at the two elementary schools in Three Rivers, especially in third grade.

He reached his hand down and said, "Come on, baby. Let's go find Sabrina, and you can sit by her."

"Does she need a Band-aid?" Etta asked.

The man swung his attention toward her, and Etta's lungs froze with the air right inside them. He sported light brown hair and deep, dark eyes. He hadn't shaved that morning, and possibly not yesterday morning either, which was just fine with Etta.

"Do you have one?" the little girl asked. "Can I have one, Daddy?"

Daddy.

Etta reached into her pocket, tore her eyes from this girl's father with great difficulty, and withdrew her makeshift first aid kit. "I have a few," she said. "The regular kind. There's a pink one, a blue one, and a couple with horses on them."

"Horses?" the girl asked.

"Hailey," her father said. "You're not even bleeding."

Etta knelt in front of the girl. "Oh, your daddy doesn't know that Band-aids do so much more than help with bleeding, does he?"

Hailey shook her head, and Etta peeled the backing off the sticky parts of the bandage. "Right here?" She touched the girl's knee, where a scrape sat.

"Yes, please," she murmured.

Etta taped the horsey Band-aid over the red part of her skin, patted it gently with two fingers, and said, "All good."

"Thank you." Hailey let go of her dad's hand and skipped into the barn while Etta got back to her feet. She stood next to the handsome man, her heartbeat thundering through her chest. She hadn't reacted to a man in this way in a very long time, and she smiled and watched the girl until she disappeared.

"Thank you," the man said.

"I'm Etta Glover," she said, turning to look up at him. He stood six or eight inches taller than her, and by all accounts, he should be a cowboy. He wasn't wearing the hat, and there were no boots in sight.

"August Winters," he said with a sigh. "She's hit this dramatic streak, and I don't know what to do with her."

Etta handed him her baggie of Band-aids and wipes. "Apparently, horse bandages do the trick." She told herself to walk away while she still had his interest and her dignity.

She did just that, rejoining her sister as the last of the

students flowed into the barn. Their teachers would already be in there, as well as many of the chaperones. August Winters remained outside, and he glanced down to the other bus, where two moms hustled up one final student.

"I'll head in," Ida said, and Etta nodded.

"Welcome to Shiloh Ridge Ranch," she said to the moms and the student. Then she gestured for August to enter too.

"Do you work here?" he asked in the small foyer of the barn.

"Yes," she said. "I'm a Glover. We own this ranch."

"Ah, I see."

Etta tilted her head at him. "Are you new to Three Rivers?"

"Yeah," he said, nodding and smiling. "Yep. Been here a couple of months now." His grin slipped. "Is it that obvious?"

"It's just...." Etta trailed off, because she didn't want to sound as arrogant as the thoughts in her head. *Everyone knows us.* She absolutely couldn't say that or anything reminiscent of it. "My family has been in this area for a long time."

"Ah, so I should know about you," he said, the smile roaring back onto his face.

"Of course not," she said, pausing in the doorway and lowering her voice. "Though my cousin did win the Christmas light show last year, and my other cousin is a huge rodeo champion. That's all." She grinned and folded her arms as she leaned into the doorway of the barn.

"How many cousins do you have?" he whispered.

"Seven," she said. "And four siblings." She nodded toward where Ida currently held everyone's attention. "She's my twin."

"Twins, huh?"

"Mm." Etta wanted to look for a wedding ring, but it wouldn't really tell her anything. Lots of men around Three Rivers didn't wear them, because they got damaged or lost out on ranches and farms. But he had a daughter, and she implied a wife or girlfriend at some point.

"All right," Ida said, finished with the rules. "We're going to go out the back door. Everyone get up and follow me."

Etta waited for the kids and other adults to go with Ida. She really was going to go slow and pick up the rear. "Why'd you come to Three Rivers?" she asked as she and August strolled through the barn.

"Uh, well, I needed a change."

Etta glanced at him, not liking that answer. "Where'd you move from?"

"Dripping Springs."

"Oh, the Hill Country is spectacular." She smiled at him. "It's much different here."

"It is," he said slowly. When he reached the door, he held it for her, so he possessed some Texas manners. Etta pushed it open further, stepped too soon, and stubbed her toe into the bottom of it.

Instant humiliation filled her, especially when August asked, "Are you all right?"

"Fine," she said, though she wanted to spit curses and give the door another good, hard kick. "That door sticks sometimes. I keep telling my brother to put a sign on it." Her toe throbbed, as she only wore tennis shoes and not boots. Everyone knew a ranch required closed-toed shoes, and they didn't allow school groups to come if anyone wore sandals. So things could've been worse.

"Come on, sweetie," she said to a dark-haired girl who'd squatted to look at something. "Everyone's going into the equipment shed."

"There's a huge caterpillar here," she said, standing up. She wore the cutest pair of glasses, and Etta grinned at her.

"Look at that," she said, pausing too. "It is huge." She noted that August stopped too, and that only made Etta's heart do cartwheels. "You won't want to miss the harvester. It's *massive*."

The little girl took off at a run, her feet making classic squelching noises in the loose gravel. Etta giggled after her and picked up her pace. "I'm supposed to keep everyone together. Come on, Mister Winters, we can't be lollygagging around."

"No, ma'am," he said, reaching up as if to tip his hat, which made Etta suspect he usually wore one.

Perfect, she thought, because Etta loved a tall, handsome cowboy about as much as she liked banana pudding and cooking with her nephews.

She'd walked this path dozens of times. Hundreds, probably. Something about August made her nervous, because the moment she reached the equipment shed, she tripped going from gravel to cement.

Down she went, her knees cracking against the hard concrete and her hands skidding enough to tear the skin. "Curses and cusses," she blurted out before she could stop herself.

Thankfully, the students were almost halfway down the building, and no one heard her. She hadn't really sworn anyway.

A warm hand landed on her back, and Etta sat back on her haunches, brushing her injured palms together to get the small rocks out of her skin.

August crouched down beside her and asked, "Do you need a Band-aid?" the plastic baggie she'd given him pinched between his fingers.

CHAPTER 28

August Winters grinned at Etta Glover, thinking about how gorgeous she was. He'd been trying to erase that thought for the past fifteen minutes, and it wouldn't go. Not when he thought about his daughter. Not when he thought about his new job in Three Rivers. Not when he thought about the reason he'd applied for and taken the job in the first place.

The change he'd needed.

Only August had brought the dark cloud of misery with him from Dripping Springs. He'd left his beloved wife there, and he'd come here. Most days, horror struck him right behind the heart, urging him to repack everything he and Hailey owned and get on home again.

Home, which wasn't here in Three Rivers.

It was, however, sparking in Etta Glover's eyes. "I could definitely use a Band-aid," she said good-naturedly.

August wondered what it would take to ruffle her feathers, and he wondered if he was up to the task.

Of course you're not, he told himself. He could barely get up in the morning and get his daughter to school and himself to work. He had no business thinking anything about Etta, or contemplating how he could get her number, or wondering if she'd go out with him at all.

He waited for the panic to hammer him in the heart, but it…didn't.

He calmly opened the bag, his thoughts now revolving around his possible alien abduction, and took out a pink Band-aid. "I think the pink one for that knee." He nodded to the spot of blood on her jeans, and Etta sucked in a breath.

"I should get it cleaned up," she said, reaching out to stand. He was the only thing nearby, and Etta latched right onto him and used him as a prop to stand. He didn't mind so much—another alarming realization. "There's a sink right over here."

Another human approached, and August straightened, his knees protesting his movement. Or maybe that crouch. "Mister Winters?" one of the third-grade teachers asked. Not Hailey's, who still stood up by Etta's twin. "Is everything okay?"

"I just stumbled," Etta said to the woman. "Sorry, Rhonda. I'll clean up quick as a wink." She held up the Band-aid. "Thank you, Mister Winters." She limped away from him, and August wanted to call her back over and tell her to just call him August.

Since he didn't know how to do that in front of a teacher—and seventy third graders, one of whom was his daughter—he said nothing. He blinked at her back and tucked the bag of bandages into his pocket where he'd stowed them previously.

"Sorry," he murmured to the teacher, and they started toward the group. "She just went down."

Rhonda looked over toward Etta, but August refused to do so. "She'll catch up," she said brightly.

August joined the kids, finding Etta's twin just as personable as she was. They weren't identical, and he noticed a gold band around her left ring finger as she gestured and spoke with her hands. Etta hadn't been wearing a wedding ring.

Of course, August knew by now that not everyone who was married actually wore their rings. His wife never had, but she'd done what the cowboys and cowgirls here at Shiloh Ridge did—she'd worked outside. A lot of men and women who worked a lot with their hands didn't wear their rings.

And the only other woman August had tried a relationship with since Josie's death hadn't worn her ring either. It really was too bad that he'd gone out with her a half-dozen times before his neighbor had told him she was married.

He'd been pretty off of women since then, but Hailey was now nine years old, and August knew she needed someone to help guide her over the next several years of her life. Girls wanted and needed a strong female in their lives, and August couldn't help looking over to Etta again.

She stood at a big, white sink, scrubbing her hands. She bent and cleaned up her knees and her jeans, and as the group started to move out, he tore his eyes from her. He watched her sister throw her a glance, and August made his decision.

"I'm going to check on Etta," he said to Rhonda. "We'll be two seconds behind everyone."

"Sounds good." The teacher herded a couple of kids away from one of the large, red tractors, and August took a deep breath. The equipment shed came with the scent of oil and rubber, and it trapped plenty of heat to amplify both.

Not exactly the kind of air August needed to be inhaling deeply. He pushed the air out and headed in Etta's direction. His heart pounded—positively pounded—in his chest, and it hadn't done that since the day he'd seen Josie leading a horse toward him for a riding lesson.

Not for him, but on his first day on her ranch, she'd brought out the horses for the children's riding lessons. Her father had hired August to help teach, and he'd fallen in love with the man's daughter, married her, and taken up a permanent place on the farm in Dripping Springs.

At least until Josie had passed away.

"Hey," he said, catching Etta's attention. "Are you okay?"

She ran her hand through her hair, and since it was wet, it made some of her dark locks stick out. He grinned at her, and she sighed, her smile not far behind. "Yeah, just embarrassed with a couple of stinging knees."

She'd put the pink Band-aid over her left one, as he'd indicated she should. He offered her his arm and his crooked smile. "I'll see no more harm or accident comes upon you."

She shook her head, the moment between them tender and quiet. "All right." She looped her arm through his, and they took their first steps away from the sink. "But if I go down again, I'm dragging you with me."

August tipped his head back and laughed. He hadn't done that in a while, and it felt good. "I think I can handle you, Etta. You can't be more than five feet tall."

"I'm five-two, I'll have you know." She straightened her shoulders and gave them a little shake. "What are you? Five-six?"

"Oh-ho," he said. "I see how it is." He was easily five-ten if he stood an inch, and no woman had ever underestimated his height.

They left the equipment shed together, immediately coming upon the children and their chaperones. Her sister stood at the front of the group, her eyes coming back to meet Etta's as she and August stepped into the sunlight.

Her twin cut off mid-sentence, and Etta hastily slid her arm out of August's. She took a big step away from him, cleared her throat as more and more people turned to look at the pair of them, and then she put that charming smile right back on her face.

"You've got to be careful around a ranch," she said in a

loud, clear voice. She held up both palms. "If you fall, you could get hurt."

A thousand tiny pinpricks touched August's skin from head to toe. He wasn't sure if he should be embarrassed that Etta had moved away from him or be glad she was smart enough to remember he was on a field trip with his daughter.

"Go on, Ida," Etta said, and her sister picked up the tour right where she'd left off. August stayed near the back and close to Etta for the rest of the trip, noting that Ida slid a look at her sister every minute or so.

They worked together to pass out the caramel popcorn balls back in the big blue barn, and August watched his daughter happily munch on hers. When Mrs. Lambert waved both hands above her head and said it was time to return to the bus so they could get down to the park for their lunch, August groaned internally while the children all did so audibly.

His heart did that booming beat again, and he wondered if he could just walk right up to Etta and ask for her number. If what she'd said was true, and the Glovers had been in Three Rivers for a while, maybe someone he knew could give it to him.

And you'll tell her what? he asked himself. *That you asked your construction manager to get her number for you?*

No, he had to get it himself. *Now,* his mind screamed at him.

She still stood near the table, the bin of popcorn balls behind her now. She hugged the children as they exited, and surprise darted through August when he saw more and more of them line up to get a hug from her.

"She's single," Ida said, and August turned toward the woman he hadn't seen nor felt come near him.

"Is she?" he asked, when he should've said, *Okay, whatever*, and walked away.

"Do you want her number?" Ida asked, something sparking in those blue-gray eyes.

August hesitated. He didn't want to get her number from her sister. Etta Glover was the first woman in ages to bring the sunlight with her. So much light that his dark cloud had disappeared the moment he'd laid eyes on her.

"I do," he said. "But I can ask her for it." He smiled at her twin and started across the hall to Etta. The line of children stretched in front of her, and she glanced up at him as he approached.

"There are extra popcorn balls," she said. "Help yourself."

"Thanks." August stepped past her and plucked a ball of popcorn from the bin. He returned to her side and smiled at the little boy who'd just gotten his hug.

"Thank you, Miss Etta," the girl next in line said, and Etta gave her a quick hug too.

"Hurry, guys," Etta said. "Mrs. Lambert doesn't like it when we hold up the departure of the bus."

Three or four children crowded in around her, and August grinned at her love for them. It filled the air it was so palpable, and he absolutely could not leave here without getting her number.

"What does a man have to do to get your phone number?" he asked as she wiggled her fingers at a couple of girls who'd linked arms and were skipping past her.

Etta abandoned the line of children and faced him. "What?"

"I mean, I gave you a Band-aid," he said, grinning at her.

She blinked, slowly thawing.

"Children," Mrs. Lambert said. "Leave Miss Etta alone. Come get on the bus now. Come on."

"Are you seeing anyone?" August tried again, his chest starting to shrink. His heart would surely be crushed any moment now.

"No," Etta said, drawing the word out.

"I'm not either," he said. "Are you opposed to going out with single dads?"

"No." Etta gave one last child a side-hug, her smile blooming on her face. She watched the boy trot toward the exit, and she turned toward August fully. "All right. Do you have something to write with?"

"No," he said, pulling his phone from his pocket. "Go. I'm ready."

Etta rattled off her number, the air horn on the bus drowning out the last digit. "You're going to get left here."

"What was that last number?" he asked, looking up at her.

"Seven," she said.

August nodded, said, "Thanks, Etta. It was great meeting you."

"You too," she said just as Mrs. Lambert returned.

She put both hands on her hips and said, "Mister Winters. We're leaving."

"Yeah, yep," he said, hurrying toward her. "I'm coming." He darted past the foreboding and terrifying Mrs. Lambert, noting that she didn't immediately follow him. He wasn't sure how close she was with Etta, and he didn't care.

He walked on light feet back to the bus and flew up the steps. Hailey sat in the back, just like before, and August had to endure the looks from all the children as he made his way toward her.

"What were you doing?" she asked, looking up at him with childlike eyes.

"Nothing," he said, tucking his phone away and patting his pocket like it held a great prize. Because it did. "How's your knee?"

That got his daughter talking, and August simply let her chat as they bumped down the dirt road to the highway, and then vroomed onward to the park to eat lunch.

He had no idea when he'd call Etta, or what he'd say, and his mind kept going round and round and round, searching for that perfect idea for such a perfect woman.

CHAPTER 29

*P*reacher didn't like the way Ward looked at him and then bent to get the box from the kitchen floor. "I can lift things," he said.

"Not today," Ward said without looking at him again.

"I'm not an invalid," Preacher called after him just as Bear entered the Top Cottage with Don, Mother's new husband.

"Who says you're an invalid?" Bear asked, twisting to watch Ward walk by.

"Ward," Preacher said, not bothering to keep his voice down. He also didn't move away from the kitchen counter where he had one palm pressed to the granite.

"He twisted his hip this morning," Charlie said, totally betraying him as she came out of the hallway that led back into the bedrooms. She carried their bald baby on her hip and grinned at Bear. "He fell all the way down, but he won't let me take him to the hospital."

"I'm fine," Preacher said.

Charlie gave him a look that said she'd get him to the hospital one way or another. She turned back to his brother. "Thank you for coming."

"Of course," he said, taking Betty from Charlie. His face lit up as he tossed the girl up and caught her on the way down. Betty giggled in her cute baby voice, and that got Preacher to smile.

"All of this?" Don asked, and he nodded. Don bent and picked up a box, moving to follow Ward outside.

"Did he confess to you?" Ward asked, coming back inside with Mister, Judge, and Cactus on his heels.

"No," Preacher growled. "I didn't do anything wrong. I was moving a box. We're *moving* today."

"He hurt himself," Ward said, barely looking at Preacher. "Charlie says it's bad, and she doesn't want him doing a whole lot."

"No problem," Cactus said. "There's plenty of us." He gestured back the way he'd come. "I brought my big boys, and they'll do whatever you want."

It wasn't that Preacher didn't want or even need the help. He simply didn't want to be sidelined today. He felt weak, and he hated that. He looked at Charlie, silently begging her to let him help.

A silent moment passed between them, and he appreciated that she didn't pity him or give him a look of sympathy. "How about you go outside and direct people where to put things?" she suggested.

"Fine," he said. He stepped away from the counter

while everyone watched, and yes, he had to limp to move. He had twisted something funny, and it did hurt. He'd landed on his hip, and that had sent white-hot shockwaves of pain through him.

They hadn't lasted long, and Preacher knew enough about a broken hip to know what one felt like. He was fine.

Or at least he would be with a fistful of painkillers and a lot of rest.

Preacher didn't get angry very often, but he felt the fury foaming within him. "Thank you," he murmured as he went past his brothers and his cousin. "We really appreciate this."

Ranger filled the doorway before Preacher could reach it, and he said, "Oakley and I put the ATVs in your shed."

Preacher froze, then kept moving, the stutter in his step ultra-obvious. "Thank you, Ranger."

Ranger stepped out of the way, a quizzical look on his face. Preacher would let someone else explain, because he didn't have it in him to do so. He didn't want to stand next to tailgates and direct people either. He just wanted the move to be done. He wanted all the boxes to be unpacked, the beds made, and the baby snuggled into his chest while they both slept.

Instead of going over to the four trucks that had been backed up to the house, he went around the corner of it. He pressed his back into the wood and breathed in, then slowly out. "Why, God?" he asked, looking up through the branches of the trees surrounding the cottage. "Why today?"

He stayed out of sight as more people arrived, and more voices joined the fray. Boots went up and down the steps, and Ward directed men as they loaded up the furniture Preacher and Charlie would be taking with them.

"I don't know where he is," he heard his wife say, and Preacher still couldn't get himself to go around the corner. Maybe they'd all just leave him behind.

Another woman said something, but someone started their pick-up truck at the same time, and the words got roared out. One truck left, then another, then a third.

Preacher sighed, feeling immature and like an invalid now, and he took the first step toward the edge of the house. Zona appeared there before he got too far, and surprise filled her expression. She glanced back toward the front of the house and then came toward him.

"You're smart," she said. "Staying out of the way."

"I was hiding," he said, not wanting her to give him any credit. "They wouldn't have let me do anything anyway."

"No, they wouldn't have." She scanned him down to his feet and back. "How are you? I heard you twisted your hip."

"I did," he admitted. "It's...going to be fine."

"Charlie said she almost called the physical therapist it was so bad."

"It hurt," he said, and it sounded like Charlie hadn't been spreading the news that he'd fallen down. He loved his wife powerfully in that moment, because she knew how much he hated not being able to be helpful and strong. "But I know the exercises to do. I've been to physical therapy a ton of times."

Zona nodded and looked off into the trees. "Bear let you get the ATVs."

"Yeah." Preacher didn't know what else to say. "Listen, Zona, I'm okay."

She nodded again, her chin trembling now. "What if I'm not?" Her eyes zipped past him again, and Preacher's heartbeat rebounded through his chest.

"What do you mean?" he asked. He and Charlie had spent a lot of time with Zona and Duke. They adored one another, and Zona liked to put on a show in a crowd, but she was quieter and more reserved at home. Charlie loved her, and she took Preacher out in their father's old, restored Corvette whenever he wanted.

She'd become a very good friend over the past couple of years, and Preacher stepped toward her. "Zona." He put his hand on her forearm. "What's going on?"

"Duke just has a ton of pressure from his dad right now." Zona shook her head, sniffled, and wiped her eyes. "It's fine. I'm just a little stressed."

"Come tomorrow for lunch," he said. "We can talk about it."

"He might will the ranch to Dawson instead of Duke." She looked up then. "Duke's devastated, and I don't know how to help him." Tears filled her eyes. "I really don't."

Preacher enveloped her in a hug and held on. "I'm

sorry, Zona." Dawson Rhinehart could only be nineteen or twenty, with Duke being quite a bit older than his half-brothers. He had left the ranch for several years, but Preacher had seen him with his father. They'd always seemed to get along fine, and he didn't know the root of why Duke had left town.

"Lunch isn't going to fix anything," she said into his chest. "It won't fix that, and it won't fix your hip, and it just doesn't fix much of anything."

"No, but you'll know you're not alone," he whispered.

"Like you do?" She stepped back and gave him a cocked-eyebrow look.

"I just—I don't want to feel useless today. It's supposed to be a great day. A new house—one Charlie and I have been waiting for over a year to move into after a ton of delays and pushbacks. *Finally*, you know? My life can begin with my wife and daughter. And instead, it's just… hip pain and embarrassment and everyone tiptoeing around me while they eye me like I'm a criminal if I lift anything bigger than a fork."

Zona grinned at him. "Yeah, you should go for a spoon. They're much smaller, and no one would say a word."

They laughed together, though it sure seemed like they had plenty *not* to laugh about. His phone rang, and he knew it would be Charlie. "Let's go." Preacher pulled out his phone and saw his wife's name. "Hey, sweetheart."

"Where are you? I thought you'd be down here, but you're not."

"I'm on my way with Arizona," he said, meeting his

sister's eye. She came to his side and linked her arm through his so they could step together. On the uneven ground, he was grateful for the steadying influence.

"Okay," Charlie said. "I need you here."

"I'm coming." The call ended, and Zona looked at him. He shouldered her eyes for as long as he could, and then asked, "What?"

"She needs you. You're not useless."

"I won't do anything," he said. "She'll ask me where I think the pictures should go and if I can feed Betty while she unpacks a box."

"Both of those are valuable things," Zona said.

"It doesn't feel like they are."

"There are different ways to be useful." Zona reached for the passenger door and opened it for him. "I've had to learn that, Preach. You being there for your wife is useful to her. Your presence is what she wants. Taking the baby? That's huge. Helping her hang the pictures makes her feel like you two are building your home together. Trust me, it's not all about hauling in a bed frame and hulking out by taking three boxes when you should take two."

He looked at his sister—really looked—and he felt and heard the wisdom in her voice. "Thank you, Zona," he said quietly as he gauged the step up into the truck.

"Duke, come help him."

"You got it." Duke jumped out from his side of the truck, and Preacher didn't mind so much that his brother-in-law put his hand on Preacher's right ribcage to steady him. "In? Up?"

Preacher used his left leg to step up first, relying on Duke to hold him on the right. With that up, he managed to slide in and sit in the passenger seat, and he let Duke close the door behind him while Zona climbed in the back.

Duke got behind the wheel again and flashed a smile toward Preacher. "Howdy, Preach," he said, and Preacher saw the lines of exhaustion around the man's eyes.

"Hi, Duke." His heart pinched for his sister and brother-in-law, and he wished he could make the hard things in their life easier. He really appreciated that Duke didn't ask him how he felt, or if he was okay.

Duke drove them all down the hill to the new farmhouse, where all of the trucks had parked. Preacher took his time getting out, and he took in the horizon. He loved it here, so close to family and yet so far away.

He let Duke and Arizona start to carry things inside while he limped over to a huge tree they hadn't taken out when they'd cleared the land. It made the new area of the ranch look old, and he leaned against the trunk and took in the scent of the bark, the grass, and the sunshine.

"Preacher."

He turned toward Ward's voice and found his cousin coming toward him. He worked closely with Ward around Shiloh Ridge, and he loved him a whole lot. "Hey, Ward."

"I'm sorry." He sighed as he came to stand beside Preacher. "Dot says I'm overprotective."

"It's fine." All the fight had left Preacher anyway. "I can't lift anything. I can't even walk."

"I can come take you to the barn and back every day," Ward said quietly, as he'd done exactly that in the early days of Preacher's recovery after his disastrous car accident.

"Charlie will make me do it," he said, smiling at his cousin.

"When she called…she was panicked, Preach. Maybe I panicked too."

"It's okay," Preacher said. "I can be a little stubborn sometimes."

"Are you kidding right now?" Ward grinned at him. "You? Stubborn? I don't believe it…."

They laughed together, the last of Preacher's dissatisfaction flying into the wide sky above. "All right," he said. "Enough feeling sorry for myself. My wife needs me to lay on the couch with our baby."

"You'll have to fight Montana for her. She says she's going to take Betty home with her tonight."

They walked back inside together, Ward taking the same slow, measured steps Preacher did. He'd done that before too, never making Preacher go faster than he wanted to. He did make him go, every day, and he had no doubt he'd be down here every single day if he had to be.

The activity inside the house nearly choked Preacher, but the moment his eyes met Charlie's, he settled. She came over to him and said, "Thanks, Ward. Can I steal him for a moment?"

"He's yours," Ward said. "No theft necessary." He

grinned at the two of them and left them standing near the back door.

Charlie met his eyes, and Preacher gave her a smile. "All right," he said. "I'm sorry I disappeared. Where do you need me?"

"I put a box right there," she said, indicating the untaped box sitting on the counter. "It's bowls and cups. I want them in the cupboard right above it."

"Yes, ma'am," he said, taking a limping step toward it.

"I set them all up like that," Charlie said, and Preacher looked down the counter, where four more boxes waited for him.

"I guess I should've embraced the idea of taking a nap on the couch with the baby."

Charlie smiled at him and pressed a kiss to his mouth. "Live and learn."

"Charlie," someone called. "Where do you want this desk?"

She looked at Judge and Bear, who currently struggled with the huge piece of furniture that usually held four computer screens. "The front room to the right, sweetheart?"

"Yes," Preacher said. "That's where your broadcast setup will be." She stepped away from him to direct the two men, who'd come further into the house than they needed to. She still did her morning broadcast for Nexus, and she still had a few partnerships. He loved playing video games with her, and he adored waking up with her to kiss at his side, and he marveled at her kindness in setting out boxes full of kitchenware so he could participate in their new life, in this new house.

He smiled to himself and started on the tasks she'd set for him, grateful for a good wife and a thoughtful sister. He'd just finished with the last box when Montana came into the kitchen with a fussy Betty.

"Preach," she said. "Your daughter needs you. We've got the nursery set up." She passed him the baby, and Preacher gazed down into his five-month-old's face. She had Charlie's light blue eyes, and absolutely no hair at all. He loved her with his whole soul, and he smiled at Betty.

"Was that code for *go rock your baby to sleep and take a nap*?" He looked around and didn't see anyone watching him. So he slipped out of the kitchen and down the hall to the second bedroom on this level. Sure enough, the crib had been set up and made up. The rocking chair had been placed beside it, as well as the changing table.

He sank into the chair, his hip firing pain through his leg and up into his back as he did. He groaned and panted, then as the pain subsided, he began to toe himself and baby Betty back and forth, back and forth, until they both fell asleep.

CHAPTER 30

Mister pulled up to the farmhouse a few hundred yards off the highway. He got out and looked back the way he'd come, expecting to hear more traffic noise. He couldn't, and for that he thanked the Lord. Preacher would've hated hearing cars and trucks drive by all the time.

He faced the house and started toward the steps, ready for his brother's attitude. Preacher had re-injured himself a couple of weeks ago, and all the reports from every family member who'd stopped by to check on him and Charlie had included his sour attitude at being checked on all the time.

Mister himself had been by several times, and he didn't feel bad about it. If he couldn't help his brother, who could he help?

He knocked on the door and twisted the knob at the same time. "It's me," he called as he entered. Preacher turned from the back wall of the house, a pitcher of lemonade in his hand. "Can I have some of that?"

"Sure," Preacher said, an actual smile on his face. He moved slowly still and watching him get up from a couch or sink into one was painful for Mister. He wanted to jump to his brother's aid, but he'd refrained. He'd restarted physical therapy, and this time, he'd added going to a chiropractor as part of his healing.

But it was slow, and that frustrated Preacher to no end. The man may be soft-spoken, but he wasn't slow, and he wanted his body to cooperate with him to get things done around the ranch.

Thankfully, now that it would be November in a couple of days, most of the harvesting was done. The cattle had been rounded up and returned to the ranch. A lot of them had been sold. Breeding happened in the spring, and as they moved into birthing season, there were plenty of men and women to help.

Preacher had been strictly forbidden from being out in the fields this winter by Bear, Ranger, and Ward, and when Mister had stopped by that day, it had been a Very Bad Time Indeed. Preacher had actually raised his voice, and there had been broken glass.

A dog trotted toward him, a big, black lab named Biscuit. Preacher had gotten him a week or so ago, and Biscuit helped Preacher get things he couldn't. Shoes, or towels off the floor. He could open doors too, and he could alert people if Preacher fell and needed help.

"Hey, buddy." Mister bent and gave the dog a cursory

pat before continuing into the kitchen. Biscuit led the way and went around to where Preacher still stood.

"Are you ready for this?" Mister asked as he pulled out a barstool and sat at the island separating the kitchen at the back of the house from the living room at the front.

"Not really," Preacher admitted. "You?" He poured Mister's lemonade and pushed it closer to him.

Mister reached the rest of the way for it. "I don't know. You know more than I do about the family meeting."

"Nothing major this year," Preacher said. "The annual report. Who we're investing in. That kind of thing." He took a drink of his lemonade. "Did you prep Libby for it?"

Mister's taste buds constricted at the sourness of the lemonade, but it sure tasted like summer and happiness. "All prepped."

Preacher nodded, and while he wasn't the Glover who normally pried into relationships, he asked, "How are things going with her?"

"Good," Mister said, his voice too high and too false.

Preacher's eyebrows went up, the silent questions firing at Mister.

"Really," Mister said with a laugh. "I may or may not have told her I loved her a couple of weeks ago, that's all."

"That's all?" Preacher sounded like he'd sucked in some helium. "That's *huge*, Mister."

"She said it back." Mister grinned just thinking about it. "We've been talking about getting married."

"You're kidding."

"Why are you so shocked?"

"I don't know," Preacher admitted, his eyes returning to a normal size. "I guess I just thought…I don't know what I thought." He smiled at Mister. "That's great."

Mister had thought so too, but Preacher's reaction sent a boatload of doubt through him. Did he really love Libby? Why was it so shocking that she loved him too?

It's just history, he told himself. He and Libby hadn't had the best of relationships for a while there before he'd left for Winterhaven. That was all.

Mister finished his lemonade and stood up. "All right. I'm supposed to get you up there for your pre-meeting meeting. Then I have to go get Libs."

"I can get myself up to the homestead," Preacher said, frowning.

"Right, sure," Mister said. "I'm on my way up anyway is all."

Preacher glared at him, and Mister gazed right on back. "Who asked you to take me?"

"I don't want to say."

Preacher folded his arms, and when he cocked his hip, a flash of pain stole across his face. "Was it Bear?"

"No."

"Ward?"

"No."

"You know I can tell when you're lying."

"It was your wife," Mister admitted. "Okay? Is it so bad that she's worried about you? Or that I am? Or Bear?" He wouldn't want anyone fussing over him either, but Preacher needed to accept that it was going to happen. "I was up at the homestead already, and she's up there helping Holly Ann and Montana with the rolls. She asked me to come get you and bring you up, because—she said—you're not supposed to drive."

"I was going to take the ATV."

"Fine," Mister said. "Take it." He'd just follow him up to make sure he got to the homestead okay. He didn't want the wrath of Charlie on him if her husband didn't get to the homestead in one piece, with as little pain as possible.

"You'll just follow me up like a stalker."

"Have you met your wife?" Mister teased. "I don't want to be on her bad side. Then she won't let me come babysit Betty."

Preacher rolled his eyes. "You've come once."

"And I liked it," he said. "Let's get going. I don't want to be late to get Libby."

"Fine." Preacher took a moment to put the pitcher of lemonade in the fridge, and then he followed Mister out to the front porch. Mister didn't hover behind him or to the side of him. He led the way, just like he would've had Preacher been just fine. He knew he wasn't, but he also knew how fiercely independent Preacher wanted to be.

"You can get in?" Mister owned a massive truck, and even he had to vault into it at times.

"I doubt it," Preacher muttered. "I really can take the ATV. It's not hard."

"I told you to take it then," Mister said. "I'll just follow at a distance to make sure you're okay. Biscuit can ride with me."

Preacher paused at the front of the truck, having made it down the steps by going slow and holding onto the railing. "Will you really let me?"

"Sure."

"Go with Mister, Biscuit." He nodded and started for the shed across the road from the house.

Mister opened the back door of his king-cab for Biscuit, and to his surprise, the dog jumped in without help. Then Mister got behind the wheel, thought about sending Charlie a text to make sure Preacher could drive the ATV, and changed his mind. Preacher was a grown man. He'd probably been driving the ATV up to the ranch since his accident.

His brother backed out of the shed and started forward easily. He looked confident and perfectly comfortable on the ATV, and Mister gave him a few seconds before he rounded the circular driveway and followed him.

Preacher arrived without incident, and Mister let Biscuit out of the back seat. Preacher whistled as he went up the sidewalk toward the house, and the dog ran to his side while Mister waved to both of them.

Twenty minutes later, he pulled up to Libby's red house to find her sitting on the front steps with Franklin. "Hey," he said as he got out.

She stood and dusted off her pants. "Stay here, Frankie. Do you want to go in?" The golden retriever's tail whapped the porch when he saw Mister, and he chuckled as he went up the steps to give him a pat.

"Hey, boy. You better get inside. It's supposed to rain today."

"Come on, Frankie," Libby said, moving to open the door. The dog got up and trotted inside, and Libby closed the door behind him.

"Hey," he said again, standing down a couple of steps as she approached. He took her into his arms, and she stood as tall as him while she stayed on the porch. He leaned in to kiss her, enjoying the sensation of her fingernails through his hair, and the way she kissed him back.

He broke the kiss and breathed in, keeping her safely and steadily in his arms. "You ready for this?"

"I've been to plenty of Glover family things," she said. "I know how many of you there are."

"This'll be different," he said.

"How so?"

Mister pulled away and reached for his cowboy hat, which had fallen to the porch. "I don't know, Libs. It just will be." He reached for her hand and led her to the truck. "My family isn't subtle, that's for sure. There will probably be oh, half a dozen people who will ask you about us."

"What have you told them?"

"Very little," he said as he opened the passenger door of his truck for her.

Her dark eyes met his. "Very little?"

"They know we're dating," he said. "Other than that...I live with Ranger, and he doesn't ask questions. Bear and

Sammy know the most probably. Preacher." He cleared his throat. "I told Preacher today that we were talking about getting married. He's the only one I've told that to."

Libby nodded and climbed into the truck. When she faced him again, she wore a beautiful smile to go with her bright yellow sweater and blue jeans. She took his breath away no matter what she wore, because he liked so much more than what Libby presented on the outside.

He couldn't believe he'd made it this far in a relationship with her, and he thanked the Lord he had as he rounded the truck and got behind the wheel.

The radio kept them company on the drive up to Shiloh Ridge, and Mister's nerves multiplied with every minute and every mile. He wasn't sure why. Libby had been up to Shiloh Ridge lots of times. She'd come to family parties before. Weddings. New Year's Eve celebrations.

For some reason, Mister felt differently about her coming to the annual family meeting and angel tree celebration, and when he pulled up to the homestead, he blew out a long sigh. "All right. I can already hear the noise."

Libby giggled and got out of the truck, and he joined their hands again when he met her at the hood.

Inside the homestead, Zona and Sammy worked to set up the tree. "Mister," they said at the same time, both of them automatically moving their eyes to Libby too. "Libby," Sammy said, abandoning the branch she'd been fanning out. "Hello. Welcome."

"Thanks, Sammy," Libby said. She stepped back, her

smile as radiant and as beautiful as always. "This is the angel tree, huh?"

"Yeah," Mister said. "So we know it's kind of crazy to set up a Christmas tree in October, but that's when my daddy died. So we do the last Sunday of the month, and we leave it up for a couple of months."

"It's a good reminder for everyone who walks into the homestead," Zona said, still pulling on branches this way and that. "To be reminded of our ancestors, and all the Glovers, and to feel like they're watching over us. At least for me."

"Mm." Mister smiled at his sister. He'd never had any problems with Arizona, but he also wasn't really close with her either. He should probably do something about that, but he had so many other things he was still working on.

"For me," Sammy said. "It's a welcoming light to the family, since I'm not a Glover by birth. Doing this—decorating the tree and putting up ornaments for *my* loved ones—reminds me of them, and how they're part of me, and that we're all part of the traditions here at the ranch."

"Like you belong," Libby said, her voice barely loud enough to meet Mister's ears.

He looked at her, surprised she needed to feel like she belonged. To him, she already did—on her ranch, and on his.

"Yes." Sammy gave her another smile and returned to her task of making the false Christmas tree look as real as possible. "Like I belong. When Bear brought me to this for the first time, I really felt like I belonged. Me and Lincoln. It was really nice."

"He's here," someone said, interrupting the moment. Mister turned toward Cactus, who came out into the foyer with his little girl, Lynn. "We're just waitin' on you, Mister."

"Really?" he asked. "Everyone else is here?" He hadn't thought he was late; the tree wasn't even set up yet.

"Yep." Cactus took him into a hug, and then did the same to Libby, who gave a slight grunt of surprise. Mister sure did feel it running through him, because Cactus had traditionally been the prickly brother.

"Heya, Lynnie," Mister said, taking the four-year-old's hand. "Did you get any of the Boston cream cake?"

"No, sir," she said.

"Ida said not until after dinner," Cactus said.

"Come with me," Mister said, leading the girl into the kitchen. He reached back for Libby too, glad when she darted forward and took his remaining free hand. "I know how to sneak past Ida."

"Mister," Cactus warned, but he just kept going into the kitchen. Ida wasn't even in the area between the island and the rest of the kitchen appliances and counter space, and Mister scooped Lynn into his arms.

Etta smiled at him, and he stepped past her to the sink. "You need a drink, baby?"

"No, sir," she said, and he chuckled as he turned on the water.

"I do." He filled a glass but didn't take a drink. He

side-stepped over to the desserts, hearing Libby's giggle amidst all of the talking and other laughter the Glovers put out. The cake hadn't been touched, and he didn't think he could mar it without getting caught.

But he'd made it past Ida.

"Can we have cake first?" he asked, and that somehow drew everyone's attention.

"If you touch that cake, I'll rearrange your face," Bishop said, lurching up from where he sat at the long picnic-style table in the dining room.

"Don't you dare," Ida said from across the room.

"No, we're not having cake first," Holly Ann said.

"Get out of the kitchen, Mister," Montana said.

"All right, all right," he said, laughing. He looked at Lynn. "We made it past Auntie Ida. If I hadn't said anything, she would've never known."

"I would've known," Ida said, arriving on the scene. "The moment I'd have seen a piece missing, I would've known it was you." She gave him a smile and took the little girl from him. "The kids can have a cookie before dinner. You better ask your mama first." She set Lynn down, and she scampered over to Willa.

Ida gave him another mock glare and then turned to Libby. "Hi, Libby. It's so good to see you." She hugged her, and Mister watched Libby's eyes close for a moment, her smile bright and wide.

"Good to see you too, Ida."

Ida linked her arm through Libby's and started around

the back of the couch. "You tell me the truth: How are things with my dear cousin?"

"Here we go," Mister said, glancing at Bishop. Libby had thought he'd been kidding about the questions. He hadn't been.

Bear got up from the table too and nodded at Judge. "All right," he said. "We're all here, so let's get started while the cakes are still intact."

"I didn't even touch them," Mister called.

Libby had been taken to a couch, and he went into the living room too. Judge obviously had a presentation set up for the television hanging above the mantle. He squeezed into a spot between Libby and Ace, glancing at his cousin. He took Gun from him and said, "Hey, baby boy."

"Mis-Mis," Gun said, and Mister laughed at the attempt to say his name. He looked past the boy to Ace. "He's going to say it soon."

"He can say his name," Holly Ann said from Ace's other side. "Gunny, tell Uncle Mister what your name is?"

"What's your name, bud?" Ace prompted.

Gun looked at him with wide, deep brown eyes. "What's your name?" his dad asked again.

"Gun," Gunnar said, and Mister squeezed him tight.

"That's right, buddy," he said. "You're so smart. *So* smart."

"Where's Cactus?" Bear asked, cutting through the chatter that had picked up again.

"Right here," he said, entering the living area.

"You're doing the charity this year."

"Right." He drew in a breath as the television came to life. "Everyone knows Willa and I became foster parents this year, so for our charity donation, the ranch is giving twenty thousand dollars to the Foster Care Parent Support Center. It's privately run here in Three Rivers, with another office in Amarillo. The money will stay here in the Panhandle, to help people like me and Willa be better at handling the challenges and caring for the children we get to have in our lives."

The screen switched, and Preacher said, "We sold one hundred and ninety four cows this year. With half of that money made, Shiloh Ridge is going to invest in boxcars."

Boxcars? Mister thought, glancing at Ranger and Ward. The two brothers did a ton of the investing and financial matters around the ranch, and Ranger had a degree in accounting.

"They're a preferred stock that pays every month," Ranger said. "No one thinks about how goods are moved around this country, but a lot of it is done by train. There's always the need for more and newer boxcars, and it's one of the most stable stocks there is."

"Any other news?" Bear asked, and Mister noted that Judge sat down at the piano.

Ace raised his hand. "Holly Ann and I are going to have another baby."

Judge immediately began to play the little diddy that their dad had introduced decades ago. Beside him, Libby turned her attention to him, and he realized he hadn't prepped her for this.

There was no time now.

Everyone in the room burst out with, "Hey, howdy, ho, it's your lucky day today. It's your *lucky* day today! Congrats to you, because it's your lucky day to-day!"

Mister sang along with all of them, and several people burst out laughing afterward.

Libby looked like she'd been hit with a two-by-four, and Mister kept laughing and put his arm around her. "Sorry, sweetheart. I forgot about this part."

"That was…something else."

"Family tradition," he said.

"You have a lot of those."

"Not a ton," he said. "But some. Do you have any?"

"Ward's going to pray," Bear said, and Libby couldn't answer. The way she kept looking around at everyone like they'd grown horns didn't comfort Mister, and after the prayer, he stayed right where he was on the couch, though he was usually one of the ones at the front of the line.

"Libs?"

"Not like this," she said.

"Your daddy makes that spitted pig."

"Yeah," she said, and she stood up. "But it's not like this." She didn't sound happy, and Mister wondered why. When he stood and looked at her again, she wore a smile on her face, and he didn't know what else to say.

So he got in line behind her, groaning when Willa asked, "How are you getting along with Mister, Libby?"

"I'm right here," Mister said.

Willa smiled sweetly at him. "I know."

CHAPTER 31

*L*ibby laughed along with Charlie and Dot, and she bounced baby Betty on her lap while she did. It seemed like no one was in a great rush to get up from the table, and Libby didn't know what came next anyway.

Mister had told her the family meeting would be boring, though sometimes they got to vote on something or have a discussion. He'd admitted that he'd video-called in last year, and the family hadn't really done anything.

Libby hadn't minded, because the act of gathering together and going over things brought this family together. She'd never done anything like that with her family. Judge had flashed figures for the year up on the screen, so every Glover knew what they were doing on the ranch. Libby had no idea how much money Golden Hour made. She helped with the round-up, but she didn't know how many cows her father had sold, or what they did with the money.

She'd never really had a need to. She had a comfortable place to live, which she didn't pay a mortgage for. She paid utilities, and that was all. She had to pay for her car, but she drove an old pick-up that had been paid for long ago.

She didn't hurt for money, but the Bellamores weren't anything like the Glovers. Mister had a ton of money, Libby knew that. It wasn't something she'd ever thought much about, and she didn't now—other than it had become apparent how open the Glovers were with their ranch finances.

Everything they did was new for Libby. Sure, her family had a couple of traditions, and they got together for holidays. It simply didn't feel anything like what Libby was currently experiencing. Charlie and Dot had immediately added her to their fold, and June, Sammy, and Willa had spent most of the meal asking her questions about Mister.

What their dates had been like, where he'd taken her, what they did at her place in the evenings. Oakley had finally told them to leave her alone, but that only allowed Montana and Holly Ann to steal her away for a few minutes of tree branch fluffing in the lobby.

"Are we ready?" Ranger asked, standing up. "Come on, Mother," he added. "Everyone, we're moving into the foyer for the angel tree decorating."

Libby passed Betty to her mother, and she stood, looking around for Mister. He'd filled a paper plate with every dessert available, and when she found him sitting in the living room with Preacher, Judge, Ace, and Duke, the plate was empty.

She shook her head as he handed it to her, his own grin matching hers. "I can't believe you ate all of that."

"He's got a hollow leg," Ace said, standing and then extending his hand to help Mister off the couch too. "He once won a hot dog eating contest." Ace smiled at her, his dark eyes all lit up. "Has he told you that story?"

"She was there," Mister said. "We're the same age in school."

"I've seen the man eat," Libby said, though she had forgotten about the hot dog eating contest he'd won during Homecoming week of their senior year in high school. She stayed out of the way as moms, dads, and children streamed past her to get into the foyer. Only with Mister at her side did she go through the arched doorway.

They stopped near the back, which made Libby happy, and she shuffled to the side a little bit so she could see Bear and Ranger, who stood shoulder-to-shoulder near the tree.

"Welcome, everyone," Bear said, and he looked at Ranger.

"Most of us are familiar with the angel tree celebration," Ranger said. "Zona's got all of Grandmother's ornaments up here. The past couple of years we've had people share what the angel tree means to them, and to kind of go along with that, this year, Bear and I thought it might be nice to get a generational perspective." He smiled out at the crowd. "I asked my mother to say a few words about Daddy, or her parents, or whatever she wants really."

"Then my mother is going to say a few words," Bear said. "Then we'll open it up for decorating."

"And there's more cake," Ranger said, gesturing back toward the kitchen. A few people chuckled, but Libby wasn't one of them. Mister had told her about the angel tree celebration, but he wouldn't tell her what ornaments he always looked for to hang for his father or grandmother. She couldn't wait to find out.

Dawna Glover stepped out of the crowd, and Ranger tucked her arm through his and stayed right beside her while Bear went to stand with his family.

Libby searched for Mister's hand and found it easily, squeezing tightly once her fingers were through his. He edged closer to her, and she liked his strength and solidity behind her.

"Coming to the Glover family was quite different for me than it has been for all of you," Dawna said, her voice a touch feeble and barely able to fill the foyer. "For one, Bull only had one brother. He'd married Lois already, but it was just the two of them, and two little boys. Lois and I shared several months of pregnancy when I had Richard and she had John.

"Bull's parents lived in what we now call the Ranch House, and Priscilla had a hand in everything around Shiloh Ridge. She could bake the best apple turnovers in the morning and go out and wrangle cattle in the afternoon. She loved her boys and her grandchildren with a power I've tried to conjure up myself. I've since learned that she was simply a special woman, and no one can do what she did.

"I hang a three-dimensional Christmas tree for her every year," Dawna said, her voice breaking. "She was the spirit of Christmas to me. She brought the party and the love and the example of Christ everywhere with her, and I love this angel tree, because it helps me remember her, the good times we had, and how very wonderful our family is."

When she didn't continue, Ranger nodded, and eased into the crowd with her.

Mister's mother stepped to the front of the crowd all alone. She didn't seem nearly as weak as Dawna, and her eyes burned like blue, blue fire. "Grandmother Priscilla would be thrilled to see all of you here." Her voice cracked, and she pressed one hand to her heart and took several long seconds to compose herself.

Libby's heart pounded through her chest, especially when she heard others sniffling too.

"I wish more of you could've known her," Lois said. "I think the men and women who did are doing a good job telling their spouses and children about her. About their fathers. About the tradition of greatness we have here at Shiloh Ridge. I came here as a very young woman, barely out of high school. I had no idea what I was doing, but I dug in and I worked.

"Priscilla taught me that, as did Grandfather. My very best friend in the world became Dawna, and there's no way I would've survived my boys in their teens without her and Priscilla, who would take them when I wanted to kick them out. She'd bake them pizzas and love them for who they were at that moment, and that was such a marvel to me.

"Now, watching all of you with your children and your problems, I understand the level of joy and love she must've received and felt from the grandkids, whether they were being brats or not." She gave a light chuckle, as did a few others.

Beside Libby, Mister reached up and wiped his eyes, and she turned toward him. She'd never seen him cry, save for one time. When his femur had been broken right in half, he'd cried. During some parts of that recovery, he'd shed a few tears, mostly from the pain he'd endured.

This was a different kind of tear, and he offered her a smile before he pressed a kiss to her forehead. He morphed right in front her, all over again, and Libby adored this tender side of him that he kept hidden.

"Anyway, I hang a bell for Priscilla and a horseshoe for Ranza, because she brought me into this family by serving me meals and taking my children, all of which started with a bell. Either a dinner bell, which she used to stand on the porch and ring, or with a telephone call, which is a type of bell. Ranza taught me how to make and throw horseshoes, and I'm still one of the best in this family." She beamed out at the group, practically challenging anyone to disagree with her.

A few scoffs and scattered laughs moved through the crowd, but no one contradicted her.

"For my dear Stone, whom I miss daily, I hang a pair of turtle doves, because they symbolize love and faithfulness. The turtle doves mate for life, and Priscilla gave us a lesson one Christmas about how the birds work together to build nests and raise their young together.

"I wanted that togetherness with Stone, and we worked hard for it. This ranch is our nest, and I'm so thankful and so blessed to see all of you living here, building your own smaller nests, and raising your own children together. Thank you for making time to come to this each year, and I hope it'll continue to be a tradition for generations to come."

Lois moved back to her spot beside her husband, and Cactus moved forward to get an ornament out of the box. Several others did too, and Libby basked in the sweet, peaceful, reverent silence that filled the homestead now.

She had no idea the Glovers could be this quiet, and while there were a few whispers, and the shuffling of feet and the movement of branches, that was all. Even the children seemed to know that they just needed to find their ornament and hang it.

"So you can pick any one you want," Mister said quietly as they got closer to the tree and the boxes beyond it. "Most people who have favorites have selected them by now."

"I have no idea what to put up," Libby said, waiting for him to go first. He moved down to a box on the end and crouched in front of it. He didn't have to look long to find what he wanted, and he straightened with a miniature version of a horse in his hand. It was crocheted with snowy white thread, but it still looked majestic and regal.

"I asked Grandmother to make this for me," Mister said. "I was maybe ten, and I had these big dreams of being in the rodeo." He grinned at the horse. "She told me she would make something, but it wasn't going to be one of 'those awful bulls.'" His smile drooped slightly. "She loved horses, and she made this. I hang it every year for her."

Libby watched him step over to the flocked Christmas tree and find a spot for the equine. "So I just pick whatever I want?"

"Yes," he said. "Some people choose things that mean something to them personally." He touched a car. "I think Oakley hangs this. Bear has a teddy bear he puts up for Grandmother every year."

"You can remember anyone," Dot said. "A family member you've lost. Someone you're thinking about."

"I hang one for my sister," Charlie said. "I don't get to see her very much."

"I do the same with my parents," Oakley said, and she moved over to the tree with a reindeer and a star.

"She seemed to know who would be in the family," June said. "I found this old TV last year, and it just felt like it was for me." She held up the ornament, her smile so honest and so open.

Libby bent and looked in the box where Mister had

taken his ornament. She didn't know what meant something to her. She was a simple cowgirl from Texas. She'd grown up in Three Rivers, still lived in Three Rivers, and wanted to die in Three Rivers.

She had no special skills. She hadn't won any racecar driving events. She didn't own a landscape company, and she had no idea what to do when her WiFi went out.

What would Priscilla Glover have made for someone like her?

She poked through the stars, the sleighs, and the snowflakes. She loved the Texas landscape, a good sunset glowing over the land, and feeling the sunshine on her skin. She loved Christmas—everything about it, from the music, to the food, to the treats, to the decorations.

She loved her family, and she loved putting on the Country Christmas.

After edging aside a tiny little drum, her eyes landed on a flatter ornament. They were all made of the same white thread, though some of the ornaments were definitely older than others. They'd aged into a yellowish color.

Not the one Libby pulled out. It was the shape of Texas, with a tiny, red heart stitched up in the Panhandle, right where Three Rivers sat on the map.

She could only stare at it, and after Mister had hung his last ornament, he came back to her. "Libs," he said. "That's perfect for you."

She looked up at him, tears pricking her eyes. "It seems to be, doesn't it?"

"It's Three Rivers, Texas," he said. "Which is everything you love." He smiled at her with such warmth and such softness, revealing yet another part of him she hadn't seen much of. He nodded toward the tree, and Libby stepped over to it and hung the Texas ornament on a branch.

She moved back and admired it. Someone flipped off the overhead lights, and only the angel tree put off the soft glow from its all-white lights, making Libby feel the magic of this ranch, these people, and this tree.

The magic of history.

The magic of belonging to something bigger and better than herself.

The magic of the Glovers.

"Silent night," a man started to sing in a rich, deep bass voice. A higher soprano joined him on the next words, and then the whole family came in with Cactus and Willa.

Libby sang along too, the prayer in her voice and in her heart one of pure gratitude that the Lord had allowed her to get out of her own way and allow Mister Glover a place in her heart and in her life.

$\mathcal{M}$ister's phone chimed several times in a row as he drove back to Shiloh Ridge, sending a double shot of anxiety through him. He knew better than to text and drive, but he hated knowing someone had texted him and he couldn't answer.

Especially so many times in a row. One more came in, and Mister grumbled, "If it's that important, they'll call," to himself. With the arrival of November, the sun set earlier, and darkness had already fallen over Three Rivers.

He wasn't going to take an unnecessary risk and look at his bright phone. He wasn't.

No one texted again, and no one called, before he turned onto the road that led up to the homestead. He pulled over across the lane from Preacher's house and put the truck in park. Only then did he allow himself to look at his phone.

Etta had texted five times, and Mister frowned. His

heartbeat also plummeted toward his boots and back to its rightful spot in his chest. She'd agreed to a date with August Winters, and Mister was the only one who knew the man's name. He'd been up late one night while Etta sat in the dark living room, curled into the couch, texting him. He'd seen the name on her phone, and she'd sworn him to secrecy.

Tonight was their first date, and she'd told Mister she might need help getting out of it early. He quickly swiped to get to the messages, hurrying to calculate how long it had been since she'd sent them.

Doing great, the first one read. *Don't panic.*

His muscles released, and he kept reading.

Thanks for suggesting the Ponderosa. It's gorgeous here, and I'm having a good time.

But…

I think Libby might be here.

His anxiety came roaring back. He hadn't been at Libby's tonight, because Dave had decided he wanted to make the move to Three Rivers permanent. He was back in town for a few days, looking at houses, and he and Mister had gotten together for burgers and drinks. Dave actually drank, but Mister didn't.

He'd given up the stuff ages ago, after his one and only drinking experience that had not ended well for him. He didn't like feeling out of control and wild, and riding bulls and broncs had been enough of a high for him.

The last text was a picture, and it took its sweet time

coming through. When it finally did, Mister definitely saw Libby sitting in a booth with another man.

Mister pulled in a breath, his mind racing. How many times had he been busy in the evenings? With Bear, or Dave, or Cactus and his kids?

Not that many, but several.

He'd thought Libby had stayed home on those evenings. She'd told him she had, but he was looking at proof that she didn't.

She was out right now.

"Well, ten minutes ago," he muttered.

I thought you said not to panic, he typed out and sent to Etta. What did she think that picture would do to him? Send him into a fantasy where he walked through a meadow and admired hummingbirds?

He tapped on the picture again and zoomed in, trying to get a better look at the guy. He couldn't tell who it was, and it wasn't like Mister knew every single man in town. He did know how to swing his truck around, and he did that.

He drove over to Golden Hour, where he'd already been once today. Just like usual, he'd come down from the hills and Shiloh Ridge in the afternoon, and today, he'd helped Libby set up their third biggest Christmas tree—a twelve-footer—and decorate it from top to bottom and side to side.

That sounded like an easy task, but it had taken hours, with lots of little baubles and three strings of lights that didn't work before they found one that did. He'd been up and down on a ladder, and he'd laughed at Frankie as the dog had demonstrated how he could climb ladders too.

He'd kissed Libby good-bye while she was still out at the Country Christmas site, and he'd headed to town to meet Dave.

His headlights cut a swath through the darkness as he turned onto the dirt road that marked the entrance to Golden Hour, and not thirty seconds later, he pulled up to Libby's house.

Her dark, no-truck-parked-outside house. No one had texted him, and Mister's pulse hummed beneath his skin as he thought about what to do.

Text her, came into his mind, but Mister pushed against it. Wasn't he the one who'd asked Libby if she trusted him or not? Didn't he trust her?

He could simply say that he'd gotten done early, and he'd stopped by and she wasn't home. He quickly typed out, *Where are you? I dropped by, and your house is dark. Maybe you're in bed.*

Before he could think too hard about it, he sent the text. He looked up and out the windshield, trying to see something on the exterior of the house. What, he didn't know. He hated the way his stomach felt, too full and too big inside his body. He hated this waiting. He hated the things stirring through his mind—all the things he'd say to her if she was cheating on him.

"She can't," he murmured to himself. "She wouldn't."

What did it say about him that he thought she might? He swallowed, trying to reason through his feelings. He'd fallen in love with Libby, and he couldn't stand the thought of not being with her. He could see their whole future right there in his headlights, and he wanted the marriage with her. The house, the kids, the ranch, the Country Christmas.

His phone chimed, and he dang near dove for it. *I went out with Scott's brother,* Libby had said. *I'll be home in fifteen minutes if you want to wait. I have leftover cake.*

She'd included a smiley emoji, but Mister's emotions thundered and lightninged through his body. She'd admitted to going out with someone else?

He tapped to call her, and her line only rang once before she answered. "Hey," she said in an upbeat voice. "I'm stuffed. You can have all of the cake."

"I don't want the cake," he said, his voice too rough and too bark-like.

Libby didn't say anything for a few seconds. "Okay," she said.

"Why were you out with Scott's brother?"

"His birthday is coming up, and Hyrum wants to do a big surprise thing for him," Libby said, her voice smaller and more wounded than it had been before.

Mister immediately kicked himself for thinking anything different. He hated that he'd made her feel anything but amazing and wonderful. "Oh."

"What did you think?"

"Nothing," he said, clearing his throat.

"Were you jealous?" Libby teased, and Mister pressed his eyes closed. Was he ready to marry Libby if he didn't even trust her? *Why* didn't he trust her? She'd given him absolutely no reason not to.

This is another flaw within you, he thought, and Mister was so tired of them manifesting themselves. This past year and a half had been difficult enough, and he'd just gotten comfortable with looking at himself in the mirror and feeling like he was doing okay.

Okay with his family. Okay with Libby. Okay with the Lord.

"I thought you might be cheating on me," he said as honestly as he could. The raw emotion in his voice nearly deafened him. "I'm sorry, Libs. I don't know why I thought that. It's really stupid, and yeah. I'm sorry."

Libby didn't say anything, and Mister wished this silence didn't carry so much weight, so much accusation, so much danger.

"When you first told me you loved me, it was very hard for me to believe," she said, her voice about half the volume it had just been. "I questioned it, the way I question everything. But I decided to simply believe it, because you've been my best friend for so long, and I know you wouldn't lie to me."

"I didn't lie to you." Even just now, he'd told her what he'd really been thinking.

"You don't trust me."

"I do," Mister said quickly. "Etta just sent me a picture, and I didn't know who that other man was, so I came over here—" He cut off, realizing how many mistakes he'd just made far too late.

"So you didn't just drop by."

"I—" He swallowed, everything changing in an instant.

"Etta sent you a picture?"

"I guess the two of you were at the same place," he said, pressing his eyes closed. "And no, I didn't drop by. I mean, I guess I did. But I was almost home when I got Etta's texts, and I came over to your place to see if you were home."

"Because you don't trust me."

"I do," he said. "I guess it was a moment of weakness I should've worked through on my own." Mister regretted everything that had happened in the past half-hour. "I'm just going to go. I know you like your leftover cake for breakfast in the morning." He put his truck in reverse and backed away from her house. With any luck, he could get out of here before she arrived.

"I'm sorry, Libby," he said.

"It's fine."

"I'll see you tomorrow?"

"It's Sunday."

"At church."

"I...think I'll sit by myself if that's okay."

"Libs."

"You got to sit by yourself when you needed space and time to think."

Mister held back his sigh, and when he reached the road, he didn't turn left to get back to Shiloh Ridge. He went straight, because that would ensure that he wouldn't run into Libby or pass her as she went home.

"You're right," he said with as much control as he could muster. "I did. So I'll see you Monday."

"Okay," she said, her voice about the temperature of a glacier. "See you then."

The call ended before Mister could say good-bye. Before he could apologize again. Before he could even take a breath.

He did let his sigh out then, but it wasn't aimed at Libby. No, this was all frustration and loathing for himself.

"What does she say?" Etta asked, tipping the bowl with the eggs she'd cracked into the bigger mixing bowl.

Mister ran his hands through his hair, wishing he was anywhere else besides sitting at the counter at the homestead while Etta made pancakes at three o'clock in the afternoon. "Today, she said she didn't need me to come, because she's just making phone calls."

He exhaled and looked up at Etta, everything in him so tired. "I've sat with her while she's answered emails and made calls before. Yesterday, she said I didn't need to come, because Jack had come to help her with the lights on the barn. The day before that it was Cord who'd helped her get the huge pine tree at the entrance of the Country Christmas decorated."

She'd said she and Cord had done it in the morning, to make use of the cooler hours of the day. That made zero sense, because the temperatures weren't getting nearly up to where they were in the summertime, and it had been overcast and cool all day a couple of days ago.

"She's dodging you," Etta said. "I'm so sorry, Mister. This is all my fault." She paused in her preparation of the batter, a desperate look on her face. "Of course I should've assumed Libby would be out with someone for an innocent reason."

"It's not your fault," he said with a sigh. He got up from the barstool and went over to one of the couches. He lay down on it, more breath expelling from his body. "At what point do I just go down there even if she doesn't want to see me?"

"I've had men cheat on me," Etta said. "I know it's not healthy, but that's immediately where my mind went." She followed him into the living room and perched on the end of the couch adjacent to him. "I'm so, so sorry. Maybe I should talk to her."

"I don't think that's a good idea," Mister said. She'd once said she thought they could make a marriage work. "We can work through this."

"Does Libby usually get upset and stay that way for a long time?"

"No," Mister said, his mind working hard. "She doesn't."

"How does she get over things?"

He sat up, his brain sparking with electricity now. "I take her something good to eat, and we hash it all out."

Etta smiled at him. "Why are you still sitting here then?"

"Because I'm stupid," Mister said. "Do I just go up to the door and yell that to her? I'm so stupid and I'm so sorry, and please forgive me?"

"Something like that," Etta said. "But I don't think any woman wants to be yelled at." She kept her smile in place.

Mister blinked, trying to get a plan made when he really just wanted to go down to Libby's house and beg her to forgive him.

"She loves the sweets at Blox," he mused. "And they're only open on weekends."

"Then we have two more days to make an amazing plan." Etta got to her feet. "I'll get the pancakes going. How does Libby feel about posters?"

"Posters?"

"I'm *really* good at making posters," Etta said. "We could easily do an amazing I'm-so-sorry-please-forgive-me-I-love-you poster…just saying."

Mister grinned at his cousin even as he shook his head. "I don't think Libby would go crazy for a poster, but she does love a good country song…."

"Let's get Ward and Cactus over here," Etta said. "I'm sure they could help with that."

CHAPTER 33

*L*ibby felt like crying as she looked at the big barn where they fed the guests who came to the Country Christmas. She'd managed to string some of the lights on the rain gutters and around the double-wide door, but she didn't trust herself to get up on a ladder or a roof.

She sniffed, pulling back on her emotions. She couldn't do this alone, and she wanted to call Mister and ask him to please, please come help her.

"You lied to him," she murmured to herself. She'd told him one of her brothers had come to help her get the barn lights up, and the other had helped decorate the large pine that acted as their main Christmas tree.

Neither were true, and both jobs sat in half-completion. "If that," she said, sighing as she turned away from the barn. She hadn't told anyone what had happened last weekend, because Mildred didn't live on the ranch anymore, and she was busy with her new husband. She came to Golden Hour every day, and she'd said nothing about Mister's sudden absence in the afternoons.

Libby's brothers had jobs of their own to do, and neither of them had the time or patience to come string Christmas lights or weave bows through boughs. Once again, a ladder was required to finish the big pine tree, and Libby wasn't even sure she could carry it.

Maybe she could hire someone to come get those jobs done. The moment she entered the smaller barn, she saw the giant wreath which had been delivered yesterday morning. She lost the fight against the tears then.

She loved hanging the wreath over the archway of the ranch, and that had traditionally been her absolute favorite part of getting ready for the Country Christmas event. That wreath welcomed everyone to the ranch as the first sign of the festival, though the lights in the arena could be seen from the highway.

And she'd stuffed the wreath here in the barn. She couldn't hang it herself. Usually, she, Mildred, and one of her brothers wrangled with it until it hung precisely where Libby wanted it, but she hadn't been able to bring herself to ask anyone to come help.

She wanted *Mister* to help her.

Reaching up, she wiped her eyes and continued past the wreath. She needed something that wouldn't remind her of Mister. But the space outside the office reeked of his cologne. It was where she'd stood, talking to him on the phone, when he'd said he loved her for the first time.

The doorway was where he'd leaned when he'd showed up after saying those words, and where she'd whispered them back.

She couldn't go home, as Mister had touched every surface in her house. He was simply *everywhere*, and Libby collapsed into the desk chair and cradled her head in her hands as she cried.

That episode only lasted for a few minutes, and then she drew in a deep breath and reached for a tissue. She wiped her eyes and blew her nose, straightening her shoulders. "Okay, enough," she told herself. "Either call him and tell him everything, or figure out how to get this job done."

She wasn't sure what she'd expected from him. She was the one who'd sent him messages about how she didn't need him to come to the ranch, and he hadn't come. For five days, he hadn't come.

She would've been angry had he ignored her and shown up anyway. And yet, there she sat, angry he hadn't ignored her and shown up anyway.

Nothing made sense. She loved Mister Glover—she had last year when he'd left town, and she did now. But she wanted someone who trusted her, and she wished on every star in the great state of Texas that she didn't know he'd immediately jumped to the conclusion that she was sneaking around with someone else behind his back. She wished she hadn't told him she'd struggled to believe he loved her.

Libby wiped her palms down her thighs and looked up to the ceiling. "What do I do now, Lord?" She'd sat alone at church, just like she'd said she would. It had felt like someone had dropped a clear tube around her. The pastor's words warbled through it, and she'd barely been able to hear him.

She could smile to other patrons, but she couldn't talk to them. She'd seen Mister, and they'd locked eyes, but he was so unreachable.

Libby felt cast out, thrown into outer space where there was no gravity and no friction. She'd just continue in a wild free-fall until she burned up or crashed into another heavenly body.

"Tell me what to do," Libby begged God. "And I'll do it. Even if I have to get down on my knees and beg someone, I'll do it."

No instant thoughts came to her mind, but Libby felt calmer after talking to the Lord. In the past, she might have been upset that she hadn't received an immediate answer, but she knew now that the Lord worked in myste-rious ways. Ways she didn't have to understand—and probably *couldn't* understand.

But He was still there. He still loved her. He had not abandoned her.

She reached for the computer mouse and woke the machine. She started searching for a handyman or someone with a lift on their truck that she could hire to

come help her get the wreath up, the lights, and the decorations. If she could get something like what the power
company used, she could ride up in that little pod and get
everything done in a couple of days.

Her mind blanked, and she didn't know how to look at
the options the Internet had spit back out to her. In that
moment, she knew hiring someone to come help wasn't
the right thing to do.

She needed to call Mister and tell him the truth, then
ask him to come help her. He hadn't lied to her, and Libby
appreciated and respected that. She was the one in the
wrong here, and though he'd apologized about five dozen
times, she hadn't said *I'm sorry* to him once.

She swallowed, because admitting she was wrong was
hard. Very hard.

She started typing, but her fingers stalled after only a
few words. That blankness in her mind returned, and
more understanding filled her mind.

This wasn't something she could or should send in a
text. This required an honest, open, face-to-face conversation. At the very least, she should call him so he could
hear her voice.

Her hands trembled, and she set her phone down on
the desk. She could tap from there, and she did so on the
phone icon on his text string, and then the green button
to get the call going.

The line rang once, twice, three times before Mister
said, "Libby." He sounded relieved, and that only sent a
second hot round of tears into her whole system. When he

didn't say anything else, Libby realized how nervous he was.

She drew in a deep breath. "What are you doing this afternoon?" she asked, her voice shaking.

"Oh, uh, I don't know," he said. "Ward and Cactus and I are…headed to town." It sounded like they were on the way right now.

"Okay," she said, a dose of frustration with herself mixing with foolishness at calling him only to ask for his help. "Listen, I—"

"Okay, that wasn't entirely true," he said. "Ward, Cactus, and I are together, but we're not going to town."

Libby blinked, trying to keep up with the situation. "Okay. And I didn't get my brothers to help me with anything for the Country Christmas."

"I—what? You didn't?"

"I lied to you," she blurted out. "I'm so sorry. I just had all these knots inside me, you know? And I needed a couple of days to figure out how to undo them, and I can't. I can't undo them without you." She breathed hard, forgetting what she said the moment she said it.

"Tell her," someone said, and she realized she was on speaker phone.

Horror moved through her, and she demanded, "Am I on speaker?"

"Yes, sorry," Mister said. "I should've said that up front."

"Heya, Libby," Cactus said. "It's just Cactus and Ward."

She pressed her eyes closed, though Cactus sounded friendly enough, and they had to know the situation.

"Tell her," Ward said again.

"How do you get this to stop going through the blasted radio?" Mister grumbled.

"I'll tell her if you don't."

"Shut your mouth, Ward," Mister said, plenty of power behind the words. He sighed in the next moment, and Libby simply waited. She'd apologized, and while she hadn't asked him to come help her specifically, she'd told him her brothers hadn't helped, and she'd asked him what he was doing that afternoon.

"Where are you, sweetheart?" he asked. "We're actually on our way to you."

"All of you?"

"Yes," he said, his voice turning a touch hard. "All of us."

"I'm in the barn office," she said. "But I can run home."

"Okay," he said. "I'll see you there in maybe five minutes?"

She adored the way he asked, and she found herself smiling and nodding. "Five minutes."

Ward said something about how someone had to do something, and Mister argued back with him before they finally got the call disconnected. Libby basked in a warm glow for about five seconds before she jumped to her feet, the reality of the situation suddenly pressing on her.

Mister was going to be here in five minutes, and then

he'd see how she'd lied to him. She'd have to look into those dark eyes and confess everything.

She hurried out of the barn and behind the wheel of her truck, because she *wanted* to do that. She wanted to be with him, and the only way to make things right was to be honest and open.

She arrived back at her house first, thankfully, and she ran up the front steps and into the house to wash her hands and face. She didn't want any evidence of tears staining her cheeks, and as she gazed into her own eyes and examined her own face, she thought she'd done a decent job of erasing that episode in the barn.

A knock sounded on the door, causing Libby to jump. "It's fine," she said. "It's Mister, and this isn't going to be the last time you need to have a serious conversation with him."

In fact, it wasn't the first time either. When he'd stopped by last year to say good-bye before he'd left for Oklahoma, Libby had thought that had been the hardest conversation in the world. He'd left Three Rivers—he'd left his family ranch—because of her.

She hadn't been herself for a few months after that, but she'd found her way back to her center. She'd found her way back to Mister.

Forcing herself to walk calmly, Libby made it to the front door. She opened it, expecting to see Mister standing there. Instead, Ward Glover waited on the front steps, his guitar in his hand. Since Libby had known the Glovers for decades, she knew Ward had once pursued a career in country music.

He grinned at her and said, "Howdy, Libby," his fingers already moving over the strings on his guitar, causing it to sing.

"Hello, Ward." She didn't want to be rude, but she looked past him, hopefully to find Mister. But Cactus stood behind Ward, who edged to the left side of the porch. He held a highly recognizable, yellow pastry box from Blox, Libby's favorite patisserie that had just come to Three Rivers six months ago.

Cactus wore the widest grin a man could, and he flipped open the box and said, "Mister wanted you to have something sweet today."

She smiled at the array of pistachio bars, the brown butter crispy treats, and the German chocolate brownies, with those big, beautiful blotches of creamy nut-caramel filling right on top.

"Thank you," she murmured.

Cactus moved to the right side of the porch, finally revealing Mister as he came up the last few steps. He lifted his eyes to hers, pure emotion streaming from him. Some regret, which made Libby's heart hurt. Some anxiety, which she felt streaming through her. Some joy, which she hoped would always enter his expression when he saw her.

Her first inclination was to blurt out another apology and throw herself into his arms, but he paused a couple of paces away from her and nodded to Ward.

The music changed from the plucking of chords he'd been doing to a recognizable tune. A smile grew on Libby's face when she realized what it was, and she burst out laughing when Mister started to step-touch to the right, and then step-touch to the left, Cactus joining in with him.

This was going to be amazing.

CHAPTER 34

*M*ister possessed decent rhythm, and while he felt like a fool dancing in front of his brother, cousin, and the woman he loved, he'd do anything he had to do to get Libby back.

Including singing and dancing to a pop song.

When he'd gone to Cactus and Ward for help, Judge had been at Bull House. Mister hadn't minded, because he got along just fine with Judge now. They weren't best friends, but they weren't enemies anymore, and they'd come a long way since Mister had left Three Rivers to grow up and become himself.

So many of his relationships were different, including the one he had with Cactus. A year or two ago, he and Cactus didn't share much of anything. Now Mister was out at the Edge Cabin weekly to see his brother, Willa, and all of their kids. He loved taking Cam and Kyle on the ATV, despite the dirty looks Bear gave him when he did.

"Dance with me under the diamonds," he started, because he'd love to hold Libby while they swayed under the stars.

He never in a million years thought he'd be singing a Justin Bieber song, but when Judge had suggested it and then played it for Mister, it was like a ray of light had come straight down from heaven.

He'd spent the past twenty-four hours memorizing the lyrics, and he and Cactus and Ward had worked out this simple routine.

It's thirty seconds, he told himself as Ward played the prompt for the next line again, and then again.

Mister roped his courage and kept going. "See me like breath in the cold," he sang. "Sleep with me here in the silence, Come kiss me silver and gold."

Cactus added his lower voice to Mister's tenor, and he sang the back-up vocals as the song increased in speed and intensity. "You say that I won't lose you, but you can't predict the future, So just hold on like you'll never let go.

"If you ever move on without me, I need to make sure you know

That

You are the only one I'll ever love.

Yeah, *you*

If it's not *you*, it's not anyone."

Ward provided vocals too, and his fingers moved expertly across the guitar, and Mister's emotions swelled as Libby cupped her hands and pressed them to her heart, tears filling her eyes. He could probably stop now, but he wanted to finish the chorus, because the lyrics were so powerful. They were everything he'd wanted to tell Libby for so long.

"Looking back on my life, you're the only good I've ever done."

"Yeah, *you*, If it's not you, it's not anyone."

He knew the second verse, and it had some great words about how forever wasn't long enough for him to show her how much he loved her. But by the look on her face, he didn't need to continue.

He glanced at Cactus and then Ward, who switched the notes quickly to wrap up the song. He was so talented, and Mister loved his family so much for how they'd immediately dropped everything going on in their own lives to come help him with this.

"Ohhh, ohhh, ohhh," he, Ward, and Cactus sung in harmony. "Ohhh, yeah."

"Yeah, *you*," Mister said, really singing out over the others. "Are the only one I'll ever love."

"Love," Cactus sang. "Loove."

"Yeah, you," Ward said. "Gotta tell you, he's gotta tell you."

"You," Mister belted. "If it's not *you*, it's not anyone."

"It's not anyone," Ward sang, with Cactus on the lower register in the same words. "It's not anyone."

Finally, the three of them came together with one final, "It's not anyone," and Ward silenced his guitar.

Mister breathed in heavily and exhaled the same way. "Libby," he said, hoping she knew exactly how he felt about her now. "I love you. I'm so sorry I made a rash and idiotic assumption. Please forgive me."

He took a step toward her just as her tears fell. He rushed her then, gathering her close to his chest as she cried. He didn't know what else to say. The song had said it all.

He heard the fading steps of his brother and cousin, and finally Libby said, "I don't deserve you."

"Of course you do," he said, inching back and lifting her chin so she'd look at him.

"I lied to you. The tree is only half-decorated, and the barn has maybe three strings of lights on it." She shook her head, pure anguish in her expression. "I got the wreath yesterday, and it's this gorgeous pine bough with all these ribbons and pine cones, and I haven't hung it yet. I can't do it alone. I can't do anything alone."

Mister offered her a wobbly, emotional smile. "I can help you wrangle that wreath." He leaned down and touched his lips to hers in a sweet kiss, appreciating the moment for what it was—pure love between a man and a woman who'd come so far together.

"I love you," Libby whispered. "I'm so sorry I pushed you away."

"I know how tight knots can be sometimes," he whispered.

"Forgive me?"

"Already done."

She smiled up at him, and if there was a sight more glorious that Liberty Bellamore grinning at him, Mister never wanted to see it. "Did you really learn a Justin Bieber song?"

He laughed lightly and rolled his eyes. "And a dance."

"And you roped your prickly brother into doing it with you."

"Right?" Mister laughed then. "Can you believe Cactus did that? I mean, even a couple of years ago, he was barely talking to me."

Libby reached up and cupped his face in her hands, making him feel cherished and claimed and completely hers. "I think it's you who's changed the most in the past couple of years. That's why he's talking to you. It's why he and Ward were here to help you."

"Judge helped too," he said. "It is miraculous how far we've come."

"Again, that's because of you."

He wasn't sure about that, because Judge had changed a ton recently too. "I have been working so hard," he whispered. "To be good enough for you."

"You have always been good enough for me," she whispered back. "Kiss me again, please."

Mister obliged, because he wanted to kiss this woman morning, noon, and night, and he would work, change, and do whatever it took to make her happy and be worthy of her.

When he finally got the wherewithal to pull away, he sighed and held her tight. "Okay, so I say we try a few desserts first, and then we tackle the tree, the barn, and the wreath. Deal?"

"Yes, please," she said quietly.

He turned back toward the front of the house. "Can you give me a ride back up to Shiloh Ridge later?"

"Of course."

"I'll go tell Cactus and Ward they can go, then." He left Libby standing on the front porch and hurried back to Cactus's truck. He rolled down the driver's side window, and Mister grinned at them.

"Thank you," he said, his voice lodging in his throat. "For everything. That was so amazing. Thank you."

"Things are good?" Cactus asked.

"Things are good," Mister confirmed.

"Happy to do it," Ward said. "Though next time, I say we do the Chris LeDoux song." He grinned at Mister and touched the brim of his hat.

Mister raised his fist to his heart and pressed it there, the way he'd seen Judge do at Ward's wedding. At the time, he hadn't realized the silent gesture meant so much in his family, but he understood it now.

As Cactus and Ward both touched their hands to their hearts, the bond between them only grew and strengthened.

"All right," Cactus said, putting his hand back on the steering wheel. "Go get back to your girlfriend. We've got work to do too."

"I'm going to need ideas for a proposal," Mister said, grinning at them even as he took a couple of steps back.

"I'm not singing again," Cactus growled. "You're lucky you got what you did today."

"I'll help," Ward called. "We'll get Bishop and Bear to join in."

Mister waved in acknowledgement and watched them back up and leave. Then he faced the red house—and Libby.

He went right back up the steps and took her into his arms again. She held the yellow pastry box out to the side and asked, "Which do you want first? I recommend the pistachio blox if you haven't had them."

"I have not," he said. But instead of taking a treat, he kissed her again, letting her know with every stroke of his mouth against hers that every word he'd sung had been perfectly true.

"To the left?" he called down a few hours later. "You sure?"

"To the left," Libby and Mildred both confirmed.

Mister couldn't tell as close as he stood to the wreath, but he sure wouldn't have adjusted it to the left. He did anyway, moving it a centimeter at a time until both Libby and Mildred yelled at him to stop.

"Right there," Libby said. "That's perfect."

Mister didn't waste any time getting down off the ladder, which they'd stabilized between the tires of Libby's truck and Mildred's car. The arch over the road leading onto Golden Hour Ranch arced at least twenty feet up, and while Mister didn't hate heights, he wasn't their biggest fan either.

His foot finally landed in the bed of Libby's truck, and relief washed through him. "All right," he said, wiping his brow, though the November day wasn't terribly hot. "That's done."

"Nice wrangling, cowboy," Libby said, and Mister jumped down to the ground as she grinned at him.

"I'm good for some things," he said, turning to fold up the ladder. "Is that it for today?"

"Yeah," she said. "I'm starving and sweaty."

"Ditto." He hefted the ladder into the back of her truck, his muscles straining to get the job done. He managed it and turned back to her. "Dinner at your place?"

"Oh, all right. If you like frozen pizza."

"Is that even a question?" He laughed with her, waved good-bye to Mildred, and went to get in the passenger seat of her truck. Exhaustion pulled through him, because it had been a long, emotional day. He'd worked at Shiloh Ridge that morning. Gone to Blox to get the desserts.

Did all that dancing and singing. He and Libby had talked during their dessert-lunch, and then he'd strung the rest of the lights along the main barn for her, and then hung the wreath.

He closed his eyes, beyond grateful for this day, but tired nonetheless. He let Libby drive, walk him up the steps, and put him on the couch with the words, "Take a nap, Mister. I'll make something to eat."

He did what she said, and he definitely nodded off, because the next thing he knew, Libby's fingers trailed along his forehead, her sweet voice saying, "Dinner's ready, sweetheart."

He opened his eyes and blinked until she came into focus. He was the one who called her *sweetheart*, not the other way around. But the way she gazed at him with such love told him that he *was* her sweetheart.

"I don't want to wait forever to be your husband," he said, his voice barely loud enough to reach his own ears. "What do you think? Long engagement or not?"

"Not," she said, stroking his hair off his forehead in such a loving way. "My mother will want a couple of months, at least."

He nodded and stayed right where he was, her touch so comforting and so calming. "And you want to live here?"

She shook her head. "No," she said. "I want to live at Shiloh Ridge."

"Really?"

"Mister," she said, her smile slipping off her face. He loved this serious, sober side of her too. Whatever she said when she looked at him with that potent edge in her eyes, she meant with her whole heart. "I've had so many fantasies about my life with you, and they all play out at Shiloh Ridge."

"I'll have to meet with Bear and the rest of the admin team to find a spot to build a house. Then we have to talk to Bishop and Montana. It'll be months out. Maybe a year."

"We can live here until then," she said. "But we belong up at Shiloh Ridge. *You* belong up there, and I do too."

He nodded, his heart so full. A sigh blew between his lips. "Okay." He sat up, his head aching just a little.

"We're going to make it," Libby said, still kneeling beside him.

He looked at her, his soul filling with love and joy. "Yeah," he said, reaching to curl his hand around the back of her neck and bring her closer for a kiss. "We are."

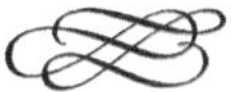

Ranger Glover held the door for his sister and then his wife. "Come on, Wilder," he said to his son, who toddled along, getting distracted by blades of grass. Seemingly. Sometimes Ranger had patience for his son to adore every little thing he saw, and sometimes he didn't.

Tonight, with his belly grumbling for food and the wind blowing so hard, he just wanted his son to make it inside.

"Daddy," Wilder said, his high-pitched voice reaching right into Ranger's heart.

"Hurry," Ranger said, shifting Fawn on his hip.

"There's a snake."

"Okay, well, he's not invited to Thanksgiving dinner." He grinned at his son as he came up the front steps one foot at a time.

"It was gween."

"Green snakes aren't poisonous, so he can stay in the grass." Ranger looked back toward the lawn, but he couldn't see any serpents. Wilder had gone inside, and Ranger made to follow him. He shut the door behind him, the chatter and laughter pouring from the kitchen in Bull House telling him a lot of people had arrived already.

Sure enough, when he turned around, he quickly counted all four of his siblings. They'd all arrived ahead of him, though he supposed he and Etta had arrived at the same time. Holly Ann stepped forward to take Fawn, saying, "Ward wants to talk to you for a second."

"All right." Ranger glanced around for his brother, finding him standing over by the door that led into the pantry. Strange, but Ranger had participated in weirder conversations.

"Howdy, Dotty," he said, pausing to kiss his sister-in-law on the cheek. "How's the baby?" He smiled at her bulging belly, and he couldn't wait to see if they'd bring home a girl or a boy. "Only a week or so now."

"Eight days," she said, putting both hands on her baby. "If you could tell Ward that Glory does not sound strange with Glover, that would be great."

Ranger chuckled at the dry, under-her-breath sentence and continued toward the pantry. He ducked inside to find Ward standing over by the bottled peaches from forever ago. Their mother used to make them all help for a whole weekend, an event she dubbed "Peach Days," and which all of the children hated.

Even as an adult, Ranger had peeled, pitted, and preserved peaches.

"What's going on?" he asked, searching his brother's face. Ward was one of the more serious Glovers, and he was a lot like Ranger in the regard that he didn't mind the spotlight when it came to him, but he didn't seek it out. Not the way Mister or Bishop did. Not even the way Ace did.

"I finished the scrapbooks," Ward said, swallowing. "I guess I'm a little nervous to pass them out, what with Mother here, and Ida wanting to make some announcement, and then Etta just told me that her new boyfriend is coming."

"Whoa, wait a minute." Ranger's mind raced. "Etta has a new boyfriend?"

"Yes," Etta said from behind him, and Ranger spun around. "She does." She smiled at him as she leaned in the doorway. "He'll be here in five minutes." She held up her phone. "Can I have a moment to address everyone right now?"

"Sure," Ward said while Ranger could only gape at her. He lived with her; how did he not know she'd started seeing someone? He narrowed his eyes at her, feeling like someone had lashed him with a bleach-laced whip.

Ward pressed past him, leaving Etta to face Ranger. "Why didn't you tell me?"

"I don't know," Etta murmured. "I—maybe I was trying to make sure it was something before I said anything." She sighed and ducked her head. "I've thought

I had three boyfriends this year, Range. I just…didn't say. I'm sorry."

"I get it, Etta." Ranger took her into a quick hug, and Ward called everyone to attention, saying, "Etta would like to speak to us for a moment."

Since the dinner tonight at Bull House only included Ranger's immediate siblings—no cousins, no one from Bear's family—it didn't take long for them to quiet down. He had two children, as did Ida, and Ace had the one. Five kids. Ten adults. He stayed in the doorway of the pantry, facing the house, as Etta went to stand beside Ward.

"All right," she said. "I invited someone to this meal, after asking Ward and Dot if it was okay. I'm counting it as a date, and it'll be our fourth official date."

"Etta," Ida said, plenty of warning in her voice. Her eyes had widened to the point where they must be so very dry.

"His name is August Winters, and we've been seeing each other for oh, I don't know. A few weeks. We can't get together very often, because he has a nine-year-old daughter. We've only been out a few times, like I said. I do not want anyone to make a big deal out of this." She pointed at Ace, who held up both hands and looked around like he was always the innocent one. "I don't want any embarrassing questions. We don't need to go into details of my life from when Dad would make us run mud trails or anything like that."

"Is he bringing his daughter?" Oakley asked, and Ranger appreciated how very calm she was.

"No," Etta said. "I haven't officially met her yet, as he's being cautious about that. I don't mind, so don't make it a big deal."

Ida wore a smile the size of Saturn now, as did Holly Ann. Even Mother looked like Etta would be married by Christmas.

"That's all," Etta said. "He's a nice man—so far—and we're just getting to know one another. But he doesn't have any family in the area, and since it's not Thanksgiving Day, I invited him."

"Can I say something really quick?" Ida asked.

"If it's about the field trip—" Etta started.

"It's not," Ida assured her. "It's about Mother." She linked her arm through Mother's and beamed at her, but when she faced the group again, she wore tears in her eyes. Ranger's pulse spiked, and his gaze volleyed back and forth between Ida and Mother.

"She had an appointment last week with the cardiologist. She's been very fatigued and out of breath, and she's not sure why. She has a little bit of anemia, but not enough to make her feel the way she does."

Ida swiped at her eyes, but the tears kept coming. Ranger took a step out of the pantry, everything inside him telling him he'd have to handle this situation. As the oldest, he should've known Mother had a doctor's appointment in the first place.

"Ida?" he asked, stepping past Ward and Etta, who both held silently still.

"I'm in the early stages of dementia," Mother said,

sparing Ida from having to say it. "I lose my thoughts from time to time."

"She's a little disoriented sometimes," Ida said, her voice barely more than a whisper.

"I live in a good place," Mother said. "They do memory care there, and Ida got me signed up with a therapist. I start next week." She patted Ida's arm, her smile wobbling but also the bravest thing Ranger had seen in a long, long time.

He reached Mother and wrapped her up in a tight hug. "I love you," he whispered.

"I love you too, son."

Ranger knew he couldn't break down. He couldn't cry. Not here, not now. Everyone would be looking to him for a reaction, and it would do no good to start blubbering and wailing. Mother was seventy-four years old, and she'd been through hip surgeries and various other health issues for over a decade.

He stepped back and allowed Ace to give her a hug. He breathed in deeply, tamping down his emotions time and time again, especially when his wife wept as she hugged her mother-in-law. Mother was very important to Oakley, and he put his arm around her as she returned to his side.

"Sorry," Ida said. "I didn't mean to ruin anything. I thought maybe we better tell you before August shows up."

Etta nodded and wiped her eyes. "Yes, thank you, Ida." She hugged her twin too, and Ranger looked at Ward, who'd stood on his right side. He reached over and took his brother's hand. They all connected each person, reaching for the one closest to them, until they made an oddly-shaped circle with Mother at the head of it.

"I'm going to be okay," she said. "Whatever happens is going to be okay. It's in the hands of the Lord."

Ranger nodded, even if that wasn't the answer he wanted. He drew in a deep breath, feeling several sets of eyes on him, though it had been Ward who'd started the group text suggesting this meal. He was in charge; this was his house.

"Ward," Ranger said. "Did you want to say something?"

He cleared his throat. "I have a surprise for everyone. I've been working on them for a long time. Years. I'm just so busy that they didn't get done until Dot stopped going to work in the past few weeks. She's been helping me get them finished up." He looked around at everyone and smiled, all traces of his anxiety now gone. "We'll pass them out after dinner."

A timer on the oven went off at the same time the doorbell rang, and the moment broke. The group released each other, but Ranger had never felt so close to his family as he had in those few minutes.

He leaned over and pressed a kiss to Oakley's forehead, seeing more frequent trips down to Nestled Oaks, the facility where his mother lived, in the future.

"Mother," Ida said. "You stay with me. We'll meet this man together."

Ranger watched Etta as she reached the door, and he

smelled the scent of freshly baked bread as Ward removed a pan of rolls from the oven. He came back to stand beside Ranger, saying, "I'm going to pray every morning and night that he's the one."

"Me too," Ranger murmured, because Etta deserved to find someone she could spend her life loving. Someone who would love her from now until forever too.

A brown-haired man stepped into the house, a smile already on his face. He glanced toward the kitchen as Etta shut the door behind him, then back to her. She smiled up at him and linked her arm through his. Everything about Etta was always so proper, and watching her loosen up the past few years had been fascinating to Ranger. She'd lost a lot of what made her intimidating, and that was a good thing in his opinion.

"Everyone," she said, stopping near the already-set dining room table. "This is August Winters. August, my mother, Dawna, and surely you remember my twin, Ida."

"I do." August said, nodding at them. "So nice to meet you, ma'am." He took Mother's hand and kissed it.

"Brady's got the twins contained," she said, indicating the man as he stood beside the two highchairs, each of them holding one almost-two-year-old. "Johnny and Judy."

"Oh, wow," August said, his grin widening. "A twin had twins."

"It happens quite often," Ida said, and Ranger thought her face would crack for how hard she was smiling.

"Nice to meet you," August said to Brady, who returned the sentiment and shook his hand.

"My youngest brother, Ace," Etta said, as Ace now stood closer than anyone else. "He's married to Holly Ann." Etta searched for her, and Holly Ann raised her hand from the kitchen. "She's due with their second child in early March, and they have a boy around here somewhere."

"Hello," August said, stepping forward and stretching to shake Ace's hand. He wore a pair of jeans and a leather jacket over a pale blue shirt, about the exact same thing Ranger had on.

"Where is Gun?" Ace asked, looking around, and Ranger had a good idea. The child could sniff out sugar better than a bloodhound, and sure enough, he was located in the kitchen with his mother, holding half a cookie.

"My other two brothers," Etta said, leading August closer. "Ward and then Ranger. He's the oldest."

"Howdy," Ward said, stealing Ranger's greeting. "My wife, Dot." He indicated her, and she came over to shake August's hand too.

"Hey there," he said, feeling stupid and out of sorts. "My wife, Oakley. We have a son and a daughter too."

"Wilder and Fawn," August said, first shaking Ward's hand and then Ranger's. He had a nice, firm grip, and Ranger liked the energy he put off. A lot. No wonder Etta liked this man.

"And that's us," Etta said.

"You said your family was huge," he said. "This is only a few people."

"There's no cousins here," she said. "There's seven more of them, with seven more spouses. That doubles us right there."

"They have more kids too," Ranger said. "My one cousin just fostered, and he's got five kids."

August nodded, but he looked like he'd just walked into a brick wall and needed a moment to get his head on straight again.

"Dinner's ready," Dot said, and that got everyone to move. They managed to all find spots around the table, with Mother sandwiched between the twins, and their significant others on their opposite sides. Ranger accepted the highchair for Fawn and started buckling her in while Oak put a booster seat on a chair for Wilder.

When everyone had finally found a place to eat, Ward looked at Ranger again. Everyone did, and he smiled around at them. "This is great," he said. "We should do smaller meals or parties or whatever more often. Less chance of getting lost or overlooked."

"I'd like that," Ace said.

"Mother," Ranger said, leaning forward to see her. "Would you pray?" He looked at Ward. "Then we'll eat, yes?"

"Yes," Ward said.

"I'd like to just quickly say how grateful I am for you all," Dot blurted out, her eyes a little wild. "I was—am—very nervous to have a baby and become a mother, and you have all been so kind and so helpful and so…great." She nodded like that was that, and she visibly relaxed.

"We could do a thankful moment," Ranger said. "If someone else has something they want to say." He glanced around, not sure if they would. The loudest of them was Ace, but he'd calmed so much in the past few years. He still loved his video games and laughing really hard, but he knew when to be reverent too.

"I'm grateful for modern medicine," he said. "And I'm grateful for a wife and a sister-in-law who worked hard to provide gluten-free rolls, and I'm really grateful that potatoes are gluten-free, because I love mashed potatoes and turkey." He grinned as a few people laughed, Ranger included.

Another few seconds of silence hung in the air.

"I'm grateful for my children," Mother said. "Your father would be so proud of all of you." She patted Etta's hand, her eyes as clear as Ranger had seen them in a while. "Each of you is so talented and so faithful. A mother couldn't ask for better children, and I love everyone you've chosen to spend your lives with too. It's wonderful to have so many new sons and daughters." Her eyes watered, and she reached for her napkin to wipe them.

Ranger didn't think anything could top that, so he nodded and said, "Thank you, Mother. You can pray when you're ready."

He closed his eyes and reached for his wife's hand. They once again joined together as a single unit while

Mother offered a beautiful prayer for good health and a good year ahead. "Bless any here who need something special that they can have it, according to Thy will." She paused, and Ranger opened his eyes to see if she needed help. Ida watched her too, and they exchanged a glance.

"We recognize Thy hand in all things, and we're grateful for the bounty Thou has always given those who come to Shiloh Ridge. Bless August that he'll find what he seeks. Bless Ranger with strength to lead the family. Bless Dot in her delivery. Bless Ward to know how very loved he is."

Ranger's eyes filled with tears, because Ward had questioned that in the past. Mother continued to bless each of them by name with exactly what they seemed to struggle with the most, and when she said, "Amen," his weren't the only stormy, nearly-wet eyes.

"That was beautiful," August said in an awed voice. "Thank you so much."

A moment later, the spirit broke, and Holly Ann started passing out the food. The mood lifted then, thankfully, because Ranger couldn't handle many more weighty items. He kept busy talking to Ace, Ward, and Holly Ann, keeping his children fed, and watching Mother. Fine, maybe he was watching Etta with August, but his eyes kept traveling across the table in their direction.

"All right," Ward said once it appeared like most people had finished. "Dot?" They got up and went into the pantry, and Ranger regretted that they'd been interrupted earlier. Ward had been nervous, and Ranger sent up a silent prayer that all would be well with him.

He and Dot returned after only a few seconds, each of them carrying a book. A big book.

"I made scrapbooks for each of the Glovers," he said. "I've been working on them for a long time. Years. I went through a lot of pictures that Mother gave me, and I went through her books for us and separated everything out into personalized books." He held up one volume, a rich, dark brown leather book roughly a foot by a foot in size.

On the front of it, *Richard* sat in silver letters. "Ranger," he said, handing the book to Ranger.

He looked at it, actually tracing his fingertip along the R on his name. A sense of awe and wonder and a higher power filled him.

"All right," Ward said, clearing his throat. "We never got letters from our dad, the way Stone wrote to his kids. And I've always felt...I don't know. I felt like I wanted something to remind me of who I am too. I thought you might each like that too. You can open them."

Ranger looked across the table to Etta, their eyes meeting. She offered him a smile, and he returned it. Then he flipped open his book. A baby picture sat there, and he wasn't so old that it was black-and-white. It was definitely weathered, with a bit of damage on the corners.

He smiled at himself, a sense of nostalgia and a longing for the simpleness of the past streaming through him. "Look," he said, tilting the book to share it with Oakley.

"Daddy, who?" Wilder asked, and Ranger held up the book so his son could see.

"It's daddy, buddy. That's me, when I was a tiny baby." Ward had put a placard below the picture that said Ranger's birthdate and when this picture had been taken. "I was only one month old."

"You?" Wilder asked, clearly confused. He looked from the picture to Ranger. "Baby."

"Yes," Ranger said. "Daddy was a baby once too."

He turned the page, and he pulled in a breath. It was him and Ward as children, and while he'd seen this picture before, it had been a very long time. "Ward," he said, and his brother looked over to him, removing his eyes from Ida's book.

Ranger held up his book, and Ward grinned. "I made a copy of that one and put it in my book too," he said, holding up his to show they had the same picture.

"This is my handprint," Ace said, the same wonder in his eyes that Ranger felt streaming through him.

"I wrote this letter to Santa when I was four," Etta said, and she turned her book to show everyone.

Ranger wanted to spend hours looking at each thing in his book, and while it wasn't a letter from his father, Ward had given them all the very next best thing—their history. A reminder of who they were and who they wanted to continue to be.

"Thank you," Ranger said, his voice getting caught in his throat. He handed his book to Oakley and stood up. He went around the table to where Ward still stood.

"Thank you, brother." He grabbed onto him and held him tight—so tight. He hoped his grip could say all the things his voice couldn't, and when Ward patted him on the back, he stepped away.

He nodded at Ranger, and Ranger nodded at him, their unspoken words, *I love you. Thank you,* going both ways.

Ranger looked around the table at the joy on his siblings' faces. At the smiles the scrapbooks produced on their spouses' faces as they learned more about their loved one and saw pictures they'd never seen before. He wanted to freeze this moment and live inside it for a while.

It felt so good to belong to a family. It felt right to be here tonight with them.

"You did something amazing," he said to Ward, who shook his head.

"Glory be to God," he said, and Ranger could echo that. Everything he had, he could give to God and die happy knowing he had.

He looked around the table, time slowing as he tried to see each person for who they were and how the Lord would see them.

He watched Ace laugh and point to something in his book, and he wanted his brother's health to continue to improve. He wanted Holly Ann to have an easy delivery.

He wanted his children to be healthy and happy, and he wanted his wife to have the same.

He wanted Ward and Dot to feel comfortable inside the larger family and to start their family with confidence and love.

He wanted Ida and Brady and their twins to enjoy good fortune.

He wanted Mother to stay with him forever, but he knew she wouldn't.

He watched Etta lean her book toward August, a bright smile on her face. August looked at her, definite adoration in his eyes before he looked at the scrapbook. Ranger wanted so much happiness for her he could hardly stand it. He wanted her to have a husband who could make her a mother, which was the deepest hope of her heart.

He wanted so much for these people he loved so much, but all he could pray was, *Please, Dear Lord. Please.*

The Lord could—and would—fill in the rest.

CHAPTER 36

*L*ibby felt like she'd left part of her brain in the house, or the barn office, or the rodeo trailer where the five cowboys she'd gotten to come do tonight's show had hunkered down with pizza, pop, and playing cards.

They didn't have to be out in the arena until six o'clock for the first wave of guests, and then again at eight o'clock for the second.

"Miss Bellamore?" Brody Baldwell, her chef for the Country Christmas, asked.

"Yes," she said, pulling the fragments of her mind back together. "We want all of the lemonade, and you better put more chicken on." She looked at her clipboard. "We're sold out for tonight."

The chef's eyes went up, and his surprise mirrored Libby's. They never sold out on weeknights, though tonight was opening night, and that usually performed well.

Mister had helped so much with getting the word out about this year's entertainment, and his connections to professional rodeo stars had tickled the interest of Three Rivers residents in a way Libby and Mildred had been missing for a while.

"Thank you," Libby said, turning away from him. She put a checkmark next to *food and drink* on her clipboard and looked up to check the lights. They all twinkled merrily, and she wasn't going to go around and re-check every string.

The barn looked straight out of the North Pole, if Santa had barns where he kept his reindeer. The huge pine that welcomed everyone to the Country Christmas practically sagged under the weight of the lights and ornaments that had been placed on it.

Their three turnstiles had been set up, and Libby herself would man one of them. Mildred would stand at another, welcoming people to the festival and checking tickets, and Mama had agreed to operate the third one tonight.

They usually only had two, but with the swelling numbers, Libby had begged for more help. Jack and Cord would be here as well, helping to get the guests where they needed to be, when they needed to be there.

She walked past the open side of the barn, glad to see the temporary help she'd hired had arrived, been trained, and were wiping down all the tables.

The wreath up front looked amazing. The signs for parking had been put up by her personally. The maps and brochures for tonight's activities and schedule waited in the podiums by check-in.

Libby drew a deep breath, tasting the energy in the air. This was going to be a great night. "Please let it be a great night," she prayed. A sense of calmness and peace came over her, a direct answer to her plea, and Libby smiled up into the evening sky.

Christmas possessed such magic, and Libby could see it everywhere she looked this year. Mister had touched everything around this part of the ranch where the Country Christmas took place, and it all seemed plated in gold, silver, and tinsel. Everything shone, even the dirt, and Libby let herself experience pure joy.

"Libs," Mister said from behind her, and she turned toward him. He jogged the last few steps toward her and lifted her right off the ground. "It's going to be great tonight."

She smiled down at him, wondering how he'd known how worried and anxious she was. His beaming smile made the nearby Christmas tree lights seem pale, and she giggled as he set her back on her feet.

"You're supposed to be in the trailer," she said. "People don't get to see the celebrities until the show."

"Mm, I know." He didn't move to go back to the huge fifth-wheel he'd rented for him and his friends to have somewhere comfortable to stay out of the limelight when they weren't in the arena. He leaned down and traced his nose down the side of her face. "I like the lighter hair. It looks real nice on you."

"Thank you," Libby said, reaching up to finger the bleached and colored locks. "Just trying something different. That's been working for me so far."

He chuckled and said, "Plus, Mother and Don said they're almost here, and I was wondering if I could sneak them in early...." He let his request trail off, his eyes so hopeful they were almost boyish.

Libby laughed and shook her head. "You've always been a mommas-boy."

His grin only got bigger. "Is that a yes? I want to show her Turtle Dove. Please, Libby. Please."

"You don't need to beg," Libby said, twisting in his arms as she heard the tell-tale sign of truck tires crunching over the dirt road.

"That's them," he said. "The gates don't open for another twenty minutes. No one will even know."

"Right, until Porter wants to bring his family in early tomorrow, and then Dave finds some woman he has to bring back." Libby acted like she cared, but she didn't. Not for Lois and Don.

Mister laughed, kissed her quick, and stepped away. As he jogged toward the big truck, which had gone around the regular parking area to the staff lot, he called, "I love you, Libs. You're the best."

"Mm hm," she said mostly to herself. "I am the best, and he better not forget it." Libby looked around, trying to think of something she'd forgotten.

Another car approached, and relief ran through her when she saw Scott driving and Mildred in the passenger seat.

She followed Mister toward the staff parking lot at a slower clip, but he had whisked his mother and step-father off quickly. She met Mildred at the door and hugged her. "Wow, you smell amazing," she said, stepping back and smiling at her. "New perfume?"

"Yes, it's from that new booth at the mall," she said, linking her arm through Libby's. "We have to go. Plus, they're doing that gift event this weekend."

"I don't see how we can go this weekend," Libby said. "Card Dalley is coming into town on Friday morning, and my whole weekend is going to be spent making sure he has everything he needs."

Mildred laughed, but Libby wasn't kidding. "He's bringing an assistant, Libs," she said. "She can go get him food or a new guitar string or whatever." She looked at her with big, pleading, puppy-dog eyes. "Come on. You can take an hour to go to the mall."

"It takes an hour just to drive there and park during the holidays," Libby said, frowning. "You have to be kidding."

"I'm not," Mildred said. "When Card gets here, I'll talk to him. Things are usually dead in the afternoon. The chef will be cooking. The show will be four days old by Saturday. Everything will be humming like a well-oiled machine. Let's go around two." Mildred always seemed to have the answer for everything, and Libby didn't want to deny her. She missed her sister and spending time with her, and her resolve faltered.

"All right," she said. "I can spare an hour from two to three on Saturday. But I have to be back here by three-thirty, because there will be things to do before dinner starts at five."

"I'm aware of what time dinner starts," Mildred said. "How are things looking tonight? Where do you need me and Scott?"

Libby turned toward her sister's husband. "Howdy, Scott."

"Libby." He smiled and leaned down to give her a friendly kiss on the cheek. "Everything looks as amazing in real-life as it does in the pictures."

Libby thought so too, and she swelled with the compliment. "Thanks," she said. "Can you see the lights from the highway?"

"You sure can," Scott said, glancing around. "Mildred said I might need to man a lemonade stand?"

"Yes," Libby said, adopting her business-like persona. "Let me show you what we do." She started back toward the main area, right where the customers would come in. "So we don't open the barn for seating until four forty-five," she said. "Guests can start arriving at four-fifteen. So there's a children's train that goes around. There's a gift shop. There's plenty of benches and shade. The lemonade is free—it comes with the meal. We just need people to hand it out or make sure it stays stocked."

"I can do that," Scott said as he walked alongside her. "Oh, I see it."

"Yeah, not hard to find," Libby said, slowing as she watched the vendor she used for lemonade carry in another huge barrel of it. "I hope I ordered enough."

"You did," Mildred said. "You've gone over everything twice, then again a third time. It's going to be amazing."

An alarm on her phone went off, which prevented her from accepting Mildred's vote of confidence. "It's time," she said. "Do you see Mama?"

"I talked to her on the way over," Mildred said. "She'll be here."

Libby hurried into the barn and put away her clipboard. She had a digital copy of everything on the paper on her phone, and she didn't want to be burdened with it while she took tickets and handed out maps.

Cars had already started to fill the lot, their parking attendants directing them so not a single inch was wasted. They kept coming and coming, and Libby was sure they'd sold too many tickets. There was no way everyone would fit in the barn for dinner, though she, Mildred, and Mister had been over and over what their maximum capacity was for the festival.

Right at four-fifteen, another alarm went off, and she and Mildred said, "Howdy, folks. Welcome to the Country Christmas Rodeo Extravaganza!" in tandem. They looked at one another, laughed, and then Libby gestured forward the first guests in line.

Mama arrived about ten minutes later, an apologetic

look on her face when she glanced at Libby but the smile of perfection when she faced the guests.

Within twenty minutes of welcoming everyone, the line had dwindled, and Libby turned to watch people sipping their lemonade, laughing, chatting, and seemingly enjoying themselves. The tractor that pulled the "train" growled behind the barn, and the scent of woodsmoke filled the air.

Libby loved the Country Christmas with her whole heart and soul. She didn't want to stop doing it, and she told herself she wouldn't have to. Mister had scheduled a meeting with Bear, Ranger, Ward, and Preacher, his brothers and cousins who ran Shiloh Ridge, and they'd be talking next week about a possible plot of land where he could build a house for him and Libby on the ranch.

She'd be able to come here anytime she wanted. She wasn't leaving for good. She was leveling up.

At four-fifty-five, an ear-splitting dinner bell rang, and a man's voice—Papa's from years ago—played over the speaker system. "All right, cowboys and cowgirls. It's almost time to eat. If you're not in the dining barn, c'mon in and find a seat. Dinner will be served in five minutes."

From there, Libby could sit back and relax. Kind of. Their system for feeding people got three hundred people through the line in under fifteen minutes, and that went off without a hitch. They had plenty of baked potatoes, baked beans, and baked chicken. People could leave the barn when they finished and go on to attend the other activities, the craft booths, or get a seat in the arena behind the dining barn.

Libby wandered that way, seeing plenty of kids at the face-painting tables and teens and adults interested in the blacksmith demonstration.

Close to six, most people started streaming toward the arena, and Libby flowed with them. She had no idea if this would be something people wanted to see or not. Mister and Wyatt had brought in the rodeo animals, and they'd all been training with them for a couple of weeks now. Everything was done by the rodeo book, with high standards for animal care and treatment, and Libby leaned against the fence where Mister would come flying out on his horse, his rope high above his head as he aimed to catch the calf who'd gotten a head-start on him.

Libby had loved watching Mister in the rodeo. He'd always looked so regal and majestic atop a horse, and he was pure perfection in events. She knew that flawless performances like that came after hours and days and months of training, and while the five cowboys here tonight hadn't been doing that, she prayed for a good show.

Precisely at six o'clock—Libby had lectured the cowboys that they must start on time, otherwise, things would overlap badly with the second wave of dinner, which was served at seven—Wyatt's voice came over the speaker.

"Well, howdy-ho, Three Rivers!" The man himself stepped out onto a platform opposite the grandstands, and the crowd seated in those bleachers went wild. Libby smiled, because getting Wyatt to come do this was a *big* deal.

The man was a *huge* celebrity. Yes, bigger than Mister.

"I'm not sure I can hear you," he said in the mic, leaning one ear forward as if the roaring crowd could get any louder. They could, and Libby laughed as hundreds of feet started stomping on the metal bleachers.

Wyatt laughed into the mic, pulled his hat off his head, and waved it at the crowd in his signature move. The noise dropped as hats came off and got waved back at him, his smile bright enough to light the whole arena should the power go out.

"Thank you, Lord," Libby murmured.

"I've got some of the biggest stars in pro rodeo here with me tonight," Wyatt said. "Give it up for Porrrrterrrrr Hangford!"

A horse bearing a man came barreling out of the end of the arena opposite of Libby, and Porter looked like he hadn't spent a day out of the saddle. The crowd stomped and whooped for him too, and he lifted his hat as he rode in front of them, his horse sprinting—positively sprinting —toward Libby. It only slowed to turn, and she marveled at the power and grace of the black beast.

"Daviiiiiid Warrrrrburton!" Wyatt bellowed into the night.

Dave came out of a chute on a bull, and even Libby wasn't expecting that. It bucked and kicked, doing every-thing it could to get him off its back. She couldn't help looking at the timer, because that was what one did when watching a cowboy ride a bull.

He needed to stay on for eight seconds. The crowd started to count as the numbers went up. "…six, seven, eight," and Libby even joined in.

They cheered and whistled when he made the bell, and then Dave jumped down, swept his hat off his head, and lifted both arms up in the air. That sent people into a frenzy, especially when Wyatt said, "No one's ridden Gone in the Night since Dave, who stayed on the bull for a full eight seconds and won the National Championship the year he rode him."

More whistles, more applause, more cheers. This couldn't be going any better.

"Say hello to Austiiiin Goodniiiiight!" Wyatt said, and a chute on the other side of him opened, and a bucking bronc came out with Austin on his back. No saddle, and again Libby found herself watching the clock. He made it the whole eight seconds, and her heart started to pound for Mister's entrance.

The horse came into the fenced area beside her, and he said, "Heya, love."

She looked up at him, and in the bright stadium lights, she fell in love with him over and over again. He wore a huge black cowboy hat, a blue and white plaid shirt, and those delicious jeans. He had his rope all ready, and his brown and white horse—which he'd named Turtle Dove—blinked lazily, like this would be just another walk through the hills.

"Good luck," she said. She knew all the cowboys wanted to put on a good performance—a National-Championship-winning performance—right out of the gate. Then they'd do a few other events, a few demos, and it would be done.

"Austin won the National Championship four years in a row," Wyatt said. "Putting up high scores in two or three events yearly, which is basically unheard of."

Austin waved both hands above his head, his cowboy hat solidly staying in place, and ran for the fence.

"And last," Wyatt said. "But certainly not least. Our own local hero, a four-time National Champion himself, from the most-talked-about and biggest working cattle ranch in the Texas Panhandle…Miiiiiiister Glooooooover!"

"Yep," Mister said, and it was a miracle Libby heard it above the insane hollering of the crowd, and he burst out of the gate in hot pursuit of the calf. She stepped up onto the bottom rung of the fence to see him throw that rope, leap from the saddle, and get the calf tied—all in under six-and-a-half-seconds.

He jumped up, his hands in the air, and headed right back to his horse as if he'd done nothing spectacular. Libby and the crowd disagreed. Just watching him get back in his saddle was like watching an artist in motion, and once the calf had been tied for the required six seconds, he released it.

"Whoo-ee!" Wyatt said. "That's professional-time right there, ladies and gents. Six-point-six-six seconds. I'm gonna have to look up what they're puttin' down in Vegas in calf roping, because that was belt-buckle-worthy." He grinned at Mister, who did wear something sparkly around his waist, and Mister lifted his fist and pressed it to his chest, right over his heart.

A particularly loud group went wild in the stands, and Libby wasn't surprised to see several rows of Glovers, right there in the front, cheering for Mister. Men, women, and children, and once they'd made themselves known, almost all of them put their fists over their hearts too.

Mister nodded and swung his horse back around to return out of the arena near where he'd come in.

With tears in her eyes, Libby went to greet him. It didn't matter if they ran out of lemonade or food for the second feeding of guests. It didn't matter if Dave didn't make it the eight seconds. The last ten minutes had been enough for Libby to call the Country Christmas a huge success.

Mister slid from his horse and asked, "So? What did you think?"

She couldn't speak. She simply threw herself into his arms and hung on. After several long seconds, she said, "Thank you, Mister. That was amazing."

He smoothed her hair back, his smile wide but personal—just for her. "If it's not you, it's not anyone," he said. "I love you."

"I love you more and more every minute," she whispered, and then she tipped up onto her toes to kiss him.

Mister paced behind the stage, telling himself again and again that he liked being in the spotlight. He, Wyatt, and the other boys weren't putting on their rodeo show tonight—a show that had been ranked number one on the Two Cents app since opening night, and a show that had helped Libby sell out the Country Christmas every night over the past few days —because she'd booked Card Dalley for this first weekend in December.

"It'll be okay," the country music sensation said as Mister turned again. "You've got to calm down." He put both hands on Mister's shoulders. "You've already sang to this woman. This is going to be easy."

"There are hundreds of people out there," Mister said. On the weekends, the bands mingled with the early crowd, and they only performed one concert for both crowds. There was seating in the grand stands, all the bleachers all the way around, and on a grassy area beyond the arena, so they could accommodate both groups. "Last time, it was just me and her." And Cactus and Ward, but they didn't account for hundreds upon hundreds of eyes.

"I'm going to be doing the singing. You're just going to get down on both knees, just like we practiced."

"How many women have you asked to marry you?" Mister asked.

"Just the one," Card said, smiling at him.

"How did you feel before you did that?"

His smile stayed as sunny as before. "Like I was going to throw up."

"Right. So let me pace." Mister turned away from him and caught sight of Bear and Preacher approaching. "You've got the ring?"

"Right here," Bear said, handing it to him. Mister cracked the navy blue box, not sure why he needed to see the diamond. He also had no idea why he seriously felt like fleeing into the night.

"You've got some serious energy flowing off of you," Preacher said, peering at him.

"I'm so nervous," Mister admitted, looking right into his brother's eyes. He had an appointment to meet with everyone about a homesite on Monday, and he really wanted to show up with Libby as his fiancée.

"It's going to go great," Preacher said, leaning against his cane for support. He wore a smile on his face, and Mister admired him so much for his strength and resiliency. "You've got everything rehearsed. Card knows what he's doing."

"Card does know what he's doing," Card said, arriving on the scene. He shook hands with Bear and Preacher. "Heard a lot about you guys. Thanks for having me and my family up to the ranch."

"Happy to do it," Bear said pleasantly. "How do you like the Panhandle?"

"Haven't been around much yet," Card said. "But we plan to explore a little bit tomorrow before we're back here for another show."

"If you want to ride this weekend, let us know," Preacher said. "We've got plenty of horses for you and your wife, kids."

"Sure," Card said. "I've been wanting to get Millie on a horse. She's a little nervous."

"There's a great equine therapy facility north of town," Preacher said. "I go a couple times a week, and they do kids classes."

"Will they be able to get in?" Mister asked.

"I don't know," Preacher said, glancing at him. "But we can call Pete and find out."

"Let me talk to Karen," Card said. "Don't worry about it right now."

"You have my number," Mister said, turning as the lights started to change colors behind him. "Is it time already?"

"Ladies and gentlemen," Libby said, and sure enough, that meant it was time for the concert to start. "Thank you so much for coming out to Golden Hour Ranch tonight to share in a Christmas tradition that is ten years old this year!"

The crowd tonight had plenty of energy and life, and they cheered enthusiastically.

"Thank you for being here with us on this Saturday night, when the biggest guitar star in Texas is going to be taking the stage and performing for us. He won Country Music Stars-On-the-Rise, landed a recording contract with Blue Jean Records out of Nashville before his nineteenth birthday, and all three of his albums have gone platinum. He's a superstar, and I'm so grateful he's here with us tonight."

She paused, and Mister heard the emotion in her voice. He knew she didn't want to cry or get sappy on the stage, and he hurried to send up a prayer to help her stay steady and clear.

"He was named Texas's Rising Guitar Star this year, and without further ado, Golden Hour Ranch and your Country Christmas Rodeo Extravaganza presents...Card Dalley!"

The men and women in Three Rivers and the surrounding small towns sure knew how to make someone feel welcome, as Mister had felt that over the past few nights when he'd come out of the chutes. It helped that Wyatt sure knew how to charm a crowd, and Mister thought if he didn't want to spend time with his wife and family, he could definitely become an announcer.

The music started with a big guitar riff, plenty of

drums, and Card himself going right into his bestselling single.

"All right," Mister said, taking the ring out of the box and sliding it into his pocket. "I'm on in two minutes. Wish me luck."

"You don't need it," Bear said while Preacher said, "You got it, bro. Good luck."

Mister drew in a deep breath and headed for the stairs that led up to the side of the backstage area. The air seemed clearer up here, and he thought he caught a whiff of the new perfume Libby had bought that afternoon when Mildred had gotten her away from the ranch so Mister could coordinate and practice with Card for this proposal.

They'd been gone for about ninety minutes, and Mister had pretended like he'd just shown up at her house when she'd returned.

Card's song finished up, and he said, "Thank you, Three Rivers!" and the crowd crowed right back at him. The guitar sound went down a notch, and the drums faded until only a slight beat remained.

Mister drew in another breath and touched the diamond in his pocket, and it somehow gave him strength. An image of his father popped into his mind, and he could see him standing in the bleachers, cheering for Mister at the Nationals when Mister had won for the very first time.

He'd come to watch this too, and he'd be cheering Mister on the same way he had years ago. That gave him the bravery he'd been lacking, and when Card said, "We've got an extra-special guest with us here tonight, so let's welcome Mister Glover to the stage!"

He plucked a melody on his guitar, and it blared out into the crowd as Mister jogged past the black curtains separating him from the bright, colorful lights swishing back and forth on the stage. The bass guitarist handed him a mic, and Mister lifted his free hand in a wave.

"Howdy, Mister," Card said, his voice made of friendliness.

"Howdy back atcha, Card." Mister slipped easily into his public persona, and when he looked out into the crowd, he could only see black. Perfect.

"I hear you've got a pressing question that needs to be asked." Card continued to play, his fingers obviously with a mind of their own, just like Ward's. Mister's throat narrowed as he thought of his family out in the crowd, because they'd all come tonight to see this.

"That I do," Mister said, clearing his throat. "But I need our amazing host back out here first." He peered toward the side of the stage where she'd exited. "Can I get Liberty Bellamore back out here, please?"

She didn't immediately step out of the shadows, and the drummer started playing a drumroll on his snare. The audience quickly joined in with their hands and feet, and Mister's throat turned dry as the seconds ticked by.

"Libby," Mister said, and Card picked up her name as a chant.

Oh wow, Mister thought. Where had she gone? He'd performed one song.

Finally, Libby came up the stairs off the front of the stage, and the spotlight swung to illuminate her way.

Mister dropped to both knees, the lights on him boiling hot too. The crowd went nuts, and he could definitely hear Duke's voice, as well as Bishop's and Ace's.

Libby reached the top of the steps, and her eyes moved to him. Her step faltered, and he gestured her to keep coming toward him. He handed the mic back to the bass guitarist, who held it for him, right in front of his mouth.

"I love this woman," Mister said, his lips brushing the metal part of the mic. "Libby, you're the part of me I've been missing for so long. You make me want to be a better man. You'd make me the happiest man in Texas if you'd say yes to being my wife."

He pulled the diamond ring from his pocket and held it up, at which point Card said, "Ho-ly cows, friends! Look at that gem!"

Mister turned it as even more lights beamed down on him and Libby. He held it in one hand and reached for one of hers with his other one, bringing her even closer.

"It's a yes or no question," he said.

"Oh, was there a question in there?" she asked, plenty of playfulness in her tone.

"Maybe not," he said, chuckling. "Will you marry me?"

"Yes," Libby said, and again, he heard the waver in her voice. Before he could put the ring on her finger, she took his face in her hands, leaned forward, and kissed him. It was a sloppy kiss, as she couldn't stop smiling, and Mister couldn't either. "Yes, I'll marry you," she said, right into the mic.

He could barely hear beyond the drums and the guitar that suddenly increased. He couldn't hear past the roaring approval of the crowd. He couldn't hear above Card yelling into his mic, "She said yes!"

But he didn't need to hear anything Libby said. He could *feel* the way she felt about him in her touch, and in her presence. He got to his feet and put the ring on her finger, kissed her properly amidst a bunch of catcalls and whistles, and turned toward the grandstands and lifted her left hand into the air.

The flashes from cameras popped in his vision, and Mister stayed put for several long seconds. Then he kept his hand in Libby's and led her toward the side curtains again.

His breath whooshed out of his mouth once he reached the cool darkness, and he didn't stop until he reached the ground off the stage completely. Only then did he turn back to Libby. "I love you."

"I love you more," she said. "For me, Mister, it's always been you."

"I can't wait to marry you," he murmured, curling his fingers around the back of her neck and drawing her closer for another, deeper kiss, this one once again saying more than words ever could.

Read on for a sneak peek at **THE HOPE OF HER HEART**, which finally features Etta Glover and all of her hopes and dreams for the future…

It'll also wrap up this series, and the enormity that is the Glover Family. I can't wait for you to read it!

*E*tta Glover bent to put baby Betty in her stroller, noting the closed door on Charlie's office. She'd picked up another sponsorship for the holidays, but Etta didn't mind coming down to take Betty and Preacher for their walk.

"Ready?" she asked once the six-month-old was all buckled in. Preacher Glover, her cousin, stood right behind the stroller, both hands on the handlebars. "I get to push Betty." She raised her eyebrows, clearly telling him to move aside.

"I can push my own daughter in a stroller," he said, his voice like a drought in Texas.

"Of course you can," she said. "But it's my turn."

"It's been your turn every day this week." He shuffled out of the way, reaching for the sideboard to steady himself.

"If we don't hurry, it'll start to rain on us while we're out there."

"I checked the weather," he said, reaching for his cane. He hated it, but Etta had been given about ten talks from Ward, her brother, about how Preacher would try to take the easy way out of his physical therapy. He went to a facility three times each week, but it was important he walk every single day. Only by forcing him to use the muscles in his back, core, and legs would they heal.

"It'll be fine through lunchtime," he said, turning toward the side door without twisting his hips. He stepped outside onto a long, narrow porch that ran toward the back corner of the house. He went right instead of left, where Ward and Bear had come built a ramp for Preacher.

Etta took an extra moment to tuck a blanket around Betty all the same, because the darling girl wouldn't like the wind should it gust up. And if anything was predictable about winter in Three Rivers, it was the wind.

"Two months," Preacher grumbled, loud enough for Etta to hear. She watched him go by the window in his slow, somewhat stilted gait. "How much longer, Lord? I'm workin' hard here."

Etta's heart bled for her cousin. He'd been in a terrible car accident over two years ago now. He'd had several surgeries, and just when it seemed like he was doing so well, something would happen. This last time, Preacher had fallen and reinjured his hip and lower back. He'd been experiencing sciatica pain since, and he'd had to relearn how to walk with the new limitations on his right leg.

He hadn't endured any more surgeries, and Etta thanked the Lord for that each day. "Come on, baby Betty," she said. "You come with Auntie Etta, and let's go walk with your daddy." She aimed the stroller through the doorway and followed Preacher down the ramp, where he waited at the bottom.

He flashed her a tight smile. "Thank you for coming," he said. "I'm sorry I'm in a foul mood."

"You're allowed," she said. "Now." She took a deep breath of the cool air, felt it infuse her lungs and life with energy, and blew it all out. "Yesterday, we walked the full circuit—down around all the cowboy cabins, back up here, across the road, along Mister's new home-site, and back in thirty-two minutes and twelve seconds."

It could only be maybe a half-mile to do all of that, so Preacher's pace wasn't anything to write home about. Still, he improved every single day, and Etta could go slow, listen to Betty babble about nothing, and enjoy time outside without having to say much.

"I'm going to set my timer for that, and our goal is to be right here, on this spot, before it goes off." She tapped on her phone, Preacher's eyes boring into the side of her head. She didn't care, not really.

Some in her family had called her stuffy in the past. Stuck-up had entered her ears a time or two. Ida, her twin sister, used to say Etta was the sophisticated one while Ida was the country girl. Etta could admit to liking nice things, fancy food at even fancier parties, and getting dressed up in pumps, pearls, and perfume just to go to church.

But in a lot of ways, she'd calmed down tremendously in recent years. Since Noah Johnson, if she were being honest. He'd been one of her high-brow cowboy boyfriends. Rich, classy, mature—he'd been a lot older than her.

Because of that, he hadn't wanted more children, and Etta had been unable to walk down the aisle and meet him at the altar. A stab of guilt poked right into her chest, though she'd come to terms with what she'd done, and she'd done her very best to make it right.

"Ready?" She looked up and away from her thoughts.

"A timer, Etta?"

"Let's go, baby," she said, pushing start on her timer. She put the phone in the cupholder on top of the stroller and took the first step. Preacher came with her, and she knew he wouldn't talk. If she had something to say, she said it, but more often than not, they just walked together. Then she'd go inside and make fresh coffee and make sure Preacher got settled on the couch. By then, Charlie had been coming out of her office, and Etta had been going back up to the homestead.

It worked out that this morning walk put her back home about time to put together lunch, and since she didn't do field trips up to Shiloh Ridge in the winter, she'd been feeding anyone who wanted to come to the home-stead for a week or so now.

After the successful Thanksgiving dinner a couple of

weeks ago, where she'd invited August Winters and things had gone well with her core family of four siblings, their spouses, children, and Mother, Etta had considered asking him to come to the ranch for lunch. Or offering to meet him in town, as he had a very busy construction job.

He'd had a very busy construction job, she corrected herself. August had just taken a new job, and he was starting on Monday. He was moving into a new place today, as Etta had learned a few days ago when she'd texted him to see if he could get together this weekend.

They didn't see one another in person all that often, because he had a nine-year-old daughter he wanted to protect. Dating was new for him, he'd said, and Etta understood the complexities of having children and trying to fit a new love interest into the situation.

She was fine going slow and being cautious. It gave her time to make sure the man she'd started seeing was being honest with her. So many in the recent past hadn't been, and perhaps Etta wore jade-colored lenses in her dating glasses.

"You're lifting your leg well," she said.

"It feels good today," Preacher said.

Betty screeched and threw her plastic keys on the ground. Etta kept right on moving, bending to swoop them into her hand as she passed. The baby started to fuss, but Etta didn't give her the keys. She set them in the cup holder with her phone and kept a steady pace.

When Betty really got herself worked up, which only happened after a few more steps, Etta reached for the bottle in the other part of the cup holder. "Okay, Betty Boop," she said. "Enough of that." She stepped next to the stroller and extended the bottle toward the girl. She had fat tears clinging to her lashes, which made Etta's whole soul light up. "Oh, you poor thing. Here's your milk. No more crying now." She made sure the girl had a good grip on the bottle and had laid back before she returned behind the stroller.

The road moved right and into the small cowboy community, and Preacher and Etta went with it. "Looks like someone's moving in," she said, noticing two cabins down at the end, both with trucks backed up to them.

"Yeah, new hires," Preacher said. "I can't really do anything with birthing season, and I hired a couple of new men."

"Two people for what you do alone," she said with a smile. Preacher did not return it, and a sigh moved silently through Etta's body. "Preacher."

"I don't need praise, Etta. Not right now."

"I'm sorry," she murmured.

"I don't even know why I'm still foreman. I've told Bear and Ranger and Ward to get Judge to do it a hundred times. They won't let me resign."

"No one wants you to do that."

"What about what I want?" he asked, sliding her glare out of the corner of her eye. "Instead, I have to hold a bogus title and then hire people to do what I can't. It's ludicrous."

"They wouldn't be foreman."

"Judge could do it."

"Judge doesn't want to do it."

"Then Mister."

"As soon as you're better, it's—"

"I'm not going to *get* better," Preacher said. "Why am I the only one who can see that?" He looked up into the sky. "Dear Lord, open their eyes to the reality of the situation I'm in."

"You *are* going to get better," Etta said, surprised by his out-loud prayer. "You're stronger and faster every single day. Why do you do the exercises if you don't believe you're going to get better?"

"So my wife won't leave me?" It sounded like a question, and Etta turned her full attention to him while she usually looked for rocks and potholes in the dirt road.

"Preacher," she chastised. "Charlie loves you just how you are. Sickness, health, fall, no fall. It doesn't matter to her."

Preacher looked away, his jaw tight. He finally said, "I know."

"Are you seeing anyone?" she asked.

"It's required to see a counselor when you do the level of physical therapy I do," he said.

"Good," Etta said. "After Noah, I—" She swallowed. "It helped me to talk to someone."

He looked at her. "I didn't know you went to a therapist after Noah."

"I did."

"You don't still feel guilty about that, do you?"

"Here and there, it jabs at me," she said. "But it doesn't hold me back the way it used to. In fact, I started seeing—" She cut off as she saw the man she'd started seeing. She and August hadn't kissed yet, but they'd held hands. They'd flirted *a lot* over text message. They'd been out five times.

"Etta?"

"He's right there," she said, her brain misfiring at her. What in the world was August Winters doing here? Taking a lamp and a frilly pink suitcase from the back of his truck? Her step slowed to the point where Preacher was moving faster than her, her eyes scanning for Hailey, August's daughter.

If he was moving in here—and it sure seemed like he was—then he'd have his daughter with him. Etta had met her, of course. Hailey had come to Shiloh Ridge on a field trip with her third-grade class a couple of months ago. August had come along to help chaperone, and that was how Etta had met him.

The handsome cowboy had asked for her number before the bus had left, and they'd been talking and seeing one another since.

"That's August Winters," she said as he disappeared into the last cabin on the right side of the road. "Did you hire August Winters?"

"Yeah," Preacher said slowly. "Why? Should I not have?"

Etta suddenly wanted to come face-to-face with him.

He knew she lived here at Shiloh Ridge. He knew her family—the Glovers—owned and operated it.

"No," she said, a bit of fire lighting inside her. "He's a great guy."

"Why do you look like you're going to rip his face off then?"

She got moving again, causing Preacher to hobble to keep up with her. August came out the front door, laughing about something. His fair daughter followed, and Etta quenched part of the flames burning through her.

August looked toward the road, and she knew the moment he'd seen her. His smile fell right off his face, and he dang near tripped over his own feet. She lifted one hand and both eyebrows, a silent demand to know what in the world was going on.

"Etta," he said smoothly, continuing toward her in a normal gait now. "Good mornin', Preacher."

"Yeah, I don't know about that," Preacher said, his gaze volleying from August to Etta and back.

"What are you doing here?" Etta asked as Hailey arrived at his side.

"Miss Etta!" she said, throwing herself into Etta's arms. She softened, because she loved children, and she'd helped this one once upon a time. "Daddy got a job here as a cowboy. A real, live cowboy. We're gonna live in this cabin, and have all these fields to roam in, and there are horses *right there*."

She looked like she'd harnessed the world in a single throw, and Etta couldn't help absorbing some of her enthusiasm. "That's amazing, Hailey. Has your daddy ever been a cowboy before?"

"Yeah, once," Hailey said, reaching up to push her wayward hair back out of her eyes. "We each get our own room here too. It's awesome."

"Hailey," August said, his voice definitely made of several emotions woven together. Etta wasn't sure how to pull them apart and analyze them fast enough. "Grab your laundry basket of dolls and take it into your new room, okay?"

"Okay, Daddy." She skipped over to the tailgate of the truck and did what her father asked.

He watched her until she went up the steps and then he turned back to Preacher and Etta. She put one hand on the stroller handlebars and cocked her hip, clearly female-speak for, *Well?*

"Surprise," he said with that devilish smile that made her stomach turn to heated marshmallow and made her mind conjure up such fantasies as tasting his mouth with hers.

"Surprise?" she repeated. "That's what you have to say for yourself?"

*A*ugust Winters swallowed and looked at his new boss. He shook his head, far too much glee on his face. Preacher Glover wasn't going to help August, that much was clear.

"I told you I got a new job," he said. "This is it."

"You know I'm a Glover."

"Yes," he said with a smile. "As you've told me a million times now."

"I have not, you rascal," Etta said, stepping out from behind that stroller to swat at his chest. He laughed as he warded off her hands, managing to grab one around her wrist.

Sparks and fireworks and entire forest fires moved through August's bloodstream. He hadn't felt anything like this with a woman since he'd met his wife, about fifteen years ago now.

Josie had been the sun to him, and he'd been willing to

be her satellite, revolving around anything and everything she did.

Etta Glover possessed the same magnetic, centrally strong pull on him that Josie had, and August had no idea what to do about it.

Etta finally stopped struggling, her own smile decorating her pretty face. She huffed out her breath and tugged on the bottom of her jacket. Her fingers slipped through his as they faced Preacher, and she said, "I was just telling Preach about this man I'd started seeing. And then, like fate, there you were. Here you are. Here he is."

August grinned at Etta, because it was rare to see her flustered. A slight pinkish hue had crept into her cheeks, and that only made August's desire for her shoot toward the stratosphere. He'd met her siblings and mother a couple of weeks ago, but not her cousins.

Well, Preacher he had, obviously.

"August Winters," she said. "I'm seeing August Winters."

Preacher lifted his right eyebrow. "Is this going to be a problem for me?"

"No, sir," August said quickly.

His boss's face melted into a smile as Etta started swatting at him, saying, "You—walk—yourself—around—Mister," with every playful whap against his shoulder and chest. August noted that she stayed on his left side, as Preacher walked with a cane on the right. He didn't know the whole story there, and he didn't need to.

He understood how some things weren't fun to talk

about—a fact that stared him in the face every single day that he continued to text and talk to Etta and he didn't bring up his late wife. She hadn't asked yet, but August suspected she would soon enough.

"We're never going to beat the timer now," Preacher said, laughing the same way August had at Etta's pretty pathetic attempts to punish him.

"Yes, we will," she insisted. "I'm just going to have to push you harder." She resumed her spot behind the stroller, the cutest, chubbiest baby girl sitting up in the front seat. "Lovely to see you, Mister Winters," Etta said, her chin aiming for the stars. "Let's go Betty Boop. Your daddy has walking to do."

She continued by him, and August watched her go, stunned that was really going to be the end of their inter-action. No other questions? No invitation to the home-stead for lunch? She'd been texting him pictures of all the delicious food she was feeding other cowboys this week, and it had taken a great deal of willpower to stay at his construction site and eat his sad peanut butter and honey sandwich.

They rounded the corner, Preacher tossing a look over his shoulder at August. Etta, however, did not. The woman was like a rock. A steel rock, and August wasn't sure if he liked that or if it intimidated him.

He turned back to his truck, plenty left to unpack. He got busy doing that, because he only had today and tomorrow to get himself and Hailey settled in this house before he had to start the job here at Shiloh Ridge.

Everything about this job was better than where he'd been for the past seven months. He hated the construction job, because he had to be clocked in by six a.m., and that made life really hard with Hailey. He had to get her up really early and completely ready for school. Then his next-door neighbor watched her until the bus came at eight-twenty, and he had to rely on his nine-year-old to text him and let him know she'd made it to school.

It had been very difficult to get time off, and he'd barely made enough to keep him and Hailey in a one-bedroom apartment. He'd slept on the couch, his long legs hanging over the end of it and the sound of the refriger-ator coming on to refill the ice-maker waking him without fail near two a.m. every night.

Here, this cabin stood tall and proud, brand-new and brilliantly white against the stormy sky threatening to drop rain at any moment. He had a front porch and a back one. No garage, but that was fine. Two bedrooms. Two bathrooms. A living room with really nice furniture—brand-new. Everything here on this part of Shiloh Ridge was new, and everything broadcasted dollar signs.

August picked up the pace with bringing in boxes when the first rumble of thunder shook the sky. He'd just managed to get everything on the covered porch before the raindrops fell, and he and Hailey could get it all in from there.

By the time he thought to check his phone, he had four messages from Etta. *Lunch at the homestead will be at noon.*

You're welcome to come.

Don't think just because you live here now that you can just come up and see me whenever you want.

Or maybe you can.

They'd all come within seconds of each other, because they had the same timestamp on them, and she must've only been around the corner from him when she sent them, because they were a good forty-five minutes old.

If you can handle two extra mouths for lunch today, Hailey and I will be there.

I suppose that's fine, Etta sent back, and August smiled at his device, at her ruse to make him think she wasn't as interested in him as she was. He could see the interest light up her dark blue eyes every time he looked at her. He wondered if he put off the same feelings, and he suspected he did. Josie told him he wore everything right on the surface, and while he'd tried to shelve things and hide them after her death, he wasn't great at it.

Were you surprised to see me? He didn't need to ask to know. She'd worn her shock as evidently as he did.

Yes, she said, and he hated texting when he couldn't see her face. He'd spent quite a bit of time with her in the past couple of months, and Etta had a quirky sense of humor buried beneath her more proper exterior.

I told you it was a good job and good move for me.

I'm glad, she said. *I really hope that's true.*

I do too, he sent, and he looked up, only getting an eyeful of the ceiling. But it was a brand-new ceiling, with pristine, white paint and the canister lights only found in the nicest, newest homes.

"Daddy," Hailey said, skipping into the kitchen from the hallway which led down toward the bedrooms and bathrooms. He even had a laundry room right here to do their wash. He'd taken so much for granted in Dripping Springs, and while he'd wanted to move to Three Rivers to give himself and Hailey a chance at a fresh start, he hadn't realized how much it would cost.

Monetarily, emotionally, spiritually, physically, mentally, it had cost him so much.

He once again paused and waited for the weight to come into his heart. When he thought of the farmhouse he'd left behind in the past, a load of bricks would settle on his chest. When he thought of how far away his wife's grave was and that he couldn't go see her whenever he wanted, someone pumped steel into his veins and his whole system turned to metal.

Today, however…it didn't. None of that happened, and August's heart kept beating blood through his body.

"I'm ready," he whispered. Josie had died four years ago, and he'd lived long enough in the darkness hanging over the farm they'd run together in the Hill Country.

"Daddy," Hailey said again, and he blinked himself back to the situation at hand.

"Yeah, sweets?"

"What do we have for lunch? I'm getting hungry."

"You know what?" August asked, grinning at his daughter. Sometimes he swore he could see Josie when he looked at Hailey, and right now was no exception. "Miss

Etta invited us up to the homestead, thinking we might not have any food."

Hailey's face lit up, making his next question unnecessary. He asked it anyway. "Do you want to go?"

"Can we?"

"I know the way," he said with a smile. "She said it would be at noon." He looked down at his phone. "We've got about a half-hour. Let's make sure our beds are set up for tonight, and after lunch, we'll go get some groceries, and then we won't have to do anything else if we don't want to."

"Okay," Hailey said, and she started a joyous skip back down the hallway. Her room was still a jumble of boxes, clothes, dolls, and a bare mattress, so despite the exhaustion in August's soul, and the fact that he had to do everything himself, he dug in and started getting his daughter's bedroom put together.

No matter what, he would not let her down. Not again.

His phone buzzed in his pocket, and he suspected it would be Etta again. After finishing with the purple pony comforter his mother had bought for Hailey on her bed, he said, "Start hanging up your shirts, little lady," and he stepped out into the hallway.

He made it into his bedroom, which needed as much work as his daughter's, but he chose his phone over making up his bed.

Etta had texted: *What are you going to tell Hailey? Do I need to be prepared to say anything? Should I tell my family to play it cool? I don't want to put you in a difficult position, and I'm really fine to follow your lead on this.*

August looked up, the curtain-less window showing him the wide world of Shiloh Ridge Ranch beyond the glass. He liked this woman. He liked Etta Glover a whole lot.

He'd never told Hailey about his feelings for anyone but her mother, and he didn't know how to get these new words about Etta to align in his throat.

Two things, he typed out, his thumbs flying to keep up with his brain. *Let's go to dinner one night next week. You tell me when you can, and I'll get a babysitter for Hailey. Two, I'd like a little more time before I tell Hailey about us. If that means you've got to tell your family something, I'm sorry. Can I have a little more time?*

He read over the text, the question in his mind—and surely the one that would be in Etta's—was, *Time for what, August?*

You can have as much time as you need, Etta responded quickly. *I'll just send them a text to let them know to keep things cool at lunch today. Not everyone comes, and most of my cousins don't know about us anyway. So this will open that can of worms…*

Sorry, he said. *Maybe just tell your siblings?*

No, Etta said. *I once hid a boyfriend for a long time from my family, and I don't want to do that. I'll just tell them about us quickly and ask them to please, please be reasonable and respectful. They can do it.*

August wanted to hear more about this other

boyfriend. August wanted to know everything about Etta, absolutely everything, and that alone made him swallow hard.

"Help me," he whispered to the stark walls around him. He wasn't sure if he was speaking to God or Josie, but he knew he'd need help from one of them to protect his daughter…and his heart.

He couldn't believe he was going to take his heart out of the box where he'd stored it years ago, but he was. As he stood in his bedroom and read over Etta's texts from the past week, he realized he already had.

It beat in a new way, and it seemed to say *Et-ta, Et-Et-ta* with every thumping sound.

"Daddy," Hailey said, causing him to jump and guilt to gut him.

"Yeah."

"It's time to go," she said. "Can we go?"

"Sure, sweets," he said, shoving his phone in his pocket. Now, he just had to figure out how to hide all of his soft feelings for the lovely Miss Etta in the time it took to drive a mile up the hill to the homestead.

Get Etta and August's romance in THE HOPE OF HER HEART and don't miss a moment of life at Shiloh Ridge Ranch and keep up with everything to do with the Glover Family!

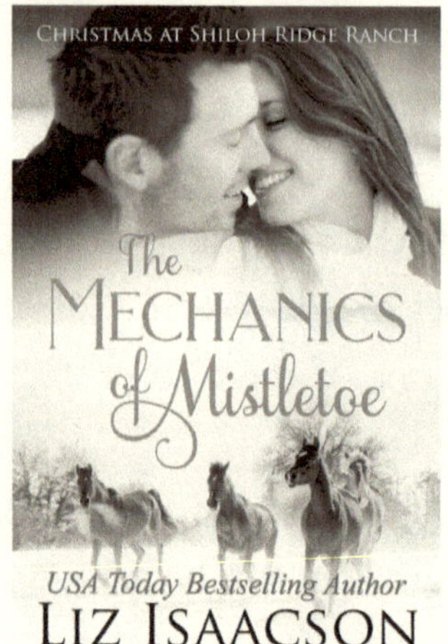

The Mechanics of Mistletoe (Book 1): Bear Glover can be a grizzly or a teddy, and he's always thought he'd be just fine working his generational family ranch and going back to the ancient homestead alone. But his crush on Samantha Benton won't go away. She's a genius with a wrench on Bear's tractors...and his heart. Can he tame his wild side and get the girl, or will he be left broken-hearted this Christmas season?

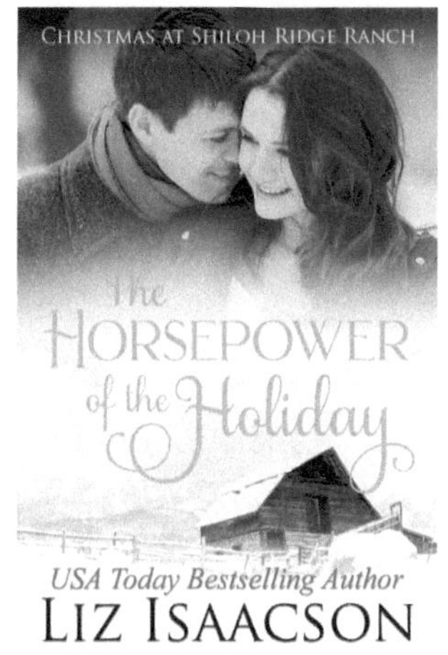

The Horsepower of the Holiday (Book 2): Ranger Glover has worked at Shiloh Ridge Ranch his entire life. The cowboys do everything from horseback there, but when he goes to town to trade in some trucks, somehow Oakley Hatch persuades him to take some ATVs back to the ranch. (Bear is NOT happy.)

She's a former race car driver who's got Ranger all revved up... Can he remember who he is and get Oakley to slow down enough to fall in love, or will there simply be too much horsepower in the holiday this year for a real relationship?

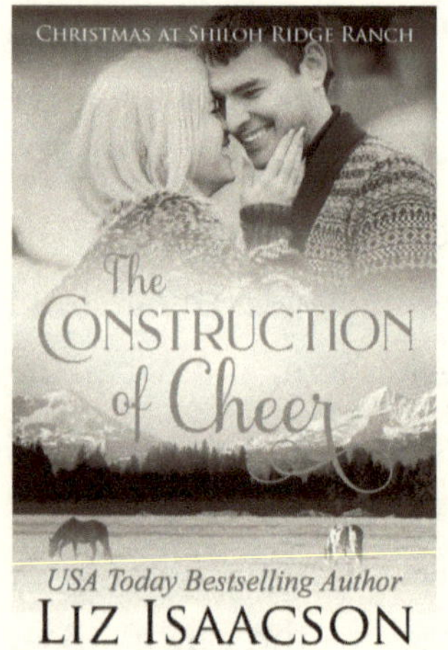

The Construction of Cheer (Book 3): Bishop Glover is the youngest brother, and he usually keeps his head down and gets the job done. When Montana Martin shows up at Shiloh Ridge Ranch looking for work, he finds himself inventing construction projects that need doing just to keep her coming around. (Again, Bear is NOT happy.) She wants to build her own construction firm, but she ends up carving a place for herself inside Bishop's heart. Can he convince her *he's* all she needs this Christmas season, or will her cheer rest solely on the success of her business?

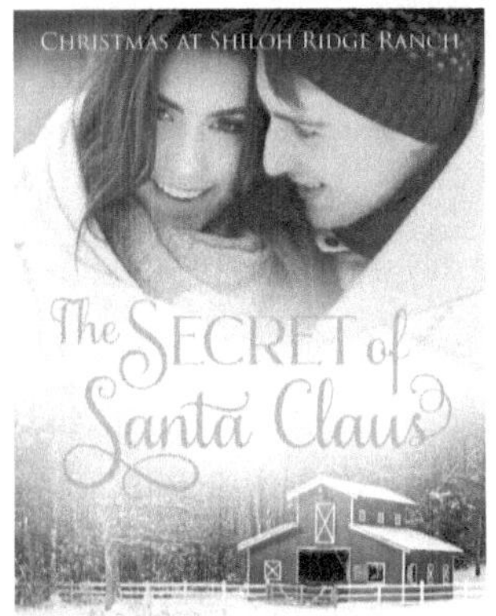

The Secret of Santa (Book 4): He's a fun-loving cowboy with a heart of gold. She's the woman who keeps putting him on hold. Can Ace and Holly Ann make a relationship work this Christmas?

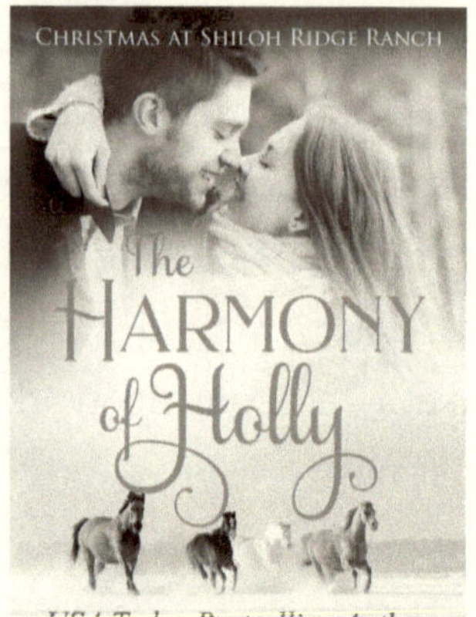

The Harmony of Holly (Book 5): He's as prickly as his name, but the new woman in town has caught his eye. Can Cactus shelve his temper and shed his cowboy hermit skin fast enough to make a relationship with Willa work?

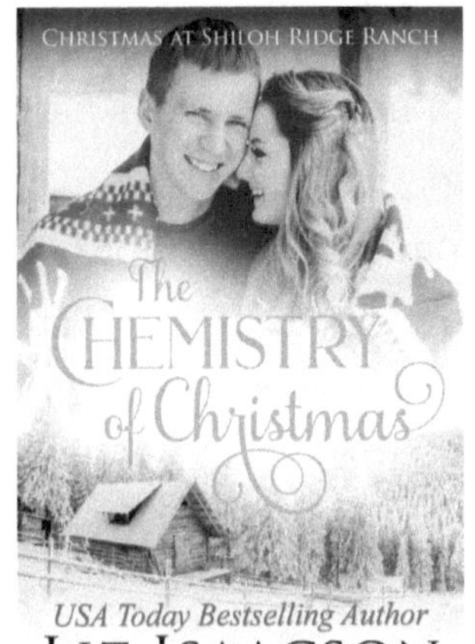

The Chemistry of Christmas (Book 6): He's the black sheep of the family, and she's a chemist who understands formulas, not emotions. Can Preacher and Charlie take their quirks and turn them into a strong relationship this Christmas?

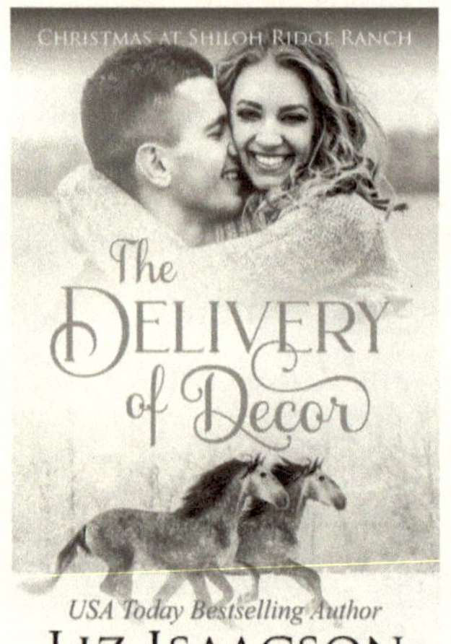

The Delivery of Decor (Book 7): When he falls, he falls hard and deep. She literally drives away from every relationship she's ever had. Can Ward somehow get Dot to stay this Christmas?

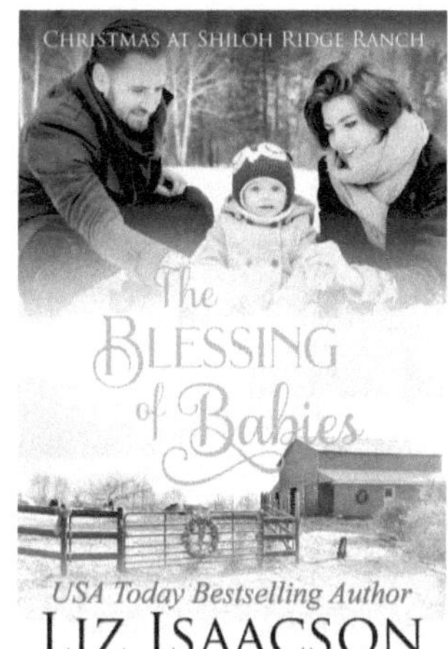

The Blessing of Babies (Book 8): Don't miss out on a single moment of the Glover family saga in this bridge story linking Ward and Judge's love stories!

The Glovers love God, country, dogs, horses, and family. Not necessarily in that order. ;)

Many of them are married now, with babies on the way, and there are lessons to be learned, forgiveness to be had and given, and new names coming to the family tree in southern Three Rivers!

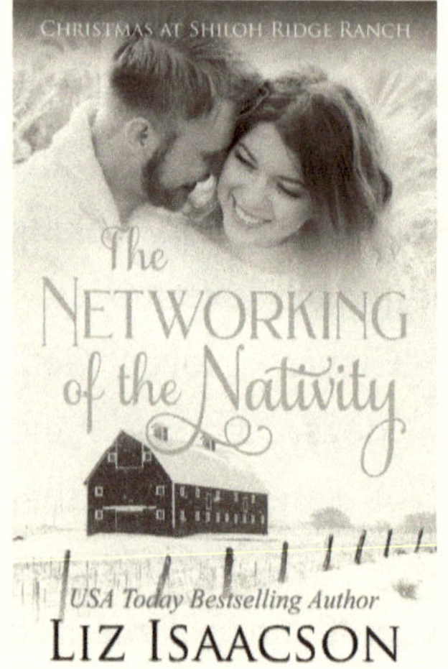

The Networking of the Nativity (Book 9): He's had a crush on her for years. She doesn't want to date until her daughter is out of the house. Will June take a change on Judge when the success of his Christmas light display depends on her networking abilities?

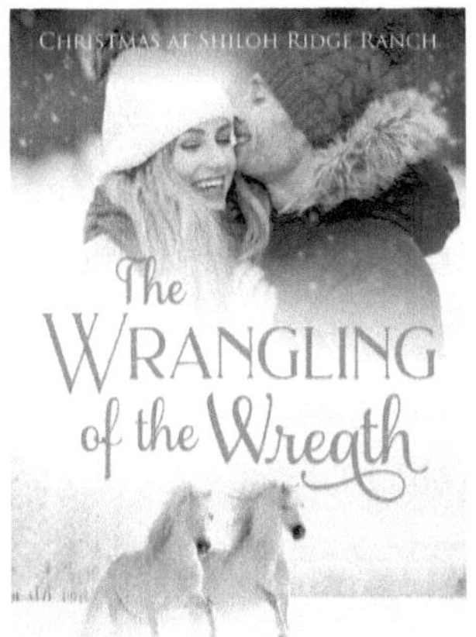

The Wrangling of the Wreath (Book 10): He's been so busy trying to find Miss Right. She's been right in front of him the whole time. This Christmas, can Mister and Libby take their relationship out of the best friend zone?

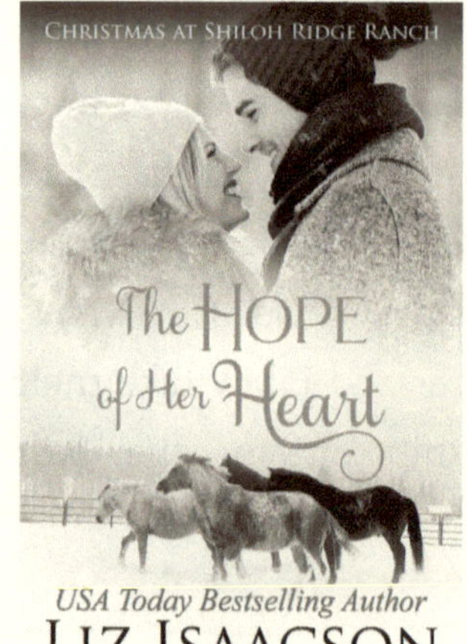

The Hope of Her Heart (Book 11): She's the only Glover without a significant other. He's been searching for someone who can love him *and* his daughter. Can Etta and August make a meaningful connection this Christmas?

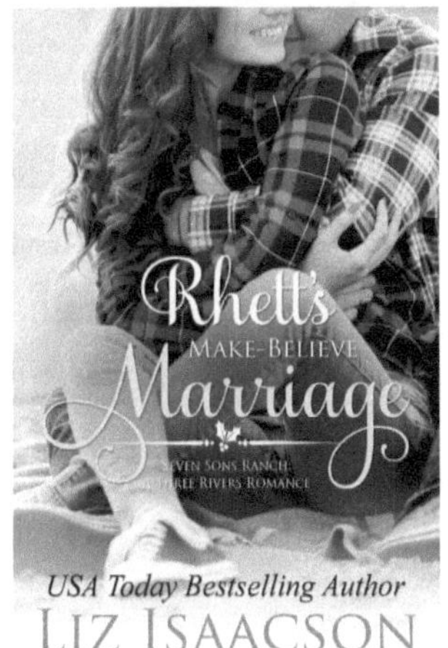

Rhett's Make-Believe Marriage (Book 1): She needs a husband to be credible as a matchmaker. He wants to help a neighbor. Will their fake marriage take them out of the friend zone?

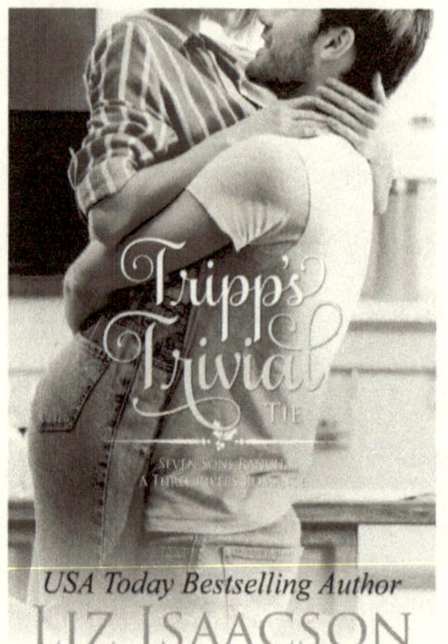

Tripp's Trivial Tie (Book 2): She needs a husband to keep her son. He's wanted to take their relationship to the next level, but she's always pushing him away. Will their trivial tie take them all the way to happily-ever-after?

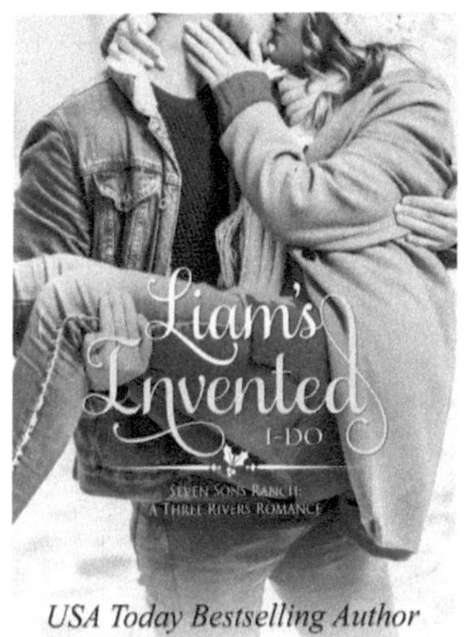

Liam's Invented I-Do (Book 3): She's desperate to save her ranch. He wants to help her any way he can. Will their invented I-Do open doors that have previously been closed and lead to a happily-ever-after for both of them?

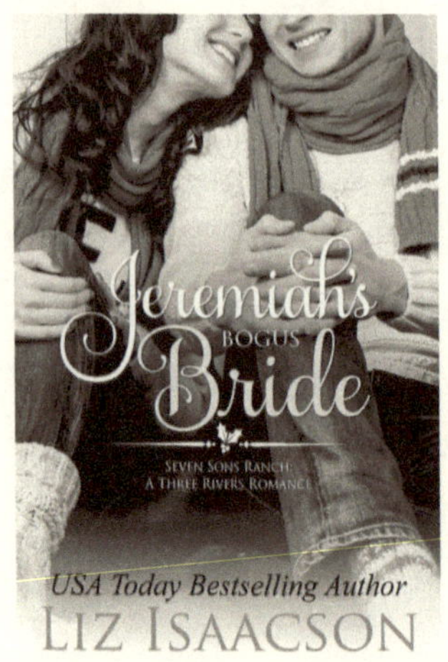

Jeremiah's Bogus Bride (Book 4): He wants to prove to his brothers that he's not broken. She just wants him. Will a fake marriage heal him or push her further away?

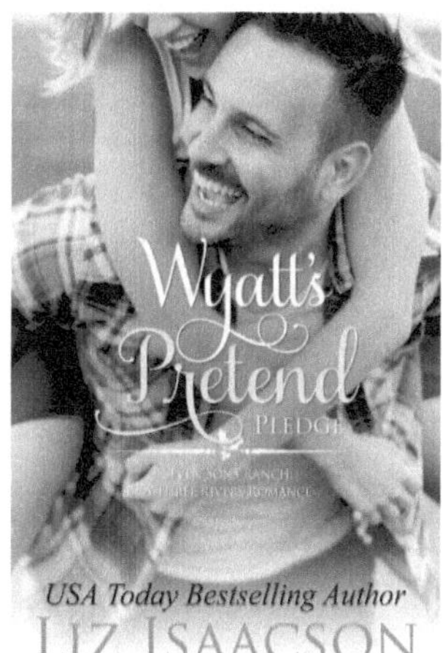

Wyatt's Pretend Pledge (Book 5): To get her inheritance, she needs a husband. He's wanted to fly with her for ages. Can their pretend pledge turn into something real?

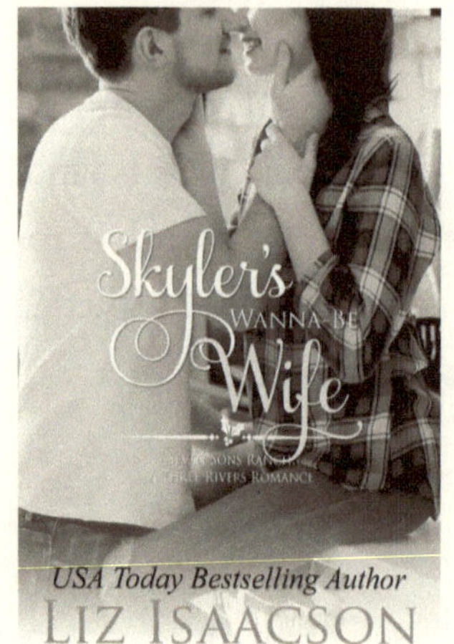

Skyler's Wanna-Be Wife (Book 6): She needs a new last name to stay in school. He's willing to help a fellow student. Can this wanna-be wife show the playboy that some things should be taken seriously?

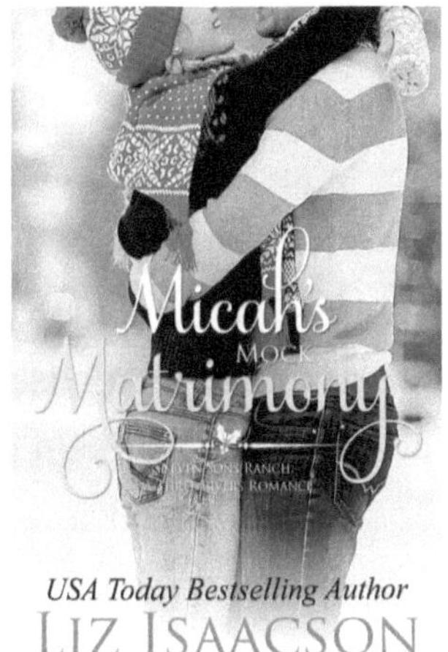

Micah's Mock Matrimony (Book 7): They were just actors auditioning for a play. The marriage was just for the audition – until a clerical error results in a legal marriage. Can these two ex-lovers negotiate this new ground between them and achieve new roles in each other's lives?

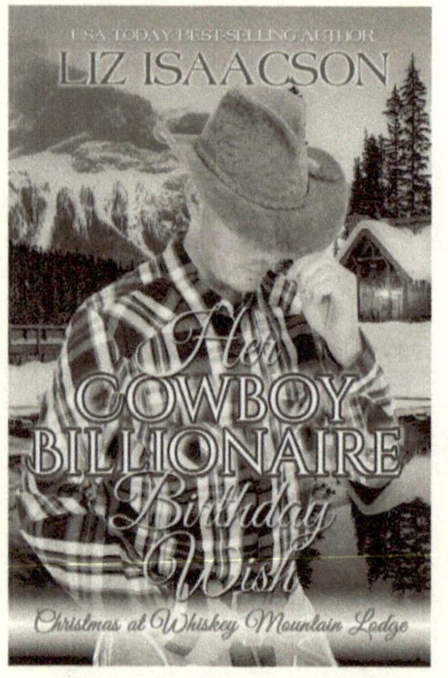

Her Cowboy Billionaire Birthday Wish (Book 1): All the maid at Whiskey Mountain Lodge wants for her birthday is a handsome cowboy billionaire. And Colton can make that wish come true—if only he hadn't escaped to Coral Canyon after being left at the altar...

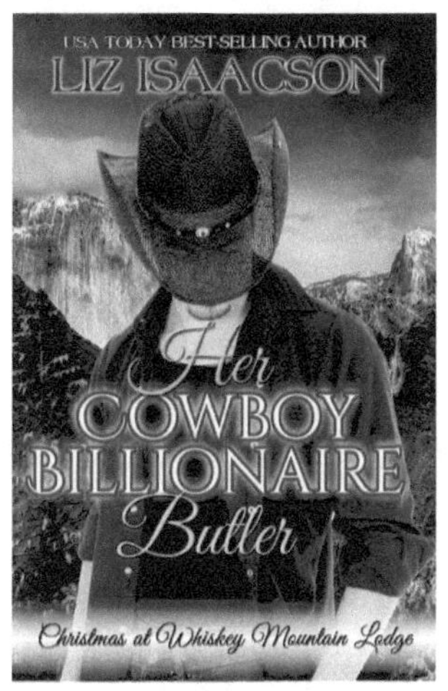 **Her Cowboy Billionaire Butler (Book 2):** She broke up with him to date another man...who broke her heart. He's a former CEO with nothing to do who can't get her out of his head. Can Wes and Bree find a way toward happily-ever-after at Whiskey Mountain Lodge?

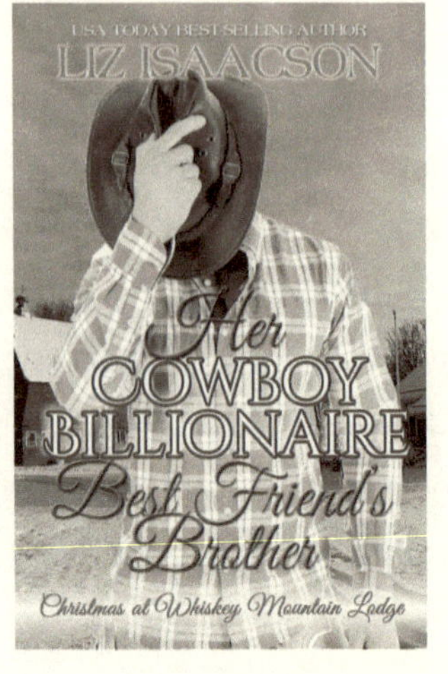

Her Cowboy Billionaire Best Friend's Brother (Book 3): She's best friends with the single dad cowboy's brother and has watched two friends find love with the sexy new cowboys in town. When Gray Hammond comes to Whiskey Mountain Lodge with his son, will Elise finally get her own happily-ever-after with one of the Hammond brothers?

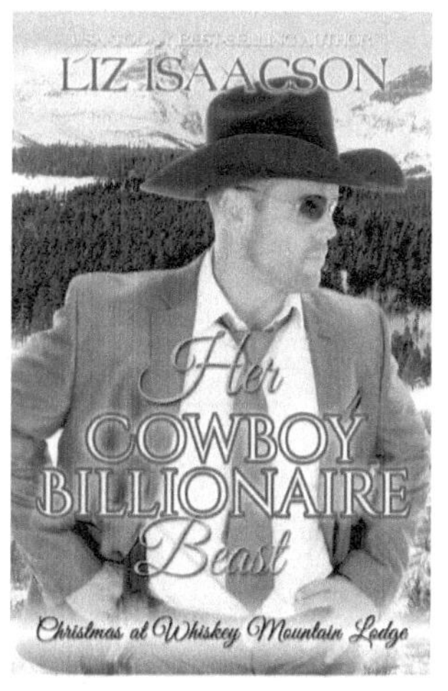

Her Cowboy Billionaire Beast (Book 4): A cowboy billionaire beast, his new manager, and the Christmas traditions that soften his heart and bring them together.

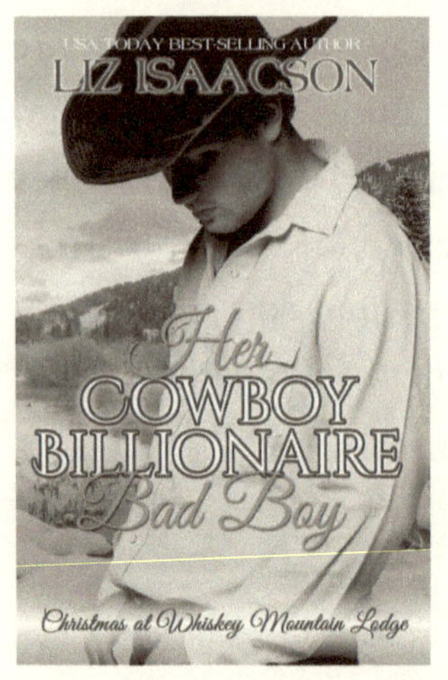

Her Cowboy Billionaire Bad Boy (Book 5): A cowboy billionaire cop who's a stickler for rules, the woman he pulls over when he's not even on duty, and the personal mandates he has to break to keep her in his life...

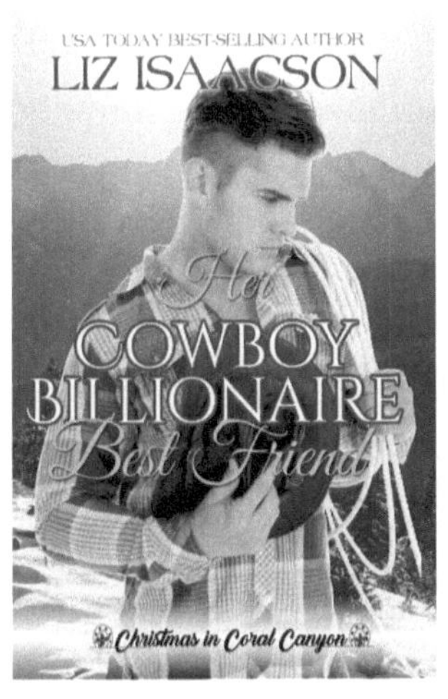

Her Cowboy Billionaire Best Friend (Book 1): Graham Whittaker returns to Coral Canyon a few days after Christmas—after the death of his father. He takes over the energy company his dad built from the ground up and buys a high-end lodge to live in—only a mile from the home of his once-best friend, Laney McAllister. They were best friends once, but Laney's always entertained feelings for him, and spending so much time with him while they make Christmas memories puts her heart in danger of getting broken again...

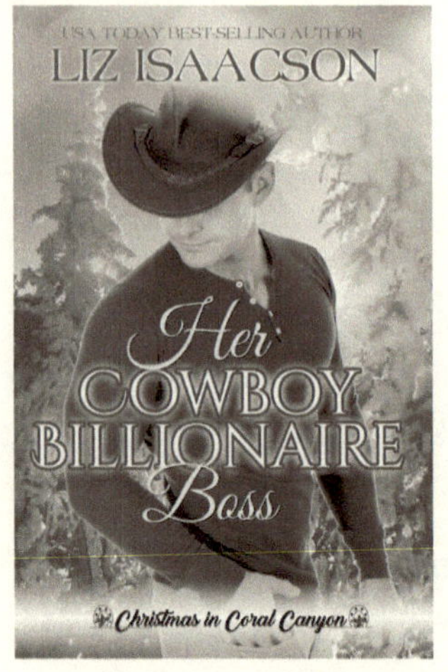

Her Cowboy Billionaire Boss (Book 2): Since the death of his wife a few years ago, Eli Whittaker has been running from one job to another, unable to find somewhere for him and his son to settle. Meg Palmer is Stockton's nanny, and she comes with her boss, Eli, to the lodge, her long-time crush on the man no different in Wyoming than it was on the beach. When she confesses her feelings for him and gets nothing in return, she's crushed, embarrassed, and unsure if she can stay in Coral Canyon for Christmas. Then Eli starts to show some feelings for her too...

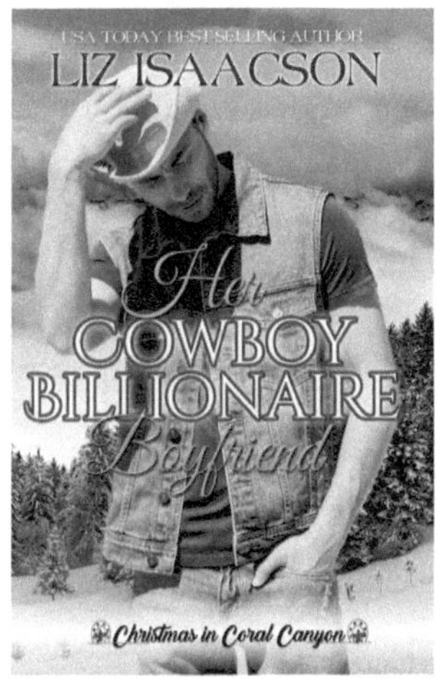

Her Cowboy Billionaire Boyfriend (Book 3): Andrew Whittaker is the public face for the Whittaker Brothers' family energy company, and with his older brother's robot about to be announced, he needs a press secretary to help him get everything ready and tour the state to make the announcements. When he's hit by a protest sign being carried by the company's biggest opponent, Rebecca Collings, he learns with a few clicks that she has the background they need. He offers her the job of press secretary when she thought she was going to be arrested, and not only because the spark between them in so hot Andrew can't see straight.

Can Becca and Andrew work together and keep their relationship a secret? Or will hearts break in this classic romance retelling reminiscent of *Two Weeks Notice?*

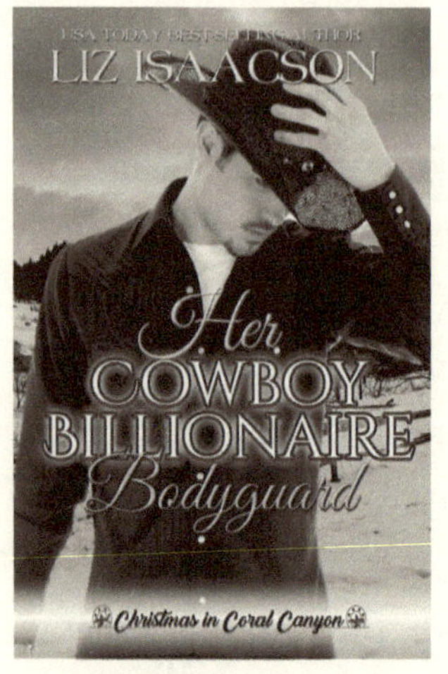

Her Cowboy Billionaire Bodyguard (Book 4): Beau Whittaker has watched his brothers find love one by one, but every attempt he's made has ended in disaster. Lily Everett has been in the spotlight since childhood and has half a dozen platinum records with her two sisters. She's taking a break from the brutal music industry and hiding out in Wyoming while her ex-husband continues to cause trouble for her. When she hears of Beau Whittaker and what he offers his clients, she wants to meet him. Beau is instantly attracted to Lily, but he tried a relationship with his last client that left a scar that still hasn't healed…

Can Lily use the spirit of Christmas to discover what matters most? Will Beau open his heart to the possibility of love with someone so different from him?

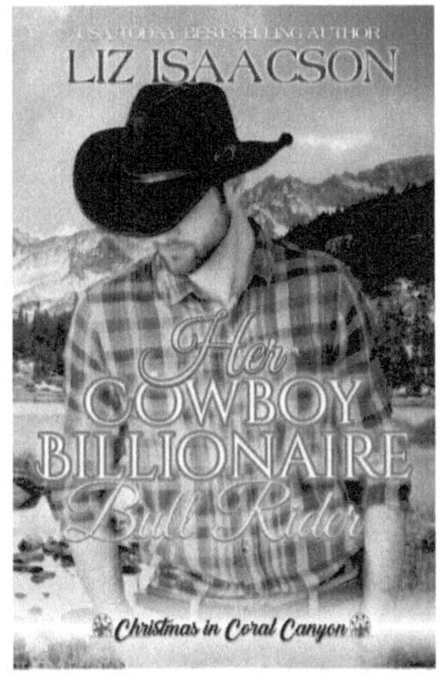

Her Cowboy Billionaire Bull Rider (Book 5): Todd Christopherson has just retired from the professional rodeo circuit and returned to his hometown of Coral Canyon. Problem is, he's got no family there anymore, no land, and no job. Not that he needs a job--he's got plenty of money from his illustrious career riding bulls.

Then Todd gets thrown during a routine horseback ride up the canyon, and his only support as he recovers physically is the beautiful Violet Everett. She's no nurse, but she does the best she can for the handsome cowboy. **Will she lose her heart to the billionaire bull rider? Can Todd trust that God led him to Coral Canyon...and Vi?**

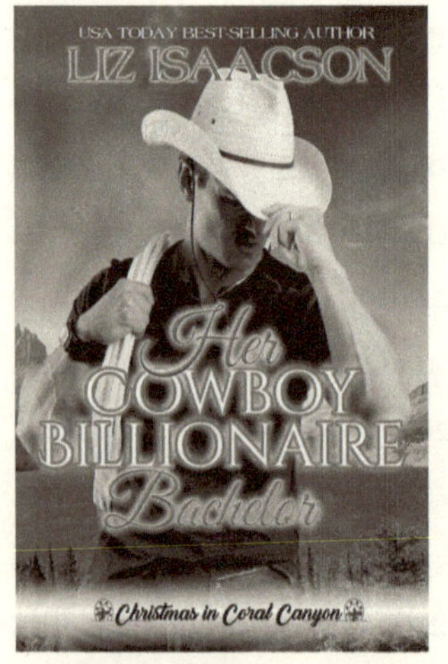

Her Cowboy Billionaire Bachelor (Book 6): Rose Everett isn't sure what to do with her life now that her country music career is on hold. After all, with both of her sisters in Coral Canyon, and one about to have a baby, they're not making albums anymore.

Liam Murphy has been working for Doctors Without Borders, but he's back in the US now, and looking to start a new clinic in Coral Canyon, where he spent his summers.

When Rose wins a date with Liam in a bachelor auction, their relationship blooms and grows quickly. **Can Liam and Rose find a solution to their problems that doesn't involve one of them leaving Coral Canyon with a broken heart?**

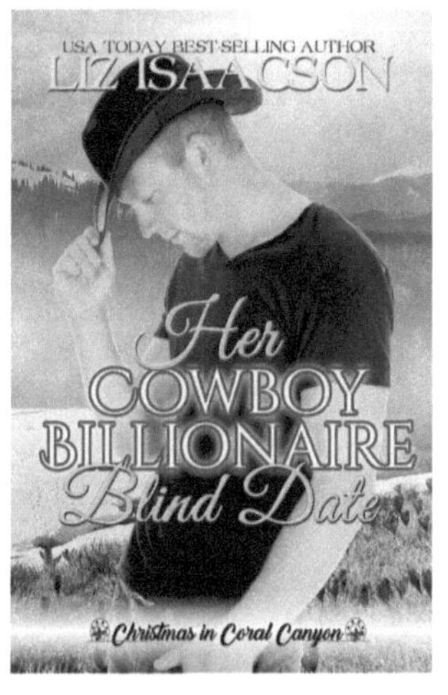

Her Cowboy Billionaire Blind Date (Book 7): Her sons want her to be happy, but she's too old to be set up on a blind date...isn't she?

Amanda Whittaker has been looking for a second chance at love since the death of her husband several years ago. Finley Barber is a cowboy in every sense of the word. Born and raised on a racehorse farm in Kentucky, he's since moved to Dog Valley and started his own breeding stable for champion horses. He hasn't dated in years, and everything about Amanda makes him nervous.

Will Amanda take the leap of faith required to be with Finn? Or will he become just another boyfriend who doesn't make the cut?

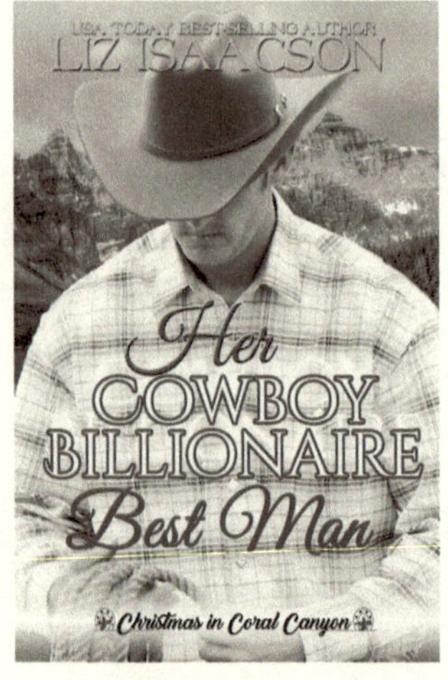

Her Cowboy Billionaire Best Man (Book 8): When Celia Abbott-Armstrong runs into a gorgeous cowboy at her best friend's wedding, she decides she's ready to start dating again.

But the cowboy is Zach Zuckerman, and the Zuckermans and Abbotts have been at war for generations.

Can Zach and Celia find a way to reconcile their family's differences so they can have a future together?

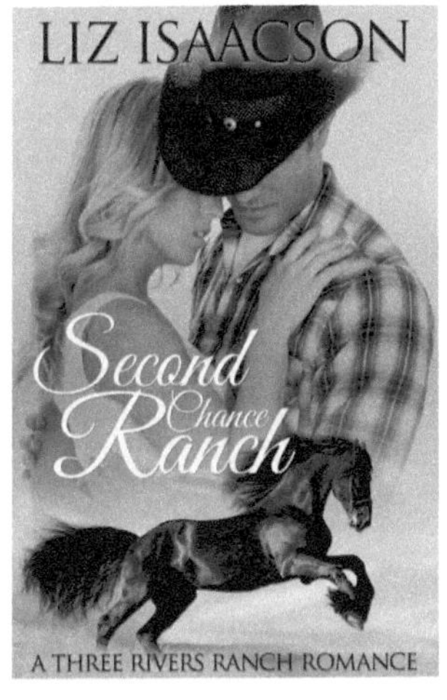

Second Chance Ranch: A Three Rivers Ranch Romance (Book 1): After his deployment, injured and discharged Major Squire Ackerman returns to Three Rivers Ranch, wanting to forgive Kelly for ignoring him a decade ago. He'd like to provide the stable life she needs, but with old wounds opening and a ranch on the brink of financial collapse, it will take patience and faith to make their second chance possible.

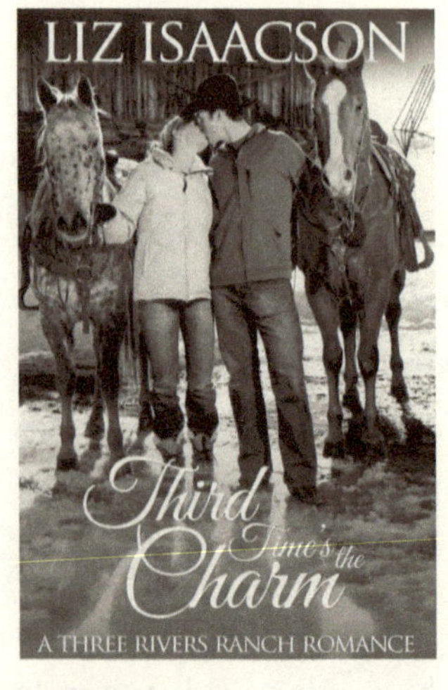

Third Time's the Charm: A Three Rivers Ranch Romance (Book 2): First Lieutenant Peter Marshall has a truckload of debt and no way to provide for a family, but Chelsea helps him see past all the obstacles, all the scars. With so many unknowns, can Pete and Chelsea develop the love, acceptance, and faith needed to find their happily ever after?

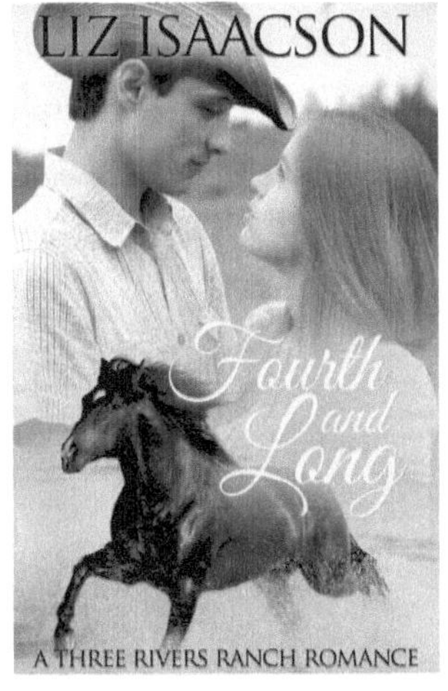

Fourth and Long: A Three Rivers Ranch Romance (Book 3): Commander Brett Murphy goes to Three Rivers Ranch to find some rest and relaxation with his Army buddies. Having his ex-wife show up with a seven-year-old she claims is his son is anything but the R&R he craves. Kate needs to make amends, and Brett needs to find forgiveness, but are they too late to find their happily ever after?

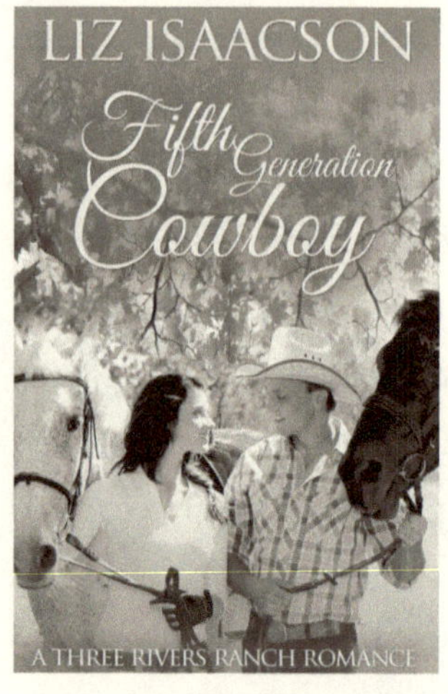

Fifth Generation Cowboy: A Three Rivers Ranch Romance (Book 4): Tom Lovell has watched his friends find their true happiness on Three Rivers Ranch, but everywhere he looks, he only sees friends. Rose Reyes has been bringing her daughter out to the ranch for equine therapy for months, but it doesn't seem to be working. Her challenges with Mari are just as frustrating as ever. Could Tom be exactly what Rose needs? Can he remove his friendship blinders and find love with someone who's been right in front of him all this time?

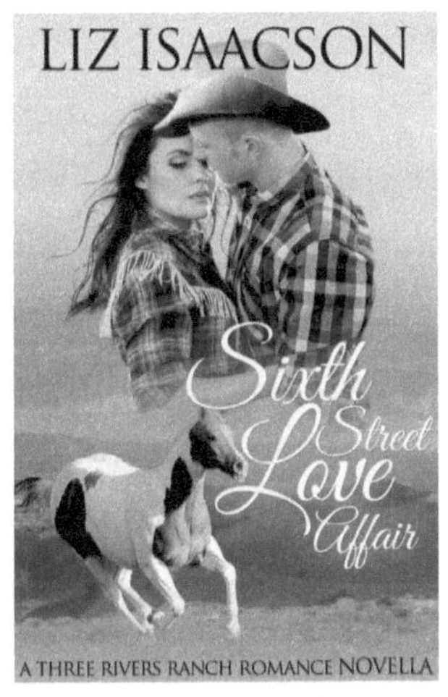

Sixth Street Love Affair: A Three Rivers Ranch Romance (Book 5): After losing his wife a few years back, Garth Ahlstrom thinks he's ready for a second chance at love. But Juliette Thompson has a secret that could destroy their budding relationship. Can they find the strength, patience, and faith to make things work?

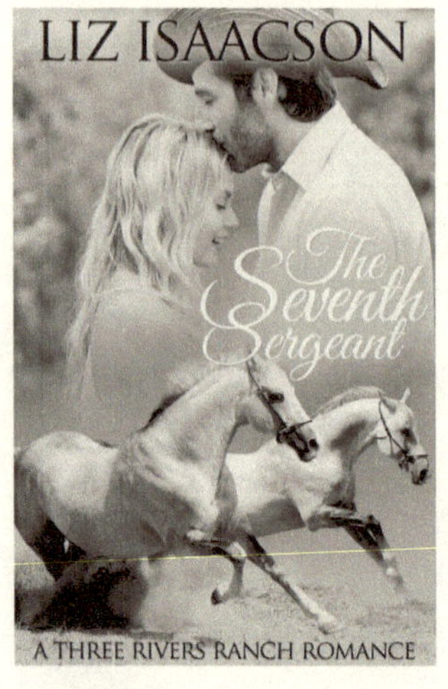

The Seventh Sergeant: A Three Rivers Ranch Romance (Book 6): Life has finally started to settle down for Sergeant Reese Sanders after his devastating injury overseas. Discharged from the Army and now with a good job at Courage Reins, he's finally found happiness—until a horrific fall puts him right back where he was years ago: Injured and depressed. Carly Watters, Reese's new veteran care coordinator, dislikes small towns almost as much as she loathes cowboys. But she finds herself faced with both when she gets assigned to Reese's case. Do they have the humility and faith to make their relationship more than professional?

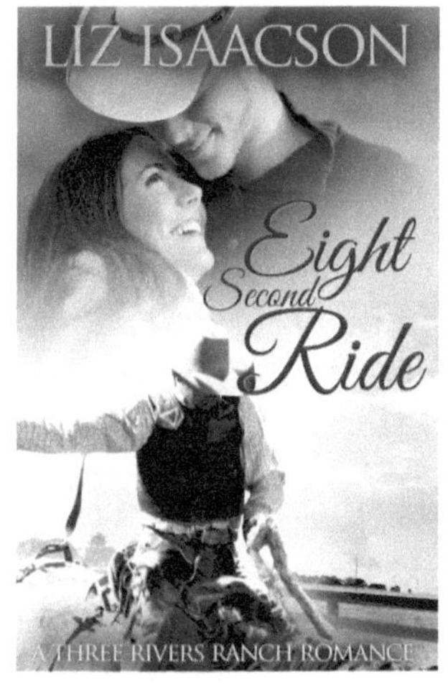

Eight Second Ride: A Three Rivers Ranch Romance (Book 7): Ethan Greene loves his work at Three Rivers Ranch, but he can't seem to find the right woman to settle down with. When sassy yet vulnerable Brynn Bowman shows up at the ranch to recruit him back to the rodeo circuit, he takes a different approach with the barrel racing champion. His patience and newfound faith pay off when a friendship--and more-- starts with Brynn. But she wants out of the rodeo circuit right when Ethan wants to rejoin. Can they find the path God wants them to take and still stay together?

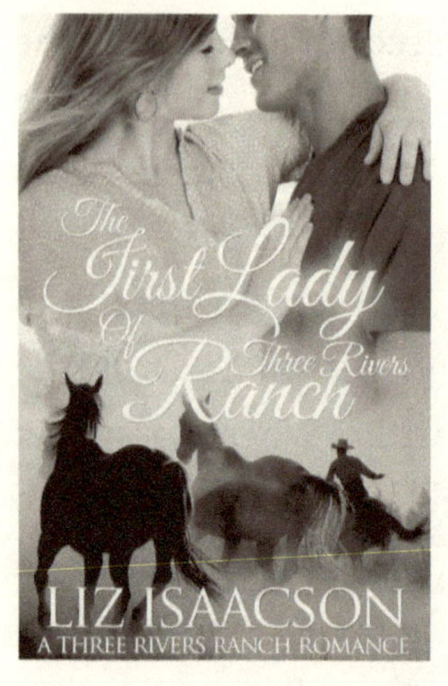

The First Lady of Three Rivers Ranch: A Three Rivers Ranch Romance (Book 8): Heidi Duffin has been dreaming about opening her own bakery since she was thirteen years old. She scrimped and saved for years to afford baking and pastry school in San Francisco. And now she only has one year left before she's a certified pastry chef. Frank Ackerman's father has recently retired, and he's taken over the largest cattle ranch in the Texas Panhandle. A horseman through and through, he's also nearing thirty-one and looking for someone to bring love and joy to a homestead that's been dominated by men for a decade. But when he convinces Heidi to come clean the cowboy cabins, she changes all that. But the siren's call of a bakery is still loud in Heidi's ears, even if she's also seeing a future with Frank. Can she rely on her faith in ways she's never had to before or will their relationship end when summer does?

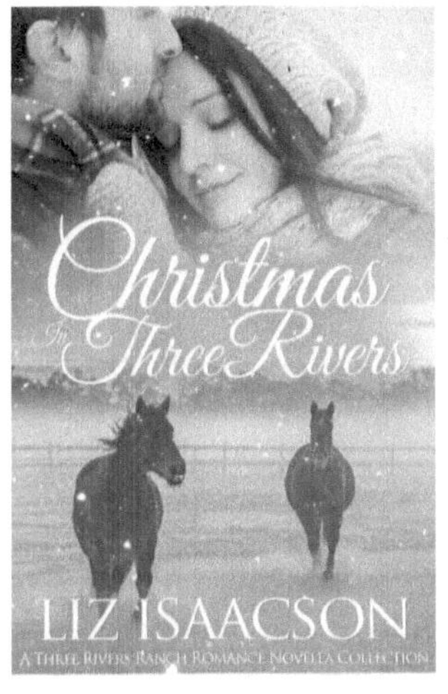

Christmas in Three Rivers: A Three Rivers Ranch Romance (Book 9): Isn't Christmas the best time to fall in love? The cowboys of Three Rivers Ranch think so. Join four of them as they journey toward their path to happily ever after in four, all-new novellas in the Amazon #1 Bestselling Three Rivers Ranch Romance series.

THE NINTH INNING: The Christmas season has never felt like such a burden to boutique owner Andrea Larsen. But with Mama gone and the holidays upon her, Andy finds herself wishing she hadn't been so quick to judge her former boyfriend, cowboy Lawrence Collins. Well, Lawrence hasn't forgotten about Andy either, and he devises a plan to get her out to the ranch so they can reconnect. Do they have the faith and humility to patch things up and start a new relationship?

TEN DAYS IN TOWN: Sandy Keller is tired of the dating scene in Three Rivers. Though she owns the pancake house, she's looking for a fresh start, which means an escape from the town where she grew up. When her older brother's best friend, Tad Jorgensen, comes to town for the holidays, it is a balm to his weary soul. A helicopter tour guide who experienced a near-death experience, he's looking to start over too--but in Three Rivers. Can Sandy and Tad navigate their troubles to find the path God wants them to take--and discover true love--in only ten days?

ELEVEN YEAR REUNION: Pastry chef extraordinaire, Grace Lewis has moved to Three Rivers to help Heidi Ackerman open a bakery in Three Rivers. Grace relishes the idea of starting over in a town where no one knows about her failed cupcakery. She doesn't expect to run into her old high school boyfriend, Jonathan Carver. A carpenter working at Three Rivers Ranch, Jon's in town against his will. But with Grace now on the scene, Jon's thinking life in Three Rivers is suddenly looking up. But with her focus on baking and his disdain for small towns, can they make their eleven year reunion stick?

THE TWELFTH TOWN: Newscaster Taryn Tucker has had enough of life on-screen. She's bounced from town to town before arriving in Three Rivers, completely alone and completely anonymous--just the way she now likes it. She takes a job cleaning at Three Rivers Ranch, hoping for a chance to figure out who she is and where God wants her. When she meets happy-go-lucky cowhand Kenny Stockton, she doesn't expect sparks to fly. Kenny's always been "the best friend" for his female friends, but the pull between him and Taryn can't be denied. Will they have the courage and faith necessary to make their opposite worlds mesh?

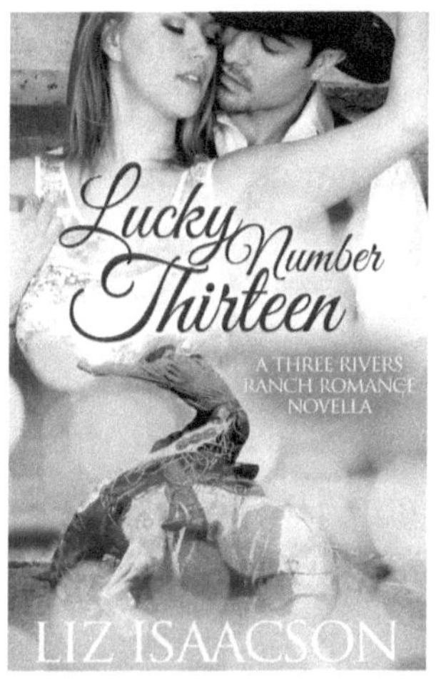

Lucky Number Thirteen: A Three Rivers Ranch Romance (Book 10): Tanner Wolf, a rodeo champion ten times over, is excited to be riding in Three Rivers for the first time since he left his philandering ways and found religion. Seeing his old friends Ethan and Brynn is thera-puetic--until a terrible accident lands him in the hospital. With his rodeo career over, Tanner thinks maybe he'll stay in town--and it's not just because his nurse, Summer Hamblin, is the prettiest woman he's ever met. But Summer's the queen of first dates, and as she looks for a way to make a relationship with the transient rodeo star work Summer's not sure she has the fortitude to go on a second date. Can they find love among the tragedy?

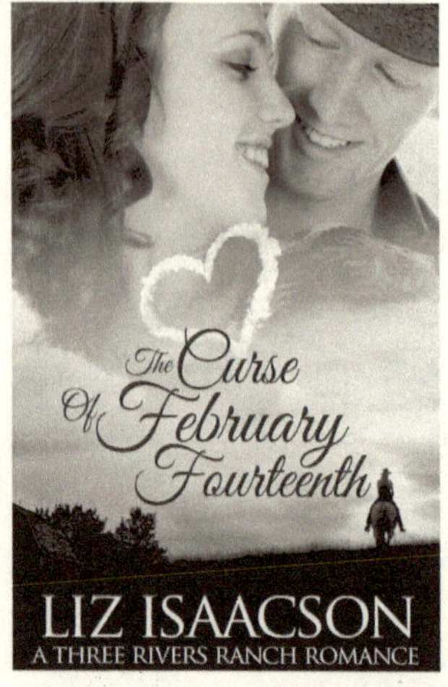

The Curse of February Fourteenth: A Three Rivers Ranch Romance (Book 11): Cal Hodgkins, cowboy veterinarian at Bowman's Breeds, isn't planning to meet anyone at the masked dance in small-town Three Rivers. He just wants to get his bachelor friends off his back and sit on the sidelines to drink his punch. But when he sees a woman dressed in gorgeous butterfly wings and cowgirl boots with blue stitching, he's smitten. Too bad she runs away from the dance before he can get her name, leaving only her boot behind...

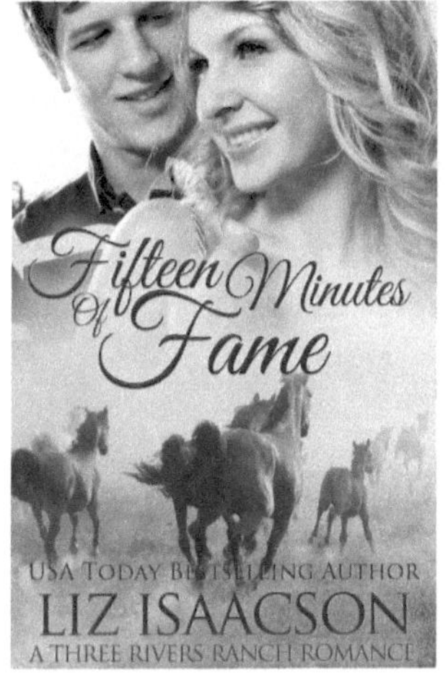

Fifteen Minutes of Fame: A Three Rivers Ranch Romance (Book 12): Navy Richards is thirty-five years of tired—tired of dating the same men, working a demanding job, and getting her heart broken over and over again. Her aunt has always spoken highly of the matchmaker in Three Rivers, Texas, so she takes a six-month sabbatical from her high-stress job as a pediatric nurse, hops on a bus, and meets with the matchmaker. Then she meets Gavin Redd. He's handsome, he's hardworking, and he's a cowboy. But is he an Aquarius too? Navy's not making a move until she knows for sure...

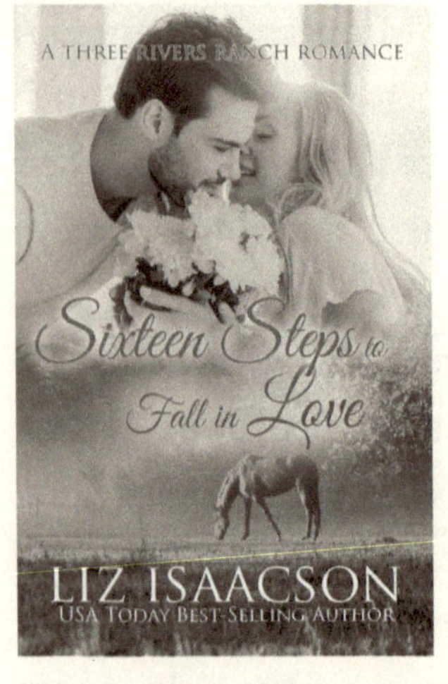

Sixteen Steps to Fall in Love: A Three Rivers Ranch Romance (Book 13): A chance encounter at a dog park sheds new light on the tall, talented Boone that Nicole can't ignore. As they get to know each other better and start to dig into each other's past, Nicole is the one who wants to run. This time from her growing admiration and attachment to Boone. From her aging parents. From herself.

But Boone feels the attraction between them too, and he decides he's tired of running and ready to make Three Rivers his permanent home. **Can Boone and Nicole use their faith to overcome their differences and find a happily-ever-after together?**

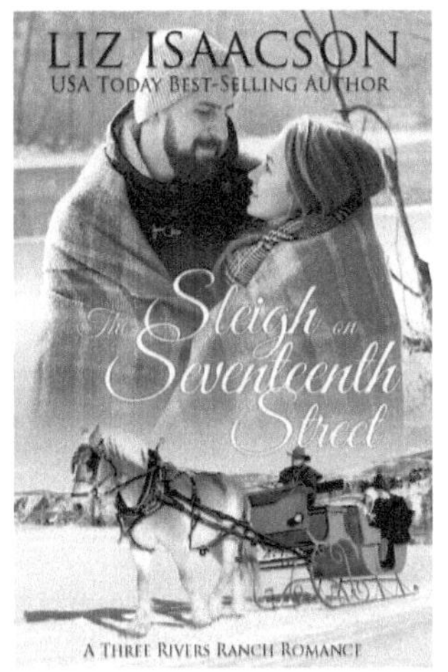

The Sleigh on Seventeenth Street: A Three Rivers Ranch Romance (Book 14): A cowboy with skills as an electrician tries a relationship with a down-on-her luck plumber. Can Dylan and Camila make water and electricity play nicely together this Christmas season? Or will they get shocked as they try to make their relationship work?

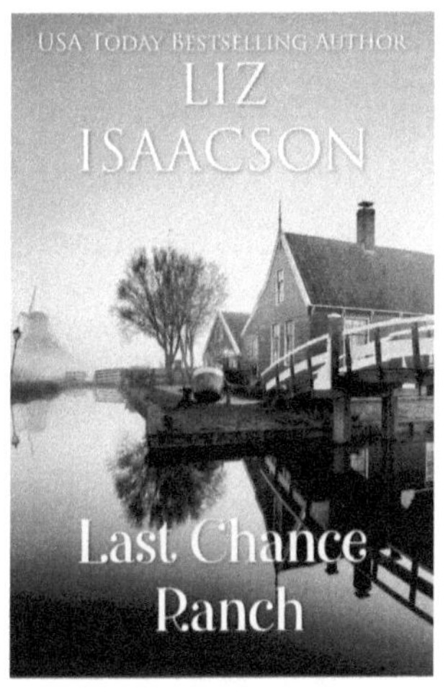

Last Chance Ranch (Book 1): A cowgirl down on her luck hires a man who's good with horses and under the hood of a car. Can Hudson fine tune Scarlett's heart as they work together? Or will things backfire and make everything worse at Last Chance Ranch?

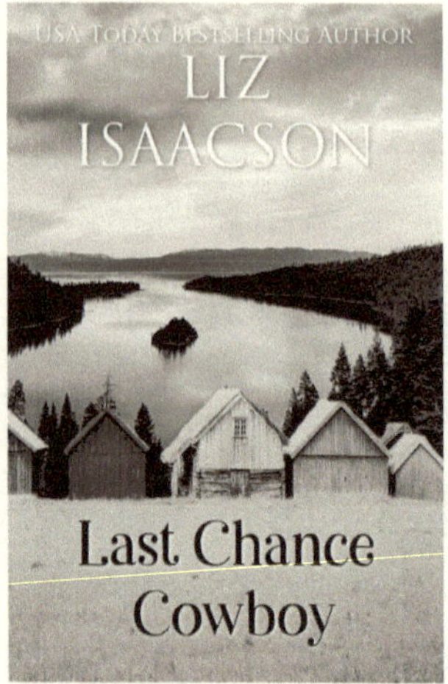

Last Chance Cowboy (Book 2): A billionaire cowboy without a home meets a woman who secretly makes food videos to pay her debts...Can Carson and Adele do more than fight in the kitchens at Last Chance Ranch?

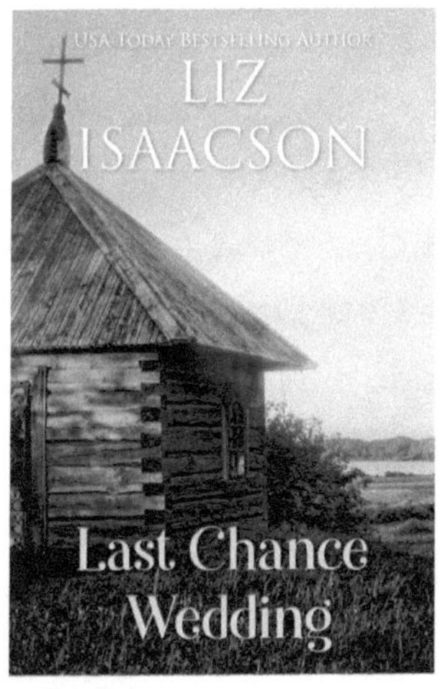

Last Chance Wedding (Book 3): A female carpenter needs a husband just for a few days... Can Jeri and Sawyer navigate the minefield of a pretend marriage before their feelings become real?

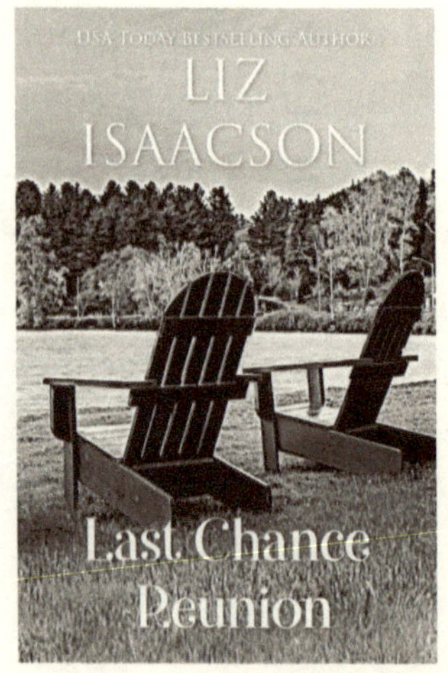

Last Chance Reunion (Book 4): An Army cowboy, the woman he dated years ago, and their last chance at Last Chance Ranch... Can Dave and Sissy put aside hurt feelings and make their second chance romance work?

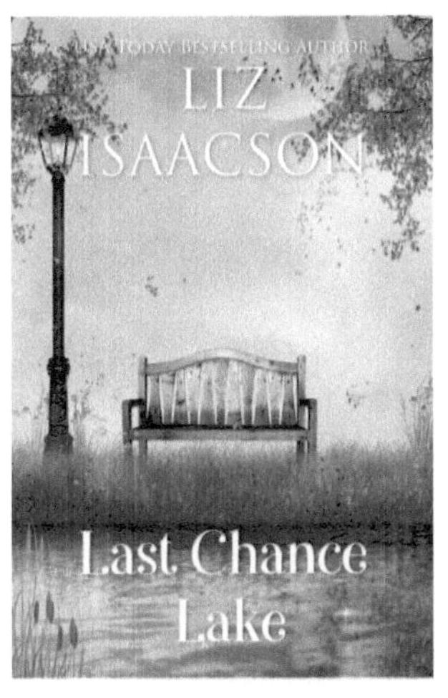

Last Chance Lake (Book 5): A former dairy farmer and the marketing director on the ranch have to work together to make the cow cuddling program a success. But can Karla let Cache into her life? Or will she keep all her secrets from him - and keep *him* a secret too?

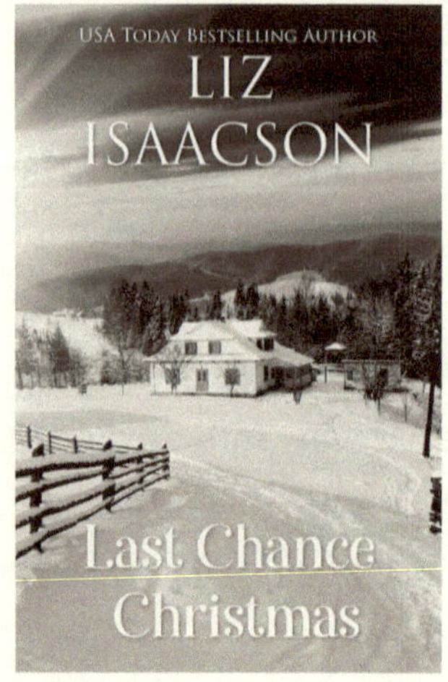

Last Chance Christmas (Book 6): She's tired of having her heart broken by cowboys. He waited too long to ask her out. Can Lance fix things quickly, or will Amber leave Last Chance Ranch before he can tell her how he feels?

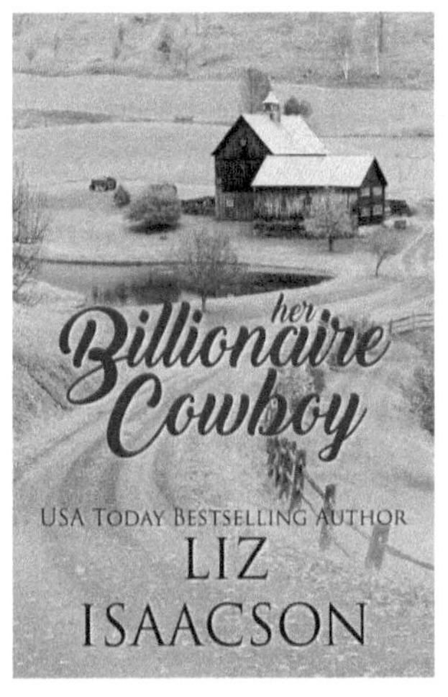

Her Billionaire Cowboy (Book 1): Tucker Jenkins has had enough of tall buildings, traffic, and has traded in his technology firm in New York City for Steeple Ridge Horse Farm in rural Vermont. Missy Marino has worked at the farm since she was a teen, and she's always dreamed of owning it. But her ex-husband left her with a truckload of debt, making her fantasies of owning the farm unfulfilled. Tucker didn't come to the country to find a new wife, but he supposes a woman could help him start over in Steeple Ridge. Will Tucker and Missy be able to navigate the shaky ground between them to find a new beginning?

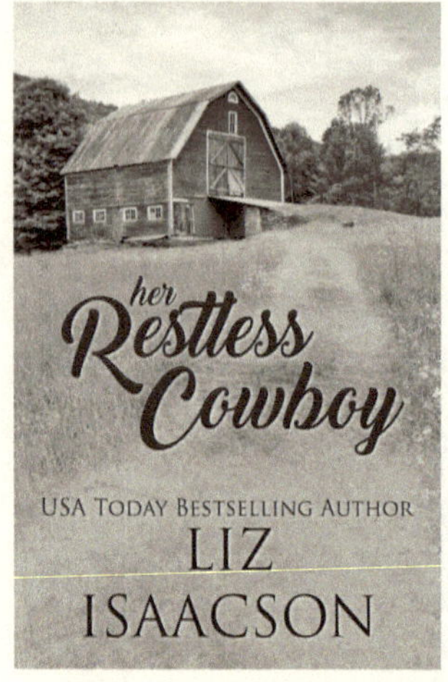

Her Restless Cowboy: A Butters Brothers Novel, Steeple Ridge Romance (Book 2): Ben Buttars is the youngest of the four Buttars brothers who come to Steeple Ridge Farm, and he finally feels like he's landed somewhere he can make a life for himself. Reagan Cantwell is a decade older than Ben and the recreational direction for the town of Island Park. Though Ben is young, he knows what he wants—and that's Rae. Can she figure out how to put what matters most in her life—family and faith—above her job before she loses Ben?

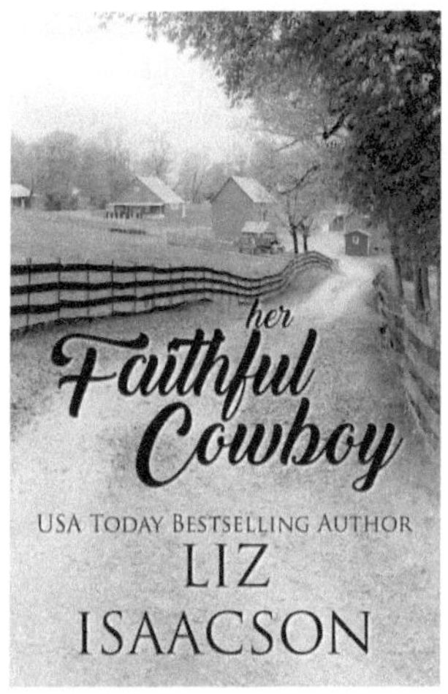

Her Faithful Cowboy: A Butters Brothers Novel, Steeple Ridge Romance (Book 3): Sam Buttars has spent the last decade making sure he and his brothers stay together. They've been at Steeple Ridge for a while now, but with the youngest married and happy, the siren's call to return to his parents' farm in Wyoming is loud in Sam's ears. He'd just go if it weren't for beautiful Bonnie Sherman, who roped his heart the first time he saw her. Do Sam and Bonnie have the faith to find comfort in each other instead of in the people who've already passed?

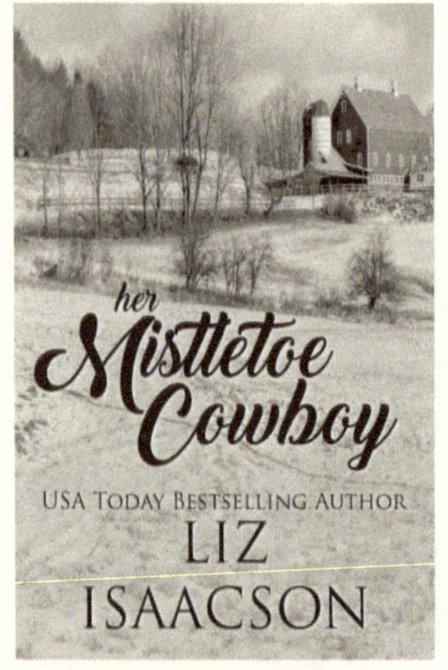

Her Mistletoe Cowboy: A Butters Brothers Novel, Steeple Ridge Romance (Book 4): Logan Buttars has always been good-natured and happy-go-lucky. After watching two of his brothers settle down, he recognizes a void in his life he didn't know about. Veterinarian Layla Guyman has appreciated Logan's friendship and easy way with animals when he comes into the clinic to get the service dogs. But with his future at Steeple Ridge in the balance, she's not sure a relationship with him is worth the risk. Can she rely on her faith and employ patience to tame Logan's wild heart?

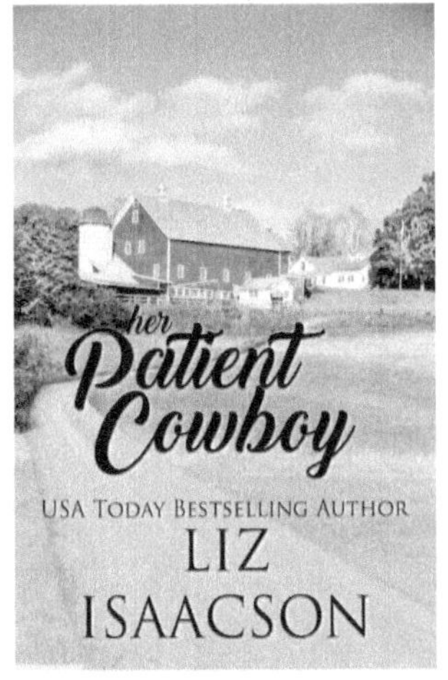

Her Patient Cowboy: A Butters Brothers Novel, Steeple Ridge Romance (Book 5): Darren Buttars is cool, collected, and quiet—and utterly devastated when his girlfriend of nine months, Farrah Irvine, breaks up with him because he wanted her to ride her horse in a parade. But Farrah doesn't ride anymore, a fact she made very clear to Darren. She returned to her childhood home with so much baggage, she doesn't know where to start with the unpacking. Darren's the only Buttars brother who isn't married, and he wants to make Island Park his permanent home—with Farrah. Can they find their way through the heartache to achieve a happily-ever-after together?

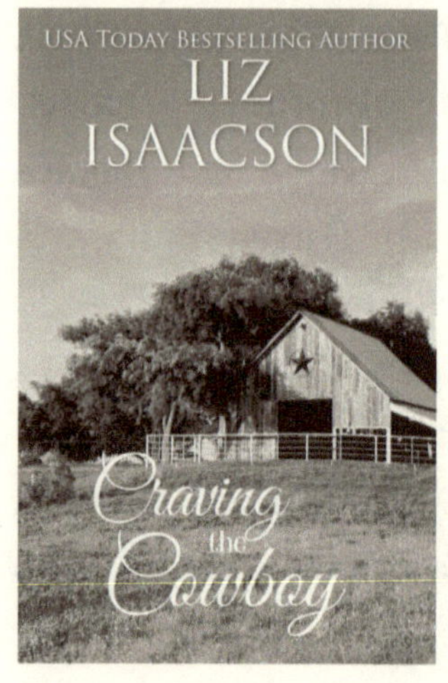

Craving the Cowboy (Book 1): Dwayne Carver is set to inherit his family's ranch in the heart of Texas Hill Country, and in order to keep up with his ranch duties and fulfill his dreams of owning a horse farm, he hires top trainer Felicity Lightburne. They get along great, and she can envision herself on this new farm—at least until her mother falls ill and she has to return to help her. Can Dwayne and Felicity work through their differences to find their happily-ever-after?

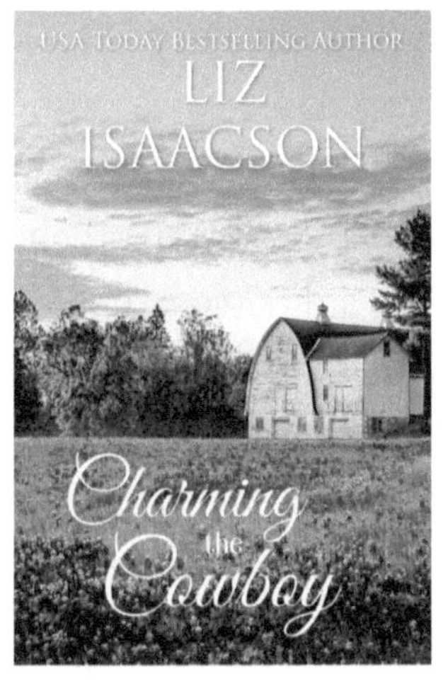

Charming the Cowboy (Book 2): Third grade teacher Heather Carver has had her eye on Levi Rhodes for a couple of years now, but he seems to be blind to her attempts to charm him. When she breaks her arm while on his horse ranch, Heather infiltrates Levi's life in ways he's never thought of, and his strict anti-female stance slips. Will Heather heal his emotional scars and he care for her physical ones so they can have a real relationship?

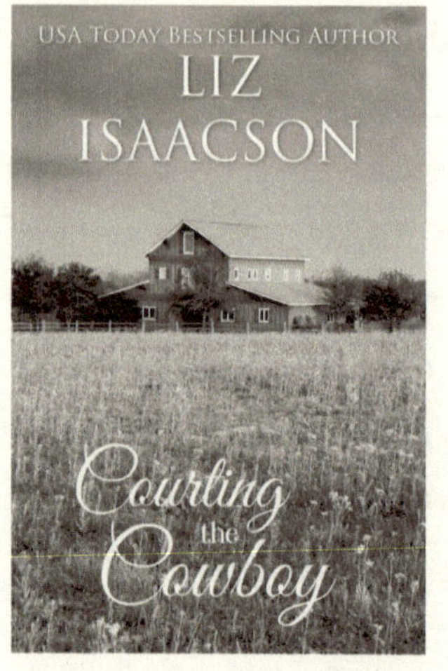

Courting the Cowboy (Book 3): Frustrated with the cowboy-only dating scene in Grape Seed Falls, May Sotheby joins TexasFaithful.com, hoping to find her soul mate without having to relocate--or deal with cowboy hats and boots. She has no idea that Kurt Pemberton, foreman at Grape Seed Ranch, is the man she starts communicating with... Will May be able to follow her heart and get Kurt to forgive her so they can be together?

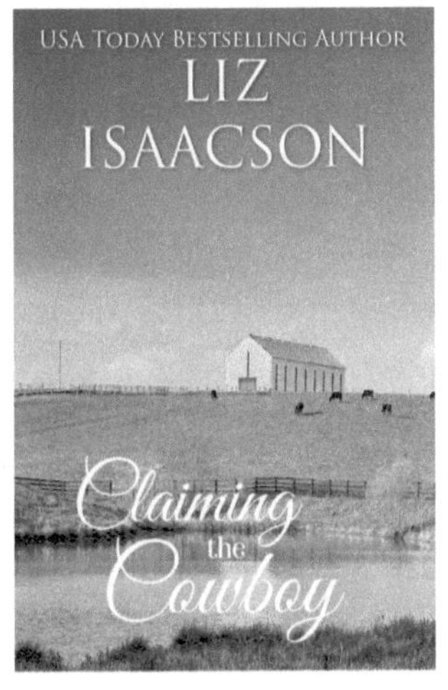

Claiming the Cowboy, Royal Brothers Book 1 (Grape Seed Falls Romance Book 4): Unwilling to be tied down, farrier Robin Cook has managed to pack her entire life into a two-hundred-and-eighty square-foot house, and that includes her Yorkie. Cowboy and co-foreman, Shane Royal has had his heart set on Robin for three years, even though she flat-out turned him down the last time he asked her to dinner. But she's back at Grape Seed Ranch for five weeks as she works her horse-shoeing magic, and he's still interested, despite a bitter life lesson that left a bad taste for marriage in his mouth.

Robin's interested in him too. But can she find room for Shane in her tiny house--and can he take a chance on her with his tired heart?

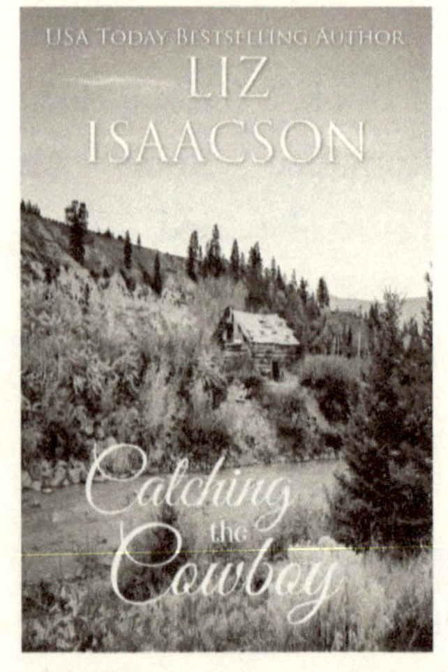

Catching the Cowboy, Royal Brothers Book 2 (Grape Seed Falls Romance Book 5): Dylan Royal is good at two things: whistling and caring for cattle. When his cows are being attacked by an unknown wild animal, he calls Texas Parks & Wildlife for help. He wasn't expecting a beautiful mammologist to show up, all flirty and fun and everything Dylan didn't know he wanted in his life.

Hazel Brewster has gone on more first dates than anyone in Grape Seed Falls, and she thinks maybe Dylan deserves a second... Can they find their way through wild animals, huge life changes, and their emotional pasts to find their forever future?

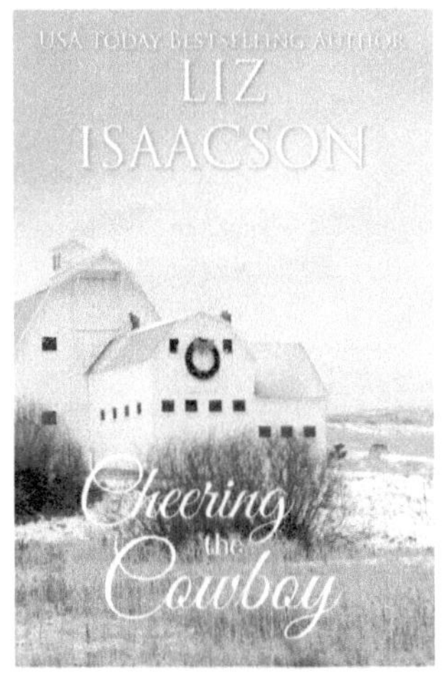

Cheering the Cowboy, Royal Brothers Book 3 (Grape Seed Falls Romance Book 6): Austin Royal loves his life on his new ranch with his brothers. But he doesn't love that Shayleigh Hatch came with the property, nor that he has to take the blame for the fact that he now owns her childhood ranch. They rarely have a conversation that doesn't leave him furious and frustrated--and yet he's still attracted to Shay in a strange, new way.

Shay inexplicably likes him too, which utterly confuses and angers her. As they work to make this Christmas the best the Triple Towers Ranch has ever seen, can they also navigate through their rocky relationship to smoother waters?

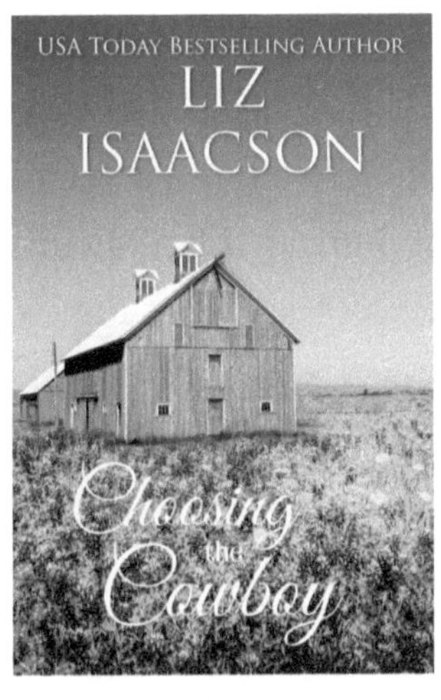

Choosing the Cowboy (Book 7): With financial trouble and personal issues around every corner, can Maggie Duffin and Chase Carver rely on their faith to find their happily-ever-after?

A spinoff from the #1 bestselling Three Rivers Ranch Romance novels, also by USA Today bestselling author Liz Isaacson.

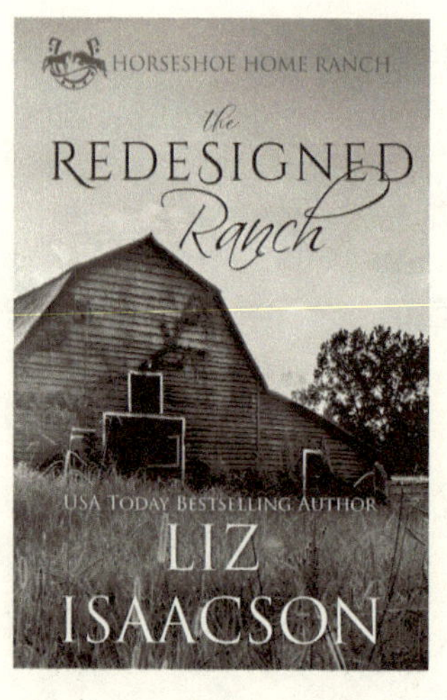

The Redesigned Ranch (Book 1): Jace Lovell only has one thing left after his fiancé abandons him at the altar: his job at Horseshoe Home Ranch. Belle Edmunds is back in Gold Valley and she's desperate to build a portfolio that she can use to start her own firm in Montana. Jace isn't anywhere near forgiving his fiancé, and he's not sure he's ready for a new relationship with someone as fiery and beautiful as Belle. Can she employ her patience while he figures out how to forgive so they can find their own brand of happily-ever-after?

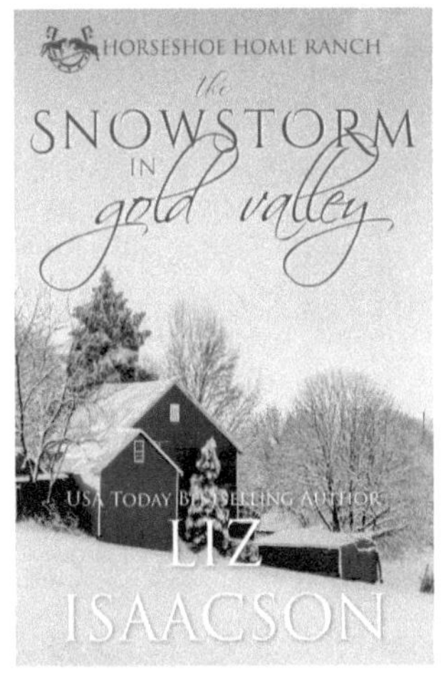

The Snowstorm in Gold Valley (Book 2): Professional snowboarder Sterling Maughan has sequestered himself in his family's cabin in the exclusive mountain community above Gold Valley, Montana after a devastating fall that ended his career. Norah Watson cleans Sterling's cabin and the more time they spend together, the more Sterling is interested in all things Norah. As his body heals, so does his faith. Will Norah be able to trust Sterling so they can have a chance at true love?

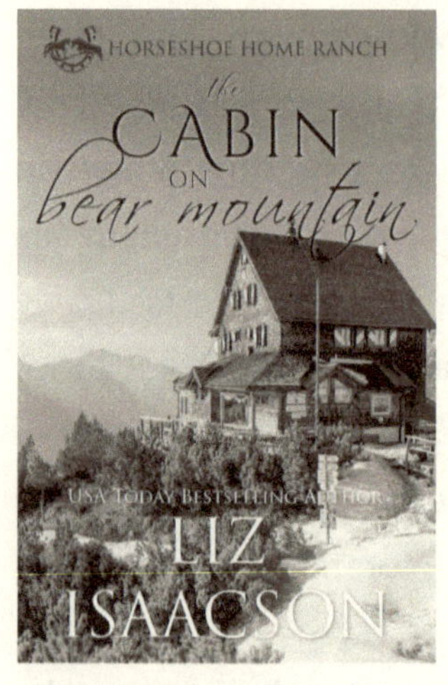

The Cabin on Bear Mountain (Book 3): Landon Edmunds has been a cowboy his whole life. An accident five years ago ended his successful rodeo career, and now he's looking to start a horse ranch--and he's looking outside of Montana. Which would be great if God hadn't brought Megan Palmer back to Gold Valley right when Landon is looking to leave. Megan and Landon work together well, and as sparks fly, she's sure God brought her back to Gold Valley so she could find her happily ever after. Through serious discussion and prayer, can Landon and Megan find their future together?

Be sure to check out the spinoff series, the Brush Creek Brides romances after you read FALLING FOR HIS BEST FRIEND. Start with A WEDDING FOR THE WIDOWER.

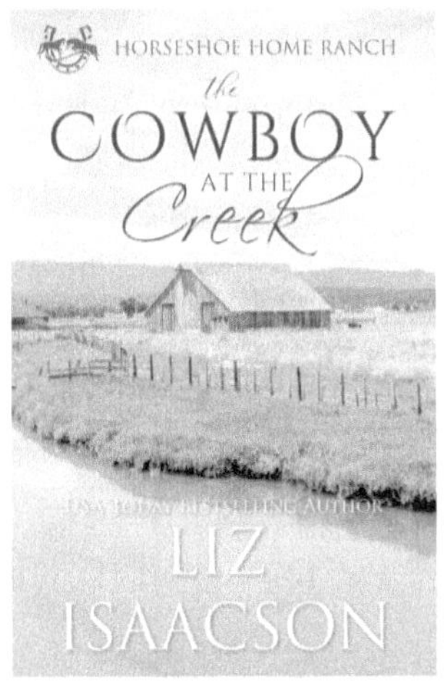

The Cowboy at the Creek (Book 4): Twelve years ago, Owen Carr left Gold Valley—and his long-time girlfriend—in favor of a country music career in Nashville. Married and divorced, Natalie teaches ballet at the dance studio in Gold Valley, but she never auditioned for the professional company the way she dreamed of doing. With Owen back, she realizes all the opportunities she missed out on when he left all those years ago—including a future with him. Can they mend broken bridges in order to have a second chance at love?

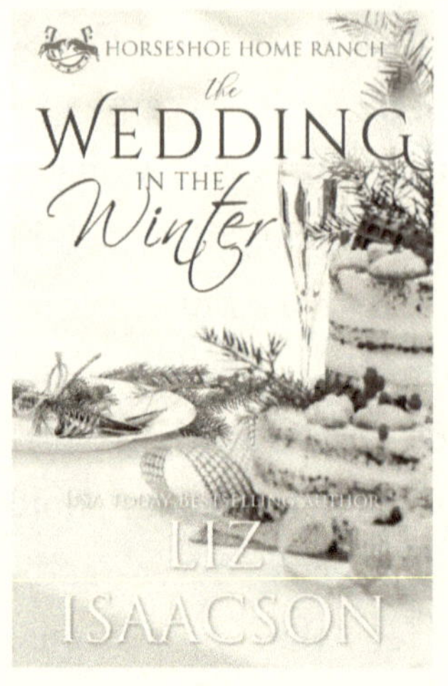 **The Wedding in the Winter (Book 5):** Caleb Chamberlain has spent the last five years recovering from a horrible breakup, his alcoholism that stemmed from it, and the car accident that left him hospitalized. He's finally on the right track in his life—until Holly Gray, his twin brother's ex-fiance mistakes him for Nathan. Holly's back in Gold Valley to get the required veterinarian hours to apply for her graduate program. When the herd at Horseshoe Home comes down with pneumonia, Caleb and Holly are forced to work together in close quarters. Holly's over Nathan, but she hasn't forgiven him—or the woman she believes broke up their relationship. Can Caleb and Holly navigate such a rough past to find their happily-ever-after?

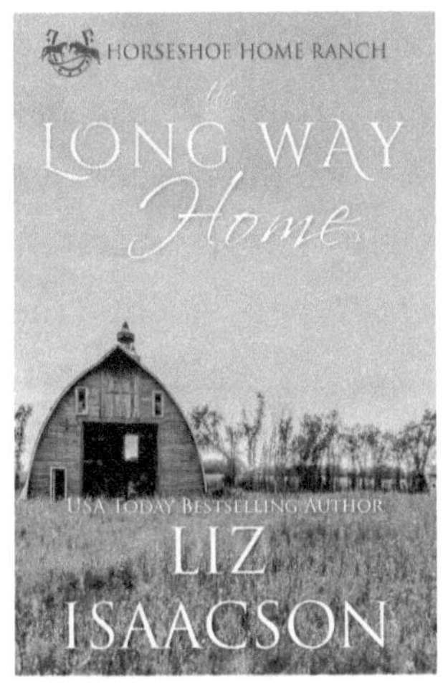

The Long Way Home (Book 6): Ty Barker has been dancing through the last thirty years of his life--and he's suddenly realized he's alone. River Lee Whitely is back in Gold Valley with her two little girls after a divorce that's left deep scars. She has a job at Silver Creek that requires her to be able to ride a horse, and she nearly tramples Ty at her first lesson. That's just fine by him, because River Lee is the girl Ty has never gotten over. Ty realizes River Lee needs time to settle into her new job, her new home, her new life as a single parent, but going slow has never been his style. But for River Lee, can Ty take the necessary steps to keep her in his life?

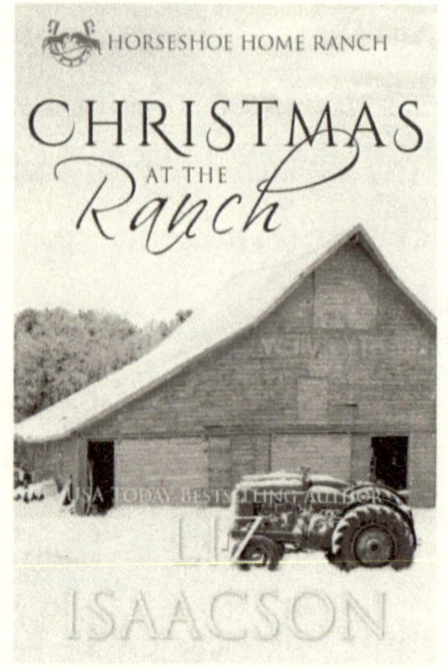

Christmas at the Ranch (Book 7): Archer Bailey has already lost one job to Emersyn Enders, so he deliberately doesn't tell her about the cowhand job up at Horseshoe Home Ranch. Emery's temporary job is ending, but her obligations to her physically disabled sister aren't. As Archer and Emery work together, its clear that the sparks flying between them aren't all from their friendly competition over a job. Will Emery and Archer be able to navigate the ranch, their close quarters, and their individual circumstances to find love this holiday season?

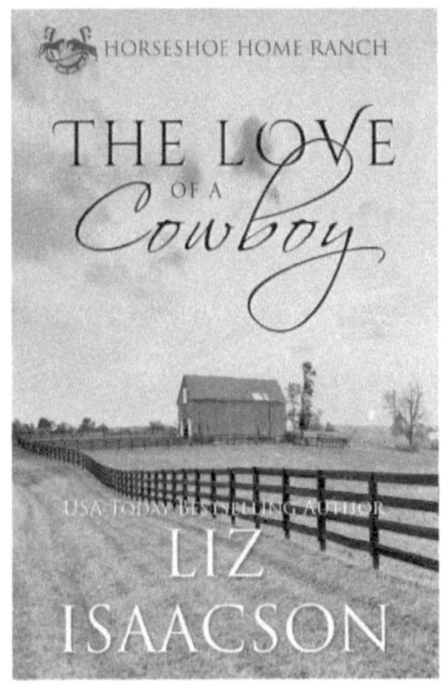

The Love of a Cowboy (Book 8): Cowboy Elliott Hawthorne has just lost his best friend and cabin mate to the worst thing imaginable—marriage. When his brother calls about an accident with their father, Elliott rushes down to Gold Valley from the ranch only to be met with the most beautiful woman he's ever seen. His father's new physical therapist, London Marsh, likes the handsome face and gentle spirit she sees in Elliott too. Can Elliott and London navigate difficult family situations to find a happily-ever-after?

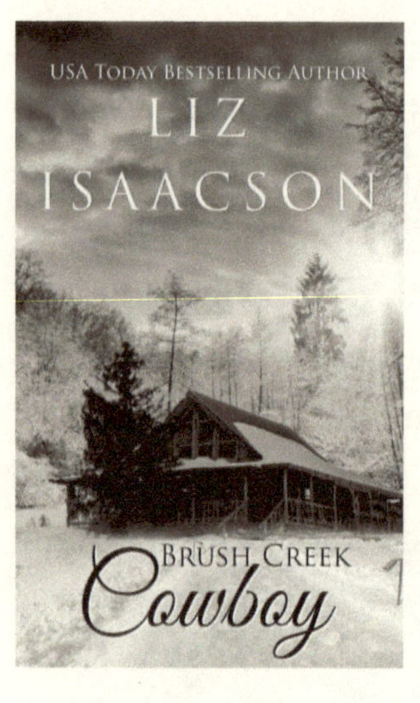

Brush Creek Cowboy: Brush Creek Cowboys Romance (Book 1): Former rodeo champion and cowboy Walker Thompson trains horses at Brush Creek Horse Ranch, where he lives a simple life in his cabin with his ten-year-old son. A widower of six years, he's worked with Tess Wagner, a widow who came to Brush Creek to escape the turmoil of her life to give her seven-year-old son a slower pace of life. But Tess's breast cancer is back…

Walker will have to decide if he'd rather spend even a short time with Tess than not have her in his life at all. Tess wants to feel God's love and power, but can she discover and accept God's will in order to find her happy ending?

The Cowboy's Challenge: Brush Creek Brides Romance (Book 2): Cowboy and professional roper Justin Jackman has found solitude at Brush Creek Horse Ranch, preferring his time with the animals he trains over dating. With two failed engagements in his past, he's not really interested in getting his heart stomped on again. But when flirty and fun Renee Martin picks him up at a church ice cream bar--on a bet, no less--he finds himself more than just a little interested. His Gen-X attitudes are attractive to her; her Millennial behaviors drive him nuts. Can Justin look past their differences and take a chance on another engagement?

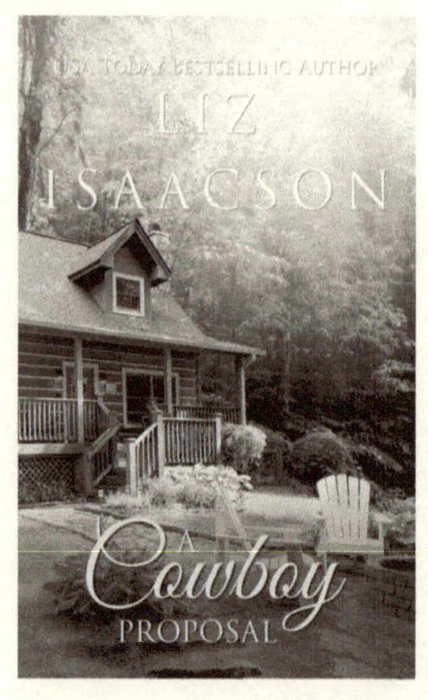

A Cowboy Proposal: Brush Creek Brides Romance (Book 3): Ted Caldwell has been a retired bronc rider for years, and he thought he was perfectly happy training horses to buck at Brush Creek Ranch. He was wrong. When he meets April Nox, who comes to the ranch to hide her pregnancy from all her friends back in Jackson Hole, Ted realizes he has a huge family-shaped hole in his life. April is embarrassed, heartbroken, and trying to find her extinguished faith. She's never ridden a horse and wants nothing to do with a cowboy ever again. Can Ted and April create a family of happiness and love from a tragedy?

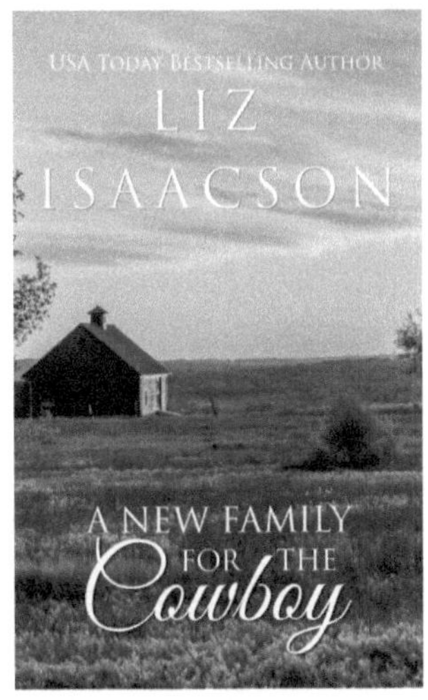

A New Family for the Cowboy: Brush Creek Brides Romance (Book 4): Blake Gibbons oversees all the agriculture at Brush Creek Horse Ranch, sometimes moonlighting as a general contractor. When he meets Erin Shields, new in town, at her aunt's bakery, he's instantly smitten. Erin moved to Brush Creek after a divorce that left her penniless, homeless, and a single mother of three children under age eight. She's nowhere near ready to start dating again, but the longer Blake hangs around the bakery, the more she starts to like him. Can Blake and Erin find a way to blend their lifestyles and become a family?

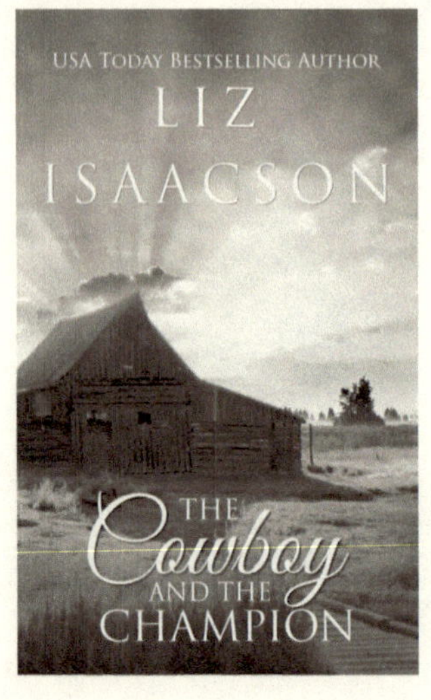

The Cowboy and the Champion: Brush Creek Brides Romance (Book 5): Emmett Graves has always had a positive outlook on life. He adores training horses to become barrel racing champions during the day and cuddling with his cat at night. Fresh off her professional rodeo retirement, Molly Brady comes to Brush Creek Horse Ranch as Emmett's protege. He's not thrilled, and she's allergic to cats. Oh, and she'd like to stay cowboy-free, thank you very much. But Emmett's about as cowboy as they come.... Can Emmett and Molly work together without falling in love?

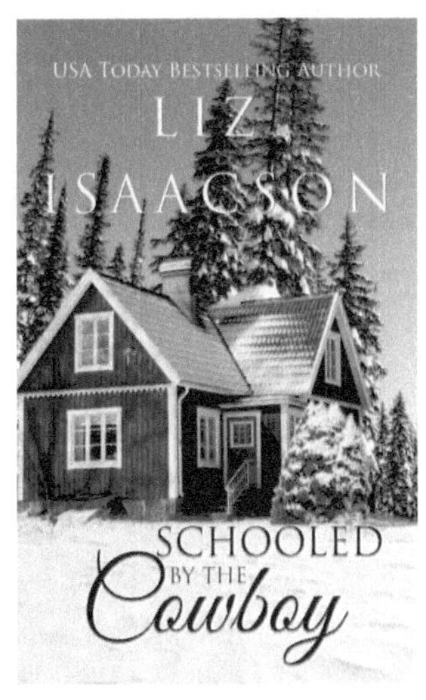

Schooled by the Cowboy: Brush Creek Brides Romance (Book 6): Grant Ford spends his days training cattle—when he's not camped out at the elementary school hoping to catch a glimpse of his ex-girlfriend. When principal Shannon Sharpe confronts him and asks him to stay away from the school, the spark between them is instant and hot. Shannon's expecting a transfer very soon, but she also needs a summer outdoor coordinator—and Grant fits the bill. Just because he's handsome and everything Shannon's ever wanted in a cowboy husband means nothing. Will Grant and Shannon be able to survive the summer or will the Utah heat be too much for them to handle?

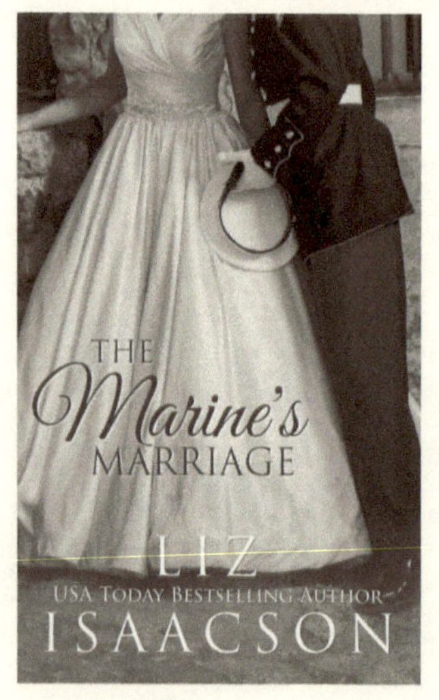

The Marine's Marriage: A Fuller Family Novel - Brush Creek Brides Romance (Book 1): Tate Benson can't believe he's come to Nowhere, Utah, to fix up a house that hasn't been inhabited in years. But he has. Because he's retired from the Marines and looking to start a life as a police officer in small-town Brush Creek. Wren Fuller has her hands full most days running her family's company. When Tate calls and demands a maid for that morning, she decides to have the calls forwarded to her cell and go help him out. She didn't know he was moving in next door, and she's completely unprepared for his handsomeness, his kind heart, and his wounded soul.Can Tate and Wren weather a relationship when they're also next-door neighbors?

The Firefighter's Fiancé: A Fuller Family Novel - Brush Creek Brides Romance (Book 2): Cora Wesley comes to Brush Creek, hoping to get some in-the-wild firefighting training as she prepares to put in her application to be a hotshot. When she meets Brennan Fuller, the spark between them is hot and instant. As they get to know

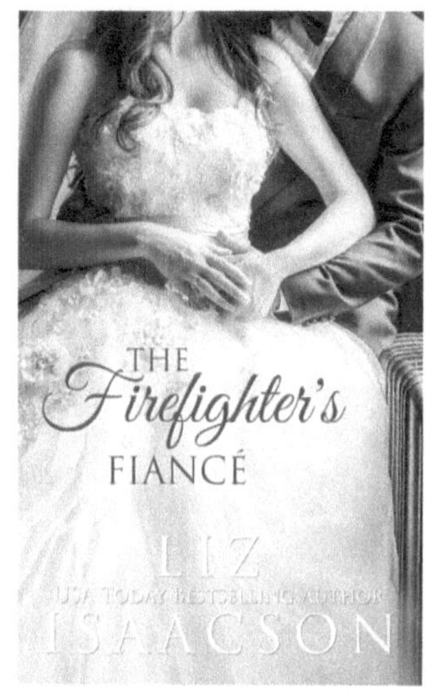

each other, her deadline is constantly looming over them, and Brennan starts to wonder if he can break ranks in the family business. He's okay mowing lawns and hanging out with his brothers, but he dreams of being able to go to college and become a landscape architect, but he's just not sure it can be done. Will Cora and Brennan be able to endure their trials to find true love?

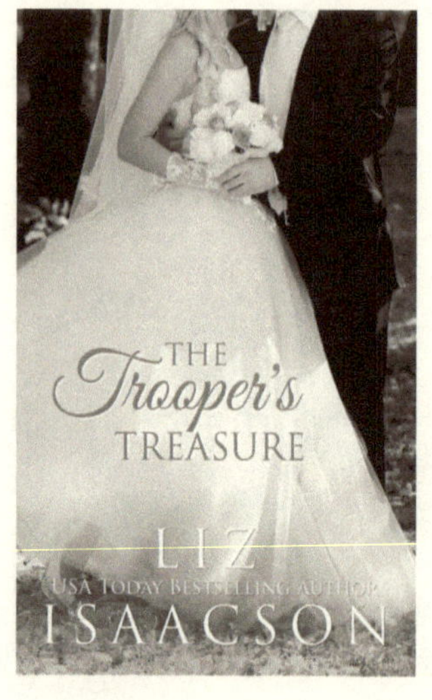

The Trooper's Treasure: A Fuller Family Novel - Brush Creek Brides Romance (Book 3): Dawn Fuller has made some mistakes in her life, and she's not proud of the way McDermott Boyd found her off the road one day last year. She's spent a hard year wrestling with her choices and trying to fix them, glad for McDermott's acceptance and friendship. He lost his wife years ago, done his best with his daughter, and now he's ready to move on. Can McDermott help Dawn find a way past her former mistakes and down a path that leads to love, family, and happiness?

The Detective's Date: A Fuller Family Novel - Brush Creek Brides Romance (Book 4): Dahlia Reid is one of the best detectives Brush Creek and the surrounding towns has ever had. She's given up on the idea of marriage—and pleasing her mother—and has dedicated herself fully to her job. Which is great, since one of the most perplexing cases of her career

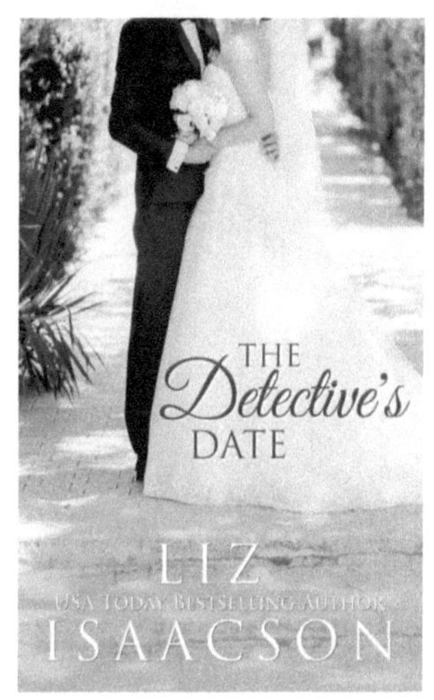

has come to town. Kyler Fuller thinks he's finally ready to move past the woman who ghosted him years ago. He's cut his hair, and he's ready to start dating. Too bad every woman he's been out with is about as interesting as a lamppost—until Dahlia. He finds her beautiful, her quick wit a breath of fresh air, and her intelligence sexy. Can Kyler and Dahlia use their faith to find a way through the obstacles threatening to keep them apart?

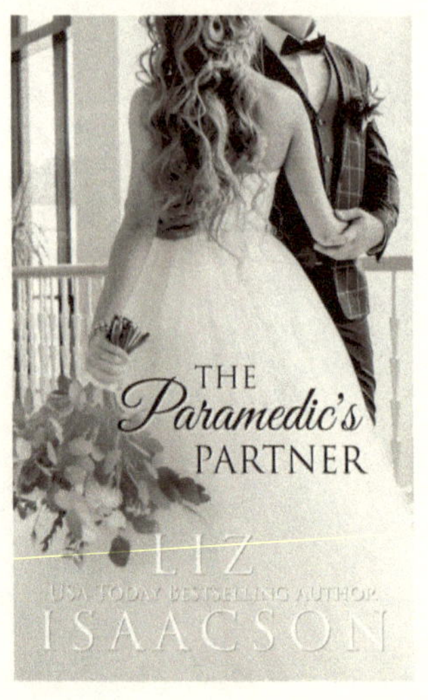

The Paramedic's Partner: A Fuller Family Novel - Brush Creek Brides Romance (Book 5): Jazzy Fuller has always been overshadowed by her prettier, more popular twin, Fabiana. Fabi meets paramedic Max Robinson at the park and sets a date with him only to come down with the flu. So she convinces Jazzy to cut her hair and take her place on the date. And the spark between Jazzy and Max is hot and instant...if only he knew she wasn't her sister, Fabi.

Max drives the ambulance for the town of Brush Creek with is partner Ed Moon, and neither of them have been all that lucky in love. Until Max suggests to who he thinks is Fabi that they should double with Ed and Jazzy. They do, and Fabi is smitten with the steady, strong Ed Moon. As each twin falls further and further in love with their respective paramedic, it becomes obvious they'll need to come clean about the switcheroo sooner rather than later...or risk losing their hearts.

The Chief's Catch: A Fuller Family Novel - Brush Creek Brides Romance (Book 6): Berlin Fuller has struck out with the dating scene in Brush Creek more times than she cares to admit. When she makes a deal with her friends that they can choose the next man she goes out with, she didn't dream they'd pick surly Cole Fairbanks, the new Chief of Police.

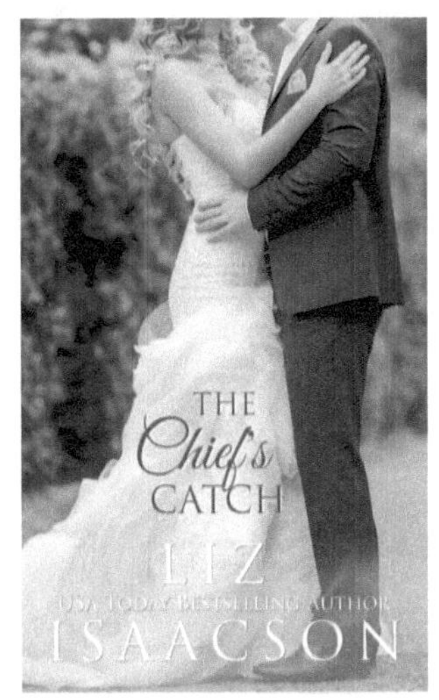

His friends call him the Beast and challenge him to complete ten dates that summer or give up his bonus check. When Berlin approaches him, stuttering about the deal with her friends and claiming they don't actually have to go out, he's intrigued. As the summer passes, Cole finds himself burning both ends of the candle to keep up with his job and his new relationship. When he unleashes the Beast one time too many, Berlin will have to decide if she can tame him or if she should walk away.

ABOUT LIZ

Liz Isaacson writes inspirational romance, usually set in Texas, or Montana, or anywhere else horses and cowboys exist. She lives in Utah, where she writes full-time, walks her two dogs daily, and eats a lot of peanut butter M&Ms while writing. Find her on her website at lizisaacson.com.